THIS TIME, THE FIGHT IS PERSONAL

Whitlock opened the folder on the desk. "What I'm about to tell you hasn't been released to any of the other Strike Force teams as yet." He stared at the page in front of him for a moment then looked up at them. "Strike Force Seven was ambushed while on assignment in London last night. Dave Swain and Jason Geddis were both dead on arrival at the hospital. Alain Mosser died in hospital in the early hours of this morning."

"We lost the whole team?" Graham said numbly, breaking the lingering silence.

Whitlock nodded grimly. "We've lost individual field operatives in the past but never an entire team."

"And it couldn't have come at a worse time," Sabrina said, shaking her head.

Whitlock continued. "Not only do you have to take over Strike Force Seven's assignment, you now also have to bring their killers to book."

"Bring them to book?" Graham said angrily. "They gunned down three of our colleagues in cold blood—"

"We can't allow that to cloud our judgment, though. This isn't a vendetta. Remember that."

Books by Alastair MacNeill

Alistair MacLean's Dead Halt
Alistair MacLean's Time of the Assassins

Available from HarperPaperbacks

Alistair MacLean's
DEAD HALT

Alastair MacNeill

HarperPaperbacks
A Division of HarperCollinsPublishers

HarperPaperbacks   *A Division of* HarperCollins*Publishers*
10 East 53rd Street, New York, N.Y. 10022

Copyright © 1992 by Devoran Trustees Ltd.
All rights reserved. No part of this book may be used or reproduced in any manner whatsoever without written permission of the publisher, except in the case of brief quotations embodied in critical articles and reviews. For information address HarperCollins*Publishers*,
77–85 Fulham Palace Road,
Hammersmith, London W6 8JB.

This book was originally published in Great Britain in 1992 by HarperCollins*Publishers*.

Cover illustration by Edwin Herder

First HarperPaperbacks printing: September 1995

Printed in the United States of America

HarperPaperbacks and colophon are trademarks of HarperCollins*Publishers*

10 9 8 7 6 5 4 3 2 1

◆ PROLOGUE

On an undisclosed date in September 1979 the Secretary-General of the United Nations chaired an extraordinary meeting attended by forty-six envoys representing virtually every country in the world. There was only one point on the agenda: the escalating tide of international crime. It was agreed to set up an international strike force to operate under the aegis of the United Nations Security Council, to be known as the United Nations Anti-Crime Organization (UNACO). Its objective would be to "avert, neutralize and/or apprehend individuals or groups engaged in international criminal activities".* Each envoy nominated one candidate for the position of UNACO Director, with the Secretary-General making the final choice.

UNACO's clandestine existence began on March 1, 1980.

*UNACO Charter, Article 1, Paragraph 1c

◆ CHAPTER
ONE

"For God's sake, we can't last out here much longer. It's getting worse by the minute. We've got to make port while we still can. It's our only chance now."

Rory Milne knew Earl Reid was right and that Reid was an experienced seaman who knew the area like his own backyard. Although Reid owned the *Ventura*, the 190-foot topsail schooner, Milne still had the final say on whether they tried to ride out the storm or whether they headed for the shelter of the nearest port. Reid had always had reservations about the arrangement but the money he was being paid had helped to ease his conscience. Now he knew his fears had been well-founded. But there wasn't anything he could do about it without Milne's authorization. He waited anxiously for Milne to come to a decision . . .

The Coast Guard had issued a storm warning for the Cape Cod area earlier that afternoon. Ten on the Beaufort Scale. Winds of up to fifty-five knots. It was due to hit Cape Cod around ten o'clock that evening. Reid had been confident they could ride it out. The

Ventura had done it before. But when it struck, Reid immediately knew it was no ordinary storm. The winds were gusting at up to eighty knots and the waves were already reaching heights of twenty feet. They were in a hurricane. And all the time the winds were increasing. The *Ventura* was reeling under the onslaught and Reid knew it would only be a matter of minutes before she foundered. They had to make for the Nantucket coast. And time was running out. Fast . . .

Reid couldn't wait any longer for Milne to come to a decision. He swung the wheel hard to starboard, a plan already taking shape in his head. He knew there was little chance of the *Ventura* reaching the sanctuary of Madaket Harbor in these conditions unless he used the huge seas to help him maneuver the schooner into the harbor. It was something he had never tried before. But he could still vividly remember the day when, as an eight-year-old, he had watched from his bedroom window as his father had used a storm off Martha's Vineyard to help him steer his crippled fishing trawler back to port. His father had turned the trawler into the path of a towering wave and used it to propel the trawler into the mouth of Edgartown Harbor. Admittedly, the trawler had been a lot closer to the harbor at the time and the storm wasn't nearly as severe as the one they were in, but Reid knew it was now their one chance of survival. The risks were enormous but he had to chance it.

He was still turning down sea when a towering wave seemed to lift the *Ventura* momentarily out of the water before crashing her down into the path of another wave which broke across the bow, smashing the wheelhouse window, and drenching the two men. A sliver of glass sliced across Milne's cheek as he was thrown back heavily against the bulkhead. Reid clung to the wheel as he fought desperately to turn the schooner toward the Nantucket coastline. Milne struggled to his feet and wiped the back of his hand across his bloodied cheek. His eyes were wide with fear. Reid glanced at him but said nothing. He wondered if he also looked that frightened. These were certainly the worst conditions he'd ever encountered in his fourteen years at sea.

"Look," Milne shouted above the howling wind.

Reid followed Milne's pointing finger. At first he couldn't see anything. Then he saw it. A flashing light in the distance. The lighthouse off Madaket Harbor. Reid checked its bearing. The lighthouse was now forty-five degrees on the starboard bow. Reid had thought he had been heading toward the light. Perhaps initially he had, but then the waves had battered the schooner back off course again.

"Make for the lighthouse," Milne yelled.

"Are you crazy?" Reid screamed back. "It's there to warn us off the rocks. I'm making for the harbor. It's our only chance now."

"Where is it—"

Milne's words were cut off as another wave smashed over the decks, sending a cascade of water into the wheelhouse. Milne was knocked back against the door with such force that it burst open and the scream was torn from his lips as he tumbled out onto the deck. A wave swept across the deck and Milne clawed desperately for the guardrail as he felt himself being washed toward the ship's side. Reid grabbed the radio handset and brusquely ordered the other three crewmen up on deck. For a moment he was caught in a dilemma. If he left the wheel to help Milne the schooner would be blown even further off course and possibly broach in the enormous seas. But what if the crew didn't reach Milne in time? Milne was essential to the whole operation. Even if they did reach port, the operation would have to be aborted without him. And that meant Reid wouldn't be paid the remainder of his money. A considerable amount of money . . .

Reid secured the wheel and as he struggled toward the door another wave buffeted the side of the schooner, throwing him to the floor. He looked around frantically for Milne, and for a moment he couldn't see anything. Then he noticed a pair of hands gripping the base of the guard rail. The rest of Milne was dangling precariously over the ship's side. Reid knew that Milne couldn't hold on for more than a few seconds. He shouted to him but the wind tore the words from his lips the moment he opened his mouth. Then he noticed the Jacob's ladder spread across the deck a few feet away from him. He made his way onto the deck to where the ladder lay. He looped his arm around the rope then, dropping onto his stomach, squirmed his way toward the guard rail. He closed his hand around the cuff of Milne's windcheater but his fingers were numb and he couldn't get a proper grip on the material. He pulled himself forward, reaching down over the side to get a hold of Milne's windcheater. He felt his fingers slipping again. At last one of the crewmen appeared behind Reid and, inch by inch, they hauled Milne up toward the deck. Then a second crewman joined him and helped to haul Milne up toward the deck. Milne's black hair was plastered against his pale face and the blood was streaming down his cheek from the gash inches below his left eye. As he reached up to grip the guard rail his rescuers saw his eyes widen in horror.

The two crewmen were still turning to look behind them when the towering wave smashed down on to the *Ventura*, hurling them overboard. Reid screamed out in pain as he was slammed face first against the hull, his arm still secured around the Jacob's ladder. The reflection of the deck lights illuminated Milne struggling in the water a few feet away from the hull. Almost within arm's length. Reid stretched out a hand toward Milne. Another wave struck the side of the boat and when Reid resurfaced Milne had disappeared.

The third crewman had secured himself to the stanchion with a rope and had managed to clamber back aboard the pitching vessel. Now he appeared above Reid and began slowly to haul in the Jacob's ladder, dragging Reid from the grip of the churning seas. Once on deck Reid slumped back against the deckhouse and wiped the hair out of his eyes. Blood poured down his face from the gash on his forehead but he was numbed by the cold and felt no pain. He scrambled to his feet and staggered back into the wheelhouse, grabbing the helm again and looking around desperately for the lighthouse beacon. It was nowhere in sight. He checked the ship's head again. The schooner was heading in a southeasterly direction. He was totally disoriented and didn't know where he was anymore so how the hell could he hope to work out a course to steer? He wiped the blood from his eyes and looked around as the crewman entered the wheelhouse. The crewman shook his head as if in answer to the question Reid was about to ask him. Now there were only the two of them. The lighthouse beacon suddenly washed across the *Ventura's* bow again, this time no more than a few hundred feet away from them. Reid swung the wheel violently as he tried to bring the schooner around in a desperate attempt to avoid the rocks. But he knew he was now at the mercy of the seas.

Seconds later the *Ventura* shuddered as the hull was sheared open on the rocks. Reid yelled abandon ship but another enormous wave dashed the schooner once more against the rocks. The crewman screamed as he lost his balance and disappeared over the side. Reid watched helplessly as another wave crashed over the man and he was gone. The *Ventura* was already listing badly and Reid knew it would only be a matter of minutes before she broke up and sank. Gripping the guard rail tightly in both hands, he made his way toward the lifeboat. Again the lighthouse beacon lit up the schooner. Reid estimated that it was now only a hundred yards away. He had to try and reach it in the lifeboat. His feet were suddenly knocked from under him as the *Ventura*'s bow slipped beneath the waves. As he struggled to regain his footing another wave smashed down onto the doomed schooner, tearing the hull in two beneath the waterline and catapulting him into the water. He fought his way to the surface but barely had time to draw breath before the next wave tossed him angrily against the hull, knocking the wind out of him.

The lighthouse beacon scythed across the water, momentarily illuminating one of the *Ventura*'s life buoys which was floating within a few feet of him. He made a desperate grab for it.

The beacon's next rotation picked up the empty life buoy as it was swept out to sea . . .

The hurricane had caught the residents of Nantucket Island completely by surprise. Fortunately there had been only minimal damage to buildings as it skimmed the edge of the island before finally blowing itself out somewhere over the Atlantic Ocean. But had the hurricane changed course the damage could have been far worse. And now the islanders were demanding an explanation from the meteorologists on the mainland as to why they had only forecast a storm warning.

But while their parents harangued the authorities that morning, the children were more interested in combing the beaches and coves in search of anything that might have been washed ashore. Ten-year-old Richard Stegmeyer had called his two best friends, Andrew Mulgrew and Tony Styles, the moment he woke up, and told them to come over to his house straight away so that they could get to Surfside Beach ahead of their schoolmates. After a hurried breakfast his mother had told him that he was to take his seven-year-old sister, Sally, with him. He had been horrified at the idea but no amount of persuasion would change her mind. If he wanted to go to Surfside Beach then he would have to take Sally with him. So when Andrew and Tony arrived the four of them set out on their bicycles for the beach. Sally had lagged behind from the start but Richard knew better than to ride off without her. He had been grounded in the past for not looking after her properly.

They didn't make for the main beach. That would already have been scoured by others. No, like most kids of their age, they had their own area where they could go when the main beach was packed with noisy tourists. They left their bicycles in a clump of trees and hurried down excitedly onto the sand. Andrew immediately made for an outcrop of rocks a hundred yards away and Richard had to stop himself from chasing after him. His mother had given him strict instructions not to go on the rocks. Normally he'd have disobeyed her but Sally would be sure to tell. Tony gave him a quizzical look then shrugged and ran after Andrew. Richard was staring disconsolately after his friends when a small hand suddenly tugged at his T-shirt.

"What's that?" Sally asked, pointing to something which lay on the sand beyond the rocks.

Richard started toward the object and as he got closer realized that it was a life buoy. He dropped to his knees in the wet sand and turned it over. The words "*Ventura*—Milford" were written around it in black letters. He knew Milford was a small fishing port on the Connecticut coastline about a hundred miles south of Nantucket Island. He shouted to Andrew and Tony and when their heads appeared above a rock he brandished the life buoy triumphantly above his head. They scrambled over the rocks, jumped onto the sand, and ran over to where he stood.

"Where did you find it?" Tony asked breathlessly.

"Right here," Richard replied, grinning.

"I saw it first," Sally added defiantly but the boys ignored her.

"Do you think it was caught in the storm last night?" Tony asked, looking out to sea.

Richard shrugged. "We could phone the Milford harbor master later this morning when my parents are at work. He could tell us about the *Ventura*."

"Yeah, neat idea," Tony said, nodding his head.

Sally suddenly tugged again at the back of Richard's T-shirt. He brushed her hand away but she continued to pull at him insistently.

"What?" he asked sharply.

"What's that over there?" she asked.

Something was bobbing in the shallows close to the rocks. Tony glanced excitedly at Andrew then, kicking off his sandals, he ran toward the water. Andrew also kicked off his shoes and sprinted after him.

"You stay here," Richard said to Sally as he slipped off his plimsolls.

"Why?"

"Because it's dangerous down there," Richard replied, tossing the plimsolls onto the sand.

"But you're going down there."

"I'm older than you," Richard retorted. "Now stay here. I'll tell you when it's safe to come down."

"Promise?"

"Yes, just stay there," he shouted over his shoulder as he ran down to the water. "What is it?" he asked excitedly.

"A crate," Tony replied through gritted teeth as he and Andrew struggled to pull it toward the beach. "Jesus, it's heavy."

"Well, don't just stand there!" Andrew chided, flashing Richard an angry look.

The three boys managed to get a grip on the wooden crate and after some difficulty finally dragged it up onto the beach.

"Now what?" Tony asked, slumping exhaustedly onto the sand.

"We open it of course," Andrew retorted.

"Yeah," Richard agreed.

"How?" Tony asked.

"There must be something we can use," Andrew replied, scanning the beach around them.

"Use your penknife," Tony said.

"It wouldn't be strong enough," Richard retorted. "The blade would snap. You two go and look amongst the rocks. There's sure to be something there. I'll wait here."

"Can I come down now?" Sally called out after the other two had headed off toward the rocks.

Richard beckoned her toward him as he took a closer look at the crate. It was roughly four feet long and two feet wide but bore no markings of origin on any of the sides.

"Maybe it's treasure," Sally said behind him.

"Yeah, sure," he muttered.

Andrew and Tony returned a minute later with a piece of driftwood they had found in a pool by the rocks. Andrew managed to wedge it under the lid and gritted his teeth as he slowly forced the lid up enough for Richard and Tony to get their fingers underneath it. He continued to lever the lid with the piece of driftwood while Richard and Andrew pulled at it with their hands. Richard gave a whoop of delight when it finally came loose under their sustained pressure. A sheet of black tarpaulin had been secured around the contents of the crate. Andrew took out his penknife and sank the blade into the tarpaulin. He sliced it open then pulled it apart. Inside was a row of wooden boxes, each roughly forty inches in length, packed between layers of polystyrene. He removed one of the boxes, noticing that there was another one underneath it. He placed the box on the sand and, using his penknife, carefully loosened the nails at one end of the box. Then, hooking his fingers under the lid, he pulled it open.

"What is it?" Sally asked, struggling to see over their shoulders.

"It's a rifle," Richard said, looking up slowly at Andrew. "Do you think all the boxes contain rifles?"

"Dunno," Andrew replied, then removed another box and used his penknife to open it. It, too, contained a rifle which, like the first, was wrapped in a transparent sheet of plastic.

"What are we going to do?" Tony asked, glancing nervously at the rifles.

"We've got to call the cops," Richard said. "You three wait here. I'll ride to the nearest pay phone and call them. OK?"

Andrew nodded.

"Put the boxes back inside the crate," Richard told the others. "And guard it with your lives."

"You can count on it," Andrew replied.

Richard swallowed nervously then turned and ran back up the beach to where he had left his bicycle.

TWO

"This is it, mate," the driver said, bringing the taxi to a stop. "The Crescent Hotel."

C. W. Whitlock peered through the rain-streaked window at the building. The paint was peeling off the whitewashed walls and the neon sign above the revolving door proclaimed the hotel's name in garish colors.

"You sure you got the right place?" the driver asked, eyeing Whitlock's expensive Armani suit.

"Quite sure," Whitlock replied with a quick smile as he paid the fare.

The driver shrugged. Whitlock picked up his attaché case and climbed out into the rain, slamming the door behind him and hurrying across to the hotel entrance. Once inside the foyer he brushed the raindrops off his jacket and crossed to the reception desk. It was deserted. A middle-aged woman sat at the switchboard in the back office. She gave him a nod of acknowledgment and went back to her telephone conversation.

Whitlock placed his attaché case on the threadbare

carpet at his feet and drummed his fingers impatiently on the wooden counter. He was a forty-four-year-old Kenyan with a light complexion and sharp features which were tempered by the neatly trimmed moustache he had worn since his early twenties. He had been educated in England and after graduating from Oxford had returned to Kenya where he had served in the army and the Intelligence Corps before joining UNACO as one of its first recruits.

UNACO, which had its headquarters at the United Nations Building in New York, had a total of two hundred and nine permanent staff worldwide, thirty of whom were crack field operatives who had been siphoned off from the military, police and intelligence services around the world. Each of the ten teams was designated by the prefix "Strike Force" and its intensive training included unarmed combat and the use of all known firearms. Whitlock had been the team leader of Strike Force Three since its inception but when the UNACO Director, Malcolm Philpott, had recently been forced into early retirement due to ill-health, his deputy, Sergei Kolchinsky, had been appointed the new Director, and Whitlock had accepted the post vacated by Kolchinsky. Whitlock had only taken the position to appease his wife, Carmen, who, fearing for his safety, had wanted him out of the field. It had helped to bridge the rift that had once threatened to break up their marriage. Deep down he still longed to return to the field, but he was far too professional to let his feelings interfere with his work . . .

"Can I help you?" the woman finally called out from the switchboard, her hand over the mouthpiece.

"Mr. Swain's room number please."

She consulted a clipboard in front of her. "Twenty-six," she announced, then went back to her telephone conversation.

Whitlock exhaled deeply and rapped loudly on

the counter to catch her attention again. "If it's not too much trouble, could you tell me which floor that's on?"

"Second," came the nonchalant reply.

Whitlock eyed the old lift with some trepidation and decided to use the stairs instead. He found the room and knocked sharply on the door, which opened immediately.

"Hello, C. W. Come on in," the man said, beckoning Whitlock into the room.

Dave Swain was the team leader of Strike Force Seven. A tall, burly man in his late thirties, he was a former presidential bodyguard who had spent ten years with the FBI's Secret Service before Philpott had recruited him. The other two members of the team were Alain Mosser, a tough-talking Frenchman, also in his late thirties, who had spent several years with the *Direction de la Surveillance du Territoire* before joining UNACO two years ago, and thirty-one-year-old Jason Geddis, UNACO's latest recruit, who had served with the Canadian Security Intelligence Service for eight years. He had only been with UNACO for four months. All three men were dressed in scruffy jeans and sweatshirts.

"When did you get in to London?" Swain asked.

"About an hour ago," Whitlock replied. "I checked into my hotel then came straight over here."

"Well, thanks for bringing the rain with you, C. W.," Geddis said with a grin as he stood up to shake Whitlock's hand.

"Always happy to oblige," Whitlock said, then turned to Mosser. "Alain, *comment vas-tu?*"

"A lot better if I didn't have to kick my heels in this damn pigsty," Mosser snorted.

"Why did you pick this place?" Whitlock asked Swain.

"We've blended in better being in a dump like this," Swain answered.

"One Frenchman. Two Americans. Yes, we really blend in well around here," Mosser added, shaking his head. "I will be glad to be out of here."

"One Frenchman, one American and one Canadian," Geddis corrected him.

"Ah, what is the difference?"

"It's like someone calling you a Swiss or a Belgian," Geddis told him.

"I hate to break up this geography lesson, but could we get down to business?" Whitlock cut in sharply. "What did you get from your informer?"

"We haven't seen him yet," Swain replied. "He cried off an hour before we were scheduled to rendezvous with him at Hyde Park this morning."

Whitlock sat down slowly in the chair behind him. "I put my neck on the block when I told Scotland Yard's anti-terrorist squad to arrest Sean Farrell when he arrived back from the continent. I assured them that we would get enough evidence to put him away for life. That's what you told me. Now what am I supposed to tell them? Let him go? Let a known IRA cell commander walk so that he can return to Europe to continue his campaign of terror against more British servicemen and their families?"

"We're meeting him later tonight," Swain said defensively. "Midnight at a multi-story car park in Hammersmith."

"And what if he cries off again?" Whitlock demanded. "It's not as if it's the first time this has happened. I thought you said you had his complete trust?"

"We do," Geddis said quickly. "We've been on this case for the last three months, C. W. We aren't about to let Farrell walk now. Not after all the work we've put into it. Our informer will come good, you mark my words."

Whitlock sighed deeply. "I hope you're right, Jason. UNACO's got a lot riding on this one. Not least our reputation. We're in a transitional period now that Colonel Philpott's gone, and that means we're being scrutinized by the other intelligence agencies around the world. They all want to see how we'll perform with a new team at the helm. Let's not give them any ammunition to use against us at some later stage."

"Don't worry, C. W., he'll be there tonight," Swain said. "And you'll have your evidence by the morning."

"Why did he put it off this morning?" Whitlock asked.

"He claims he thought he saw one of Farrell's team watching his flat last night," Swain told him. "But when he went outside the man was gone."

"It's probably nothing," Geddis said. "He's totally above suspicion as far as the IRA are concerned. He's one of their top contacts here in London."

Whitlock looked at his watch. "You've still got six hours to kill before you meet him. Have you eaten yet?"

"We were going to grab a bite later at McDonald's," Geddis said.

"The food here is terrible," Mosser added, pulling a face. "We have been eating nothing but pizzas and hamburgers ever since we got here."

"Come over and eat with me tonight," Whitlock said, getting to his feet. "We'll put it down to expenses."

"You're on," Swain said with a grin. "Where are you staying?"

"The Churchill on Portman Square."

"Very nice," Swain said, whistling softly.

"Being on the management side does have its compensations," Whitlock said, then paused as he reached the door. "What if your informer wants to get hold of you tonight?"

"I carry a beeper," Swain said. "He can have me paged if I'm not here."

"OK, let's say seven-thirty in my room. We'll order up from room service. That way we can talk freely." Whitlock opened the door then looked back at them. "Oh, and gentlemen, tidy yourselves up before you come over tonight. I don't have to tell *you* how important it is to blend in, do I?"

It was twelve forty-five by the time they reached the multi-story car park in Hammersmith. The rain had stopped earlier in the evening and as the clouds continued to drift northward, a brisk southeasterly wind had sprung up across the capital. Geddis brought the hired Ford to a halt in front of the boom gate. He paid for a ticket and the boom gate opened automatically. As arranged earlier with their informer, he drove to the underground level, pulled up in the space closest to the lift and switched off the engine. Swain, who was in the passenger seat, unbuckled his safety belt and got out of the car. He looked around slowly, surprised by how well lit it was compared to car parks in New York. There they stole the cars *and* the light fittings. He took a pack of Marlboro from his pocket and lit one.

"Quiet, huh?" Mosser said behind him.

"That's obviously why he chose the place," Swain replied, proffering the cigarettes to Mosser, who took one and lit it.

"Better make sure though," Mosser said.

The two men moved off in different directions to carry out a quick, but thorough, search of the basement area. Satisfied they were alone, they returned to where Geddis was now leaning against the side of the car.

Swain looked at his watch. Eleven fifty-six. "OK, time to take up your positions. Jason, I want you to keep the engine running in case we need to get out of here in a hurry."

Geddis nodded then climbed back behind the wheel and started the car. All three men were armed. Unlike many of the other intelligence agencies, UNACO didn't insist that their field operatives use one particular type of handgun. The choice of weapon was left entirely up to the individual. Swain carried a 10mm Colt Delta Elite, a variant of the old Colt M1911 that he had used in the Security Service; Mosser the French 9mm PA15 automatic and Geddis a Beretta 92, the most popular handgun amongst UNACO field operatives. Mosser took up a position beside a pillar where he could observe both the lift and the door which led onto the stairs. Swain crossed to the wall at the side of the door and took a last drag on his cigarette before dropping it onto the ground and crushing it underfoot. He could see Mosser and the car from where he stood but was out of sight of the door, the lift and the ramp leading up to the exit. He looked at his watch again. Eleven fifty-eight.

Mosser stubbed out his cigarette then loosened his tie and unfastened the top button of his shirt. He hated wearing suits but Swain had insisted they dress smartly to humor Whitlock. The meal had been delicious. Swain, as usual, had ordered a porterhouse steak. Mosser had realized within weeks of joining Strike Force Seven just how fanatical Swain was about his red meat. The two men had become firm friends from the start and, unlike most of the other Strike Force teams, they enjoyed socializing outside work, which usually meant barbecues at the Swains' house on Long Island. Swain's wife and two teenage daughters treated him like family. It had all helped to soften the blow of his bitter divorce only months before he had come to America. Joining UNACO had been the best move he had ever made and he couldn't imagine life again outside the organization . . .

The door opened fractionally and Mosser instinctively touched his holstered automatic. For a moment nothing happened then a face peered cautiously around the edge of the door. Mosser exhaled deeply and let his hand drop to his side. The man who emerged from behind the door was in his early thirties with a thin, sallow face and long black hair that hung down untidily onto his shoulders. He was wearing a brown bomber jacket and faded jeans torn at the knees. Gerard McGuire had been Sean Farrell's London contact for the past four years and a UNACO informer for half that time. When Swain recruited him McGuire had laid down one proviso—he would only deal with Swain. It had proved an awkward arrangement in the past when other teams had needed information on IRA activities on the British mainland but McGuire steadfastly refused to compromise his situation. He trusted Swain. Nobody else. It had often meant pulling Swain off an assignment and flying him to London to meet with McGuire. But his information had proved so invaluable in the past that both Philpott and Kolchinsky had been willing to play it by McGuire's rules. It had been a small price to pay.

McGuire closed the door silently behind him and glanced furtively in the direction of the car. Geddis, his hands resting lightly on the steering wheel, raised a finger to acknowledge him. McGuire ignored him and looked questioningly at Mosser who led him over to where Swain was standing out of sight behind a wall. Mosser then left the two men to talk. He took up a position close to the lift and although he could still see the two men he could only hear snatches of the conversation.

Suddenly there was a roar of acceleration as a white Rover Montego screeched into view and sped toward them, its lights on full. Swain watched in horror as a silenced Uzi snaked out from the back window and cut Mosser down. Geddis immediately slammed the Ford into reverse.

"Get in," Swain yelled, grabbing McGuire's arm to bundle him into the backseat.

McGuire broke free and fled toward the door. Swain sprinted after him. Geddis got off a shot at the Rover before a burst from the Uzi punctured the windscreen. Two of the bullets took him in the head and the Beretta slipped from his fingers as he slumped forward onto the steering wheel. The Ford careered backward out of control. McGuire flung open the door and a row of bullets peppered the wall inches away from him. He stumbled and fell through the doorway. Swain heard the car behind him and was still turning around when it smashed into the door, ripping it off its hinges, crushing him between the door and the wall.

The driver of the Rover dimmed his lights as two masked figures got out of the car. The taller one, who was over six feet tall, was still clutching the Uzi when he ran across to the Ford and switched off the engine.

"You go after McGuire," the tall one shouted out to his colleague in a strong Irish accent. "I'll make sure these three are dead."

The driver of the Rover, who was also wearing a balaclava, spun the car around and sped back toward the ramp, still hoping to cut McGuire off before he reached the street.

There was a "ping" sound and a laughing couple emerged from the lift. The woman screamed in terror when she saw the man swing the Uzi toward them.

"No!" his colleague shouted, pushing the barrel downward. It was a female voice. "Come on, let's go."

The two of them ran up the stairs, the woman pulling the balaclava off her head as they went. Fiona Gallagher was an attractive twenty-six-year-old with pale blue eyes and short, spiky blonde hair and a petite figure, which was disguised under the baggy clothes. As they reached the door leading out into the street her companion also removed his balaclava. Liam Kerrigan was in his late thirties with cropped black hair and the face of an ex-boxer. He reached for the handle but Fiona quickly pushed her palm against the door and gestured angrily to the Uzi in his hand. He slid it discreetly under his jacket and they stepped out into the street. The Rover was already parked outside the door. Hugh Mullen had also discarded his balaclava. He was two years Fiona's senior with curly brown hair and wore wire-rimmed glasses.

"He's gone," Mullen said. "He could have disappeared up any of these side streets. You want to look for him?"

"No, we've got to get out of here," Fiona said, shaking her head. "We left a couple of witnesses down there. It won't be long before they call the police."

"You should have let me kill them," Kerrigan snapped.

"We don't kill innocent by-standers," she retorted, then got in beside Mullen.

Kerrigan climbed into the back and slammed the door shut. He glowered at her but said nothing. Mullen engaged gears and drove away, careful to keep within the speed limit. There would be another chance to get McGuire. And he already knew how they could track him down . . .

Sergei Kolchinsky had just entered his flat when the telephone rang. It was Whitlock. Kolchinsky listened, pale and frowning, as Whitlock told him about the ambush in London two hours earlier. Swain had been killed instantly. Geddis had died in the ambulance. Mosser was in intensive care at the Charing

Cross Hospital, his condition serious. The doctor who had operated on Mosser had told Whitlock that even if he did make a full recovery, it would be very unlikely that he would ever be able to walk again. UNACO had lost field operatives in the past but never an entire Strike Force team. Both men knew it would certainly renew calls amongst its critics to have the organization disbanded. There were those governments who had felt for some time that UNACO was little more than a group of vigilantes working outside the law. And the grumbling disquiet had certainly intensified since Philpott's departure. Kolchinsky had barely settled into his new post and he was already facing the most serious problem of his professional career.

Kolchinsky was an overweight, fifty-two-year-old Russian with a doleful face and thinning black hair. He was a brilliant tactician whose meteoric rise through the ranks of the KGB had been abruptly curtailed when he had dared to speak out against the inhuman methods used by the KGB to interrogate prisoners. He had spent the next twelve years as a military attaché in a succession of Soviet embassies in the West before returning to a desk job at the Lubianka. When Philpott's deputy, a former KGB operative, was sent back to Russia in disgrace for spying, Kolchinsky's name was one of those put forward as a suitable replacement. He was Philpott's first, and only, choice. Kolchinsky had been Philpott's deputy for three years before his promotion to UNACO Director. But at that moment Kolchinsky would gladly have exchanged the mundane desk job at the Lubianka for what he knew was going to be a very rough ride over the next few weeks . . .

"I'll need you back here as soon as possible, C. W.," Kolchinsky said, reaching for his cigarettes on the coffee table in front of him. "As you can imagine, I'm going to be tied up in an endless succession of meetings with the various ambassadors once they've been briefed by their governments."

"I guessed as much," Whitlock replied. "I've already booked myself on a flight to JFK at eleven tomorrow morning, British time. That means I'll be back in New York for breakfast."

"Good. I doubt I'll even get into the office tomorrow. I should think most of the day will be spent going over the events with the Secretary-General. Can you send a fax through to headquarters giving as much info as possible on what actually happened over there tonight? At least then I'll have something to work from when I meet with the Secretary-General."

"I'll get on to it straight away," Whitlock replied. "Which team are you going to bring in to replace Strike Force Seven?"

"There is only one team I'd trust to handle something as delicate as this," Kolchinsky said, lighting his cigarette. "Your old team. Strike Force Three."

"Yes, I'd have gone for Mike and Sabrina as well. But what about Fabio Paluzzi? He hasn't actually worked on an assignment with them yet."

"Fabio's a good man. He proved that during his transitional period with Strike Force Five. He'll be all right."

"It'll be some baptism of fire for him," Whitlock said at length.

"He's got to start somewhere," Kolchinsky replied, glancing at the clock on the mantelpiece. It was almost eight-thirty. "I'll ring the duty officer at headquarters and tell him to put the three of them on a Code Red standby. What time do you want to brief them in the morning?"

"Make it nine-thirty to be on the safe side."

"Fine. Nine-thirty."

"Are you going to break the news to the families?"

"It's part of the job," Kolchinsky replied grimly.

"I'll ring Ann Swain as soon as I've spoken to the duty officer. Jason wasn't married, was he?"

"No, engaged. His fiancée lives somewhere in Alberta, I think."

"I'll get the details from the duty officer. Well, I'll see you when I see you. I think that's the best way to put it."

"Good night, Sergei."

Kolchinsky replaced the receiver and poured himself a stiff bourbon before dialing the number for the duty officer at UNACO headquarters.

"I don't know," Fabio Paluzzi said after a moment's thought. "What do you think?"

"I don't believe this," Claudine Paluzzi retorted, looking despairingly at her husband. "Fabio, which of the two colors do you prefer? The cream or the pale blue?"

Paluzzi looked at the two diagonal streaks of paint his wife had applied to the wall then shrugged. "You know I'm no good with color schemes."

"Forget about color schemes. All I want to know is which of the colors *you* prefer."

"The pale blue, I guess."

"You guess?"

"The pale blue. Definitely. Satisfied?"

She sighed deeply but said nothing. He went into the kitchen, opened the fridge, and helped himself to a beer.

He was a thirty-six-year-old Italian with a stocky physique, cropped brown hair and a gaunt face which was offset by a wide mouth and square jaw. Like his father, he had joined the carabinieri on leaving school and spent several years with them before being recruited by the *Nucleo Operativo Centrale di Sicurezza*, Italy's elite anti-terrorist squad. He was then twenty-seven years old. By the age of thirty-

three he had reached the rank of major. He was the
unit expert on the Red Brigades and had worked with
UNACO on an operation in Italy which had first
brought him to the attention of Malcolm Philpott. But
it was only when Philpott discovered that Paluzzi
was at loggerheads with his superior that he made a
move to bring him to UNACO. It was a challenge
Paluzzi readily accepted.

He had spent the first few months in New York in
a small UNACO safe house with his wife and their
ten-month-old son, Dario. They had spent much of
their spare time searching for a place of their own,
but nothing took their fancy. Then one of his UNACO
colleagues had told him about the apartment on the
lower East Side. It belonged to a friend who wanted
to sell quickly. Claudine had loved it the moment she
saw it. They had moved in three days earlier . . .

He moved to the door and looked at his wife, who
was crouched on the bare wooden floorboards reading the instructions on the side of the paint tin. She
was a former Air France stewardess, five years his
junior, with a pretty face and long brown hair which
was tied in a ponytail at the back of her head.

She looked up at him and her eyes automatically
locked on to the bottle in his hand. "How many beers
have you had tonight?"

"What's that supposed to mean?" he retorted defensively.

"It's your fourth, isn't it?"

"So what?" he demanded.

"You never drank like this when we lived in
Italy," she said, getting to her feet.

"You never nagged like this when we lived in
Italy," he snapped back angrily.

His raised voice woke Dario.

"I'll see to him," Paluzzi said tersely.

"You're not going near him in that mood," she
shot back and disappeared into the bedroom.

Four beers and she was acting like he was a hopeless alcoholic. When was the last time he had been drunk? His stag party two years ago. No, it wasn't the beers. It went a lot deeper than that. He knew she was homesick. She'd never told him in so many words but it was obvious by the way she had been acting in the last month. He even wondered if she had really wanted to move into the apartment or whether she'd just used it as an excuse to get out of the small, cramped safe house where they had been at each other's throats over every little thing. And now it was starting again . . .

A deep, thudding vibration suddenly reverberated through the floorboards. A stereo in one of the apartments down the hall. He waited for the noise to abate, assuming that the volume had been turned up accidentally. Nothing happened; indeed it was getting louder. Claudine appeared at the door, Dario cradled in her arms.

"It sounds like one of our neighbors is having a party," Paluzzi said. "I think it's time I went over and introduced myself."

"Leave it, Fabio, it probably won't go on for very long."

"And if it does? What about Dario?"

"How hypocritical can you get? It's all right for you to wake him up with your shouting but let someone else disturb him and you're on the warpath."

"He's my son," Paluzzi retorted.

She looked down at Dario. His eyes were closed. "He's almost asleep now. I'll close the bedroom door, he won't hear a thing."

Paluzzi put his beer down and walked to the front door. "I'll sort it out, don't worry."

She knew it was pointless trying to stop him. He'd made up his mind to go, and that was it. "For God's sake don't get into a fight. We've only just moved in, remember?"

Paluzzi slipped out into the corridor, closing the door quietly behind him. The noise came from the apartment two doors down. He rapped sharply on the door. It opened and the smile faltered on the youth's face when he saw it wasn't one of his friends. Paluzzi could see a handful of teenagers already congregated inside the apartment. All wore jeans and studded black leather jackets with the names of their favorite heavy-metal bands printed on the back.

"What do you want?" the youth demanded.

"My wife and I have just moved in down the hall. Apartment Seventeen. We have a little boy, he's not even a year old. The music woke him up. I'd be grateful if you'd turn it down so that we can get him back to sleep."

"No, man, I ain't turning it down," the youth replied with a sneer. "This is America. It's a free country. You can do what you want, when you want, and how you want. Capish?"

Paluzzi clenched his fists at his sides but wisely kept his emotions in check. He could take the youth apart with one hand tied behind his back. But that wasn't the issue. Claudine was right. He couldn't afford to get involved in a brawl. Not only would it reflect badly on their tenancy but it could also bring unnecessary attention on himself which, in turn, could jeopardize his position at UNACO. He had to be diplomatic.

"OK, here's the deal. Either the music's been turned down by the time I get back to my apartment or else I'm going to call the cops. I've got a feeling they might be interested in the contents of those skins you and those dummies in there are smoking. You could flush them down the john but it's the smell that lingers, isn't it? You just can't get rid of it." Paluzzi held up a finger as if he'd just had a sudden thought. "You could try telling the cops that this is America. It's a free country. You can do what you want, when you want, and how you want. I'm sure they'd capish, don't you?"

The music had been turned down before the youth had closed the door behind Paluzzi.

Claudine was waiting at the front door. "I'm impressed. Persuasion without violence. You're definitely mellowing in your old age."

"How's Dario?"

"He seems to have settled again."

Paluzzi retrieved his beer and was about to take a sip when he saw that Claudine was watching him. "OK, I won't drink any more. You know, you're getting more like your mother every day."

The telephone rang and Claudine answered it. It was for her husband and she put the receiver down on the table without a word. He knew he shouldn't have mentioned her mother. It was always a touchy subject. Paluzzi picked up the receiver. The duty officer asked him to identify himself by the ID number he'd been given when he joined UNACO. It was also the number on his personnel file which was kept under lock and key in the Director's office. Paluzzi repeated the number.

"You're on a Code Red," the duty officer informed him. That meant he was officially on standby. "The briefing will be held at nine-thirty sharp in the Director's office tomorrow morning." The line went dead and Paluzzi replaced the receiver thoughtfully. It would be his first assignment with Mike Graham and Sabrina Carver since his transfer to Strike Force Three. Sure, he had worked with them in Italy when he was with the *NOCS* but that was different. Now they were his partners. He would have to slot into Whitlock's old position. It would be difficult but he was confident he could do it . . .

* * *

Sabrina Carver hated blind dates. Especially when they turned out to be real jerks . . .

She had only agreed to make up the foursome because she knew how much it would mean to her close friend, Simone Forrest. Simone, a leading New York fashion model, had rung her the previous night to say that Steve Rutherford, the Canadian photographer she had met earlier that month on a shoot in Toronto, was in New York on a short visit. But there was a snag. His best friend, Doug Keeble, was with him. He wanted a partner for the evening and Simone had told him she knew just the person . . .

Sabrina had liked Rutherford straight away. He was just as Simone had described him. Polite, affable and strikingly handsome. She could well understand how Simone had fallen for him. So why did he have a friend like Doug Keeble? Admittedly, Keeble was also good-looking, but that was where the comparison with Rutherford ended. He was loud with a vulgar sense of humor and a bad case of wandering hands. She'd already given up counting the number of times she had had to prize his hand off her knee. She had even spoken to him discreetly about it but he had only laughed it off. Simone certainly owed her for this one. Then, after Rutherford had settled the bill, Simone announced that they were off to a nightclub. Sabrina knew Simone wanted to be alone with Rutherford. But she was damned if she was going to entertain Keeble for the rest of the evening . . .

"Where should we go now?" Keeble asked after Rutherford and Simone had left the restaurant. He slipped his hand over hers. "You know New York."

Sabrina eased her hand out from under his. "*We* aren't going anywhere. I'm going back to my apartment, I've got a busy day ahead of me tomorrow."

"It's still early. We can have a few drinks somewhere and take it from there." He grinned. "I'll see that you're in bed in good time for your beauty sleep."

Sabrina inhaled sharply. She was struggling to control her temper. If there was one thing she hated, it was being patronized. Especially by someone like Keeble. It was the same kind of chauvinism that she had encountered when she first arrived at UNACO from the FBI two years earlier. She supposed it was to have been expected as she had been the only female field operative in the organization: nonetheless she had found it irritating. But she had managed to overcome her critics with her gritty determination and her unswerving belief in her own ability. Those same critics now regarded her as their equal. Not that anyone outside UNACO, apart from her parents, knew that she was a member of Strike Force Three. As far as her friends were concerned, she was a translator at the United Nations. Secrecy was essential to the organization.

"Come on, let's go," Keeble said, reaching for her hand.

She pulled her hand away roughly from his and stood up, her eyes blazing. "I really don't give a damn where you go. But one thing's certain, it won't be with me. Understood?"

She turned sharply on her heel and walked to the door. Every man in the restaurant watched her leave. She was a strikingly beautiful twenty-eight-year-old with shoulder-length blonde hair tinted with auburn highlights, and a near perfect figure accentuated by the contour-hugging velvet dress she was wearing. She emerged onto the street then paused to retrieve her car keys from her purse.

"Hey, wait up," Keeble shouted breathlessly from behind her. "What the hell are you playing at?"

She looked around at him. "What does it look like? I'm going home."

"And what about me? Steve's got the car, you know."

"So get a cab," Sabrina retorted. "You want me to hail one for you?"

"What's wrong with you?" Keeble demanded. "You get a free meal and this is how you show your appreciation. You embarrass me in the restaurant then storm out like some spoiled brat. I think you'd better get your priorities right."

Sabrina stared at Keeble in disbelief. She opened her mouth to say something then abruptly changed her mind. What good would it do to try and reason with someone like him? The guy was still firmly entrenched in the Dark Ages. Better just to walk away.

"Don't turn your back on me," he snarled, grabbing her arm.

She broke his grip with ease but resisted the temptation to dump him on the sidewalk. It wouldn't be difficult. Not with a black belt in karate. But he wasn't worth it. Instead she levelled a finger of warning at him. "You touch me again and you'll be spending the rest of the night in a police cell."

"At least the company would be better," Keeble snapped.

"In your case, you'd probably be right," she retorted sarcastically as she walked to her champagne-colored Mercedes-Benz 500SEC which was parked at the end of the street.

Keeble cursed angrily but he seemed to have given up on her at last and hailed a cab.

Sabrina watched as it disappeared into the traffic, then started up her car and drove back to her Manhattan apartment. The night porter looked up from the magazine he was reading to greet her as she entered the black and white tiled foyer. She smiled back at him then unlocked the door of her small flat which led directly into the sparsely furnished lounge. Kicking off her high-heeled shoes, she crossed to a shelf lined with an impressive collection of modern jazz compact discs, selected the latest Bob Berg, and fed it into the Wadia transport. She switched the kettle on in the kitchen then went to her bedroom to change out of her dress. She was about to take a gray track-suit from the cupboard when the telephone rang. Well, at least it couldn't be Doug Keeble. He didn't have her number. She sat on the edge of the bed and was about to answer it when a thought struck her. What if he had asked Simone for her number? She wouldn't have given it to him, would she? There was only one way to find out. She picked up the receiver.

"Miss Carver?" a male voice inquired.

"Speaking," she replied.

"This is Llewelyn and Lee," the man continued.

She gave a sigh of relief. "Llewelyn and Lee" was the name Philpott had devised as a cover for UNACO's thirty unlisted telephone lines. The recep-tionist during the day, or duty officer at night, would only drop the pretense if the second party could iden-tify themselves by means of either an ID number or a password. Sabrina gave him her ID number, and the duty officer repeated his message once more.

"I'll be there," Sabrina replied.

"You wouldn't happen to know where Mr. Gra-ham is, would you?" the duty officer asked after a moment's pause. "I can't seem to get hold of him on the phone and he's not answering his beeper either."

"I know where he'll be," she told him. "Leave it to me, I'll pass the message on to him."

"I'd appreciate that. Could you give me a ring once you've spoken to him so that I can log it in the diary?"

"Sure, I'll do that. Oh, and don't mention to Mr. Kolchinsky that you couldn't get hold of him."

"It's regulations, Miss Carver. The Director specif-ically asked me to make a note of any operative not responding to a call."

"Just this time," she said softly. "I promise I'll have a word with him about it. And if it does happen again, you can report him. Please."

There was another pause. "I guess it'll be OK so long as he gets the message."

"He will. And thanks."

"Sure," the duty officer replied, then the line went dead.

Sabrina replaced the receiver then crossed to the cupboard again where she selected a pair of designer jeans and a baggy white T-shirt. She knew Graham would be at the Manion Hotel in Yorkville. He traveled down from his home in Vermont every Wednesday to put fresh flowers on the graves of his wife and son and stayed overnight at the Manion before returning home the following day. She tucked her jeans into a pair of brown ankle boots, grabbed the leather jacket from behind the door, and left the apartment.

"Excuse me, Mr. Mitchell, we're running a bit low on bourbon."

Peter Mitchell looked up from the chessboard and nodded to the barman. "OK, Leo, I'll get some from the cellar." His eyes flickered across to the man seated opposite him. "I won't be a minute, Mike."

Mike Graham shrugged. "Take as long as you want, Mitch. The *coup de grâce* can wait."

"*Coup de grâce?*" Mitchell snorted. "It's a temporary hiccup, nothing more."

"Really?" Graham replied with a knowing smile.

Mitchell dismissed him with a wave of his hand then got to his feet and followed Leo to the bar. Graham took a sip of Perrier water and looked around him slowly. The bar was busy for a Wednesday night. He had been going to the Windmill Tavern for the past five years ever since he found out, quite by chance, that it was owned by Mitchell. The two men had become friends while serving in Vietnam together but had lost contact when Mitchell was injured in combat and flown back to the States for treatment. It was only when the two men had met up again that Graham discovered Mitchell had lost his right arm as a result of the injury.

Graham put the glass down then sat back to await Mitchell's return. He was an athletically-built thirty-eight-year-old with a youthfully handsome face and tousled auburn hair which hung untidily over the collar of his shirt. He was a native New Yorker who, after graduating from UCLA with a degree in Political Science, had fulfilled his childhood dream by signing for the New York Giants as a rookie quarterback in the early seventies. A month later he was drafted into Vietnam where a shoulder injury put paid to a promising football career. He had liaised closely with the CIA in the last year of the war and was recruited by the elite Delta unit when he returned to the States.

Eleven years later he was promoted to leader of Squadron-B. His first mission was to take a unit into Libya and destroy a known terrorist base. They were about to close in on the base when news reached him that his wife, Carrie, and five-year-old son, Mikey, had been abducted by masked men outside their New York apartment. He was offered the chance to abort the mission but chose instead to give the order to advance. The base was destroyed but the two main targets, Salim Al-Makesh and Jean-Jacques Bernard, managed to escape. A nationwide hunt was mounted for his family but no trace of them was found. He was retired from Delta at his own request and the Delta Commander forwarded his dossier to UNACO as a possible field operative. Although the Secretary-General had turned him down on the strength of his psychiatric report, Philpott had personally overruled him.

Graham's maverick tendencies had quickly put him at odds with his superiors and it had come to a head when he undertook an unauthorized mission to track down Bernard, the man he held responsible for the disappearance of his family. Although Bernard was subsequently killed, Graham found out that it was actually a senior CIA official who had ordered the kidnapping to give Bernard, who was working for him, time to escape. He also discovered where the bodies of Carrie and Mikey had been buried and, after the remains were exhumed, he had them reburied side by side in the grounds of the church where he and Carrie had been married. The Secretary-General had wanted Graham dismissed; Philpott had again overruled him. But it had been made perfectly clear to Graham that the next time he overstepped the mark he would be out. He knew it was a threat not to be taken lightly . . .

Mitchell returned to the table and sat down again. He studied the pieces then scratched his head thoughtfully. "You're right, it doesn't look good. Not good at all."

"All you have to do is topple your king and hand me the twenty bucks we wagered on the game."

"And go down without a fight?" Mitchell retorted. "You know me better than that, Mike."

"I know you're a tight-fisted son-of-a-bitch when it comes to handing over money," Graham replied with a grin.

Mitchell made the move Graham had anticipated. The net was closing in on Mitchell. Graham put Mitchell's king in check.

"That wasn't very nice . . ." Mitchell trailed off and whistled softly to himself as he looked past Graham. "Now she *is* nice."

Graham looked round and cursed softly under his breath. Sabrina was standing in the entrance, her hands dug into the pockets of her leather jacket, her eyes scanning the room for him. He turned back to Mitchell. "She's a friend of mine."

"I'm sorry, Mike, I didn't know."

"Forget it," Graham replied. "Make your move."

"Aren't you going to signal to her? She's obviously looking for you."

"She'll find me. Now make your move, Mitch."

Sabrina finally saw Graham. He was sitting at a corner table with his back to her. She headed for the table. A hand suddenly grabbed her arm and spun her around.

"Looking for some action, baby?" the man asked without releasing the pressure on her arm.

"Would you mind letting go of my arm?" she said politely.

"Sit down," he said, and indicated to one of the other two men at the table to pull up a chair for her.

Mitchell looked past Graham, his eyes narrowed anxiously. "Mike, trouble."

Graham looked around irritably. Three men in their early twenties. Probably city kids. "She can look after herself," he replied with a dismissive shrug then gestured to the board. "I'm still waiting for you to make your move, Mitch."

"Mike, we can't just leave her over there!" Mitchell said sharply. "It's three against one."

Graham grabbed Mitchell's arm as he tried to get up. "I told you already, she can handle them. Now make your move, or forfeit the game."

Sabrina pulled her arm free just as the chair was pushed roughly against the back of her legs. She managed to keep her balance but when she tried to get past the table the man got to his feet and blocked her way.

"What's the hurry? Sit down and have a drink with us," he said, indicating the chair.

"Would you let me through?" she said sharply. "I won't ask you again."

"I'm really scared," the man said, grinning at his companions. "Sit down!"

He made the mistake of grabbing her wrist to try and force her down onto the chair. She jerked her arm toward her body, pushed her wrist up sharply against his thumb, forcing him to break his grip, then kicked him savagely on the knee. He cried out in pain and fell to the ground, clutching his knee in agony. One of his friends smashed a beer bottle on the edge of the table and sprang to his feet. Graham decided it had gone far enough. He got to his feet and crossed to where Sabrina was standing, her body tense as she waited for the man to lunge at her.

"It's OK, Mike, I can handle this," she said without taking her eyes off the broken bottle.

"I know that. But do they?" Graham looked at the two men. "She could take you both on with her eyes closed and still put you in hospital for the next six months. Think about that before you do anything stupid."

The second man held up his hands. "Hey, I don't want any part of this. I'm out of here. Joe, you coming?"

Joe's eyes flickered between Graham and Sabrina, then he tossed aside the bottle and grabbed his jacket from behind the chair.

"And don't forget to take your garbage with you," Graham said, indicating the man who was still writhing on the floor.

The two men hauled their friend to his feet and half carried, half dragged him from the bar.

"OK, the floor show's over," Mitchell announced to the other customers.

A coin was fed into the jukebox and a Dire Straits track selected. Within seconds a certain normality had returned to the bar.

"Sabrina, this is Peter Mitchell," Graham said, indicating Mitchell behind him. "We go back a long way."

"I'm sorry about those three, they're not the usual sort of clientele we get in here."

"Yeah, they're usually a lot worse," Graham added.

"Speak for yourself," Mitchell said good-humoredly. "What can I get you to drink, Sabrina? On the house. It's the least I can do after what's just happened."

"Nothing, but thank you anyway." She turned to Graham. "Can I have a word with you outside?"

Graham nodded then held out his hand toward Mitchell. "I'll take that twenty bucks now."

"The game's not over," Mitchell protested.

"It's checkmate in two and you know it." Graham snapped his fingers. "The money, Mitch."

Mitchell took two ten-dollar notes from his pocket and handed them to Graham. "I intend to win it back, Mike. Be warned."

"I'll be in New York again next Wednesday. Same time, same place?"

"It's a date."

"See you, Mitch."

Mitchell patted Graham on the arm and smiled at Sabrina. "Nice to have met you."

"Likewise," she replied then followed Graham from the bar.

"How did you know I'd be here?" Graham asked once they were in the street.

"I went to the Manion and the desk clerk told me where you were."

"What's wrong?"

"We're on a Code Red standby."

"When did this come through?"

"About half an hour ago," Sabrina replied. "Not that you'd know that, of course. You're up to your old tricks again, aren't you?"

"What the hell's that supposed to mean?"

"You're not answering your beeper."

"It never went off!" he shot back defensively.

"You're talking to me, Mike. I know all your tricks by now. Where is it? At the hotel?"

"In here," he retorted, patting his jacket pocket. But it wasn't there. His brow furrowed quizzically as he checked his other pockets. It wasn't in any of them.

"You haven't got it on you. Now that is a surprise."

"You can cut the sarcasm, Sabrina!"

"You're supposed to be the team leader now that C. W.'s gone over to the management side. That means you should be setting the example, not regressing back to your old ways again."

"I had it with me when I went to the cemetery this afternoon. It must still be in my suit pocket. I honestly thought I'd brought it with me. It was a genuine mistake."

Sabrina exhaled deeply and touched Graham's arm. "I'm sorry I went off at you like that. It's just been one of those nights."

"Sergei's going to crucify me when he reads in the duty officer's book that you had to come over here personally and tell me about the Code Red. That memo he circulated was very specific about field operatives carrying their beepers around with them at all times."

"He won't know I came out here," Sabrina said. "I had a quiet word with the duty officer. He's agreed not to mention it in the book."

"Thanks, I owe you one."

"Buy me a coffee and we'll call it quits."

"You're on," Graham agreed. "Do you have somewhere in mind?"

"As a matter of fact I do. And it has a live jazz band."

"You've convinced me."

"We can go in my car," she said, taking the keys from her pocket.

"Where are you parked?"

"Not far from here." She slipped her hand under his arm. "Come on, I'll show you."

◆ CHAPTER

THREE

He sat motionless in the back of the car, a blindfold secured firmly over his eyes. The two men on either side of him were both armed, their revolvers tucked into shoulder holsters which were hidden discreetly underneath loose-fitting, lightweight jackets. He knew he wasn't in any danger. But he was still apprehensive. He pushed the uncertainty from his mind and let his thoughts drift back over the events of the day . . .

It had been raining when he had left his New York apartment for John F. Kennedy Airport that morning. A hard, driving rain which had reduced visibility to a few feet. He had made it to the airport with minutes to spare, but the 747 had developed engine trouble as it was preparing for take-off and the passengers had been transferred to another Jumbo. The flight for Bogotá, Colombia, had finally taken off two hours behind schedule. When it had touched down at El Dorado Airport five hours later, a chartered Cessna had been waiting to fly him on to Medellín.

A taxi had taken him to the Intercontinental Hotel

where a reservation had already been made for him in the name of Warren. It was the name on his passport, not his real name. He had to take every precaution. A letter was waiting for him at the reception. He opened it in his room. More bad news. One of the men he was to meet that afternoon had been unavoidably delayed out of town and couldn't make it back in time for the original meeting. A new meeting had been rescheduled for eight o'clock that evening.

As instructed, he had left the hotel at seven-thirty and taken a taxi to the Joachim Antonio Uribe Botanical Gardens. A Mercedes was waiting to take him to the meeting. The guards had blindfolded him before they set off: the stakes were too high on both sides and it was a precaution he was prepared to accept. That had been a good twenty minutes ago. Perhaps more. He had lost track of time. Not that it mattered. He had no idea where they were going anyway . . .

When the Mercedes finally stopped the back door was opened and Warren was helped out of the car. A voice barked out an order in Spanish and the blindfold was removed. He was standing in front of a log cabin in a small clearing surrounded by dense jungle. He counted eight guards standing on the perimeter of the clearing. All carried Uzis. Another two guards stood on either side of the cabin door. One of them knocked on the door which was opened by a swarthy, thickset man in his early thirties. A holstered automatic was visible under his jacket. His name was Miguel Cabrera, the elder son of Jorge Cabrera who presided over one of the most powerful drug families in Colombia. The two men had already met several times during the past five months. Cabrera smiled as he approached Warren and extended a hand of greeting.

"I must apologize for the way you were brought here tonight," Cabrera said in faultless English. "But you must appreciate that we cannot afford to take any unnecessary risks. I am sure you understand that."

"Yes, of course."

"Excellent. I must also apologize for delaying the meeting today but, as I explained in the letter, I was unavoidably detained in Manizales. And as I am the only member of the family who speaks English, it was essential that I be here." Cabrera gestured to the open cabin door. "Please, after you."

Warren entered the cabin. A mahogany table dominated the small room. Eight matching chairs were positioned around it, and a leather padded chair stood at its head. Two men sat at the table. Ramón Cabrera was in his mid-twenties with long black hair which he wore in a ponytail at the back of his head. The brothers were complete opposites. Ramón was the brawn, Miguel the brains. That suited the cartel perfectly. Miguel had set up numerous international deals, using all the business acumen he had learned from his father. It was no secret that he was being groomed to run the family when his father stepped down. Ramón had been head of security for the cartel for the past four years and in that time he had become one of the most feared and hated men in the country. Despite their differences, the brothers were inseparable.

Twenty-two-stone Jorge Cabrera was fiercely proud of his sons. He sat at the head of the table, a handkerchief in one hand, a cigar in the other. He dabbed his sweating face with the handkerchief then placed the cigar in the ashtray beside him and beckoned Warren into the room. Miguel closed the door and made the necessary introductions. Ramón reluctantly shook Warren's extended hand. Jorge Cabrera ignored it.

"Please, won't you sit down?" Miguel said to Warren, indicating a chair. "Can I get you something to drink?"

"Bourbon if you have it," Warren said, sitting down.

Miguel poured a generous measure from a decanter on the sideboard and placed the glass in front of Warren. He then took his seat on the right of his father. Ramón, who was seated directly opposite Miguel, leaned forward and whispered something to him under his breath. His father banged his fist angrily on the table and ordered him to be quiet.

Miguel looked at Warren. "My brother does not trust you."

Warren swallowed nervously. Miguel smiled ironically. "Do not worry, he does not trust anyone. I sometimes wonder if he even trusts me."

Jorge Cabrera spoke quickly in Spanish, his eyes never leaving Warren's face; and when he'd finished he pushed the cigar back into his mouth and dabbed his forehead with the damp handkerchief.

"My father welcomes you to Colombia. He says he has been looking forward to meeting you ever since I first told him about your proposed deal."

Jorge Cabrera nodded as if he understood what his son had said then launched into another bout of Spanish. Miguel was quick to translate whenever his father paused to take a draw on the cigar.

"You said the decision to deal with us was based mainly on the fact that we are one of the most powerful families currently exporting narcotics to Europe and America. This may be true. But how do you gauge power? Is it financial? Is it how much influence we can exert within the government? Is it the number in our workforce? We could speculate all evening. What is true, however, is that we are the leading family when it comes to the processing and distribution of cocaine. In fact, that is now our sole export. Cannabis and barbiturates we leave to the other families. Neither of them has the drawing power of cocaine. I will tell you something that your Drug Enforcement

Agency would give their right arm to know. We exported almost fifty percent of the cocaine which was sent from Medellín to your country last year. But most of it was channelled through Florida. And we lost a considerable amount of that because your DEA is getting wise to our routes. After all, there are only a limited amount of routes into Florida. That is why your plan was like a breath of fresh air to us. Not only would it be a new route outside Florida but, more importantly, only we would have access to it. We already have a distribution network in the area. It can be enlarged without any difficulty at all. It's now up to you to give us the go-ahead and we can send out our first shipment."

Warren took a sip of bourbon then turned the glass around slowly in his hand. He finally looked up at Jorge Cabrera. "We're ready whenever you are."

Miguel translated for his father. Jorge Cabrera nodded and spoke softly to Miguel who then turned back to Warren. "My father has asked that you and I work out a date between ourselves before you fly back to New York."

"I was hoping to fly out tonight."

"Impossible," Miguel replied, shaking his head.

"I don't understand," Warren said warily.

"The airport only operates during the day. Medellín is surrounded by mountains. It is far too dangerous for an aircraft to take off or land at night. I will see to it that you are booked on the first flight out in the morning. But tonight you are my guest. Do you like seafood?"

"Yes."

"Then we will dine at Las Lomas. It serves the best seafood in town. Some would even say the best in the country. We can talk further over dinner."

Jorge Cabrera nodded to Ramón who got up and retrieved an attaché case from the sideboard. He

placed it in front of Warren then returned to his seat
and sat down again.

"Open it," Miguel told him.

Warren unlocked the case and lifted up the lid.

"Two hundred and fifty thousand dollars. All in
untraceable notes," Miguel told him. "It is merely a
gesture of goodwill on our part."

Warren flipped through one of the bundles then
looked up at Jorge Cabrera. *"Gracias."*

Jorge Cabrera nodded then stubbed out the cigar
to signify the end of the meeting.

Miguel got to his feet and moved to the door. "I
am afraid you will have to be blindfolded again for
the journey back to your hotel. I will have a car pick
you up at, say, nine-thirty to take you to the restaurant."

"Yes, that would be fine."

"Until then," Miguel said, shaking Warren's hand.

Warren smiled to himself. It was all going according to plan . . .

◆ CHAPTER

FOUR

Graham parked his battered white '78 Ford pickup in the car park adjacent to the United Nations Headquarters then made his way across to the Secretariat Building and showed his pass to the guard at the main door. Entering the main foyer, he crossed to the lifts and pressed the button for the twenty-second floor. Dressed in a pair of faded blue jeans, a white T-shirt, black sports jacket and a New York Yankees baseball cap, he drew disparaging looks from some of the more somber-suited men in the lift with him. Philpott had chided Graham for his unorthodox dress sense when he first arrived at UNACO but Graham had been adamant—he would not wear a suit and tie to a briefing. Philpott hadn't pushed the issue, but Graham's stubbornness had made it more difficult for Philpott to choose an authentic cover for him at the United Nations. Whitlock and Sabrina had both been assigned covers that related to their backgrounds. Whitlock was an attaché with the Kenyan delegation and Sabrina, because of her degree in Romance languages from Wellesley, was a translator at-

tached to the General Assembly. Graham, because of
his degree in Political Science and his military background, had finally been given the cover of a freelance adviser on Central American policy to the
American ambassador at the United Nations.

He was the only person to disembark on the
twenty-second floor and he waited until the doors
had closed before walking to an unmarked door at
the end of the corridor. He punched a numerical code
into the bellpush on the adjacent wall; moments later
there was a metallic click and the door opened. He
entered the small, neatly furnished room and closed
the door behind him. It was the antechamber to
UNACO headquarters. The wall opposite the door,
which was constructed of rows of teak slats, had two
seamless sliding doors built into it which could only
be activated by miniature sonic transmitters. The
door on the right led into the Command Center
where teams of analysts, using the latest high-tech
equipment, worked around the clock to monitor the
fluctuating developments in international affairs. The
door on the left led into the Director's private office.

Sarah Thomas greeted him when he entered. She
was an attractive thirty-one-year-old with short
blonde hair who had been the Director's personal
secretary for the past four years.

"Am I the first one here?" Graham asked, glancing
at his watch. "I thought I was late."

"You are," Sarah replied with a smile. "Don't
worry though, the show hasn't started yet. Sabrina
and Fabio are in the Command Center."

"What are they doing in there?"

"Passing the time until C. W. gets here. He should
be along any time now. Do you want to go through?"
she asked, gesturing toward the right-hand side of
the wall.

Graham shook his head and sat down on the
burgundy-colored sofa.

"Can I get you a coffee?"

"No thanks," Graham said, shaking his head. "I had enough of it last night."

Sarah smiled. "So Sabrina was telling me."

"Oh?" Graham said suspiciously. "And what exactly did she tell you?"

"That you two were out till two this morning at a club in Greenwich Village. Sounds like you had a good time."

"Yeah, we did," he admitted grudgingly. "We went to Sweet Basil's. It's a jazz club on Bleecker Street. You know it?"

"Of it," Sarah replied. "I'm not really into jazz."

The door to the Command Center opened. Sabrina and Paluzzi emerged into the office and the door slid shut behind them again.

Paluzzi shook Graham's hand. "So how was last night?"

"The jazz was great," Graham retorted sharply and gave Sabrina a dirty look.

"I think I'll have that coffee you offered me earlier," Sabrina said quickly to Sarah. She held up her hand when Sarah made to stand up. "Don't get up. I'll make it myself. You want one?"

"No thanks," Sarah replied.

"Fabio? Mike?"

"Not for me, thank you," Paluzzi said, shaking his head. "I only drink freshly ground coffee. That stuff's liquid mud."

"On a good day," Sabrina said with a wry grin. She looked at Graham. "Mike?"

Graham shook his head then crossed to where she was standing at the dispenser. "Did you have to announce to the whole world that we'd been to Sweet Basil's last night?" he hissed under his breath.

"I'd hardly call Sarah and Fabio the whole world, would you?" she replied tersely.

"Why did you have to tell them?"

"I don't understand what all the fuss is about. We went to a jazz club together. That doesn't mean we're dating."

Graham glanced across at Sarah and Paluzzi who were talking together. He turned back to Sabrina. "These kind of situations can be misinterpreted. That's how rumors start."

"Don't worry, Mike, I promise you it won't happen again. Because from now on we'll only see each other at work. That way there can be no misinterpretation. Satisfied?"

Before he could reply Whitlock entered the office. He greeted them both warmly then activated the miniature transmitter which operated the sliding door to the Director's sanctum.

"Sit down," Whitlock said, gesturing to the two black leather sofas against the wall. He moved around behind Kolchinsky's desk and sat down, then used the transmitter to close the door again.

Sabrina sat beside Paluzzi. The gesture wasn't lost on Graham. She smiled at Whitlock. "I still can't get used to seeing you behind that desk, C. W. I'm so used to having you sitting here with us."

"Well, you'd better get used to it," Whitlock shot back. He held up his hand in apology. "I'm sorry, Sabrina. It's been a long night. I only got in from London an hour ago."

"Where's Sergei?" Graham asked.

"With the Secretary-General. And he'll be with him for the rest of the day. And probably tomorrow and the next day as well. We're facing one of the most serious crises in UNACO's history. Perhaps the most serious."

"The Code Red assignment we've been assigned to cover?" Graham asked.

Whitlock nodded. "Strike Force Three was chosen because you and Sabrina are the best field operatives we have at UNACO. And you're going to need all

your wits about you to crack this one." His eyes flickered toward Paluzzi. "It's going to be a tough baptism of fire for you, Fabio, but I'm confident you can
handle it."

"I'm used to being thrown in at the deep end,"
Paluzzi replied with a shrug.

Whitlock opened the folder on the desk. "What
I'm about to tell you hasn't been released to any of
the other Strike Force teams as yet. I've asked those
not on assignment to come in this afternoon for a special briefing. Those on assignment will be told in due
course." He stared at the page in front of him for a
moment then looked up at them. "Strike Force Seven
were ambushed while on assignment in London last
night. Dave Swain and Jason Geddis were both dead
on arrival at the hospital. Alain Mosser died in hospital in the early hours of this morning."

"We lost a whole team?" Graham said numbly,
breaking the lingering silence.

Whitlock nodded grimly. "We've lost individual
field operatives in the past but never an entire team.
This is exactly the kind of ammunition our critics
need to pressurize the Secretary-General into dis-
banding UNACO."

"And it couldn't have come at a worse time," Sabrina said, shaking her head. "Colonel Philpott's
hardly cleared out his desk and this happens."

"Sergei and I are going to take a lot of flak over
this," Whitlock replied. "But that's not your concern.
You've got enough to worry about as it is. Not only
do you have to take over Strike Force Seven's assignment, you now also have to bring their killers to
book."

"Bring them to book?" Graham said angrily.
"They gunned down three of our colleagues in cold
blood—"

"I'm just as gutted as you are about what happened last night, Mike," Whitlock cut in sharply.

"They were a good, reliable team but more importantly they were also our friends. We can't allow that to cloud our judgment though. This isn't a vendetta. Remember that. We're here to uphold the law, we're not vigilantes out to settle a score. And you can be sure that the Secretary-General will be monitoring every move we make in this case. If you can bring them in alive then it's going to put us in a better light when it comes to answering our critics."

"What have we got to go on?" Sabrina asked.

"Strike Force Seven had been on a case for the past three months," Whitlock replied, sifting through the papers in front of him. "They've left a lot for you to go on."

"Such as?" Graham asked.

"Well, we're pretty confident we know the identities of their killers," Whitlock replied, holding up his hand before Graham could speak. "We're jumping the gun here, Mike. Let's put the case in perspective first, shall we?"

Graham nodded and sat back, his arms folded across his chest.

"The case they were working on involved a senior IRA cell commander. His name's Sean Farrell."

"Farrell?" Paluzzi retorted, spitting out the name.

"Do you know him?" Whitlock asked.

"Of him. I first came across the name about eighteen months ago when the *NOCS* were investigating the possible links between the Red Brigades and the IRA. I even heard it said that he was being groomed as a future IRA leader."

"Not if we can help it," Whitlock replied tersely. "He was arrested two days ago by Scotland Yard's anti-terrorist squad when he returned to Britain from the continent. I made the arrangements to have him arrested because Dave Swain had assured me he had an informer who could put Farrell away for life."

"Not McGuire?" Sabrina said suspiciously.

Whitlock nodded. "Yes, and Strike Force Seven were ambushed when they went to meet him. But there was no sign of McGuire when the police got there."

"Who is this McGuire?" Paluzzi asked.

"Gerard McGuire is a top UNACO informer," Whitlock told him. "He knows everything there is to know about the IRA. But there was a snag. He would only deal with Dave Swain. Nobody else."

"Which means Strike Force Seven's killers must know that McGuire was an informer," Paluzzi deduced.

"We have to assume that, yes," Whitlock agreed.

"He won't talk to us, C. W., you know that," Sabrina said. "Especially now that Dave's dead."

"If McGuire's still alive, that is," Paluzzi reminded her.

"That's what you've got to find out. And if you do find him, you make sure he does talk. Because without his testimony Farrell will be free by the weekend. But that's not the only reason why we need to find him before the IRA do." Whitlock took another sheet of paper from the folder and put it on the desk. "I managed to speak to Alain last night when he first arrived at the hospital. He was able to give me a very sketchy account of what happened at the rendezvous before he lapsed into a coma. I'm not going to read it out to you. There's a copy included in your dossiers. There is, however, one significant point that needs to be addressed now. Although he wasn't able to hear what McGuire was saying to Dave, he was positive that he heard Dave say the name 'Jack Scoby'."

"Jack Scoby, who's just been elected the new senator for New York State?" Sabrina asked.

"We have to assume that's who he meant," Whitlock replied. "I spoke to his office earlier this morning and found out that he's due to fly to London at the end of the week for a short, unofficial visit to the

United Kingdom. Included in the agenda is a trip to Ireland where his grandparents are buried."

"And you think the IRA are planning something against him?" Sabrina asked.

"Find McGuire and you'll have the answer," Whitlock replied. "But until then we can only assume the worst. I've got an appointment to see Scoby later today. I'll try and talk him into postponing his visit until we're satisfied his life's no longer in danger, though I don't hold out too much hope on that score. He can be very stubborn when he wants to be as I'm sure you all know from the television interviews he gave during his recent election campaign."

"Why would the IRA be planning something against an American senator?" Graham said at length. "Especially one as popular as Scoby. It would do irreparable harm to their image outside the United Kingdom. And it would certainly affect the flow of money they receive from their sympathizers over here. It doesn't make any sense."

"This is all just conjecture at the moment," Whitlock replied. "McGuire holds the key to this whole affair. Find him and you've solved half the case."

"And the other half?" Graham said, his eyes suddenly riveted on Whitlock. "Strike Force Seven's killers? You said earlier that you're pretty confident you know their identities."

"Two eyewitnesses arrived on the scene moments after the attack on Strike Force Seven," Whitlock told him. "There were two assassins, both were wearing balaclavas and baggy clothes. One was a woman."

"And?" Graham prompted.

"We think it could be Fiona Gallagher. She's Farrell's lover as well as his deputy cell commander. They're inseparable and rumor has it that she's taken his arrest very badly. She's prepared to go to any lengths to get him released."

"Sounds like a nice girl," Paluzzi muttered.

"Make no mistake, Fabio, she's every inch a professional. And she won't stop until she's found McGuire and silenced him."

"What about the other one?" Graham asked.

"We're positive the second man is Liam Kerrigan. The couple described him as being over six foot with a limp on his right leg. Kerrigan is six-three and was shot in the right leg at a loyalist rally eight years ago. There had to be a wheelman and we think that would have been Hugh Mullen. He recruited Gallagher for the IRA when they were both at Bristol University. She now regards him almost as an older brother. And both men work in Farrell's cell. It's too much of a coincidence for it not to be his team."

Whitlock took three manila envelopes from the drawer. Inside were details of the assignment, to be destroyed after reading; airline tickets; maps of their ultimate destination; written confirmation of their hotel accommodation; character sketches of any contacts as well as a sum of money in the currency of the country where they would be based. All field operatives also carried two major credit cards in case of emergencies. There was no limit to the amount of money they could use during an assignment, but it all had to be accounted for on their return to New York. He handed an envelope each to Graham and Sabrina. "Inside are mugshots of Kerrigan and Mullen. But there are no known photographs of Fiona Gallagher on file. You'll be working with Scotland Yard's antiterrorist squad on this one. Your contacts in London will be Inspector Keith Eastman and his deputy, Sergeant John Marsh. They've been on the case from the start."

"Where do I come in?" Paluzzi asked, pointing to the third envelope still lying on the table.

"You'll be approaching the case from a different angle," Whitlock said. "Ideally I'd have liked to have paired you off with either Mike or Sabrina as this is your first assignment with Strike Force Three, but under the circumstances it won't be possible. At least not for the time being. Mike and Sabrina work well as a team and for that reason I don't want to break up the partnership with such a lot at stake."

"I understand," Paluzzi said. "So what exactly is this 'different angle'?"

"Two nights ago a schooner sank in a storm off Nantucket Island. It's an island about two hundred miles northeast of here," Whitlock added, noticing Paluzzi's frown. "There were no survivors but some of the wreckage was washed ashore. It included a box of brand-new Armalite rifles. We don't know the size of the cache, and I doubt we ever will, but what we do know is that the schooner was bound for Ireland. Sligo Bay to be precise. From there the arms would have been smuggled over the border into Northern Ireland. Normally we wouldn't get involved in something like this. It's an FBI matter. But this particular cache was being minded by a man called Rory Milne, a New Yorker with strong ties to Noraid, the American organization sympathetic to the IRA cause. He also happened to be Sean Farrell's main contact here in America. He wasn't listed as being on board the *Ventura*. We only found out through an FBI informer within the Noraid organization. So far we've managed to keep both the fact that Milne was on board and the arms find out of the newspapers. But we won't be able to keep it out indefinitely. What we need to know is who was behind the shipment. If we can tie Farrell in directly with either the shipment or the seller then it will strengthen the case against him when it does go to court." Whitlock handed the third manila envelope to Paluzzi. "The schooner came from Milford, a port sixty miles south of here. I'd suggest you start there. One of our cars is parked outside for you to use. Sarah has the keys."

"I'm on my way," Paluzzi said, getting to his feet.

"What time's our flight to London?" Sabrina asked.

"The twelve o'clock flight from JFK," Whitlock replied.

Sabrina glanced at her watch then looked at Graham. "We'd better get moving as well."

"Yeah," Graham muttered and stood up.

"I want regular reports on your progress," Whitlock told them.

"What do you call regular?" Graham asked.

"I want you to report in at least three times a day. That way we can keep the Secretary-General updated." Whitlock picked up the sonic transmitter then looked at each of them in turn. "Sergei and I stuck our necks out this morning when we assured the Secretary-General that you were the best team in the organization. It's now up to you to prove us right. Because if you can't, and we don't find this IRA cell, there's every chance UNACO will cease to exist. It's a pretty sobering thought, isn't it?"

Paluzzi and Sabrina left the room. Graham paused at the door and looked around at Whitlock. "We'll crack it, C. W. You can count on it."

Whitlock held Graham's stare but said nothing. As Graham disappeared into the outer office, Whitlock closed the door after him and replaced the transmitter on the desk. He only hoped Graham was right. Because if he wasn't . . .

Jack Scoby's New York offices were located on the top floor of the Melrose Building, one of the many towering skyscrapers in the heart of the city's financial district. Having run the gauntlet of the strict security measures in force in the building, Whitlock sat in the reception area awaiting the senator's appearance. He looked slowly around the room. The walls were lined with framed posters from Scoby's election campaign. He recalled having seen many of the posters splashed across the city in the run-up to the election. He also recalled how Scoby's tough, hard-hitting campaign speeches had so enthralled a New York population ready and eager for change. Scoby had constantly criticized the lenient sentences handed out to criminals across the country, especially those involved in drug-related crimes, and although this had brought him into conflict with the liberal element who saw therapy, rather than punishment, as the answer to the problem, he had been swept to victory with what turned out to be the biggest majority ever recorded in an election in the state of New York. The sheer size of his victory had catapulted him into the political limelight and he had quickly become a hero for the far right of the party. There was already talk on Capitol Hill of him standing for the Presidency at the next election.

He had all the attributes needed to succeed in the political arena. His telegenic good looks and charismatic personality appealed to a wide audience; his uncompromising, often vitriolic speeches, laced with old-fashioned patriotic values, appealed to the conservatism of the middle and upper classes. Most political analysts regarded it as a foregone conclusion that Scoby would one day lead his party. It was only a question of *when* it would happen . . .

"Mr. Whitlock, I'm Jack Scoby."

It wasn't difficult to understand Scoby's appeal. He was a strikingly handsome forty-year-old with a rich tan and thick black hair which was beginning to gray at the temples. He smiled and extended a hand of greeting.

"C. W. Whitlock," Whitlock said, shaking Scoby's hand.

"Shall we go through?" Scoby asked, gesturing to his office.

It was a spacious room with a heavy teak desk and

three leather armchairs positioned equidistant from each other against the adjacent wall. The customary American flag hung in the corner of the room.

A man, who had been sitting in one of the armchairs, got to his feet and smiled quickly at Whitlock. He was in his late thirties with thinning brown hair and wire-rimmed glasses. Whitlock knew who he was before Scoby introduced him.

"Mr. Whitlock, this is Ray Tillman, my right-hand man and the brains behind my election campaign."

Tillman shook Whitlock's hand but said nothing.

Scoby closed the door. "Please, won't you sit down, Mr. Whitlock?" He waited until both men were seated then moved around behind his desk and sat down. "It's a bit of a coincidence you coming around here today. I'd actually made a note in my diary to ring UNACO sometime this week to introduce myself. We're in the same boat, aren't we? A new team in office. It certainly won't be easy trying to follow in Colonel Philpott's footsteps though. He had an exemplary record as UNACO Director."

"Did you know the Colonel?" Whitlock asked.

"I met him a couple of times at embassy functions," Scoby replied. "But I knew him better by his reputation. And that's what really counts, isn't it? Now take his successor, Sergei Kolchinsky. He's something of a dark horse for those of us outside UNACO. Certainly an interesting choice as the new Director."

"I take it from the tone of your voice that you don't wholly approve of his appointment?" Whitlock said, frowning.

Scoby clasped his hands together on the table. "He's a former colonel in the KGB who's from an era when the Cold War was at its peak. And now he's in charge of an international anti-crime unit working out of the United States. I find it hard to reconcile myself to those facts."

"Sergei's loyalties lie firmly with UNACO," Whitlock shot back, angry at any insinuation to the contrary.

"I'm sure they do," Scoby replied without much conviction. He was quick to give Whitlock one of his disarming smiles. "It goes without saying that Sergei Kolchinsky will have my full support for as long as he remains UNACO Director. And hopefully I'll be able to meet him at some point in the near future. Perhaps the three of us can get together for lunch after I return from my trip to the United Kingdom?"

"I'll have a word with him next time I see him," Whitlock said. "Actually, the reason for my being here concerns your proposed trip to Britain at the end of the week. We received some information which may make you want to change your mind about going."

Scoby frowned. "Really? What kind of information?"

Whitlock explained what had happened the previous night in London. He left nothing out, knowing it would only be a matter of time before Scoby received a report of the events anyway.

Tillman sat forward once Whitlock had finished talking, his arms resting on his knees. "What are the chances of this IRA cell being apprehended before Mr. Scoby leaves for London?"

"It's impossible to say," Whitlock replied truthfully then looked at Scoby. "That's why I asked to see you. We'll do everything possible to find them but if they're still at large by the end of the week it might be wise for you to postpone your trip."

"That's out of the question," Scoby cut in quickly, shaking his head. "I won't be threatened. I intend to fly to London on Friday, irrespective of whether you've found these terrorists or not."

"The senator's views on the IRA are well known but I still don't understand why they would plan a hit on him," Tillman said. "It would damage their image abroad. Especially here in the States."

"We don't know what they're planning, Mr. Tillman," Whitlock was quick to correct him. "And that's why we're pulling out all the stops to find this informer. Naturally I'll let you know of any developments in the case."

"I'd appreciate that," Scoby said.

"Well, I'd better get back to the UN," Whitlock announced, getting to his feet.

"Thank you for coming." Scoby walked Whitlock to the door. "If you call and I'm unavailable I'll make sure you're put through to Ray."

"Fine," Whitlock replied. "Hopefully we'll have sorted this out before you leave for London."

"I know you'll do your best." Scoby opened the door then shook Whitlock's hand again. "It's been a pleasure meeting you. We'll discuss that lunch further when I get back after the weekend."

Whitlock smiled and left the room. Scoby closed the door behind him and looked across at Tillman. "Well?"

"It doesn't make any sense. The IRA have got nothing to gain and everything to lose if they carry out this operation."

Scoby bit his lip pensively. "Agreed. But what if they're not working for the IRA?"

"Whitlock seemed convinced they were an IRA cell," Tillman replied.

"I'm sure they are," Scoby was quick to point out. "But what if they're a rogue IRA cell in it purely for the money? Enough money to buy them new identities where the IRA would never find them." He crossed the room and perched on the edge of the desk, his arms folded across his chest. "And let's face it, I've got enough enemies in my own party, never mind amongst the Democrats, who would love to see me silenced. Permanently."

"You think this whole operation could have been planned from Capitol Hill?"

"Why not?" Scoby nodded thoughtfully. "And what better way than to use an IRA cell in Britain to do their dirty work for them? That way, no comebacks."

"Do you want me to have someone look into it?"

Scoby shook his head. "Let UNACO handle it. That way it's all legit. They've got the resources and the contacts to get to the bottom of this, but more importantly, Kolchinsky and Whitlock will be desperate to impress the Secretary-General after the loss of their team in London. Which means the truth won't be suppressed. And if the plot did originate on Capitol Hill, the newspapers will have a field day. I'll see to that."

"And you'll be seen as the innocent party, strengthening your hand as a candidate at the next election."

"Precisely," Scoby replied with a knowing smile.

"We're overlooking one thing though," Tillman said anxiously. "That cell is still out there somewhere. Your life's in danger until they're caught."

"It's a risk I've got to take. Imagine what the press would say if they found out I'd postponed my trip because of a possible terrorist attack. That would seriously damage my public image. And I'm not about to jeopardize that. Not with so much at stake." Scoby smiled to himself. "You know, Ray, this could actually be a blessing in disguise. It can only improve my standing, both here and abroad, and that can't be a bad thing, can it?"

"Not if everything falls into place," Tillman agreed.

"I'm sure it will, Ray. I'm sure it will."

* * *

Paluzzi parked outside the harbor master's office and climbed out of the car. It had taken him an hour to drive from New York to Milford. He felt he'd made good time. He locked the car, pocketed the keys, then entered the building and walked over to the reception desk. A youth in his early twenties sat at a desk against the back wall. He seemed to be the only person on duty. He finished an entry in the ledger in front of him before he got to his feet and crossed to where Paluzzi was standing.

"Afternoon," he said without much enthusiasm. "Can I help you?"

"Hopefully," Paluzzi replied with a smile. He took a forged Press card from his pocket and showed it to the youth. It identified him as Franco Pasconi, a journalist for the Italian newspaper, *La Repubblica*. It had been included in the envelope Whitlock had given him in New York. "I'd like to ask you some questions about the *Ventura*."

A look of fear flashed across the youth's face. "I ain't got nothing to say to you, mister."

"I'm prepared to pay for any information," Paluzzi told him. He removed an envelope from his jacket pocket. Inside were twenty hundred-dollar bills. He took out two bills, folded them in half, and held them up between his fingers. "Well?"

The youth's eyes flickered toward the notes but he quickly checked himself. "I said I got nothing to say to you, mister. I got work to do."

"What's wrong?" Paluzzi asked, leaning closer to the youth. "What are you frightened of?"

"I ain't frightened of nothing," the youth shot back.

"Then talk to me."

"I told you, I got nothing to say."

"Well, can you at least tell me where the *Ventura* was berthed when she was in port? It's worth a hundred to you."

The youth looked at the notes between Paluzzi's fingers. "Two hundred."

"OK, two hundred," Paluzzi agreed.

The youth pulled a ledger out from under the counter and leafed through the dog-eared pages until he found the entry he wanted. "Wharf Three."

"And how long was she there for?" Paluzzi asked.

"Hey, I said I'd tell you—"

"I've still got the money," Paluzzi reminded him.

The youth glared at Paluzzi then consulted the ledger again. "It docked there at seven-forty on Monday morning. It left again at five that afternoon." He slammed the ledger over then reached out and plucked the notes from Paluzzi's fingers. When he was sure Paluzzi had gone the youth returned to his desk and dialed out a three-digit number. It was answered immediately at the other end. "Jess?"

"Yeah, who's that?"

"Jess, it's Billy."

"What do you want?" came the curt reply.

"I've just had a guy in here asking about the *Ventura*. He had one of those Press card things. Foreign accent."

"What kind of foreign accent?"

"Jeez, how should I know?" Billy retorted.

"What was the name on the Press card?"

"I didn't see it properly."

"What did you tell him?"

"Nothing, honest, Jess. I've sent him to Wharf Three."

"What the hell did you go and do that for?"

"He ain't going to leave without some kind of answers. I thought it best if you spoke to him. Hey, and I told him the *Ventura* was berthed at Wharf Three. Play along with that."

"Yeah," came the thoughtful reply. "Well, he'd

better not try and dig too deep or he ain't gonna
leave. Period."

The line went dead.

Paluzzi returned to his car and took the Beretta
from the glove compartment. He fed the clip into the
butt then pushed it into the holster he was wearing at
the back of his trousers. He didn't want to carry the
gun. It was hardly in keeping with his cover as a journalist. But he couldn't afford to take any chances.
What had alarmed him was the fear in the youth's
eyes when he mentioned the *Ventura*. It was obvious
he had been told to keep his mouth shut. But by
whom? That's what he was hoping to find out . . .

He slid on a pair of sunglasses then walked the
short distance to the docks. He stopped the first man
he saw to ask directions to Wharf Three. On reaching
his destination he paused and looked around him.
Fifty yards ahead of him was a towering crane which
was loading wooden crates into the hold of a small
freighter. To his right was a warehouse. A large "3"
was painted on the side of the building as well as on
the corrugated-iron roof. Two men sat on an empty
packing crate which had been pushed up against the
wall adjacent to the door. Both were wearing torn
jeans and grease-stained T-shirts.

"Afternoon," Paluzzi called out as he approached
them. He took the Press card from his pocket and
held it up. "Franco Pasconi. I'm a journalist with the
Italian newspaper, *La Repubblica*. I'd like to ask you
some questions about the *Ventura*. I believe it was
moored here before it sailed on Monday night?"

One of the men shrugged and took another drag
on his cigarette.

The other drew his forearm across his sweating
face then wiped it on his T-shirt. "Dunno," he said.

"Surely you must have seen it?" Paluzzi said.

"We see a lot of boats," the one with the cigarette said.

"You're not being very helpful," Paluzzi said. "The *Ventura* was registered here in Milford. The crew were all locals."

"That's right," the one with the cigarette replied. "Our people. Our friends. Not so, Randy?"

"Yeah," the other man muttered.

"How well did you know Earl Reid?" Paluzzi asked.

"What the hell do you want to know 'bout Earl for?" Randy demanded.

"Background," Paluzzi replied.

The man with the cigarette pointed a finger at him. "Shove your background, mister. Earl was a friend of ours. And that's all you need to know about him."

"What about the rest of the crew? How well did you know them?"

"We knew them," Randy replied. "Right, Tom?"

"Right. We've had enough of your questions, mister. I suggest you get your ass out of here while you've still got one. We don't like outsiders prying into our affairs. Especially at a time like this."

"Why's everyone clamming up around here?" Paluzzi asked. "What are you hiding?"

Tom stubbed out his cigarette on the side of the crate then jumped nimbly to the ground. "I told you to get your ass out of here. You don't listen, do you?"

"All I want are some answers . . ." Paluzzi trailed off when Tom pulled a switchblade from his back pocket.

"That's enough!"

Paluzzi looked around, startled by the voice behind him. The man was in his late thirties with thick sandy hair and a rugged, weather-beaten face. He was wearing jeans with a white shirt and a red tie open at the collar.

"This guy's a journalist. He's been asking questions

'bout Earl," Randy said. "We told him to beat it but he don't listen."

"Get back to work," the man ordered, then glanced at the switchblade in Tom's hand. "And put that away. I'll deal with this."

Tom glowered at Paluzzi then pocketed the switchblade again before disappearing into the warehouse. Randy spat onto the ground inches from Paluzzi's feet and followed Tom into the warehouse.

"Thanks," Paluzzi said, extending a hand toward the man. "The name's Franco Pasconi."

"Jess Killen, I'm the wharf foreman," the man replied, purposely digging his hands into the pockets of his jeans. "Why are you asking questions about Earl?"

"It's background for a story I'm writing."

"A story? What about? Hell, ships go down around Nantucket all the time. So why the interest in the *Ventura?*"

Paluzzi's mind was racing. Wharf foreman. That meant Killen would almost certainly be in on any of the deals that were struck up in or around the dockyard. And that included the loading of Armalite rifles onto the *Ventura.* He had to play his ace. But he had no idea how Killen would react. "Do you know a man called Milne? Rory Milne?"

Killen's eyes narrowed fractionally. He shook his head. "No, can't say I do. Should I?"

Paluzzi sensed that Killen was lying. "He was on the *Ventura* when it went down. But there wasn't an official passenger list. And he wasn't listed amongst the crew either. I wondered if you knew why he was on board?"

"I've no idea."

"Rory Milne was a member of Noraid. Does the name mean anything to you?"

"No."

Again Paluzzi sensed that Killen was lying. But

Paluzzi was determined to press ahead, hoping for some kind of reaction. "Noraid is an American organization that gives financial support to the IRA. I assume you have heard of them."

"Of course I've heard of them," Killen snapped, stung by Paluzzi's sarcasm. He stared at his feet for a moment then looked up at Paluzzi again. "Earl Reid was a good friend of mine. So were the rest of the crew. They were all decent, hard-working men. And they all had families. But that doesn't seem to bother you newspapermen, does it? All you're after is another story, irrespective of whether there's any truth in it or not. Well there isn't a story here, mister. Earl was taking a consignment of grain to Ireland. It's a trip he's been making every few months for the past eight years. Ask the port authorities in Sligo Bay. They'll verify what I've told you. I assume you've heard of Sligo Bay?"

Paluzzi nodded. "I know Sligo Bay. Well, thank you for your time, Mr. Killen. It looks like I'll just have to try somewhere else for my story."

"Then you make sure it's outside Milford," Killen said, pointing a finger of warning at him. "Because if I hear you've been bothering Sheila Reid, or any of the other families, I'll personally see to it that you never write again." He started to walk away then turned and eyed Paluzzi coldly. "You're not welcome here, mister. Get out while you still can." He turned on his heel and walked off.

Paluzzi sighed deeply and shook his head slowly. Killen would try and ensure that nobody spoke to him though he knew there was always a chance that one of the men would be willing to talk, given the right financial incentive. But how would he know which of them to approach? He could report back to Whitlock and ask him to run a check on the workers to find out which of them could be susceptible to a bribe, but that would take time.

He walked back slowly to where he had parked his car outside the harbor master's office. He took the keys from his pocket and was about to get in when Billy appeared in the office doorway. He looked agitated. He looked around nervously then beckoned Paluzzi toward him. Paluzzi slid the keys back into his pocket and crossed to where Billy was standing. Billy grabbed his arm and pulled him into the office. He looked outside again and, satisfied they hadn't been seen, closed the door behind them.

"What's going on?" Paluzzi demanded, his hand resting lightly on the Beretta at the back of his trousers.

"I can tell you everything you want to know about the *Ventura*. I was there, see. But it'll cost you."

"How much?"

"Ten thousand dollars."

Paluzzi snorted in amazement then shook his head. "I don't have that kind of money."

"Get it if you want to know who paid Killen to put those guns on the *Ventura*."

"Why the sudden change of heart?" Paluzzi asked suspiciously. "You obviously tipped Killen off about me after I'd spoken to you."

"I had to," Billy replied quickly. "He'd have been suspicious if he'd found out you'd been here and I hadn't told him about it."

"So you keep him informed on everything that happens in here?"

Billy nodded. "Look, we can't talk here. If Jess or any of his men found me talking to you like this I'd be dead. Meet me tonight at the back of the warehouse on Wharf Three. Midnight. And bring the money with you."

"I told you, I can't raise that kind of money."

"You want the story, you bring the money. And if you don't have the money, don't come."

"I could manage five grand, but I guess that won't

be enough for you," Paluzzi said with a shrug and moved to the door.

"Hey, wait," Billy called out after him.

Paluzzi paused at the door, his hand resting lightly on the handle. He looked around slowly at Billy. "Well?"

"Make it seven and a half—"

"Five," Paluzzi cut in quickly. "That's my final offer. I'll bring it with me tonight. It's up to you whether you want to show or not."

Billy swallowed nervously and nodded. "I'll be there. And have the money in used bills."

"I'll only hand the money over when I'm sure you're telling me the truth. And that means I'll need more than just your word."

"I've got the paperwork to back up anything I say," Billy retorted. "Now get out before someone finds you here."

Paluzzi left the office and got into the car. He smiled to himself as he started up the engine. Five thousand dollars. Pin money to UNACO. He knew Whitlock would have authorized the ten thousand if he'd needed it. But he was damned if he was about to give in to some greedy kid. Let him sweat a bit. Paluzzi engaged the gears and drove away. He knew he was going to enjoy the rest of the afternoon.

Killen was on the telephone when Tom and Randy entered his office. He acknowledged them with a nod then returned to his conversation. There were two chairs in front of Killen's desk but neither man made any move to sit down. And they knew Killen wouldn't offer them a chair either. He kept a certain aloofness from the men underneath him which had ensured that they treated him with the respect he felt he deserved. He was a tough, often brutal, foreman who ruled the docks with an iron fist. But he was also the first to reward loyalty. And men like Tom and Randy had made a lot of money through Killen's numerous illegal deals involving the loading and unloading of drugs and arms from ships in port. Killen had become known amongst the east coast underworld as a man who could keep his mouth shut. And he expected the same discipline from his men . . .

He replaced the receiver then lit a cigarette and swung his feet up onto the desk. "Yeah, what is it?"

"We've got a problem, Jess," Tom told him. "We followed that reporter back to his car. Billy offered to tell him everything about the *Ventura* for ten grand."

Killen drew on his cigarette then exhaled the smoke up toward the ceiling. "Ten grand? That's a lot of money for Billy."

"The reporter talked him down to five," Tom said. "They're meeting at Wharf Three tonight. Midnight."

"Billy? I treated him like my own kid." Killen dismissed the thought with a shrug. "No matter. Meet me here at nine-thirty tonight."

"What you gonna do 'bout the reporter?" Randy asked anxiously. "He's an outsider, Jess."

"I warned him to get out of Milford while he could. It's too late now." Killen took another drag on his cigarette. "Did either of you catch the name of the paper he's working for?"

"Hell, he did say," Randy said, scratching his curly brown hair. "You remember, Tom?"

"Something about a 'Republic', I think," Tom replied with a desperate shrug. "Sorry, Jess, that's all I remember."

"That's OK," Killen told him, then gestured to the door. "I'll speak to you guys later. I've got a call to make."

The two men left the room, careful to close the door behind them.

Killen picked up the receiver again and dialed a

number he had memorized in his head. It was answered immediately.

"It's Killen," he said when the man had identified himself.

"I told you never to call me on this number unless it was an emergency," the man told him.

"This is an emergency," Killen shot back. "You know any Italian newspaper that's got the name 'Republic' in it?"

"*La Repubblica*," came the immediate reply. "It's one of the leading papers in Rome. Why?"

"There was a guy here just now claiming he worked for the newspaper. He was asking some awkward questions about the *Ventura*."

"What sort of questions?"

"He knew about Milne."

"How?" came the startled reply.

"I don't know," Killen answered.

"What did you tell him?"

"Nothing," Killen replied. "You'd better run a check on him. See if he's on the level. He said his name was Franco Pasconi."

"Pasconi," the man muttered as he wrote down the name.

"He's meeting one of my staff here at midnight tonight."

"You set him up?"

"No, this particular staff member's suddenly got greedy. Don't worry, I'll deal with him. Nobody double-crosses Jess Killen."

"Do what you want with your own man but don't touch the journalist until I've had a chance to check him out. Is that understood?"

"Whatever you say," Killen replied with a shrug. "But if you want him silenced it'll cost you."

"Doesn't it always?" came the sarcastic reply.

"That's the price you have to pay if you want to

keep your hands clean," Killen said with a faint smile.

"Remember, leave the journalist alone unless I tell you otherwise." The line went dead.

Killen replaced the receiver, stubbed out his cigarette, then swung his feet off the desk and went in search of Tom and Randy.

It was almost nine o'clock before Kolchinsky finally returned to his apartment in the East Tremont suburb of New York. He dropped his attaché case on the chair in the hall then went to the kitchen where he helped himself to an ice cold Budweiser from the fridge. He poured the beer out into a glass then took it through to the lounge and settled down in his favorite armchair opposite the television set. But he didn't reach for the remote control on the table beside him. He closed his eyes, savoring the silence for the first time that day.

The doorbell rang.

He groaned and rubbed his eyes wearily. For a moment he was tempted to ignore it. But he knew he couldn't. He placed the glass on the table then hauled himself to his feet and went to answer the door.

"Malcolm?" Kolchinsky said in surprise.

"Hello, Sergei," Malcolm Philpott replied.

"Come in," Kolchinsky said, holding open the door.

Philpott was in his mid-fifties with gaunt features and thinning red hair. He limped heavily on his left leg, the result of a shrapnel wound in the last days of the Korean War. He now walked with the aid of a cane.

Kolchinsky led him into the lounge and gestured toward the couch. "Can I get you a drink?"

"Anything but coffee. I had three cups in that diner down the road while I was waiting for you."

Philpott sat down and leaned the cane against the wall. "I wouldn't say no to a whiskey though, if you have it."

Kolchinsky crossed to the drinks cabinet in the corner of the room. "I thought you were supposed to be visiting your sister in Scotland."

"I lasted ten days over there," Philpott replied. "I got back a couple of days ago."

"You make it sound like it was an ordeal," Kolchinsky said, handing the glass to Philpott.

"It was," came the blunt reply. "My sister and her husband live in a small cottage about ten miles outside Edinburgh. It's in the middle of nowhere. I suppose most people would regard that as paradise. The solitude almost drove me crazy. I couldn't wait to get back to New York. I guess I'm just addicted to the big city atmosphere."

"What I'd give to be in that cottage right now," Kolchinsky muttered as he sat down again.

"I heard about what happened to Strike Force Seven," Philpott said grimly.

"How?" Kolchinsky replied in amazement. "That's supposed to be classified information."

"I still have my contacts at the UN." Philpott shook his head. "Don't worry, they're not in UNACO. So who have you brought in to replace them?"

"Malcolm, you know I can't discuss this with you."

"I'm hardly going to sell the story to the Press, am I?"

"That's not the point. You're not part of the organization anymore," Kolchinsky told him.

Philpott raised the glass but it froze inches from his lips. "It's Strike Force Three, isn't it?"

Kolchinsky said nothing.

"I thought as much," Philpott said, nodding his head. "I'd have used them as well."

"I didn't say they'd been brought in," Kolchinsky said defensively.

"But you'd have denied it if it wasn't true. How are Mike and Sabrina?"

"OK," Kolchinsky replied tersely.

"And Fabio Paluzzi? How's he settling in?"

"OK."

Philpott smiled. "And I suppose C. W.'s OK as well."

Kolchinsky nodded. "Look, Malcolm, I don't want to appear rude, but it's been a very long day. Ten hours cooped up in the same room being grilled continually by a succession of foreign ambassadors about the events in London last night."

"You don't know how lucky you are, Sergei," Philpott said at length.

"Lucky?" Kolchinsky retorted in amazement. "I haven't even been in this job for a month and already UNACO's facing the most serious setback in its short history. There's even talk of the organization being disbanded. That would look great on my CV, wouldn't it?"

"UNACO won't be disbanded, and you know it," Philpott said.

"I don't know it, Malcolm," Kolchinsky replied quickly. "You should have heard some of those ambassadors today. If they had their way, UNACO would already be history."

"They're politicians, Sergei. Lots of talk. But fortunately it's not up to them, is it? The ultimate decision lies with the Secretary-General. And I know he's a hundred percent behind you and the organization."

"You've spoken to him?"

"I've spoken to someone close to him," Philpott replied.

Kolchinsky took his cigarettes from his jacket pocket and lit one. "Have you started smoking again?"

"No, but I still carry my favorite pipe with me," Philpott said, patting his jacket pocket. "It's reassuring. I won't start again. The heart attack was the incentive I needed to give up."

"So what are you doing with yourself now that you're a man of leisure?"

"Nothing," Philpott replied, shaking his head. "Absolutely nothing. And I don't know how much more of it I can take."

"You need a hobby."

"Can you imagine me growing orchids or joining some amateur dramatics society? UNACO was my life, Sergei. It's what kept me going. That's what I meant just now about you being lucky. I'd sell my soul to the devil to trade places with you right now."

"I'd settle for a straight swap," Kolchinsky said with a weary sigh. "You come back and I'll take early retirement."

"I'd jump at the chance but I doubt my doctor would agree to it." Philpott drank down the whiskey then reached for his cane and got to his feet. "Thanks for the drink. And the company. I'll leave you to get some rest. You look like you need it."

Kolchinsky stood up and walked with Philpott to the door. "You know you're welcome here anytime, Malcolm. I mean it."

"I know," Philpott replied, patting Kolchinsky on the arm. "And I might just take you up on that offer. When things quieten down again."

Kolchinsky closed the door behind Philpott then returned to the lounge and sat down again. He retrieved his cigarette from the ashtray and was about to take another drag when he abruptly changed his mind and stubbed it out. He switched on the television to catch the last five minutes of the news. He was already asleep by the time it finished.

◆ CHAPTER
FIVE

The flying time by Concorde between New York and London is three and three-quarter hours.

Graham and Sabrina had spent the first hour of the flight assimilating the contents of the dossiers which Whitlock had given to them at the United Nations. Graham had then replaced the dossier in his overnight bag and promptly fallen asleep. Although tired, Sabrina had decided against trying to catch a couple of hours' sleep as well. She knew from experience that she would only wake up feeling even more tired. She spent the remainder of the flight reading a paperback she had bought at JFK.

The rain splattered the window beside her as the Concorde began its final descent toward the runway at Heathrow Airport. She closed the paperback and looked out over the illuminated London skyline. It brought back so many memories. Good memories. Her father had been appointed to the Court of St. James's as the US ambassador to Britain when she was ten years old and the family had spent eight happy years in London before returning to the States.

New York was unquestionably her favorite city. But London ran a close second. A home from home . . .

She turned to Graham and smiled faintly to herself. He looked so peaceful with his head nestled against her arm. She shook him gently. He stirred, muttered something under his breath, but his eyes remained closed. She shook him again. His eyes opened. He immediately sat up and glanced guiltily at her arm. She bit her lip to stop herself smiling at his obvious discomfort. He noticed the gesture and, to her surprise, gave her a wry grin. She could remember a time when he would have bitten her head off for less. He now seemed more at ease with those around him. But, more importantly, he seemed more at ease with himself. She sensed that he was beginning to come to terms with the guilt he'd felt over the loss of his family . . .

It was nine-fifteen p.m. by the time they were cleared through customs but there was still no sign of their contact, Inspector Keith Eastman of Scotland Yard's anti-terrorist squad. Graham went to collect their suitcases, leaving Sabrina to wait for Eastman. By the time Graham returned, Eastman had arrived. He was a tall, gangly man in his early forties with a pale complexion and short brown hair. Sabrina introduced him to Graham.

"You'll have to excuse my not shaking hands, Mr. Graham," Eastman apologized, holding up his black-gloved right hand. "An IED, an improvised explosive device, blew up while I was trying to defuse it. It cost me two fingers and part of my thumb."

"Yeah, I read about it in your file," Graham said. "You used to be a bomb-disposal man before you joined Scotland Yard's anti-terrorist squad."

"We prefer to call ourselves ATOs. Ammunition Technical Officers. I was with the Royal Army Ordnance Corps for five years, which included three tours of Northern Ireland. I came to know IRA tactics pretty well in that time. That's why the anti-terrorist squad recruited me after I was retired from the army."

"Is there any news of McGuire?" Sabrina asked as they walked toward the exit.

"His car was found abandoned in Dover this afternoon. My sergeant, John Marsh, has taken a team down there to check it out. It could be a decoy to make the IRA think he's fled to the continent. We won't know any more until John gets back."

"When's he due back?" Graham asked.

Eastman shrugged. "It all depends on what they find down there. That's my car over there."

They crossed to a white Ford Sierra and loaded the suitcases into the boot.

"I'd like to make a stop before I take you to your hotel," Eastman said. "The pub McGuire frequents is in Soho. I've had it staked out all day but there's been no sign of him. Not that I thought he'd show anyway. I'm more interested in the two friends he drinks with there, Frank Roche and Martin Grogan. They're both expatriate Irishmen with strong Republican links. They won't talk to me or any of my men, not with so many other villains in the pub. But they might talk to you."

"And they might not," Graham retorted.

"It's worth a try," Eastman said, glancing at Graham in the rearview mirror. He started up the car and headed toward the exit.

It had stopped raining by the time they reached Soho.

Eastman opened the glove compartment and removed two Beretta 92Fs. "I was asked to get these for you. The shoulder holsters will be delivered to my office in the morning."

"Are Grogan and Roche dangerous?" Graham asked, taking one of the Berettas from Eastman.

"Grogan's been inside for armed robbery but I doubt he'd try anything," Eastman replied. "But it's best not to take any chances."

"Agreed," Sabrina said, pushing the Beretta into the pocket of her leather jacket.

"Do you want to take another look at their mugshots before you go in?" Eastman asked, indicating the envelope on the dashboard.

They shook their heads.

"OK, I'll wait out here for you," Eastman replied. "I've got a team staked out around the pub so if either Roche or Grogan try and make a run for it, they'll be on hand to grab them."

Graham and Sabrina climbed out of the car.

"You watch the back door," Graham told Sabrina. He noticed her scowl. "You heard what Eastman said, the place is full of ex-cons. If you go in there they'll be all over you, offering you drinks and God knows what else. What chance will you get to talk to Grogan and Roche in private?"

She knew he was right. "OK, I'll take the rear door."

"I'll call you when I'm through."

She disappeared up the alleyway at the side of the pub. Graham zipped up his jacket to conceal the Beretta tucked into his belt and entered the pub. The jukebox, situated near the door, was blaring out an old Robert Palmer hit. He slowly looked around the room. It was packed. He eased his way through the customers to the bar.

A barmaid immediately approached him. "What'll it be, luv?"

Graham rarely touched alcohol. But considering the situation, and his surroundings, he asked for a beer.

"You're an American," the barmaid said with a quick smile.

"Yeah," Graham muttered.

"We sell Budweiser if you want it."

"Sure," Graham replied absently as he scanned the faces around him. No sign of either Grogan or Roche.

"Where you from?" she asked, returning with a glass and a bottle of Budweiser.

"New York. I'm looking for a couple of guys. Martin Grogan and Frank Roche. Do you know if they're here?"

"Martin didn't come in tonight. Frank's at his usual table over there," she said, pointing into a crowd of customers.

"What does he drink?"

"Guinness," came the quick reply.

"A pint of Guinness then."

He paid for the drinks then made his way carefully through the crowd until he spotted Roche at a table in the corner of the room.

"Frank Roche?" Graham said when he reached the table.

Roche looked up sharply. "Who wants to know?"

"I'm a friend of Gerard McGuire's," Graham replied then placed the Guinness in front of Roche. He pulled up a chair and sat down.

Roche's body tensed and his eyes automatically flickered toward the door.

"I have both the front and back doors covered," Graham said, opening his jacket just enough for Roche to see the Beretta. "And you'd have to get past me first."

"What do you want?" Roche asked, wiping a drop of sweat from his forehead.

"I've got five hundred pounds in my pocket for you. But how I give it to you is entirely up to you."

"What do you mean?" Roche replied suspiciously.

"Well, if you cooperate I'll pass it to you under the table. If not, I'll make sure enough people around here know it's for information you passed on to the cops. I don't think they'd take too kindly to having a snitch in their midst, do you?"

"I ain't no tout, mister," Roche shot back, using the IRA's term for an informer.

"Try explaining that to them," Graham said, gesturing around him.

"You say you're a friend of Gerry's. How come I don't know you?"

"I guess we just move in different circles," Graham replied. "Where is he?"

Roche shrugged. "Your guess is as good as mine."

"I hope not, for your sake."

"Look, I don't know where he is."

"It's your funeral," Graham said, reaching into his jacket pocket.

"Wait!" Roche hissed. "I haven't seen Gerry for a couple of days. I heard a rumor that he left town in a hurry last night. But I don't know why or where he's gone."

"Has he got any close friends on the continent?"

"I don't know all his close friends. I don't know you, do I?"

"We were never that close," Graham replied, then pushed aside his Budweiser and leaned forward on the table. "You didn't answer my question. Is there anyone he'd go to if he were in trouble?"

"Is he?" Roche countered.

"Yeah."

"Who with? The law?"

"The IRA," Graham said.

"Jesus," Roche muttered and rubbed his hands over his face. He looked up at Graham. "I've got nothing more to say to you, mister. I don't want no trouble with the Provos."

"It's a bit late for that now. If word leaks back to them that you've been touting—"

"That's a lie," Roche cut in sharply.

"That's not how they'd hear it."

Roche was sweating. "OK, I'll tell you what you want to know. Then you leave me alone."

"Suits me," Graham replied.

"He has a sister living somewhere in Belgium," Roche said at length. "I don't know where. He's also got a couple of friends in France."

"Names?"

"I don't know. One of them lives near Paris. He's a builder. That's all I know about him."

"And the other one?"

Roche shrugged. "I don't know. Honestly, I don't."

"What about here in Britain?"

"Martin was his closest friend."

"Martin Grogan?"

"Yes. They're like brothers."

"So I believe," Graham replied.

"He lives in Stroud Green. Granville Road." Roche looked around him nervously. "OK, I've kept to my side of the bargain. Now you keep yours. Get out of here and leave me alone."

"One last question," Graham said, remembering what Eastman had told him in the car. "Where's this so-called safe house that only the three of you know about?"

Roche went pale. "How do you know about that?"

"I have my sources. But like everyone else, they don't know where it is."

"We've managed to keep its location a secret for the past six months. From the law and from the Provos. And I intend to keep it that way."

"Fair enough. I'll get on to my contact in Belfast. He's just waiting for the word to stitch you up. You'll be lucky to see out the week by the time the Provos have finished with you," Graham said, making to get up.

"It's a flat in Leyton," Roche blurted out. "Fifty-six Mews Heights. Langthorne Road. Close to the cemetery."

"That wasn't so difficult, was it?" Graham said, reaching for the money in his pocket.

"I don't want your money, mister," Roche spat indignantly.

"I know you won't let on to the IRA about our little chat. You'd have too much explaining to do. But you might think about warning Grogan. If I find out you have contacted him, the Provos will receive an anonymous call tonight telling them that you're a police tout."

"Get out," Roche snarled, stressing each word carefully.

Graham got to his feet, snaking his way through the crowd and out into the street. Eastman was talking to someone in the shadows of the alleyway across the street. Graham was curious as to who it might be but first he headed up the alley to find Sabrina. She was perched on the edge of a dustbin outside the back door.

"Well?" she asked, standing up.

"I spoke to Roche. It's possible that Grogan may know where McGuire's hiding out."

"Was Grogan there?"

"No, but I've got the address." They crossed the street to where the Ford was parked. "Who was that you were talking to when I came out of the bar?" he asked Eastman as they got back into the car.

"One of my colleagues. As I said, I've had a team watching the pub all day. They're cold, tired and well pissed off that McGuire didn't show." Eastman started the car. "Any luck with the safe house?"

As Graham gave the address Eastman immediately set off for Leyton.

* * *

Martin Grogan was drunk. A bottle of whiskey stood on the table beside his chair. It was almost empty. He poured himself another measure then picked up the remote control and flicked through the channels on the television set. As usual, nothing worth watching. He cursed loudly but settled on a pop concert on Channel 4. Though he hated pop music the noise seemed strangely comforting.

He had been drinking steadily for most of the day in an attempt to forget. He was torn between two loyalties. A friendship and a cause. McGuire had been his best friend for over thirty years. They had grown up together in the slums of Belfast. A tough, uncompromising childhood. They had joined the IRA in their late teens and served in the same unit for eight years in their twenties. When McGuire decided to head for London five years earlier, it had seemed only natural for Grogan to go with him. Those were the good times . . .

Then McGuire had called him the previous evening. Distraught, agitated, and clearly in fear for his life. An IRA cell had just tried to kill him. Grogan didn't believe it. Well, at least not at first. Why would the IRA want to kill one of their most trusted operatives on the British mainland? Then McGuire had told him. He had been a tout for the past two years. And now the IRA had found out about his deception. He begged Grogan to help him. He was his last chance. Although devastated by McGuire's admission, Grogan had reluctantly agreed to take him some money and a change of clothing. But after that he was on his own. The friendship was over . . .

There was a knock at the door.

Grogan cursed angrily and got unsteadily to his feet. He tossed the remote control onto the chair and crossed the room to the door. "Who is it?" he demanded, his words slurred.

"Frank, Frank Roche," came the reply.

"God, Frank, what do you want at this hour?"

"Open the door, Martin!"

Grogan fumbled with the latch and unlocked the door. The moment he opened the door it was kicked hard from the outside, sending him sprawling to the carpet. Kerrigan burst into the room and hauled him to his feet, punching him savagely in the stomach and forcing him to his knees. Grogan was retching convulsively, his hands clasped over his belly, his eyes unfocused and his expression bewildered. Kerrigan grabbed him by the hair, jerked back his head, and was aiming a punch at his exposed face when Fiona appeared in the doorway.

"That's enough!" She looked the length of the deserted corridor then entered the flat and closed the door behind her.

"He's pissed out of his mind," Kerrigan said angrily, letting go of Grogan's hair.

"Get him up."

Kerrigan yanked Grogan to his feet.

"Where's Gerry McGuire?" she snapped without looking around at Grogan.

"Gone," Grogan muttered. He shook his head, desperately trying to clear his thoughts.

"Where?" Fiona asked.

"Far away from you," Grogan replied with a sneer.

Kerrigan grabbed the whiskey bottle off the table and smashed it across the side of Grogan's head. Grogan cried out in agony and clasped his hand over his ear. The blood seeped out between his fingers.

"Where?" she repeated calmly.

"I don't know," he whimpered. "Jesus, I don't know."

The two-way radio on Fiona's belt crackled into

life. She unhooked it and put it to her lips. "What is it, Hugh?"

"We've got company," Mullen announced. "It could be the cops."

"OK, we're on our way. Drive round the back and wait for us there." She clipped the radio back onto her belt. "McGuire must have said something about where he was going."

"He didn't," Grogan replied in desperation. "All I did was bring him two hundred pounds and a change of clothes. He left straight away."

"Describe the clothes," Kerrigan snapped.

"Jeans. A white shirt. Leather jacket."

"Color?" Kerrigan prompted.

"Brown."

Kerrigan glanced at Fiona. She nodded. He hit Grogan in the stomach again and shoved him backward into the chair. Then, taking a Walther P88 from his pocket, he attached a silencer to the barrel and shot Grogan once through the heart.

"Let's go," she snapped, opening the door and peering out into the corridor. It was still deserted. Kerrigan pocketed the automatic and hurried after her.

The bell for the lift sounded at the end of the corridor just as Kerrigan closed the door behind him.

"Masks," Fiona snapped, already pulling the balaclava from her pocket. She tugged it over her head then took a Heckler & Koch automatic from her pocket and hurried toward the fire exit. Donning his balaclava, Kerrigan followed her.

Sabrina was the first to emerge from the lift. Kerrigan fired then ducked through the doorway after Fiona. The bullet chipped the wall several feet wide of Sabrina. Pulling the Beretta from her pocket, she gave chase, Graham and Eastman running after her. Reaching the fire exit, she took up a position beside the door, then, slowly reaching out a hand, pulled the door open and swiveled around to fan the stairs with the Beretta. They were deserted. She ran through the doorway.

"You check the apartment," Graham called to Eastman as he followed Sabrina down the stairs.

They reached the third-floor landing and Sabrina paused at the emergency door which was still closing slowly. They exchanged glances. Had the two masked figures fled along the third-floor corridor? Or was it a trick just to make Graham and Sabrina think they had gone that way? Graham pointed to the door. He would check it out.

Sabrina continued down the stairs. She heard the footsteps as she neared the first-floor landing. They were coming from the stairs below her. Then she heard the sound of a door being slammed back against a wall. She bounded down the stairs just as Kerrigan was about to disappear through the doorway.

"Freeze!" she ordered, levelling the Beretta at Kerrigan's back.

Kerrigan stopped in his tracks and the door slowly closed in front of him.

"Drop the gun, now!" Sabrina ordered, slowly descending the stairs. "And get up against the wall, hands outstretched."

Kerrigan made a show of releasing the Walther and it clattered noisily to the floor.

Fiona Gallagher, who seconds earlier had ducked through the door leading onto the first floor, appeared on the landing behind Sabrina. "Now you drop your gun," she commanded, levelling her Heckler & Koch at Sabrina's back. "And don't try anything stupid. I wouldn't miss from this range."

Sabrina cursed angrily under her breath. She reluctantly let the Beretta fall from her fingers. Kerrigan quickly retrieved his Walther and pushed the Beretta into his belt. Fiona eased past Sabrina, the Heckler &

Koch still trained on her. She reached the foot of the stairs and levelled the handgun at Sabrina. Suddenly the door at the top of the stairs was kicked open and Graham dived low onto the landing, the Beretta gripped in both hands. But he couldn't get in a clear shot for fear of hitting Sabrina. Kerrigan got off two shots at Graham before Fiona grabbed his arm and bundled him through the doorway behind them. They clambered into the getaway car and the tires shrieked in protest as Mullen pulled away from the building. By the time Graham had got to the door the car was already out of range. He cursed furiously and holstered his Beretta again.

"You OK?" Graham asked, turning back to Sabrina.

"Sure."

"Did they get your gun?"

She nodded grimly. "I can't believe I allowed myself to be drawn into their trap so easily. Dammit!"

"Don't blame yourself," Graham said, putting a reassuring hand on her shoulder. "We have to take those kinds of risks. It's all part of the job. You know that. Come on, we can't do anything more here."

They made for Grogan's flat. Sabrina's mind was racing. Why hadn't Fiona Gallagher put a bullet in her when she had the chance? Had she intended to use her as a hostage? Or would she have killed her if Graham hadn't showed when he did? There was a third possibility. One which seemed quite bizarre. Had she purposely let her live? The authorities have always been legitimate targets for the IRA. No, it didn't make any sense. She couldn't shrug off the lingering doubts in her mind but she decided against voicing her thoughts. They were best kept to herself.

Eastman was on the phone when they entered the flat. A blanket had been draped over Grogan's body. Graham crouched beside the body and lifted the edge of the blanket. It had been a professional hit. He let the blanket drop back over Grogan's face and stood up again.

Moments later Eastman replaced the handset. "Well, what happened?"

They told him.

Eastman moved to the window and looked down onto the courtyard below. "I'll have to wait here and straighten things out with the local CID. I'll arrange to have you taken back to your hotel."

"Who else knew we were coming here tonight?" Graham asked.

Eastman frowned. "Just the three of us."

"You didn't mention it to any of your surveillance team?" Graham asked.

"What was the point? I had no way of knowing whether you'd find out about this place when you went into the pub tonight. It was a long shot that paid off. Unfortunately we got here just too late."

"Exactly," Graham agreed. "Only McGuire, Roche and Grogan knew about this flat. That much Roche told me. So don't you think it a little strange that the IRA arrived on the scene only minutes before we did?"

"What are you getting at?" Eastman demanded.

"Well, if you didn't tell any of your people we were coming out here, it only leaves us with two possible explanations. Either someone overheard me talking to Roche in the bar, which I doubt, or else your car's been bugged."

"That's preposterous," Eastman shot back. "Our cars are checked every morning by a team of specialists. It's a security precaution."

"And that includes debugging?"

"Everything," Eastman retorted, holding Graham's stare. "We're a tightly knit team, Mr. Graham. We trust each other."

"I'm glad to hear it. But it still doesn't answer the

question of how the IRA found out about this place within minutes of my telling you."

"We'll bring Roche in for questioning first thing tomorrow morning," Eastman said at length.

"And have the car checked."

"I'll do it myself," Eastman replied coldly then held out a hand toward Graham. "Or better still, we can have it checked out together. Would that satisfy you?"

"Mike's not saying that any of your men are necessarily in league with the IRA," Sabrina said, trying to defuse the sudden tension between the two men. "But let's face it, it wouldn't have been very difficult for the IRA to find out who was leading the murder investigation, would it? So if the car has been bugged, it's more than likely that the transmitter was put in place *after* the car was checked this morning."

"I'm not out to antagonize you, Inspector," Graham assured him. "I'm just trying to look at the situation from a practical point of view."

Eastman sighed deeply. "I know. I'm sorry if I got a bit edgy just now. I get very protective of my team. They're a great bunch. And I know they're all fiercely loyal to the unit."

"I don't doubt it for a minute," Graham was quick to add.

"I'll have the car put in the pound this evening. Nobody will be allowed near it until I get there in the morning." Eastman crossed to the telephone again. "Well, I'd better ring for a car to take you over to your hotel. There isn't much else either of you can do here tonight."

Fiona Gallagher took a long hot shower after they returned to the boarding house in Cricklewood. Then, slipping on her robe, she wound the towel around her head and returned to her room. She

closed the door behind her then sat down on the edge
of the bed and rubbed her hands slowly over her face.
The Army Council, who were responsible for direct-
ing the IRA's military operations, had put her in temporary charge of the unit while Farrell was in
detention. They had put their trust in her. Their directive had been simple: silence McGuire. She wouldn't
let them down. And she knew she wouldn't have
any qualms about killing him either. He knew too
much . . .

There was a knock at the door.

"Who is it?" she asked.

"Liam," came the curt reply.

Kerrigan. The man revolted her. She sometimes
wondered just how she'd managed to stand him for
so long. "What is it? I'm about to get ready for bed."

"I want to talk to you, Fiona," Kerrigan called out
loudly. She could hear from his voice that he'd been
drinking. He was known to be a heavy drinker but
the Army Council had never cautioned him about it.
He could hold his tongue when he drank and that's
all they were worried about. She knew he wouldn't
go away until he'd spoken to her. She tied the robe
tightly around her waist then crossed to the door and
opened it.

He pushed past her into the room. He had a bottle
of brandy in his hand. She found it strange that a
fiercely patriotic Irishman like Kerrigan loathed the
taste of whiskey. Farrell had given him some stick
about it in the past. But he was the only one who
could get away with it. Nobody else dared, at least
not to his face.

"What do you want, Liam?" she demanded, closing the door behind him. "It's late and I want to get
some sleep."

"You want a drink?" he asked, holding out the
bottle toward her.

"Just say your piece then get out!" she snapped angrily.

"My piece?" Kerrigan said, then sat down on the wooden chair by the window. "Why didn't you kill that bitch tonight?"

Fiona controlled her anger. Kerrigan was trying to bait her. But she was damned if she would bite.

"Because it wasn't necessary," she replied matter-of-factly. "We've been given a directive by the Army Council. Find McGuire before the authorities do. And that's what we're going to do. With the minimum amount of bloodshed in the process."

"I always thought you were spineless. This proves it."

"I'd mind my tongue if I were you, Liam. You've already disobeyed orders when you shot those two undercover cops last night. It wasn't part of the operation. You can be sure that will be in my report to the Army Council. And you'd have killed that couple as well if I hadn't stopped you. You're psychopathic, Liam, do you know that? Why do you think the Army Council turned you down when you put in a request to lead the cell in Sean's absence? Because they couldn't trust you to carry out their orders objectively and with the minimum amount of bloodshed."

"I know Sean wouldn't have chickened out like you did. He'd have put a bullet in her back without a second thought."

"I'm not Sean," she said softly. "But I am in charge of his cell and until he gets back you'll do exactly as you're told or else you'll find yourself up in front of the Army Council on a disciplinary charge. And I don't have to tell you how the Army Council views mutiny in the ranks. Now get out of here."

Kerrigan's hands were trembling with rage as he slowly got to his feet. He stood directly in front of her. "You think you've got it made, don't you? Cute face. University degree. Screwing the Army Coun-

cil's blue-eyed boy. You may have taken Sean in, but
your kind doesn't fool me. Not for one minute.''

"My kind?"

"What would you call someone who's slept their
way into favor with senior management? In my
books that's a whore.''

She suddenly brought her knee up savagely into
his groin. As he buckled over, groaning in agony, she
brought her elbow up sharply against the side of his
face. He crashed into the chest of drawers and the
bottle slipped from his fingers as he fell to the floor.

Mullen heard the noise from the adjoining room.
He dashed out into the corridor, burst into the room,
brushed past Fiona and crossed to where Kerrigan
lay.

"He's out cold," he said, looking up at her. "What
happened?"

She told him.

Mullen sat down slowly on a chair and bit his lip
anxiously.. "What are you going to do? Have him replaced?"

She shook her head. "You know the orders. We're
only to contact the Army Council in an emergency. I
don't think they'd be too pleased to hear about this,
do you? No, I'll ask to have him replaced once we've
seen this through."

There was a knock at the door.

Mullen's eyes flickered nervously from Kerrigan
to Fiona. She crossed to the door and opened it. It was
the manager of the boarding house.

"What's going on in here?" he demanded, trying
to peer over her shoulder into the room. "We've received several complaints from other guests about a
loud noise coming from this room."

She gave him a sheepish smile then stepped aside
and pointed to Kerrigan. "We were having a few
drinks in the room to celebrate his birthday. He had a
little too much and passed out. He fell against the

chest of drawers. Don't worry though, the party's
over. I'm sorry if we disturbed the other guests."

"Will he be all right?" the manager asked, looking
over at Kerrigan.

She nodded. "He's got a head like a Challenger
tank. He'll be fine in the morning."

"Well, I'd appreciate it if you kept the noise
down," the manager said, glancing in Mullen's direction. "There are other guests to consider as well."

"We will," Mullen promised him.

Fiona closed the door and looked around at Mullen. "Wake him up and get him out of here."

Mullen filled a plastic cup with water from the
sink in the corner of the room and splashed it over
Kerrigan's face. It took another minute before Kerrigan was finally able to sit up. A discolored bruise had
already formed on his cheek where Fiona had caught
him with her elbow.

"Let's go," Mullen said, reaching out a hand to
help Kerrigan to his feet.

"I can manage," Kerrigan snapped, but when he
tried to get up a stabbing pain shot through his groin.
He inhaled sharply then slowly got to his feet and
moved gingerly to the door. He paused, his fingers
curled around the handle, and looked around at
Fiona. "This isn't over, not by a long way."

"It is for tonight," she replied. "Now get out!"

She locked the door behind the two men then took
the Heckler & Koch from her hold-all. She paused
briefly in thought. Kerrigan was a professional,
surely he wouldn't do anything to jeopardize the operation? But could she be so certain? Her decision
made, she put the automatic under the pillow. It
made her feel more secure. She couldn't afford to
take any chances . . .

* * *

Paluzzi parked the car out of sight of the dockyard. He took the Beretta from the glove compartment, pushed it into his holster, then picked up the black hold-all from the passenger seat and got out of the car. He glanced at his luminous watch. Eleven seventeen p.m. He was in good time. He avoided the main entrance, which was patrolled by an armed guard, and followed the perimeter fence until he reached a point opposite the back of the warehouse on Wharf Three. He opened the hold-all and removed a pair of wire-cutters. It only took him a few seconds to cut a hole in the fence big enough for him to slip through. He left the wire-cutters in a clump of overgrown weeds by the fence then eased the Beretta from his shoulder holster and moved cautiously toward the warehouse. A car turned into the road behind him and he instinctively ducked down as it drove past. He waited until the engine had faded into the distance then got to his feet again and covered the remaining ten yards to the back of the warehouse. He peered around the side of the wall. The fishing trawler which had been berthed at the wharf that afternoon was gone. He kept close to the wall as he made his way slowly toward the front of the warehouse. A single security light above the closed warehouse doors illuminated the deserted loading bay. He looked at his watch again. Eleven twenty-two. Well, all he could do was wait.

He was about to return to the rear of the warehouse when he heard a rustling sound somewhere behind him. He turned sharply, Beretta extended, but he couldn't see anything in the darkness. Slowly he edged his way back along the wall. He reached the end of the wall and pivoted around, fanning the area with the Beretta. Nothing. Nerves. He cursed himself silently. Get a hold of yourself. He put the hold-all down. Then he heard another noise, this time a branch snapping underfoot. He swung the Beretta toward the bushes on his right.

"Come out slowly," he commanded. "I'm armed, so don't try anything foolish."

A figure emerged from the bushes. The face was hidden in the shadows. But Paluzzi recognized the physique straight away. Jess Killen.

"Good evening," Killen said, stepping from the shadows. He smiled faintly, seemingly unaffected by the Beretta aimed at his chest. "Don't tell me, you were out taking a walk and you lost your way."

"Take your hands out of your pockets, very slowly, and place them on your head. Do it now!"

Killen shrugged then eased his gloved hands out of his pockets and held them up to show Paluzzi he wasn't armed. "Now it's your turn. If you look behind you, very slowly, you'll see that Tom and Randy are both armed. You remember Tom and Randy, don't you?"

Paluzzi's stomach was churning as he slowly looked over his shoulder. Tom and Randy were standing twenty yards behind him, both armed with Mini-Uzis. Like Killen, both men were wearing leather gloves.

"If you fancy your chances, you could try and take them out on the turn," Killen told him. "If not, I'd be obliged if you'd throw down the gun."

Paluzzi knew he could take out one of them on the turn. But both? Armed with Mini-Uzis, each with a twenty-round magazine? He'd have to be fast. And suicidal. He tossed the Beretta onto the ground.

"Wise move," Killen said. "If you'd like to follow Randy, he'll show you to the warehouse. We can talk in there."

Randy stepped back and gestured with the Mini-Uzi for Paluzzi to move ahead of him. Paluzzi did as he was instructed. Tom retrieved the hold-all and the Beretta, handed them to Killen, then went ahead to open the warehouse doors. Paluzzi was ushered into the dimly lit warehouse and Randy gestured to the wooden chair in the middle of the concrete floor. Paluzzi sat down, his eyes constantly flickering between Tom and Randy. Both Mini-Uzis were trained on him. Killen appeared, tossed the hold-all onto the floor, then closed the door behind him. He took a packet of cigarettes from his inside pocket, pushed one between his lips, and lit it.

"Cigarette?" he said, offering the packet to Paluzzi.

Paluzzi remained silent.

Killen shrugged and tossed the packet to Randy who helped himself to a cigarette. "So, your name's Pasconi. Franco Pasconi, a freelance reporter for *La Repubblica*. Correct?"

Paluzzi still said nothing.

Tom stepped forward to strike him with the Mini-Uzi but Killen waved him away. "Well, I know that already. I had you checked out earlier this afternoon. But what troubles me is why a reporter would be carrying this." He held up the Beretta. "Hardly standard issue for a foreign correspondent, is it?"

"I'd say that depends on the story you're running," Paluzzi replied coldly.

"The story? Of course. I believe Billy was going to tell you everything for five grand. A bargain at the price. But then you were dealing with Billy. I presume that's the money in there." Killen gestured to the hold-all. "Well, Billy's already here but he won't be telling you about the *Ventura*."

"Who's Billy?" Paluzzi said, holding Killen's stare.

Killen turned the Beretta around thoughtfully in his hands. "Tell me, how did you know about Rory Milne?"

Paluzzi was silent.

"Do you have a contact in Noraid?" Killen prompted.

Silence.

"I don't particularly want to let Tom and Randy work you over. I've seen them do it before. It's certainly not for the faint-hearted." Killen glanced at Tom and Randy. "Get Billy."

The two men went to a small office at the far end of the warehouse. When they re-emerged they were half-carrying, half-dragging the unconscious Billy between them. His hands had been tied behind his back. They dumped Billy onto the floor in front of Paluzzi. Killen crouched down, grabbed Billy's hair, and jerked his head back. Paluzzi winced at the sight of Billy's face. His nose had been broken, several of his teeth had been knocked out and he could make out several discolored bruises under the mask of blood. Paluzzi couldn't look at him for more than a few seconds.

"It's not a pleasant sight, is it?" Killen removed a bloodstained handkerchief from one of Billy's pockets and opened it. Paluzzi recoiled in horror. Inside was a tongue. "If you have a loose tooth, you take it out. So surely the same principle should apply to a loose tongue?"

Paluzzi clasped his hands over his face as he struggled not to throw up. When he was finally able to look up again Killen had stuffed the handkerchief back into Billy's pocket.

"Now, perhaps we can get a little cooperation from you," Killen said, getting to his feet. "Who are you?"

"You know who I am," Paluzzi retorted.

"I know who you say you are," Killen replied. "There is a Franco Pasconi working for *La Repubblica*. He's abroad, that's all we could find out about him."

"I am Pasconi," Paluzzi insisted.

"I might have believed that before you pulled this on me," Killen said, holding up the Beretta.

"I'm Franco Pasconi, freelance reporter for *La Repubblica*," Paluzzi told him.

"OK, let's say for argument's sake that you are Pasconi. How did you know about Milne?"

Paluzzi's mind was racing. He had to make up a believable story. But what? He wasn't quick enough. Killen nodded to Tom who stepped forward and brought the butt of the Mini-Uzi down hard onto Paluzzi's shoulder, knocking him off the chair. He landed inches away from where Billy lay. Killen kicked him savagely in the stomach, catching him agonizingly in the kidneys.

Killen looked down at Paluzzi. "Now, let's try that again. How did you know about Milne?"

"Go to hell," Paluzzi hissed through gritted teeth.

Killen grabbed Paluzzi's hair, jerked back his head then placed the Beretta's barrel in the center of his forehead. "Next wrong answer and I pull the trigger."

Paluzzi stared in horror at Killen.

"How did you know about Milne?"

"I have a contact in Noraid," Paluzzi replied quickly.

"Name," Killen said.

"I don't know his name," Paluzzi replied.

"Wrong answer—"

"Wait!" Paluzzi yelled in desperation. "I only know him by a codename. That's how it's been for the last five years."

"Five years?" Killen spat angrily. "What's his codename?"

"Havana," Paluzzi said, using the first word that came to mind. Havana? Why had he thought of that? He'd never been there in his life.

"Why Havana?" Killen asked suspiciously.

"How should I know? It was his choice, not mine," Paluzzi shot back.

"Where's he from?"

"New York as far as I know. That's where I contact him."

"You've seen him?"

"No, we use a locker at the Grand Central. We each have a key. I put the money there and when he collects it he leaves an envelope in its place. He knew Milne was on board the *Ventura* but he didn't know who was behind the arms shipment. That's why I came here, looking for a story."

"You've just found one," Killen replied then turned the Beretta on Billy and shot him through the head.

Paluzzi wiped a fleck of blood off his cheek then stared at Killen in disbelief. "You're mad. You're all mad."

"On the contrary," Killen replied with a smile. "We're actually very clever. Billy's dead. Your gun was used. It has your fingerprints on it, not mine. So, if the cops do ever find your bodies, they'll deduce that you shot Billy over an argument about the money. He was behind the wheel of his car at the time which then careered off the edge of the pier and you were drowned when it sank. The perfect scenario."

"And what about the state of Billy's face? And the fact that he's got no tongue? The police aren't going to turn a blind eye to that, are they?"

"He could have bitten through his tongue when the car hit the water. And the bruises, hell, he could have hit his face on the windscreen. But it doesn't matter what the cops make of it. The main thing is that there's nothing to link the three of us to any of this. And that's the beauty of it."

Paluzzi made a desperate grab for the Beretta in Killen's hand. Then everything went black.

Tom, who had knocked Paluzzi out, shouldered his Mini-Uzi and glanced at his watch. "Pete should be here by now with Billy's car. Christ, it was only parked a couple of hundred yards away."

"Relax," Killen told him, then took his cigarettes from his pocket and lit one.

The bell rang and Randy opened the door. "What kept you, Pete?"

"Someone stopped at the gate to ask for directions just as I was about to fetch the car."

Randy took the keys from the guard.

"OK, put them in the car," Killen ordered.

Billy's body was bundled into the front of the battered Ford Cadillac and Paluzzi was stretched out on the backseat. Killen dropped the Beretta onto the seat beside Paluzzi and Randy tossed the hold-all onto the passenger seat. Satisfied, Killen slammed the back door shut then nodded to Tom who climbed behind the wheel and started the engine. It spluttered and died. He tried again. The same result. Cursing angrily, Killen moved around to the driver's side and peered through the window. Tom shrugged helplessly as he continued to turn the key in the ignition.

"Nothing," Tom snapped, banging his fist angrily on the dashboard.

"We'll have to push it off here," Killen said, beckoning Randy toward the car.

"Here?" Tom asked anxiously, looking up at Killen. "I thought we were going to sink it further down the pier."

"So did I," Killen retorted sarcastically. "Now get out and push."

Tom released the handbrake then climbed out. Slowly they eased the car toward the edge of the wharf. It toppled, bonnet-first, over the side and began to sink slowly into the murky water. The water bubbled angrily as the tail section finally disappeared under the water. Randy unhooked a flashlight from his belt and began to play it across the water.

Killen waited a couple of minutes then patted

Randy on the shoulder. "He's dead. Come on, let's go back to the warehouse. We never did finish that hand of poker we were playing, did we?"

Randy switched off the flashlight then followed Killen and Tom back to the warehouse, closing the door behind him.

Paluzzi had regained consciousness as the water flooded through the open windows. It was pitch-black. And the water was freezing cold. He forced himself not to panic. That would be fatal. He fumbled for the door handle. Where was it? Billy's hand brushed across his face. Then his arm. Paluzzi lashed out in the darkness, frantically trying to keep the body away from him. Don't panic, he said to himself. He had to stay calm, conserve the air in his lungs. He reached out his hand again, this time feeling for the door. If he could find that, he could locate the handle. After what seemed an eternity his fingers finally touched the door's wooden panel. Feeling his way across the panel, he finally reached the metal handle. He jerked hard on it then pushed on the door with his feet, desperately trying to force it open. How much longer could he last underwater? The door inched open slowly. Forcing himself feet first through the opening, he propelled himself upward. As he neared the surface he saw the beam of light playing across the water. They were still there, waiting. His lungs were bursting. His only chance was to make for the pier. If he could get underneath it then he would be safe. He swam until he felt himself getting dizzy from lack of oxygen. But had he reached the safety of the pier? He couldn't see the light on the surface of the water anymore. He had to chance it and go up for air. He pushed himself upward and silently broke the surface of the water. He'd made it. He clung on to one of the wooden beams under the pier as he struggled to catch his breath. He had a splitting headache and when he touched the back of his head he could feel the blood on his fingers. He remained where he was until they returned to the warehouse then made his way cautiously to a metal ladder and climbed up onto the wharf. He paused again to make sure he was alone then ran, doubled-over, to a row of metal drums twenty yards away from the ladder and, slumping down behind them, exhaled deeply. What now? He was supposed to be dead and had no intention of letting Killen and his cronies think otherwise. Which meant he couldn't use his car again. He had to get to a payphone and call UNACO headquarters. They would send a car down for him. He'd probably have caught pneumonia by then, but what else could he do?

He was about to discard his jacket when a pair of headlights swept across the wharf. He ducked down quickly but the black Mercedes stopped before the headlights reached the drums. The driver dimmed the lights then climbed out and opened the back door. Paluzzi squinted through an aperture between the drums to see the face of the man who got out. It was too dark. Then, suddenly, the warehouse door opened, illuminating the face. Paluzzi had never seen him before: mid-thirties, collar-length black hair, deep-set eyes. He was wearing a brown suit and a cream shirt open at the neck.

"Well?" the man asked Killen.

"It's done."

"Any problems?"

Killen shook his head. "Did you bring the money?"

The man took a brown envelope from his pocket and handed it to Killen. "Compliments of the boss."

Killen slit the envelope open with his finger and looked inside. "It's a pleasure doing business with you."

"I'll be in touch," the man said, climbing back into the Mercedes.

Paluzzi ducked down again as the car did a U-turn, momentarily illuminating the drums. Then it was gone. Killen returned to the warehouse, closing the door behind him.

Paluzzi looked at his watch. It was almost midnight. All he wanted to do was change out of his wet clothes and climb into a hot bath. But he couldn't return to his hotel. Not now. He had to call New York. He patted his back pocket. At least his wallet was still there. He slowly got to his feet then looked around quickly before hurrying back to the fence and clambering through the opening he'd cut for himself earlier that evening. He shivered as a light wind cut across the deserted street. Was this really happening to him? Claudine was right. He had to be crazy to be in this line of work. He dismissed the thought. He had to find a payphone. He knew his best bet was to head back toward the town center: sooner or later he'd have to come across one. Well, in theory . . .

◆ CHAPTER

SIX

The telephone rang.

Graham turned over slowly in his bed and reached out in the darkness. His fingers touched the corner of the bedside table and he patted around its surface until he found the telephone. He lifted the receiver to his ear.

"Mike?"

"Yeah," came the sleepy reply. "Who's that?"

"It's Keith Eastman. I think we've found Gallagher and her two cronies."

Graham immediately sat up and switched on the bedside lamp. "Where?"

"At a boarding house in Cricklewood. I'm on my way over there now. I've sent a car for you. It should be at the hotel in ten minutes."

"I'll tell Sabrina," Graham said, stifling a yawn.

"Fine. See you in a bit."

The line went dead. Graham picked up his watch. Two minutes past seven. He rang Sabrina's room then scrambled out of bed and went through to the bathroom. He hated cold showers. Especially first thing in the morning. But it was the one sure way he knew to wake himself up. Fast. He stepped into the shower cubicle then gritted his teeth as he turned on the cold tap on the wall in front of him.

Eastman was waiting for Graham and Sabrina in a quiet side street in Cricklewood. "Morning," he said with a quick smile, opening the back door of his car. "Get in, we can talk more privately in here."

Inside the car, Eastman introduced the blond-haired man behind the wheel as his deputy, Sergeant John Marsh. He then took a Beretta from the glove compartment and handed it to Sabrina. "A replacement. You may need it this morning."

She took the automatic from him, checked the magazine, then slipped it into the shoulder holster hidden under her fawn blouson. "Where's the boarding house?"

"On the next block," Eastman replied. "I thought it best if we approach it on foot."

"How did you find them?" Graham asked.

"We don't know it definitely is them," Eastman corrected him, then took a copy of the *Times* from the dashboard and handed it to Graham.

Graham opened it. Mugshots of Kerrigan and Mullen had been displayed prominently on the front page. The headline underneath read: KILLER IRA UNIT. "Why weren't we told that you were going public on this? Who authorized it?"

"Commander Palmer, head of the anti-terrorist squad, and your Mr. Kolchinsky," Eastman told him.

"Sergei?" Sabrina said, taking the newspaper from Graham. "Why didn't he say anything when I spoke to him last night?"

"They only agreed to go ahead with the story minutes before the papers went to press last night," Eastman told them. "I was only told about it at midnight.

I didn't see any reason to ring you at the hotel. You both looked like you needed the sleep."

"How very considerate," Graham said sarcastically, folding up the newspaper and handing it back to Eastman. "We're supposed to be working as a team. Remember that next time."

"No harm's done," Marsh said.

"Not this time, fortunately," Graham replied.

"Who raised the alarm?" Sabrina asked, breaking the tension.

"The manager," Eastman said. "He had reason to go up to one of their rooms last night. He spoke to a man and a woman. And he's certain the man was Mullen."

"And Kerrigan?" Graham asked. "Where was he?"

"Unconscious on the floor," Eastman replied. "She gave the manager some story about it being Kerrigan's birthday and that he'd had too much to drink."

"And Kerrigan's known to be a heavy drinker," Marsh added.

"What if they've already seen the papers?" Graham said.

"It's doubtful," Eastman told him. "I told the manager to keep all newspapers hidden until we got there. So the only other way they could have seen a paper is if someone had gone out and bought one. And none of them has been out of the hotel this morning."

"You mean none of them has been past the reception desk," Graham corrected him.

"Would you use the fire escape to go and buy a newspaper?" Eastman shot back.

"Depends on the circumstances," Graham replied. "What about back-up?"

"I've got two men on the roof of a warehouse at

the back of the boarding house. They're both armed with sniper rifles."

"And that's it?" Graham said.

"We've got to take them by surprise. And we won't do that if we've got policemen crawling all over the street. I've got a back-up team on standby a couple of blocks from here. I'll bring them in once we've apprehended the cell. I've also let the local boys know what's going on but they won't come near the place unless we specifically ask for their help." Eastman opened the passenger door. "Let's go."

The four of them got out of the car and walked the fifty yards to the front of the boarding house.

"Sabrina, you and John take the fire escape," Eastman said. "Mike, you and I'll go through the front. We'll meet up outside their rooms."

Sabrina nodded and followed Marsh around the back of the building. Eastman and Graham made their way up the narrow pathway to the front door. They went inside, closing the door silently behind them.

Eastman approached the woman behind the reception desk. "Morning, could I speak to Mr. Fields please?"

The woman nodded and disappeared into the back office. She returned moments later with the manager.

"Mr. Fields?" Eastman asked.

"Yes," Fields replied suspiciously.

"I'm Inspector Keith Eastman. We spoke on the phone earlier about the photographs in the newspaper."

"Do you have a warrant card?" Fields asked.

Eastman held out his ID card to identify himself. Fields looked at Graham.

"He's with me," Eastman assured him.

Fields nodded then swallowed nervously. "I'm sure it's them, Inspector. Especially the one called

Mullen. I didn't get a proper look at the one on the floor. Had I known they were terrorists I'd never have let them stay here."

"You weren't to know who they were," Eastman said, trying to pacify him. "We'll take it from here."

"There won't be any . . . shooting, will there?" Fields asked, glancing from Eastman to Graham.

"I hope not," Eastman replied truthfully. "Thank you for calling us so promptly. We appreciate it."

Fields wrung his hands nervously as he watched them cross to the stairs at the end of the corridor. Eastman waited until he reached the top of the stairs, out of sight of the reception area, then removed the Browning from his shoulder holster. He glanced at Graham then pivoted around, Browning extended, to fan the corridor. Marsh and Sabrina were already in position at the other end of the corridor and Marsh gave him a thumbs-up sign. Eastman beckoned Graham to follow him. He held up a hand when they reached the two doors.

"Sabrina and I'll take one room," Graham said softly. "You two take the other room."

"Right," Eastman agreed.

"Wait!" Sabrina hissed under her breath. "Which is her room?"

"This isn't some vendetta—"

"Which one?" she cut across Marsh's words.

Eastman pointed to the door nearest her. "And no shooting unless it's absolutely necessary."

Graham glanced at Marsh and they both kicked open the doors simultaneously. Sabrina was first into the room, Beretta held at arm's length. Graham switched on the light behind her then cursed angrily and let the Beretta drop to his side. The room was empty. She drew the curtains. The window was open.

"Come on," she said quickly. "Eastman and Marsh may have something."

They ran back into the corridor to see the policemen

emerging from the other room. Eastman shook his head to answer Sabrina's unspoken question.

"How could they have known?" Sabrina demanded.

"Someone tipped them off, that's how," Graham retorted bitterly. "What other explanation can there be?"

Eastman followed Graham and Sabrina back into the room they had searched. "We can only have missed them by minutes."

"That's twice in less than twelve hours that we've missed them by minutes," Graham said, looking around at Eastman. "I suppose you're going to put this down to coincidence as well."

"I'm not putting it down to anything until I've had a chance to study the facts," Eastman retorted. "And unless you have some irrefutable evidence of your own pointing to one of my men being an IRA stooge then I suggest you keep your insinuations to yourself."

"You cops are always the same," Graham said with thinly veiled disgust. "You'll protect your own, no matter what the cost."

Marsh entered the room before Eastman could reply. He was holding a copy of the *Guardian* delicately between his thumb and forefinger. "Guv, I found this under the bed in the other room. It's today's."

Graham stared at the photographs of Mullen and Kerrigan on the front page then strode angrily from the room.

"What was all that about?" Eastman asked, turning to Sabrina.

She looked down into the deserted alleyway. "You know Mike's family was murdered by terrorists, don't you?"

"Yes, I read about it in his file. But what's that got to do with this investigation?"

"The FBI received a tip-off from an informer minutes after the kidnapping telling them where Carrie and Mikey were being held. The FBI officer in charge of the case didn't follow up the tip-off for more than an hour. By then Carrie and Mikey had been moved. Had the FBI acted quicker they might still be alive today. Their blunder turned Mike against all law enforcement agencies. He doesn't trust any of them. The anti-terrorist squad included. That's why you'll find he follows his own hunches and plays by his own rules. It's just the way he is. And nothing you can say or do will change that."

"So I'm just supposed to say nothing when he insinuates that someone in my team is working for the IRA?"

"Mike's hunches are rarely wrong," she said softly.

"Well, it looks like he's got it wrong this time, doesn't it?" Eastman said, gesturing to the newspaper lying on the unmade bed.

"I'd keep an open mind if I were you," Sabrina said as she left the room. She found Graham sitting at the top of the stairs. "Are you OK?"

"Yeah," he replied without looking around at her. "Eastman's being a real pain in the ass, that's all. Christ, it's obvious someone's tipped them off."

"Perhaps," she replied noncommittally.

"Come on, Sabrina—"

"It's one of your hunches," she cut in quickly. "And until you can prove it you'd better stop stepping on his toes. He's well pissed off with you right now. And understandably so."

"The feeling's mutual."

"Bite the bullet, Mike. UNACO's got its back against the wall. Right now we need all the friends we can get. And that includes Eastman. He's been assigned to this case because he's the best. Remember that."

"The voice of reason," Graham said disdainfully.

The sarcasm wasn't lost on her. She smiled. "Come on, we've got work to do."

"Sabrina?" he called out after her. "What do you think?"

"I'm keeping an open mind," she replied as she disappeared back through the nearest doorway.

"You would," Graham muttered, clambering to his feet and striding after her.

"Morning, C. W.," Kolchinsky said, entering his office.

"Morning, Sergei," Whitlock replied, getting up from behind Kolchinsky's desk.

"I'm not staying," Kolchinsky said, motioning Whitlock to sit down again. "I just stopped by to get the latest update from London so that I can brief the Secretary-General over breakfast."

Whitlock handed Kolchinsky a folder. Inside was the text of Graham's latest telephoned report. "Mike was saying you authorized the release of photographs of Kerrigan and Mullen to the Press."

Kolchinsky nodded then sat down on one of the black leather sofas. "I got a phone call from Commander Palmer, the head of Scotland Yard's anti-terrorist squad, in the early hours of the morning. It was obvious he'd already made up his mind to forward the photographs to the Press. I had no objections."

"Mike's a bit miffed that you didn't tell him."

"Palmer said Eastman would tell him," Kolchinsky replied.

"He did, this morning."

"So what's the problem?"

Whitlock indicated the folder in Kolchinsky's hand. "It seems there's a bit of a personality clash between Mike and Eastman. Mike felt that you should have let him know instead of him having to rely on Eastman."

"That's ridiculous!" Kolchinsky shot back. "The next time he contacts you, tell him to get his act together. And if he can't work with Eastman, I'll have him replaced."

"I've already had a quiet word with him," Whitlock assured him. "But I thought you should know in case Palmer mentions it in passing."

"Thanks," Kolchinsky said, rubbing his face wearily. "How did Fabio get on?"

"His report's in the folder."

Kolchinsky opened the folder and leafed through Paluzzi's four-page report. "Brief me. I won't have time to digest all this before I see the Secretary-General."

Whitlock explained what had happened in Milford the previous evening.

"How did he get back?" Kolchinsky asked.

"He phoned the duty officer, requesting a car to pick him up. It's amazing he doesn't have double pneumonia by now."

"Where is he?"

"He's using the identograph in the Command Center to try and put a name to the man he saw paying off Killen last night."

"What have you got on this Killen?"

"He's clean. No previous record."

"And his henchmen?"

"Randolph Woods and Thomas Natchett. Natchett's the only one with a record. Five years for armed robbery."

"And what about the dead man?" Kolchinsky asked.

"Billy Peterson. He'd been an inveterate gambler since his teens. He owed almost four thousand dollars to bookies in Milford and New York. He could have wiped the slate clean with the money we were going to pay him."

"Where's the money now?" Kolchinsky asked suspiciously.

"At the bottom of Milford harbor," Whitlock replied.

"Wonderful," Kolchinsky said, shaking his head slowly to himself. "It's going to look great on our expense sheet."

"We'll recover the money when the car's brought to the surface."

The door behind Whitlock slid open and Paluzzi entered the room from the Command Center. The door slid closed again.

"Ah, just in time," Kolchinsky said.

For a moment Whitlock thought Kolchinsky was going to raise the issue of the missing money. It would be typical of him. Whitlock knew only too well from first-hand experience how pedantic Kolchinsky could be in his approach to the field operatives' expense accounts.

"I was just on my way out. Any luck with the identograph?" Kolchinsky asked, much to Whitlock's relief.

Paluzzi gave Kolchinsky the computer printout he was carrying. "That's the man I saw paying off Killen last night."

Kolchinsky stared at the face for some time before skimming through the accompanying text. "Well, this is interesting."

"Who is he?" Whitlock said, unable to keep the exasperation from his voice.

"Anthony Varese," Kolchinsky said, handing the printout to Whitlock. "Martin Navarro's right-hand man."

"Navarro's one of the senior lieutenants in the Germino family," Whitlock replied, looking at the picture.

"Which ties the New York Mafia in with Billy Peterson's murder," Paluzzi concluded.

"It ties Varese in with his murder," Kolchinsky corrected him. "That's all. We don't have enough evidence at the moment to have Navarro arrested. And he's the one I really want, especially if it turns out that he was behind the arms shipment bound for Ireland."

"So how do we get that evidence?" Paluzzi asked.

"We don't," Kolchinsky replied. "At least not for the time being. If we pulled any of them in now for questioning it could seriously damage the case. You're supposed to be dead, remember that. If you start poking your nose around Navarro and Varese it'll only complicate matters. I'll detail one of the other Strike Force teams to keep tabs on them."

"What do you want me to do?" Paluzzi asked.

"Baby-sit," Kolchinsky replied, getting to his feet.

"Who?"

"Jack Scoby," Kolchinsky said as he crossed to the door. "He's officially your responsibility from now on. C. W., let me out, will you? I'm due at the Secretary-General's office in ten minutes."

"Sergei?" Paluzzi called out as the door slid open. "Does Scoby know about this?"

"Not yet," Kolchinsky replied with a quick smile.

Whitlock activated the transmitter on his desk to close the door after Kolchinsky had left. "I'll call Scoby and arrange a time for you to meet with him."

Paluzzi stifled a yawn and grinned sheepishly at Whitlock. "Sorry, I only got to bed at four this morning."

"I'll arrange for you to meet him later this afternoon," Whitlock said. "Go home and get some sleep."

"I'll be OK," Paluzzi assured him. "A couple of cups of coffee—"

"Go home," Whitlock cut in. "That's an order. I'll

expect you back here at three o'clock. I want you sharp and alert when you meet Scoby. It's important that you make a good impression on our new senator."

Martin Navarro was a tall, commanding figure in his early forties with a penchant for designer suits and expensive jewelry. He sat behind a large oak desk in his office on the top floor of West Side Electronics, one of the many legitimate businesses which had been set up in New York to launder the proceeds of the multimillion-dollar drug network which had helped to make Carmine Germino one of the most powerful and respected Capos in the country. But Germino had paid a bitter personal price for his power. His eldest son had been ambushed and killed by a Hispanic gang four years earlier. Then, two years later, his youngest son had tried to seize control of the family in a bloody gun-battle in a restaurant on Rhode Island. Navarro had saved the Capo's life and his loyalty had been rewarded with an honorary position within the family itself. And with it came the position as head of the syndicate's ever expanding drug network. He had become, in effect, second only to Carmine Germino in the family hierarchy.

The intercom buzzed and he flicked a switch on the console. "Yes, Marsha?"

"Mr. Varese's here to see you, sir."

"Send him in."

Navarro switched off the intercom, instinctively glancing at the framed photograph beside the telephone on his desk. His seven-year-old daughter, Angela. She was the spitting image of her mother. And Julia was a beautiful woman. They had been married for eleven years but his infidelities had finally become too much for her and she had walked out on him, taking Angela with her. They now lived in

Florida where she had gone back to work as a croupier. She had never asked him for money and only allowed him access to Angela during the school recesses. But, despite the fact that she had enough on him to put him away for life, she had always refused to help the authorities in their attempts to bring him to justice.

"Morning."

Navarro looked up at Varese who was standing by the door. He replaced the photograph on the desk and beckoned Varese into the room. "Well?"

"We won't be having any more trouble from Signor Pasconi," Varese replied.

"He seems to be doing a good job down there," Navarro said when Varese had finished describing Killen's handiwork. "He's loyal and reliable. I admire those qualities in a man."

"You pay him the sort of money that ensures loyalty and reliability."

Navarro smiled sadly. "You can be very cynical at times, Tony."

"It comes with the job." Varese got to his feet and helped himself to a coffee from the percolator on the sideboard. "You want one?"

"No." Navarro sat back and clasped his hands together. He formed a steeple with his index fingers and tapped them thoughtfully against his chin. "Now that's out of the way, we can concentrate our attention fully on the next little problem. Or perhaps I should say our next *big problem?* Senator Jack Scoby."

Varese took a sip of coffee then placed the cup on the table beside the chair. "Are you going to confront him personally?"

Navarro shook his head. "I'll call his lackey, Tillman, and arrange to meet him before they fly out to London tomorrow morning."

"What are you going to say to him?" Varese asked, sitting forward, his arms resting on his knees.

A knowing smile spread across Navarro's tanned face. "Enough to worry him, but not enough to give the game away."

"Come," Eastman called out in response to the sharp rap on his office door.

Marsh entered the office, acknowledged Graham and Sabrina with a nod, then looked across at Eastman and shook his head. "Nothing, guv. It's clean."

"I asked John to select a team of his own to go over the car we used last night," Eastman said to Graham. "And you heard the verdict. It's clean."

"We checked every inch of it," Marsh assured Graham. "If there had been a device, we'd have found it."

Graham said nothing.

"I thought you'd feel better if John was there to oversee the operation. An independent, so to speak," Eastman said, the satisfaction of Marsh's findings evident in his voice.

"Yeah, sure," Graham grudgingly agreed.

There was another knock on the door. Marsh answered it, taking delivery of a folder which he handed to Eastman, who skimmed quickly through its contents.

"It's been established from prints taken from the two rooms that Kerrigan and Mullen were definitely at the boarding house last night."

"We already knew that," Graham said.

"We assumed it was them, but we didn't have the proof," Eastman replied, lighting himself a cigarette. "And this is it. Now we know for certain that we're dealing with Farrell's cell."

"Anything on Fiona Gallagher?" Sabrina asked.

Eastman sat back in his chair. "I've no doubt her prints are there but we've got no way of verifying that. As you already know from your records, we don't have a thing on her. No photos, no fingerprints. Nothing. She's even said to change her appearance every few months so we can't even rely on eyewitness reports to build up a picture of her. She's good, I'll give her that.''

"Farrell did a good job on her,'' Marsh added.

Eastman nodded. "It's no secret that he taught her everything he knows about terrorism and counterterrorism. And when I tell you that he's widely regarded within the IRA as one of the leading experts on those subjects you'll get an idea of just what we're up against.''

"She's also got this,'' Marsh said, tapping his head. "She was a top student at Bristol University. Graduated with a First. Farrell plays by the book which means he can be predictable at times. She doesn't, and that's what makes her that bit more dangerous.''

"So why isn't she in charge of the unit instead of Farrell?'' Graham asked.

"She may be smarter, but he's a better leader,'' Marsh replied. "And that combination's what makes their cell so effective.''

"So the current situation could be to our advantage,'' Sabrina deduced, and immediately noticed the puzzled look on Eastman's face. "Well, they'll be weakened without Farrell. And if she's not a natural leader, they could run into problems. They may make mistakes but more likely there may be internal dissent, especially from Kerrigan. It's obvious from his file that he and Farrell were very close until she came along. I may be reading between the lines, but I doubt there's much love lost between the two of them. And now he's having to take orders from her. I can't see him being too thrilled about that, can you?''

Eastman glanced at Marsh and both men nodded simultaneously.

"That's a valid point,'' Eastman agreed. "But there is one drawback to it. And I think John will agree with me on this. Kerrigan's a die-hard Provo. A stickler for the rules. Which is why he and Farrell get along so well. That means he'll toe the line irrespective of how he feels about her being in charge of the cell in Farrell's absence."

"Everyone has their breaking point," Graham said. "Including Kerrigan."

The telephone rang.

"Excuse me," Eastman said, answering it. His eyes narrowed as he listened attentively then, grabbing a pen from the holder on his desk, he scribbled furiously on the pad at his elbow. "No, don't do anything, sir. We'll be there as soon as possible." He nodded as he listened again. "Yes, I'd appreciate it if you'd clear things with your people. We don't want any delays when we get there. Thank you for letting me know so promptly."

"Well?" Marsh asked excitedly after Eastman had replaced the receiver.

"That was the Swiss Police Commissioner. McGuire's holed up with a known IRA sympathizer outside Lausanne." Eastman tore off the sheet of paper and gave it to Marsh. "Get four seats on the first available flight to Switzerland."

Marsh stuffed the paper into his jacket pocket and hurried from the room.

"Now all we have to do is hope the IRA don't get to him first," Graham replied somberly.

"Not this time," Eastman replied confidently. "Apart from the Swiss police, only the four of us know he's there. No, I think fortune's finally beginning to swing our way."

Fiona Gallagher stood at the window staring absently at the passing traffic on the A1 two hundred yards away from the house. It had been a close call back at the boarding house. Too close. But she also knew that without the advance warning they would all be in custody by now. It certainly paid to have a mole inside the anti-terrorist squad . . .

She had been woken in the early hours of the morning by the beeper she always carried with her. It was only ever used in an emergency. She'd immediately rung a pre-arranged number from the payphone in the corridor and was told that the manager had recognized Mullen and Kerrigan from the photographs released to the Press the previous evening. She'd woken Mullen and Kerrigan and they'd fled the boarding house minutes before the authorities arrived. They had driven north, away from the city center.

It was Mullen who had spotted the isolated Tudorstyle house on the outskirts of Hatfield. It was set back from the road and surrounded by a grove of oak trees. It would prove a useful temporary safe house until they decided on their next move. They had donned their balaclavas once more, and Mullen had driven up to the house. They had found the owners, an elderly couple, having breakfast on the back porch. Kerrigan had brandished his Uzi menacingly at the couple before Fiona had quickly put a stop to his stupidity and told Mullen to take the couple into the lounge where he'd bound their wrists. That had been an hour ago . . .

The door opened behind her. She made to pull the balaclava back over her face when she saw it was Mullen. He closed the door behind him and jerked the balaclava off his head.

"Jesus, it's hot," he said, wiping his sleeve across his sweaty forehead.

She nodded then crossed to a chair and sat down. "How are the old couple bearing up?"

"OK," Mullen assured her. "It turns out the old guy takes some kind of pills for his heart. He wouldn't take them at first because I'd gone to get them for him. But the old lady gave him a bit of a ticking off and he ended up taking them like a good little boy. He hasn't been any trouble since then."

Fiona smiled then glanced at the door. "And Liam?"

"He's already eaten through half the contents of the fridge," Mullen replied with a helpless shrug. "But at least he hasn't started on the booze."

"Yet," she added.

"You gave him a big fright last night," Mullen told her. "I don't think he'll be drinking again in a hurry."

She sighed deeply then got to her feet and returned to the window, her hands dug deep into the pockets of her camouflage trousers.

"What's on your mind?" Mullen said softly behind her.

"There are family photographs on the mantelpiece in there," she said, indicating the door leading into the adjoining room where Kerrigan was guarding the couple. "And most children keep in touch with their parents. What if one of them calls? No answer. Next minute the whole family's up here to check on them. Then what? Invite them in for tea and scones?"

"If someone calls, get the old lady to answer it. She seems the more cooperative of the two. And she'll be especially cooperative if Liam's holding an Uzi to the back of the old man's head."

"You sure you don't want to take the reins around here?" she said, half-jokingly.

"Once was enough," Mullen replied, holding up his hands defensively.

"I didn't know you were ever in charge of a cell," Fiona said in surprise.

"Not a cell as such. The Army Council put me in charge of a three-man team several years ago. Our target was a retired RUC officer in Newry. I led them straight into an SAS ambush. I was the only survivor."

"You've never mentioned that before."

"Would you? It's not exactly something I'm proud of."

The door opened again and Kerrigan looked in. "Will someone come out here a moment? I need to take a leak."

Mullen pulled the balaclava back over his face and walked to the door.

The beeper on Fiona's belt suddenly activated and she quickly switched it off. They both looked around at her. "It's the 'Fortune Teller.' I'd better ring him straight away."

"The 'Fortune Teller'?" Kerrigan said suspiciously.

"The Army Council's contact in the anti-terrorist squad."

"The same guy who saved our arses this morning?" Kerrigan asked.

"The same."

"The 'Fortune Teller'?" Kerrigan muttered, chuckling to himself. "It's an appropriate codename. Do you know who he is?"

"You must be joking. His identity's known only to the senior members of the Army Council." She crossed to the telephone and dialed a number. It was answered after the first ring. "This is 'Rebel Woman'."

"And this is 'Fortune Teller'," came the reply. "McGuire's been spotted in Switzerland. Have you got a pen there to write down the address?"

"Right here," she said, picking up the pen which lay beside the telephone. She wrote down the address on the notepad, tore off the top sheet, and slipped it into her pocket. "What sort of head start do we have?"

"How long do you need?"

"A couple of hours would be great," she replied, more out of hope than anything else.

"You got it," came the confident reply.

"How are you going to manage that?"

"You let me worry about that. Now, about your flight. There are two flights to Switzerland in the next few hours. Both are from Heathrow. One's a Swissair flight, direct to Zurich. We're already booked on that one. It leaves at two o'clock this afternoon. It's the quicker flight. The other is a BA flight to Rome, stopping at Paris and Zurich. It leaves at midday. Take that one. I know it doesn't give you much time but there are still seats available."

"Got it," she said, scribbling furiously on the pad again.

There was a sudden pause. "Someone's coming. Call me when you get back."

"Will do," she assured him.

The line went dead. She replaced the receiver then gestured to the door. "Keep an eye on those two. I need to make some calls."

"Excuse me," Doris Matthews said, addressing herself to Fiona. "My husband needs another one of his pills."

Fiona nodded to Mullen who retrieved the bottle from the mantelpiece and tipped a single pill into his palm. He picked up the glass of water off the sideboard and crossed to the old man's chair. Herbert Matthews glared at Mullen but, unlike the last time, he made no attempt to turn his head away when Mullen pushed the pill between his lips. Matthews took a sip of water to wash down the pill then looked away sharply, his eyes riveted on an imaginary spot on the wall. Doris Matthews could see the anger in his eyes. It was certainly an anger she shared. Their home had been invaded. Their privacy abused. Their lives would never be the same again . . .

She looked across at the three masked figures talk-

ing in whispers by the door. The big one frightened
her. Psychopathic was the word that came to mind.
She was sure he could be extremely dangerous if pro-
voked. The smaller one seemed more relaxed, more
at ease with the situation. She had immediately as-
sociated them with the IRA when she first heard the
two men's voices. She knew she could be wrong. But
she certainly knew her accents after thirty years as a
drama teacher in London. The big one had a strong
Irish accent. Guttural. Although the smaller man had
less of an accent it was still noticeable in the way he
stressed certain words. But it was the woman who really fascinated her. She had no discernible accent at
all. Hers was a calm, soothing voice. But also authori-
tative when the need arose. She felt strangely at ease
when the woman was in the room. It was as if she
knew nothing would happen to either her or her husband as long as the woman was there . . . .

Fiona broke away from the others and crouched
beside Herbert Matthews.

"We'll need to borrow your car, Mr. Matthews."

"How do you know my name?" he demanded.

"It's the name on the envelope on the hall table,"
she replied matter-of-factly.

"We don't have a car," he said brusquely.

"Please don't insult my intelligence, Mr. Matthews," she said in a soft, menacing tone. "It's a blue
Rover Montego, and it's parked in the garage at the
back of the house. Where are the keys?"

"You can go to hell," Matthews retorted.

Fiona indicated Kerrigan behind her. "If I let him
hit you, he'd probably kill you. Is your car worth
that?"

"The keys are hanging on the rack by the back
door," Doris Matthews interceded quickly, the tears
welling up in her eyes. "Just take the car and leave us
alone. Please, just go away."

"Bring the car round to the front of the house,"

Fiona said to Mullen. She glanced at Kerrigan. "Get the stuff out of the other car and put it in the Rover."

"What about them?" Kerrigan asked suspiciously.

"Out!" Fiona snapped.

Mullen grabbed Kerrigan's arm and led him from the room.

"A word of warning," Fiona said to the couple. "Don't try to struggle against the ropes after we've gone. They've been tied in such a way that the more you struggle, the tighter they'll become. It could get very uncomfortable. I'll see to it that you'll both be freed within the hour." She moved to the door then turned back to them. "I'm sorry this had to happen. I really am."

Doris Matthews stared at the door after Fiona had gone. There was no doubt in her mind that Fiona *had* meant what she said. They would be free within the hour. But more astonishingly, the apology had been sincere. It had been in her voice. And Doris Matthews knew voices . . .

They knew something was wrong the moment they saw the row of police cars parked outside the main terminal at Heathrow Airport.

"Park there until we find out what's going on," Eastman said to Marsh, indicating the space between two panda cars.

Marsh reversed into the space. Challenged by an armed policeman, he held out his ID card. "What's going on?" he asked, switching off the engine.

"Bomb scare, sir," the policeman replied.

"In the terminal?" Marsh continued.

"No, sir. One of the planes, I believe. I don't know which one though."

"I think I can guess," Graham said from the backseat.

"Let's not jump to conclusions," Eastman replied as he got out of the car. "Are the ATs here yet?"

"The ATs, sir?" the policeman said with a frown.

"The ATOs . . ." Eastman trailed off when he spotted a figure in army fatigues emerging from the terminal. "It's OK, I've just seen one." He hurried after the man. "Chippy? Chippy Woodward?"

The man turned around and a wide grin spread across his face. "Keith, good to see you."

"I'm not sure yet whether I can say the same about you," Eastman replied. "Which plane is it?"

"A Swissair Airbus. It was due out in forty minutes. We've got it parked on one of the outer runways just in case the bastard does blow. But we haven't found anything up to now."

"Isn't that just bloody marvelous?" Marsh said angrily behind Eastman.

"You know Sergeant John Marsh, don't you?" Eastman said to Woodward.

"Yes, we've met before," Woodward replied, shaking Marsh's hand.

"And this is Mike Graham and Sabrina Carver, two of our American cousins," Eastman added, using the euphemism for the CIA. There was no point mentioning UNACO.

Woodward shook hands with them. "So what's the problem . . . ?" He trailed off and nodded to himself. "You were booked on that Swissair flight, weren't you?"

Eastman nodded. "How long before you'll be able to give the all clear?"

Woodward shrugged. "You know the drill, Keith. An hour, perhaps ninety minutes. The guy who called the airport seemed to know a bit about explosives. That's why we're treating this one with extra caution."

"So it'll be a good two hours before we can even

take off," Graham said, struggling to control his temper.

"More like two and a half," Woodward said, glancing at his watch. "Well, if you'll excuse me, I'd better go and see how the lads are getting on. Good to see you again, Keith."

"Likewise, Chippy," Eastman replied.

"Are there any other flights to Switzerland in the next hour or so?" Sabrina asked after Woodward had gone.

"One flew out half an hour ago," Marsh replied. "Ours is the next scheduled flight to Switzerland."

"So why weren't we booked on the earlier flight?" Graham demanded.

"Because this one was due to reach Zurich first," Eastman told him.

"Couldn't we charter a private plane?" Sabrina said.

"It wouldn't get us there any quicker," Eastman replied. "I'll phone the Commissioner in Zurich and have him double the men watching the chalet where McGuire's holed up. If this is an IRA tactic to make sure they get to McGuire first, then he'll have the men on hand to apprehend them."

"You've suddenly changed your tune," Graham said with thinly veiled sarcasm.

"I'm not taking any chances, that's all," Eastman retorted brusquely.

"Coffee, anyone?" Sabrina asked, breaking the lingering silence.

"Sounds good to me," Marsh responded quickly. "Guv?"

"I'll meet you in the cafeteria. I've got to call Zurich first."

Sabrina turned to Graham but he was already walking toward the terminal. She gave Marsh a helpless shrug and they went after him.

* * *

Ingrid Lynch studied the passengers as they emerged through customs at Zurich's Kloten International Airport. She was an attractive redhead in her mid-twenties who had met her husband, Dominic, a year earlier at an IRA rally in Belfast. They had returned to Zurich together where she taught as a primary school teacher. He was now regarded as one of the IRA's main contacts in Europe and had helped to arm several of the IRA's active cells in both Germany and France.

"Ingrid?"

She looked around, startled by the voice behind her. It was a woman with black shoulder-length hair and tinted sunglasses. Her eyes narrowed uncertainly. Did she know her?

The woman removed the sunglasses and grinned. "Don't you even recognize your chief bridesmaid when you see her?"

"Fiona," Ingrid said, hugging her more out of relief than anything else. "I did not even recognize you."

"Good," Fiona replied. "Then neither will any of the security staff around here."

"What have you done to your hair?"

"It's a wig," came the reply. "Where's Dominic?"

"He stayed in the car. He did not want to take any chances."

"It's good to see he's not become complacent," Fiona replied, then introduced her to Mullen and Kerrigan.

"Have you got your luggage?"

"We didn't bring much," Fiona replied, tapping her shoulder bag. "We don't expect to be here very long."

They left the terminal and Ingrid led the way across the car park to where her husband had parked the Audi. Dominic Lynch, a short, stocky man in his late twenties, jumped out of the car the moment he saw the reflection of his wife in the rear-view mirror. Fiona hurried toward him and they embraced warmly.

"You're looking good, girl," Lynch said, holding her at arm's length. "But I preferred you as a blonde."

"It is a wig," Ingrid chided her husband.

"It's very good," Lynch replied, then turned to Mullen and pumped his hand vigorously. "It's good to see you again, Hugh."

"And you, Dom," Mullen replied. "How are you settling down out here?"

"I still miss the comforts of home. Like Guinness." Lynch smiled at Kerrigan. "And how is my old drinking partner?"

Kerrigan shook Lynch's hand. "Good, man. And how's marriage treating you? Have you finally settled down and become a bit more responsible?"

"Not a chance," Lynch replied with a smile. "So how did you manage to get past security at Heathrow? I hear your faces were splashed across all the morning papers over there."

"We took the necessary precautions," was all Fiona would venture.

"I get it," Lynch said with a knowing smile. "What I don't know can't hurt me."

"Did you get the chopper, Dom?" Mullen asked, changing tactics.

"It's ready and waiting for you, Hugh," Lynch assured him.

"And what about the weapons?" Fiona asked.

"They haven't turned up yet," Lynch replied apologetically.

Fiona banged her fist angrily on the roof of the car. "You assured me on the phone that you'd have them by the time we got here. You know we can't make a move without them."

"They'll turn up, don't worry," Lynch replied, trying to pacify her.

"When?" she challenged.

"When the courier arrives," Lynch shot back defensively. "The weather's been atrocious over here for the last twenty-four hours. He's probably been held up somewhere."

"That's not my problem, is it?" she snapped.

"That's enough, Fiona," Kerrigan said behind her. "It's not Dom's fault that the weapons aren't here yet."

She swung around, her eyes blazing. "This doesn't concern you, Liam. Get in the car."

"Like hell—"

"You'll do as you're told unless you want to go up in front of the committee on a charge of insubordination," she snarled, levelling a finger of warning at him. "And it wouldn't be the first time that's happened to you, would it?"

Kerrigan glared at Fiona then cursed furiously as he climbed into the back of the car, slamming the door after him.

Lynch led Fiona away from the others. "What's got into you treating him like that?"

"Let go of my arm, Dom," she said softly.

Lynch released his grip on her arm. "I know Liam better than any of you. You can only push him so far before he'll snap."

"This is my cell, Dom, and I'll run it as I see fit."

"What's really troubling you, girl? Is it Sean?"

She stared at her feet for a moment then let out a deep sigh. "I'm sorry I snapped at you just now. I guess I'm just a bit edgy, that's all. Come on, let's go."

They returned to the car. Lynch shivered suddenly, as if someone had just stepped on his grave. This wasn't the calm, rational Fiona he'd once known in Ireland. And that worried him. Had the burden of responsibility become too much for her? Much as he liked Mullen, he knew he couldn't talk to him. He was too close to her. But Kerrigan was an old friend. Yes, he'd have a word with Kerrigan when they got back to the house. And he'd take the situation from there . . .

◆ CHAPTER

SEVEN

There's a Mr. Tillman here to see you, sir."

"Show him in, Marsha."

Navarro rose from behind his desk to greet his visitor. "Mr. Tillman, I'm Martin Navarro," he said, approaching Tillman.

Tillman eyed Navarro's extended hand with disdain. "I'm not in the habit of shaking hands with wise guys."

Navarro smiled. "The only difference between us, Mr. Tillman, is that a politician's crimes are legal."

"I didn't come here to be insulted," Tillman snapped.

"No, of course not," Navarro replied then gestured to the man sitting on the couch against the wall. "Tony Varese, my right-hand man."

"Is that what you call him?" Tillman retorted sarcastically. "I would have thought 'hatchet man' would have been a better description of his duties."

Varese chuckled softly to himself. "Then it would seem we have something in common, Mr. Tillman."

"Tony, that's enough," Navarro interceded before

Tillman could say anything. "Please, sit down, Mr. Tillman. We've got so much to talk about."

"You can begin by telling me why you called me this morning threatening to release certain information to the Press—which, you claimed, would destroy Senator Scoby's reputation—unless I met with you here today. What is this, some kind of blackmail scam? Because if it is—"

"Sit down," Navarro repeated, indicating the chair to the right of his desk. "Would you like a coffee? Or perhaps something a little stronger?"

"Nothing," Tillman replied, sitting down.

Navarro moved around behind his desk and sat down. "Did you tell Scoby you were coming here?"

"Certainly not," Tillman retorted indignantly. "The less the senator knows about this the better."

"Of course," Navarro said with a smile.

"Navarro, my time is limited," Tillman snapped. "Will you get to the point!"

"What if I told you I knew all about the deal you finalized earlier this week with the Cabrera cartel in Medellín?"

Tillman's face went pale but he was quick to regain his composure. "I don't know what you're talking about."

"Let's bypass the denial stage, shall we? It's not fooling anyone."

"I tell you, I don't know about any deal made in Medellín," Tillman snapped back.

Navarro removed a folder from the drawer in front of him. "There's enough evidence in here to put you and Scoby in San Quentin for the next twenty years. Let's see what we've got here. A copy of the reservation card from the Intercontinental Hotel in Medellín. The name on it is Charles Edward Warren. Your handwriting, I believe? And then there're the photographs which were taken at the various meetings you've had with Miguel Cabrera, both here in

New York and in Medellín, over the last five months." He tossed a dozen photographs onto the desk in front of Tillman. "Any one of these photographs could ruin Scoby's career."

Tillman swallowed nervously then picked up the nearest photograph. It showed him dining with Cabrera at a small restaurant in Medellín. He dropped the photograph back onto the desk. "The senator knew nothing of this. The whole thing was my own idea."

"Your loyalty's very touching." Navarro opened another drawer and removed a shoe box. Inside, neatly arranged in chronological order, was a row of audio cassette tapes. "All your meetings with Miguel Cabrera were recorded secretly on tape. They proved that Scoby's been involved with it from the very beginning."

"And if that wasn't enough, we can even prove that Jorge Cabrera provided Scoby with financial aid to help with his election campaign," Varese said, getting to his feet. "I doubt any of this would go down very well with the public, do you? Especially as Scoby won the election on such a strong anti-drugs campaign."

"Tony, I think Mr. Tillman may need that drink after all," Navarro said to Varese.

Varese crossed to the drinks cabinet in the corner of the room. "What would you like, Mr. Tillman?"

Tillman stared at Navarro. "Miguel Cabrera gave you this information, didn't he?"

"We do have a mole in the cartel," Navarro replied evasively.

It had to be Miguel Cabrera. He must have known the risks. What if his father had discovered his duplicity? Kinship would have counted for nothing. If anything, it would have made it even worse for him. Family betrayal. But why?

"Your drink," Varese said, breaking Tillman's train of thought.

Tillman drank the bourbon down in one gulp. He handed the glass back to Varese. "It's Miguel Cabrera, isn't it? It has to be."

"Who it is doesn't concern you," Navarro replied.

"I want to know!" Tillman yelled, the blood rushing to his face. "I want to know," he repeated, this time in a calm voice.

"Why?"

"Wouldn't you want to know if you were in my position?"

Navarro looked up at Varese who gave him a noncommittal shrug. "Yes, it was Miguel Cabrera."

"But why? The Colombians and the Mafia have been archenemies for years."

"Pour me a small bourbon, Tony," Navarro said, then got to his feet and crossed to the window. He turned back to Tillman. "Miguel Cabrera wants to take over the cartel from his father. And that means he needs money to finance his power base. We agreed to provide him with that money in return for this information." He took the glass from Varese. "You see, Miguel has a vision of the future. The strongest cartel in Colombia uniting with the most powerful family in the United States. The Cabrera cartel and the Germino family. And, in doing so, creating a complete monopoly on the movement of drugs into the United States."

"It could never work of course," Varese added.

"So you've deliberately set him up?" Tillman said.

"We played along to get the information we wanted. But he doesn't know anything about our plan to intercept the drugs and distribute them as our own. So, when the time's right, he'll be dealt with accordingly."

"So where does my deal with Cabrera come into all of this?"

Navarro returned to his desk. "First, let's run through the basic points of this deal you made with

Jorge Cabrera. You have senior customs officials
who, in return for the right kind of financial incentive, would see to it that each month several large
shipments of cocaine, all sent by the Cabrera cartel,
were allowed to pass undetected through certain customs checkpoints in New York State for distribution
across the United States. And, in return, the Cabrera
cartel would be willing to allow some of their smaller
shipments to be seized by the same customs men to
give the impression that they were carrying out
Scoby's tough anti-drugs measures successfully.
How am I doing?"

Tillman just nodded.

"And, for every shipment that was successfully
smuggled through customs, Scoby would receive ten
percent of its final street value. That money, in cash,
would then be distributed amongst certain right-
wing governments in South and Central America."

"The senator has no personal interest in the
money: it's purely a political venture," Tillman said
proudly. "The world believes that Marxism is dead
now that Russia's finally decided to turn its back on
the old-style communism. They couldn't be more
wrong."

"Spare us the political rhetoric," Navarro said disdainfully. "Now, let me put our proposal to you.
Your deal with the Cabrera cartel remains the same.
But once the cocaine gets through customs, your people will tip us off as to its ultimate destination. We'll
then intercept some of those shipments before they
reach their destination and distribute them as our
own. But only some." He held up a finger to stress
the point. "We don't want it to appear suspicious.
Well, at least not at first. And in return we'll pay
Scoby fifteen percent of its street value. The money
will be laundered through our legitimate businesses,
like West Side Electronics, and forwarded to any government of his choice. So not only will the deal

provide more financial aid for the death squads in
South and Central America, it'll also give us the edge
over the Colombians in the drugs war."

"And what's going to happen to the senator and
myself when Cabrera finds out what's happened?"

"What can he find out?" Navarro replied, shrug-
ging his powerful shoulders. "You've kept to your
side of the deal. We won't touch any of the shipments
until they've cleared customs. That puts you in the
clear. We'll be taking all the risks."

"And how will we explain the loss of the shipments to the cartel? Cabrera's going to get suspicious
after a while."

"Get your senior men to throw a couple of their
minnows to the cartel every now and then to keep
them satisfied." Navarro gathered together the
photographs, put them back in the folder, then
placed it on the desk in front of Tillman. "Show them
to Scoby. I've got the negatives locked away in a safe
place. You can take the tapes as well if you want. I've
got copies."

Tillman took the folder and the box of audio cassettes. "And if the senator refuses to go along with
your plan, you'll see to it that the negatives and a set
of the tapes are made public?"

"You're very astute," Navarro replied with a
smile. "I believe you're off to England for the weekend. It'll give the two of you time to consider my
more than generous offer. When are you flying
back?"

"Monday morning."

"Then I'll expect your answer by Tuesday. Shall
we say ten o'clock, here in my office?"

"Very well," Tillman replied tersely as he packed
the last of the cassettes into his attaché case.

"There is one other thing," Navarro said. He nodded to Varese who produced an attaché case and
placed it on the desk. Navarro unlocked it and

opened the lid. "Two hundred and fifty thousand dollars in cash. All in untraceable notes. We can match whatever the Colombians gave you. Just a little incentive to help you make up his mind."

"I didn't know we had a choice," Tillman replied, eyeing the money which was laid out in neat bundles in the case.

"Of course you have a choice," Navarro replied, locking the case again. "After all, isn't that what America's all about?"

Varese placed the case at Tillman's feet.

"Well, it's been a pleasure meeting you," Navarro said, extending his hand again.

Tillman ignored Navarro's hand then, picking up both attaché cases, walked to the door.

"Oh, I almost forgot," Navarro said as Varese opened the door for Tillman. "*Bon voyage.*"

Tillman eyed Navarro coldly then turned and left the room without a word.

It was already dark by the time the Swissair Airbus finally touched down, nearly three hours behind schedule, at Kloten International Airport. A thick blanket of snow covered the perimeter of the airfield and the snow plows were continually having to clear the fresh snow as it drifted down across the city. And, according to UNACO's weather charts, the situation was set to deteriorate over the next twelve hours. Eastman had been assured before he left London that the Swiss authorities would assist them in every way possible once they touched down at Zurich. Their contact in Lausanne would be Captain Philippe Bastian, one of the most experienced officers in the Swiss anti-terrorist squad.

A black Mercedes was waiting for them on the runway when they disembarked. The driver, a plain-clothes police officer, immediately drove them to another section of runway where a police helicopter was waiting to fly them on to Lausanne.

"You wanted to see me, Dom?"

Lynch looked around at Kerrigan who was standing in the doorway. "Come in, Liam. And close the door."

Kerrigan entered Lynch's study and closed the door behind him.

"It's a breathtaking view during the day," Lynch said, gesturing to the darkness beyond the window. "I'm really lucky to have got this place."

"I'm sure you didn't ask me here to discuss the view from your window," Kerrigan said bluntly.

"No, of course not," Lynch replied, turning back to Kerrigan. "Sit down, Liam. Drink?"

Kerrigan eased himself into the armchair by the door. "No drink. I'm going to need my wits about me if we're to get McGuire tonight, especially in these godforsaken conditions."

"Yes, it's definitely getting worse," Lynch muttered, crossing to the drinks cabinet and pouring himself a whiskey.

"Still no news of the weapons?"

"Nothing yet," Lynch replied with an apologetic shrug. "And this weather won't help matters any either."

Kerrigan banged the chair arm angrily with his fist. "Those pigs will probably be in the country by now. Christ, if those guns don't arrive soon they'll get to McGuire first."

"The weather's going to work against them as well, you know." Lynch sat down behind his desk and looked across at Kerrigan. "I want to talk to you about Fiona."

"What about her?" Kerrigan retorted suspiciously.

"I think she's cracking under the pressure of being put in charge of the cell in Sean's absence."

"Cracking?" Kerrigan snorted. "I guess that's one way of putting it. But the Army Council made the decision to put her in charge and until they relieve her of that responsibility, there's nothing any of us can do about it."

"You don't like her, do you?"

"Not particularly, no. But she's Sean's girl and that's why I tolerate her."

"That's where we differ." Lynch took a sip of whiskey then turned the glass around thoughtfully in his hand. "Sean and Fiona are good friends of ours. He was my best man. She was Ingrid's chief bridesmaid."

"I was at the wedding, you know," Kerrigan was quick to point out.

"It upsets me to see her like this. You said just now that there was nothing any of us can do about it. Well, that's where you're wrong."

"You know the rules, Dom. I can't call the Army Council unless it's an emergency. What would I tell them? That she's cracking? Where's my evidence? The Army Council don't deal in suspicions and rumors. Only facts. And anyway, they think she's bloody marvelous. That's Sean's fault for falling so heavily for her."

Lynch finished his drink and placed the glass on the desk. "You can't call the Army Council. But I can."

Kerrigan's eyes narrowed. "And tell them what?"

"What I've seen since she got here. What can they do to me? I'm not part of your cell. And I'd only be calling because I'm worried about her, which will be true."

Kerrigan chewed his lip thoughtfully. "When are you going to call them?"

"When you've gone," Lynch replied.

"It's good thinking, Dom. For her, and for the cell."

"I'm doing it for her. Period. And only because she's got a hell of a future ahead of her with the Provos. I don't want to see her burnt out before she's thirty."

"You always were a pragmatic one, Lynch," Kerrigan said with an edge of sarcasm. He got to his feet. "You call, mind."

"I'll call," Lynch assured him. "But in the meantime you do as she says, no matter what she tells you to do."

"As if I wouldn't," Kerrigan replied with a look of mock innocence.

"I know she's riding you, Liam. But let it go. Because if you cross her you're going to find yourself in a whole load of trouble when you get back home. You remember that."

"I can look after myself, Dom. Don't you worry yourself about that."

There was a knock at the door. Kerrigan opened it.

Ingrid looked around the door at her husband. "Alain's here."

"At last." Lynch stood up and looked at Kerrigan. "The guns have arrived."

"Then let's go," Kerrigan said.

Fiona waited until the voices had died away then eased open the door and peered out cautiously into the hallway. It was deserted. She emerged into the hall and closed the door silently behind her. She automatically glanced toward the study door. Her suspicions had first been aroused when she had overheard Lynch asking Kerrigan to meet him in his study. Why the secrecy? Now she knew. She had overheard the entire conversation. Well, almost all of it before she had to duck into the room opposite when she had heard Ingrid approaching. Lynch was going to call the Army Council. She doubted they would listen to him. As Kerrigan had said, there was no evidence to taint her reputation. But what if Lynch's call planted a seed of doubt in their minds? What if she was recalled after the operation? No, she couldn't afford to take that chance. Not with so much at stake . . .

She went into the bathroom further down the hallway, flushed the toilet, then made her way to the lounge.

"We were about to send out a search party for you," Lynch said as she entered the room.

"I was in the toilet," Fiona replied. Her eyes flickered to the man beside Lynch.

"This is Alain," Lynch told her. "The weapons have finally arrived. Hugh and Liam are busy transferring them from Alain's car to my car. I'll pick my car up in the morning."

"Thanks, Dom."

"You still think you'll be able to find your way over to the helicopter?" Lynch asked.

"I might not but Hugh's great at memorizing routes."

Alain said something to Lynch in French. Lynch shook his hand and Alain left the room. Moments later the front door banged shut.

"He's a good man," Lynch said. "Very reliable. And he doesn't speak a word of English."

"Perfect," Fiona replied softly.

"Something wrong?" Lynch asked, putting an arm around her shoulder. "You seemed to be in another world just now."

"I guess I'm just tired. It's a real bitch running the show now that Sean's in custody."

"I can believe that. But it'll all be over after tonight."

"It will be if we don't get McGuire," Fiona replied with a sigh. "The Army Council will crucify us. But even if we do tag him, what's to say the Army Council won't want us to carry out another operation? We're on a run. Why pull us in now?"

"They'll call you back after this," Lynch said.

"How can you be so sure?" she said, eyeing him suspiciously.

"I'm not," Lynch replied quickly. "But why push you to the limit when Sean's due out at the weekend?"

"Which brings us back to McGuire. We have to get him, Dom."

"You will," Lynch said, squeezing her arm. "Hey, I almost forgot. I've got something for you." He took a Glock 17 automatic pistol and a silencer from the top drawer of the sideboard. "Recognize it?"

"It's Sean's," Fiona said in surprise, taking it from Lynch. "He told me he'd lost it."

"He left it behind the last time he was here," Lynch replied. "I know he'd want you to have it."

She slipped it into the pocket of her windcheater. The front door opened and Mullen and Kerrigan came inside, their windcheaters flecked with snow.

"God, it's cold outside," Mullen said, rubbing his gloved hands together. "We're set, Fiona."

"Great," Fiona replied. "Then let's say our good-byes and get the show on the road."

Mullen and Kerrigan shook hands with Lynch.

"You two go on out to the car," Fiona said to them. "There's something I need to talk to Dom about. It'll only take a minute."

"Sure," Mullen replied. "But don't shilly-shally. We're already running late."

"I told you, it'll only take a minute."

Lynch waited until Mullen and Kerrigan had gone before looking at her. "What is it, girl?"

"Can we go to your study?"

"Sure, come on." Lynch led the way down the hall and opened the study door for her. Closing it behind them, he moved to a window before turning back to her. "Well, what . . . ?" He trailed off when he saw the silenced automatic in her hand.

"I heard everything you said to Liam earlier," she announced, holding his stare. "You were going to call the Army Council and tell them I wasn't fit to run the cell, weren't you?"

"Fiona, it's not what you think," Lynch said anxiously, his eyes riveted on the automatic in her hand. "I was only concerned about you. You and Sean are like family to me. I'd never hurt you, you know that."

"Family aren't supposed to betray each other, are they?" she replied coldly.

"Fiona, listen . . . listen to me," Lynch stammered. "Put the gun down, girl. We can talk about this."

"The time for talk's over," she said, squeezing the trigger.

The bullet took Lynch in the forehead. He was dead before he hit the floor. She left the study, closing the door behind her, then made for the kitchen where Ingrid was busy loading the washing machine. She looked up and smiled as Fiona entered the room.

"I've just come to say good-bye," Fiona said, returning the smile.

"Then do it properly," Ingrid replied, arms outstretched.

"I will," Fiona said and as they embraced she pressed the tip of the silencer against the back of Ingrid's head and pulled the trigger. She caught Ingrid's limp body as it fell and eased it onto the floor. Wiping her fingerprints off the automatic she tossed it into the bin. She then walked calmly down the hall, zipped up her windcheater, opened the front door, and went out into the cold night air.

Two police cars were waiting for the plane when it touched down at Lausanne's La Blecherette Airport.

Eastman and Marsh got into the first car. Graham and Sabrina shared the second. The sirens were switched on and the cars headed for Les Paccots, a ski resort thirty kilometers from Lausanne.

When the two police cars finally pulled up behind a mobile police van close to Les Paccots the four of them were ushered inside. Half a dozen policemen, all wearing white Gortex overalls, were seated at two long tables on either side of the van, poring over charts and reports.

"We're looking for Captain Bastian," Eastman said to the man.

"*Capitaine Bastian?*" The man pointed to the figure at the end of one of the far tables. "*Là-bas.*"

"Over there," Sabrina translated.

Eastman crossed to the man. "Captain Bastian?"

"*Oui?*" the man snapped without looking up from the map he was studying.

"I'm Inspector Keith Eastman, Scotland Yard. I believe Commissioner Mansdorf told you to expect us?"

"Of course," Bastian replied with a quick grin. He pulled off the white peaked cap he was wearing and got to his feet. He was a sturdy man in his mid-thirties with short cropped brown hair and a craggy, weather-beaten face.

Eastman introduced him to the others and was glad when Bastian didn't extend his hand in greeting.

"Please, sit down," Bastian said hesitantly in a thick accent. "You understand, my English is not good."

"It's a lot better than our French," Graham assured him as he sat down. "So where exactly is McGuire? All we've got is an address. And that doesn't mean anything to us."

"I will show you on here," Bastian said, gesturing to the map on the table beside him and stabbing his finger at a point where a group of lines intersected each other.

"Where is it in relation to us?" Marsh asked.

"We are here," Bastian replied, pointing to an "X" marked on the map.

"So we're not far from the chalet?" Eastman asked.

"Not far, no," Bastian agreed. "About three kilometer."

"A couple of miles," Graham said. "How long has the chalet been under observation?"

"Since this afternoon."

"What about the man in the chalet with him?" Eastman asked. "Do you have any information about him?"

"A little," Bastian replied. "We have taken a photograph of him when he go to the shop this afternoon. We then send the picture to Interpol. They say he has long criminal record. A friend of the IRA."

"Is he Swiss?" Sabrina asked.

Bastian shook his head. "He is from France. Paris."

Graham and Eastman exchanged glances.

"Are you thinking what I'm thinking?" Graham asked.

"The man Roche told you about in the pub?" Eastman nodded and turned back to Bastian. "Is this man a builder?"

Bastian nodded slowly. "He is a builder. But how do you know?"

"One of McGuire's friends in London told us about him," Graham explained. "But he didn't give us a name."

"I have his name," Bastian said, taking a battered notebook from his overall pocket. He leafed through it then held up his index finger when he found the entry. "Marcel Bertranne. You want his address?"

"Not at the moment," Eastman replied. "How many men have you got watching the chalet?"

"Always four men. They change every hour. You understand it is very cold on the mountain."

"Yeah," Graham agreed. "Has McGuire left the chalet since your men started watching it?"

"He did not leave, no."

"So how do you know he's even in there?" Marsh asked the obvious question.

"He often go to the window. My men see him then."

"And your men haven't reported anything suspicious since they've been up there?" Eastman asked.

"Suspicious?" Bastian replied with a frown. "I do not understand."

"Haven't you been told that there's an IRA cell out to kill him?" Eastman asked.

"I was told that he is hiding from the IRA. But the *Commissaire* told me that they do not know he is here in Switzerland."

"I wouldn't be too sure of that," Graham replied, then asked Sabrina to explain to Bastian in French what they knew about the Provo unit.

"I did not know this," Bastian said when Sabrina had finished talking. Then, opening the safe in the corner of the room, he handed each of them a Heckler & Koch MP53 machine-pistol and a twenty-five-round magazine.

"So how do we get to the chalet?" Graham asked.

"There is a cable car not far from here. It is the only way up the mountain. You will all put on the white ski suits before you go? Then you will not be seen in the snow."

"More to the point, will *we* be able to see in the snow?" Graham said after the ski suits were brought for them.

"It's definitely getting worse out there," Marsh agreed.

Bastian looked at Graham. "We can wait until the storm has gone."

"No," Graham retorted as he put on his ski suit. "If the IRA cell's already in the area then you can be damn sure they won't be put off by these conditions. That's why it's essential we get to McGuire first."

"You think they're already in Switzerland, don't you?" Eastman said to Graham.

"I think there's a good possibility of it, yes," Graham replied, slipping a pair of goggles over his eyes.

"I hope you're wrong."

"So do I," Graham said.

"The skis and ski boots are outside," Bastian announced once they had finished dressing.

"Then let's go," Sabrina said and followed Bastian to the door.

One of Bastian's men was on hand when the cable car docked at the first of the funicular's four landing stages. He opened the door and they gratefully piled out onto the concrete platform.

"Now I understand why the Pope kisses the ground when he gets off an airplane," Marsh said, shaking his head slowly to himself.

Sabrina smiled. "It was a bit rough out there, I agree."

"Now there's an understatement for you," Marsh replied. "We took a right buffeting out there. It's a miracle the cable car wasn't blown away."

"Just be glad we don't have to go any further," Eastman told him.

"I am, guv."

Bastian had a brief word with his colleague before turning back to the others. "You are ready?"

"We're ready," Graham told him.

"Good. There is a rope outside that will lead us down the mountain to where my men are waiting for us. You understand?"

"Yeah," Graham told him. "How far are your men from here?"

Bastian consulted again with his colleague before answering. "About three hundred meters."

"And the chalet?" Eastman asked.

"It is also there. But my men cannot be seen. They are hidden in the trees." Bastian tapped the harness attached to his white overall. "You fasten this to the rope. Then you will not get lost."

"After you," Eastman said.

Bastian led the way down the steps to the door at the foot of the platform. They snapped on their skis then Bastian braced himself and pulled open the door. The wind burst through the doorway like an unwelcome intruder and whistled eerily around the interior of the station. Bastian stepped out into the snow, guided only by the light above the doorway. He pulled a flashlight from one of his pockets and switched it on. The rope had been looped through a pole beside the door and secured firmly by a figure-of-eight knot. He attached his harness to the rope then looked around at Graham and gave him a thumbs-up sign. Graham stepped out into the night. After each of them had secured themselves to the rope, Bastian switched off the torch. He couldn't risk it being seen from the chalet. They would have to move in complete darkness. Slowly, and arduously, they made their way down the slope to where Bastian's men were staked out below. In one gloved hand they held their ski poles, using the other to grip the rope tightly. They repeatedly stumbled into each other in the darkness, their heads bowed against the driving snow that lashed against them. At one point Marsh lost his balance, but was saved by the harness which ensured he didn't stumble away from the rope. But, like the others, he was comforted in the knowledge that they were being led by a competent guide. Bastian obviously knew his way around the slopes, even in these treacherous conditions.

It seemed to take forever for them finally to reach the edge of the small grove of trees though, in reality, less than ten minutes had passed. Bastian tugged twice on the rope, the prearranged signal for them to stop. He stood for a moment, listening, as a message was relayed to him via the small transmitter which was tucked firmly into his ear under the thick padded hood. Satisfied, he tugged three times on the rope. The signal to continue. Seconds later the group noticed through the falling snow the flickering light marking a snow cave. The entrance had been purposely built facing away from the clearing which housed the chalet, allowing one of the men to guide them in with a powerful flashlight. Once they had all scrambled inside the cave a block of snow, which acted as a door, was replaced to keep out the snow. Bastian pulled back his hood then sat down and spoke to the two men at some length.

Sabrina listened in on the conversation, mentally recording anything that needed to be passed on to the others, so that when Bastian turned to brief them she was able to tell him that she could give them the gist of what had been said. Bastian gave her a grateful smile then reached for the thermos flask and poured himself a coffee.

"A spotlight's been mounted on the edge of the clearing," Sabrina explained. "So once we're in position at the chalet, they'll switch it on, hoping McGuire will panic and try to escape. We'll then be on hand to grab him the moment he opens the door."

"And if he doesn't take the bait?" Graham asked.

"Then we go in," she replied.

"And pray he doesn't have a Kalashnikov," Eastman said.

"McGuire's the least of our problems."

"You're still convinced the IRA are going to get to

him first?" Eastman said. "How are they going to do it? The cable car's guarded by Bastian's men. What does that leave? A helicopter? Jesus, what lunatic would take a chopper up in these conditions?"

A radio crackled into life and one of the men passed the handset to Bastian. Sabrina's eyes widened in horror as she listened to the communiqué. She looked around at Eastman. "An unidentified helicopter's just been picked up on police radar. It's heading this way. ETA: five minutes. Two police helicopters have been scrambled from Geneva but they won't be able to intercept it before it gets here."

"Assuming it's coming here," Eastman said, but there was no conviction left in his voice.

"We've got to get McGuire out of there before the helicopter gets here," Graham said, moving to the door. "God only knows what kind of arsenal they'll have with them."

"You have a plan?" Bastian asked.

"Sabrina and I will go to the chalet," Graham replied, holding up his hand before Marsh could say anything. "We know him. It's our only chance."

"What do you want us to do?" Eastman asked.

"You could start praying," Graham replied, moving to the door. "Captain, we'll need two-way radios to keep in touch with you."

Bastian snapped an order at the two men and they unclipped their radios and gave them to Graham and Sabrina.

"I'll call you once we're in place," Graham said. "That's when you switch on the spotlight."

"We can switch it on now. It will make it easier for you to reach the chalet."

"Sure it would, but you're forgetting the back door. The moment you switched on the light McGuire could duck out of the back and we wouldn't be any the wiser." Graham looked at Sabrina. "Ready?"

"Ready," she replied, pulling the goggles back over her eyes.

"Good luck," Eastman said, patting them both on the shoulder. "Call us if you need us."

"You can count on it," Graham assured him.

"You will follow me?" Bastian said, putting on his skis, pushing aside the block of snow and ducking out into the night.

Graham and Sabrina were right behind him. They harnessed themselves to another section of rope which led from the door to where the spotlight had been mounted at the edge of the trees. Bastian tapped Graham's arm and pointed into the darkness. Graham could just make out a light, barely visible through the falling snow. But it was enough for him to get his bearings. He tugged Sabrina's sleeve and she gave him a thumbs-up sign. She had also seen it. Bastian switched on his torch and one of the men manning the spotlight took a length of rope from his haversack and looped it through their harnesses. He secured it with an overhand knot which could be easily untied once they reached the chalet. Sabrina tugged Graham's sleeve then stepped out into the clearing. Graham, who had expected to take the lead, cursed sharply under his breath but quickly went after her. She dug her ski poles into the snow as she struggled against the fierce wind. She was determined to stay on her feet; one slip and they would both fall. And they could ill afford to get tangled up on the ground. Every second was precious to them now.

The light, which came from behind the drawn curtains of a window facing out over the clearing, became more defined with each stride. Then, suddenly, the silhouette of the chalet appeared through the falling snow. It was barely ten yards in front of them. Graham tugged sharply on Sabrina's sleeve, indicating that she should go to the rear of the chalet. Again she nodded and gave him a thumbs-up sign. Stealthily they moved closer to the chalet until there was enough light for her to untie the rope binding them together. Sabrina held up her index finger, indicating that she wanted a minute to get into place as she moved off around the side of the chalet. Graham made his way cautiously to the front of the chalet. He reached the door, counting out another thirty seconds before unclipping the two-way radio from his belt. Praying that his voice could be heard above the wind, he crouched down, his body in the lee of the wall and, pressing the radio against his lips, shouted his instructions to Bastian as loudly as he dared. For a moment Graham thought Bastian hadn't heard him. Then suddenly the spotlight snapped on, bathing the chalet in a bright, piercing light. Graham unclipped his skis, unslung the machine-pistol from his shoulder, then pushed down hard on the door handle. The door was locked.

The explosion knocked Graham off his feet. He landed painfully on his side and wrapped his arms around his head as debris rained down onto the snow around him. He lay there, momentarily winded, still struggling to comprehend what was happening. Above the howling wind, another sound pierced his consciousness. Horrified, he looked up to be blinded by the dazzling beam of a second spotlight directly above him, one being operated from the open cabin door of a helicopter. A burst of gunfire from the helicopter scored a direct hit on the police spotlight and darkness descended over the trees. Graham clawed frantically in the snow for the machine-pistol which had slipped from his grasp when he hit the ground. It was gone. He cursed furiously. He could have taken out the helicopter's light if he'd had it. Another rocket grenade hit the roof and the chimney disintegrated in a hail of bricks. Graham, now without his skis, stumbled on through the snow to the chalet and was about to smash one of the windows when a row of bullets peppered the wall above him. He flung himself to the ground seconds before the window disintegrated in a hail of bullets.

The front door swung open and a figure was momentarily illuminated in the doorway. It was McGuire. He was wearing skis and his face was partially obscured by a hood. Graham yelled at him to get back into the chalet but the wind whipped away the words the moment he opened his mouth. McGuire looked up in terror at the helicopter then launched himself out of the doorway. A moment later the builder, Bertranne, followed him onto the snow. Graham stayed down, watching helplessly as McGuire and Bertranne stumbled blindly down the slope. In the sky the helicopter was banking around steeply, coming in low behind them, stalking their clumsy movements like a giant bird of prey. A burst of gunfire from the helicopter hit Bertranne in the back; as he fell one of his ski poles sliced into McGuire's leg and both men tumbled headlong into the snow. The helicopter descended to within twenty feet of the ground and a masked figure in the doorway emptied the machine gun into the two men. Immediately the spotlight clicked off and the helicopter banked sharply to the right before disappearing over the trees.

Graham sat up slowly and looked around him, still struggling to come to terms with what he had just witnessed. It had all happened so fast that it was almost like something out of a nightmare. He couldn't see McGuire or Bertranne in the darkness but he knew they were dead. Nobody could have survived that onslaught. Irrelevantly, he wondered which member of the cell had been responsible for such a clinical, cold-blooded execution. Not Mullen, he would have been the pilot. Which left Kerrigan or Gallagher. It had to be Kerrigan. He had a history of extreme violence. And he would have enjoyed it. But he knew it didn't really matter who had pulled the trigger. All that mattered now was that UNACO were back to square one again. And Scoby was due in London the next day ...

Lights appeared out of the darkness as Bastian skied over to where Graham was slumped against the side of the chalet. He directed the flashlight onto Graham's face. "Are you all right?"

"Yeah," Graham retorted, then a look of horror suddenly crossed his face. "Sabrina?"

Bastian put a restraining hand on Graham's shoulder. "You stay there. We will go and check on her."

"She's my partner." Graham brushed Bastian's hand off his shoulder then got to his feet and stumbled through the knee-deep snow to where Marsh and one of Bastian's men were crouched at the back of the chalet. Sabrina lay motionless by the door. The blood, which was seeping out from under her hood, had already stained the cushion of snow behind her head.

"She'll be OK, Mike," Marsh was quick to reassure him.

"Don't touch her," Graham snapped as Marsh was about to lift her up. "I'll take her. You get the door."

Marsh didn't argue and set about breaking down the locked rear door with the help of one of Bastian's men. Easing his hands underneath Sabrina, Graham cradled her to his chest, carried her into the chalet and laid her down gently on the sofa in the lounge.

"What happened?" Eastman asked, appearing in the doorway behind them.

"It looks as if she was hit by some falling debris," Marsh replied.

"How is she?" Eastman asked anxiously.

"Do I look like Dr. Kildare?" Graham snarled. "Get me some towels. And see if you can find a pair of scissors."

Marsh hurried from the room.

"McGuire and Bertranne are both dead," Eastman said.

"Tell me something I don't know," Graham replied, brushing the stray strands of hair from Sabrina's face. "I was there when it happened. Neither of them stood a chance."

Marsh returned with two bath towels, and Bastian appeared behind him with a pair of scissors he'd found in the kitchen. Graham carefully severed the elastic strap which held the goggles against her face, then, cutting away part of the hood, tilted her head gently to one side to get a better look at the wound. She had a deep gash at the base of her neck which would require stitches. That meant hospital.

"Are your police choppers equipped with stretchers?" he asked Bastian.

"No, but I have radioed for a mountain rescue helicopter. It has a stretcher." Bastian looked down at Sabrina. "Is it serious?"

"It's a nasty cut but she'll be OK once she's seen a doctor. How long before the chopper gets here?"

"It will be here soon," Bastian assured him. "The station is not far away."

Sabrina's eyes fluttered open. "So which one of you is going to give me the last rites?" she asked of the anxious faces peering down at her.

Graham crouched beside her. "How you feeling?"

"OK, apart from the bulldozer in my head. What happened? All I remember is an explosion. Then nothing."

Graham explained briefly what had happened after she blacked out.

"So McGuire's dead?"

Graham nodded grimly. "He was dead the moment he opened the door. That was obviously the idea. Send down a couple of rocket grenades to panic him into trying to make a run for it. That way they could track him with the spotlight and pick him off almost at will. It was also the only way of making sure they killed him. Poor bastard, he didn't stand a chance."

"Any casualties on our side?" she asked.

"One of my men was hit in the leg," Bastian replied. "But it could have been a lot worse. It was fortunate that most of the bullets hit the spotlight. They stopped firing at us after that."

"That's because they weren't after us," Graham said, looking up at Bastian. "That's not to say they wouldn't have killed us if we had got in the way. Hell, they took a shot at me when I tried to break into the chalet. But that was because I could have got to McGuire and prevented him from leaving. No, they knew exactly what they were doing. And, like true pros, they were out of here the moment the job was done."

"Leaving us with more egg on our faces," Marsh said.

"Yet again," Graham added, staring significantly at Eastman.

Eastman remained silent. One of Bastian's men appeared to announce the arrival of the mountain rescue helicopter and Bastian hurried from the room.

"Mike?" Sabrina said softly.

"Yeah?"

"Thanks."

"Don't start getting sentimental now," he said gruffly.

She grinned then winced as a pain shot through the back of her head. "Don't make me laugh. It hurts."

"Next thing I know you'll be wanting me to hold your hand on the way to the hospital."

"Would you?" she replied with a mock innocent look, then inhaled sharply as she struggled not to laugh again.

Bastian returned with one of his men. "It is too dangerous for the helicopter to land. They will lower a stretcher for Miss Carver."

"I can manage—" Sabrina tried to sit up but gasped as a spearing pain pulsed through her head. Gritting her teeth until the pain subsided, she slowly lay back on the sofa. "Then again, maybe not."

A paramedic, lowered from the helicopter, came into the room, his ski suit still flecked with snow. He spoke briefly to Bastian then crossed to the sofa and kneeled beside Sabrina. As he examined her wound, Sabrina was aware of Graham standing over him, watching his every move. She looked up at him, her eyebrows raised questioningly; Graham muttered something under his breath and stepped back. The paramedic took a hypodermic syringe from his bag, pulled back her sleeve, and inserted the needle into her skin. Within seconds she began to feel drowsy and when she looked over at Graham, who had now taken up a position at the foot of the sofa, she smiled contentedly to herself. She knew he'd be there to watch over her. Then she drifted into unconsciousness.

◆ CHAPTER

EIGHT

A penny for them."

Fiona looked around at Mullen who had entered the lounge silently behind her. "It's nothing."

Mullen crossed to the window and put a comforting arm around her shoulder. "Hey, since when do we have any secrets from each other?"

"It's hardly a secret. I was just thinking that, under different circumstances, this could have been a pretty romantic setting. A chalet in the Swiss Alps with a blizzard raging outside. All that's missing is the bearskin rug and a bottle of vintage champagne."

"And Sean," Mullen added softly.

She stared thoughtfully into the darkness beyond the window then ducked out from under Mullen's arm and went to the hearth to toss another log onto the open fire. "Dom did well to get this chalet for us at such short notice. Nobody's going to find this place in these conditions. And, according to the weather forecast, the blizzard's here for the night."

Mullen sat down in front of the fire and held out his hands toward the flames. "We got here just in time. Another ten minutes and I'd have had to put down somewhere on the mountain."

"You were fantastic up there tonight," Fiona said, sitting in the armchair opposite him. "I still don't know how you managed to keep the chopper steady in those crosswinds."

"Frankly, neither do I," Mullen replied, pouring himself a small brandy from the bottle on the table beside him. "The winds can get pretty strong at times along the Irish coast but they're nothing compared to the conditions we experienced out there tonight. But at least the blizzard held off until we'd put down here. If the storm had set in half an hour earlier we'd have had to abort the operation. Controlling a chopper in high winds is one thing but being caught in a blizzard is another matter altogether."

"What are you going to do about the chopper?"

Mullen took a sip of the brandy. "Leave it out there. It's probably half submerged in the snow by now. By the time it's spotted from the air we'll be long gone. And it's clean so there's nothing to tie us in with McGuire."

The door opened and Kerrigan entered the room, towelling his wet hair. It was obvious that he had been drinking. He tossed the towel aside then pulled up the third armchair and sat down. "Ah, that's better. I don't think I've ever enjoyed a bath so much in my life. I feel almost human again."

"Brandy?" Mullen asked, holding up the bottle.

"Make it a double," Kerrigan said, running his hand through his hair.

Mullen handed the glass to Kerrigan then raised his own glass toward Fiona. "You certainly put on quite a show out there tonight. But then you always were one of the best shots in the organization."

Fiona touched her coffee mug against Mullen's glass. She had been a teetotaller since leaving university. "We all did well tonight. It was always going to be a difficult operation even without the added problems of the adverse weather conditions. But we pulled it off without a hitch. I know the Army Council will be pleased with the results." She raised her mug toward Kerrigan. "Good work, Liam."

"Sure," Kerrigan snorted. "Working the goddamn spotlight. Big deal."

"That was an important part—"

"Don't patronize me." Kerrigan cut angrily across her words. "It's done, let's leave it at that. Hugh, give me another drink. To hell with it, give me the bottle. I'll pour it myself."

"You've already got a bottle. There were two bottles on the table when we arrived. Now there's only one. I haven't taken the other bottle and Fiona doesn't drink. That leaves you."

"A brilliant deduction, Holmes," Kerrigan snarled, rising to his feet and hurling the empty glass angrily into the fire. "I didn't realize I had to ask your permission whenever I wanted a drink."

Mullen eyed Kerrigan contemptuously. "Look at you. We haven't even been here an hour and already you're pissed."

"And what are you going to do about it?" Kerrigan shot back sarcastically. "You're always bitching about my drinking but you've never tried to stop me, have you? You're all mouth, Hugh. And that's all you ever will be. You don't have the guts to stand up to me, do you? Well, do you?"

"That's where you're wrong," Mullen said, getting to his feet.

"That's enough!" Fiona snapped. "Sit down and stop acting like a couple of adolescent kids."

Mullen's eyes flickered toward Fiona. He knew she was right. But he was damned if he was going to be humiliated by Kerrigan. Not in front of her.

"Hugh, sit down!" she commanded, stressing each word in turn.

Mullen exhaled sharply then slowly sat down again, his eyes fixed on Kerrigan's face.

"Liam, you too."

"I've taken my last order from you," Kerrigan said to her, his eyes blazing. "The operation's over and I'll do as I please from now on."

"Really?" she replied contemptuously. "I remember the last time you crossed me. You didn't come out of it very well, did you?"

"You caught me by surprise," Kerrigan retorted defensively. "I promise you it won't happen again."

"You're right, it won't," she replied, then slipped her hand under the cushion behind her and withdrew a Colt .45, one of the pistols included in the consignment which had been delivered to Lynch's house earlier that evening. She levelled it at Kerrigan. "I don't want to see your face again until we leave in the morning. Now get out."

Kerrigan looked from the pistol in her hand to the cold aloofness in her eyes. "You'd kill me too, wouldn't you?"

Fiona said nothing.

Kerrigan stormed out of the room, slamming the door angrily behind him.

"He'll be back," Mullen said, staring at the door.

"Perhaps."

"Perhaps? You humiliated him, Fiona. Nobody does that to Liam, especially not when he's had a drink."

"What should I have done? Let him beat the hell out of you?"

"Your faith in me's really touching," Mullen replied, stung by her words.

"Come off it, Hugh. You're no street fighter. He could have taken us both on and still won. He was right about me catching him by surprise at the boarding house. But you can bet he's learnt from that."

"This is turning out to be some night," Mullen said, pouring himself another drink.

"We've still got the edge. I'm armed. All the other weapons are still in the helicopter. He couldn't get to them even if he wanted to. Not in these conditions. No, I don't think he'll trouble us again tonight."

"I hope you're right."

"So do I, for his sake," Fiona replied, picking up her mug and drinking down the remainder of the coffee.

"For his sake?" Mullen repeated.

"If he sets foot in my room tonight I'll kill him."

Mullen felt a shiver run down his back. He drank the brandy but checked himself as he was about to refill the glass. He had the feeling he was going to need a clear head for whatever lay ahead that night. He only wished he knew what to expect . . .

Mullen woke suddenly. The light was still on. The dog-eared paperback he had been reading was lying on the floor by the bed. He didn't remember falling asleep. He looked at his watch. It was almost two a.m. He'd only been asleep for a couple of hours. He swung his legs off the bed, rubbed his eyes sleepily, then stood up. What had woken him? Had someone banged on the door? He crossed to the door and opened it. The hall was deserted.

Then he heard a noise. It had come from somewhere outside the chalet. Fear gripped him. What if it was the police? But how could they have found them? He switched off the light then moved cautiously to the window. Tweaking back one of the curtains, he peered out into the darkness. The blizzard was over. Everything was still. Then he saw it. A single beam of torchlight coming from beyond the pine trees in the exact spot where he had left the helicopter. It had to be the police. Was the chalet already surrounded? Suddenly the beam swung around toward the chalet. He pressed himself against the wall, his face only inches away from the window, as he peered tentatively toward the light. A hunched figure was moving slowly toward the chalet, the beam shifting unsteadily with every jarring step. Mullen felt a brief surge of relief. Surely the police would have been on skis for easier mobility: it had to be either Fiona or Kerrigan out there. The silhouette's build suggested Kerrigan and Mullen felt a renewed sense of alarm. Why would Kerrigan have gone out to the helicopter unless to arm himself? He let the curtain fall back into place and hurried out into the hall. The front door opened and Kerrigan entered, his head still bowed against the biting wind. He was carrying an AK-47 in his gloved hand.

"What the hell's that for?" Mullen snapped.

Kerrigan went into the lounge without answering him. When Mullen entered the room he found Kerrigan standing in front of the fire. The AK-47 was now propped against the wall. Kerrigan peeled off his leather gloves then crouched down in front of the fire and extended his hands toward the flames. "Dom and Ingrid are dead."

"What?" Mullen said in disbelief.

"You heard," Kerrigan snapped.

"You're still drunk, Liam. Go and sleep it off."

"I'm not drunk," Kerrigan replied, looking around at Mullen.

Mullen had to admit that Kerrigan didn't seem drunk, but he did look agitated. Very agitated.

"I couldn't sleep so I came through here to watch a bit of telly," Kerrigan continued. "The news came on. And one of the reports was about Dom and Ingrid. They're dead, Hugh. Dead."

"And I suppose the news was conveniently in

English. Or perhaps you just happened to have the necessary phrase book handy to translate the report?"

"I didn't need any damn phrase book!" Kerrigan snarled. "A picture of Dom and Ingrid came up on the screen. It was one of the snaps you took at their wedding reception. Then there was a live report from outside the house. Christ, man, the reporter was standing almost exactly where you parked the car. As he was talking two bodies were brought out on stretchers from the house behind him. And the sheets were pulled up over their faces. In my book, that means you're dead. And I know who killed them."

Mullen sat down slowly and ran his fingers through his tangled hair. "Dom and Ingrid dead? God, no."

"Didn't you hear me? I said I know who killed them. Fiona."

"What are you talking about?" Mullen snapped back. "She was with us all the time."

"Oh no she wasn't. She stayed behind when we went out to the car. Remember?"

"And how was she supposed to have killed them? All the guns were in the boot of the car. Remember?"

"She killed them. Who else could have done it?"

"You don't have a shred of evidence—"

"I may not have the evidence, but I know why she did it," Kerrigan cut in. "Dom told me confidentially that he was going to call the Army Council and tell them he thought she was cracking under the pressure of being in charge of the operation. They would have listened to him. And that would have put paid to her chances of running a cell of her own one day. She obviously found out somehow and that's why she had to silence him. It's the only logical explanation. But I'm damned if I'm going to let that bitch talk her way out of this when she gets back home. Because she will. The Army Council think she's so bloody great, they'd believe anything she tells them. I'm not going to let her get away with it. Not this time."

"I've always known you despised her but even I didn't think you could sink this low. God, you disgust me. I know Dom would never have plotted against her like that. He loved her as if she were his own sister. If he'd had something on his mind, he'd have confronted her with it. I can't believe you could say something like that with Dom only hours dead. You're sick, Liam. This obsession's going to destroy you."

"You're a fine one to talk about obsession," Kerrigan snorted contemptuously. "What about your obsession with Fiona? You've wanted her since you first laid eyes on her. But you don't have Sean's good looks and quick wit so she was never interested in you. So instead you've tagged along behind her like a little puppy, believing all that crap she fed you about you being her confidant and best friend. If you want her so badly why don't you just ask her her price? Every whore has a price."

Kerrigan sidestepped Mullen's lunging punch and brought his elbow up sharply into the small of Mullen's back, propelling him face first into the wall. He followed through with two vicious kidney punches which left Mullen on his knees, gasping for breath. Kerrigan was turning to get the AK-47 when he saw Fiona standing in the doorway, the Colt .45 in her hand.

"Don't even think it," she said menacingly. "Now step away from the gun. Slowly."

Fiona noticed Kerrigan's eyes flicker toward the AK-47. She knew he was wondering whether he could get to it before she pulled the trigger. But she was a good shot. One of the best. No, he wouldn't risk it. He stepped away from the AK-47, his hands half raised in the air. She glanced across at Mullen. He was doubled over on the floor with his back to them, still struggling to catch his breath. Perfect. She smiled coldly then shot Kerrigan in the chest. He was punched back against the wall and was still raising his head to look at her when she shot him again, this time through the heart. His body slid lifelessly to the floor, the disbelief still mirrored in his sightless eyes. She kicked the AK-47 away from his outstretched hand and checked for a pulse.

Mullen struggled to his feet, his face still twisted in pain. "Is he dead?"

She nodded slowly then slumped into the armchair behind her. "I told him to get away from the gun. But he wouldn't move. He just stood there. Then he made a grab for it. I had to shoot him, Hugh. I had no choice. You must understand that."

Mullen took the Colt from her fingers, placed it on the table and squeezed her arm reassuringly. "I heard you tell him to get away from the gun. You gave him every chance. If you hadn't shot him he'd have killed us both."

She sat back and closed her eyes tightly. "Sean's going to be devastated. He and Liam were really close."

"That wasn't the Liam Sean knew. He hasn't been himself these last few days. And tonight's news finally sent him over the edge. You heard what happened?"

She nodded. "I could hear the two of you from my bedroom. Do you really think Dom and Ingrid are dead?"

"Liam seemed very sure of his facts," Mullen replied softly.

"Oh God." She rubbed her moist eyes then suddenly looked Mullen in the face. "You don't think I . . ."

"I know you didn't kill them," Mullen replied quickly.

"I heard Liam say something about Dom calling

the Army Council. I didn't catch everything he said though.''

Mullen told her.

''Why would he do that? If Dom had something on his mind, he'd have talked it out with me. He's always done that . . .'' She trailed off and swallowed quickly. ''He always did that with me in the past.''

''No, I don't think he would have called the Army Council either. It was Liam's last attempt to try and turn me against you.''

''The sooner we get out of here, the better.''

''Agreed. What are we going to do about Liam?''

''Leave him here,'' she replied. ''If we tried to bury the body the disturbed snow would be seen from the air. And if whoever did kill Dom and Ingrid are after us as well, then we don't want to encourage them to find this place in a hurry. Certainly not until we've got a chance to report back to the Army Council. Then at least they can investigate the matter more fully.''

''What are you going to tell them about Liam?'' Mullen asked.

''The truth. What else can I do? I only hope they believe me. He was a valued member of the organization.''

''I'll back you up, you know that.''

''You're a good friend, Hugh. Thanks for always being there for me.''

''That's what friends are for.'' Mullen moved to the door. ''I know I'm not going to get to sleep for a while. You want a coffee?''

She nodded. ''Please. But not in here.''

''I'll take it through to my room,'' Mullen replied as he went off to the kitchen.

Fiona slumped back in the chair and cast a side-long look at Kerrigan's body. A job well done. She had known she would have to kill him as soon as she'd overheard him talking to Lynch the previous afternoon. But she had still needed him to help kill McGuire. After that, he was as good as dead. She couldn't let him report back to the Army Council about the conversation he'd had with Lynch. It would have been too risky. She suddenly remembered what Kerrigan had said about Mullen being infatuated with her. But then she'd known that for years. Kerrigan had been right, she did feed Mullen crap about him being her confidant and best friend. But it kept him happy. It made him feel wanted. A little puppy, following her wherever she went. She smiled to herself. Well, as long as he followed her for just a little bit longer. Then, like Kerrigan, he would become expendable. And when that time did come, she certainly wouldn't have any qualms about killing him either . . .

Maurice Palmer replaced the receiver then got to his feet and left his study, closing the door behind him. He was a tall, angular man in his early fifties who had been commander of Scotland Yard's elite anti-terrorist squad for the past four years.

His wife, Sheila, looked up from the *Times* crossword she was doing when he entered the lounge. Her eyes followed him as he crossed to the drinks tray and poured himself a small Scotch. Although he didn't show it, she knew he was agitated. It was the only time he would take a drink. He sat down in his favorite armchair and held the glass between the palms of his hands, his eyes fixed on an imaginary spot on the wall above her head. She never questioned him about his work. And he never ventured anything. But she still worried whenever he was troubled. And she had done a lot of worrying in thirty-two years of marriage . . .

"Finished?" he asked suddenly, indicating the newspaper in her lap.

"No, there's a couple of stinkers I can't begin to fathom out," she replied, shaking her head in frustration. "You might be able to make something out of them. I know I can't."

He held up his hand when she extended the newspaper toward him. "I wouldn't be much use to you tonight. My mind's elsewhere."

"So I noticed," she said, glancing toward the glass still clenched between the palms of his hands.

"You should have been the detective, not me," he said with a smile and placed the glass carefully on the table beside him.

"Why don't you go for a walk?" she asked. "You know it helps you think."

"No, I need to stay by the phone." He glanced at the clock on the mantelpiece. Two minutes to ten. He used the remote control to activate the television in the corner of the room. He always watched ITV's "News at Ten." Sheila Palmer folded the newspaper over, placed it on the carpet beside the chair and turned her attention to the screen.

The telephone rang and Palmer rose quickly to his feet to answer it.

"Good evening, Commander. It's Sergei Kolchinsky. Can we talk?"

"Not on this line. I'll transfer the call to my scrambler line." Palmer pressed a button on the telephone, replaced the handset, then went through to the study and picked up the receiver on his desk. "We can talk now, Mr. Kolchinsky."

"Good."

"I've been expecting your call ever since I received the report on what happened in Switzerland earlier tonight."

"So you've been fully briefed?" Kolchinsky asked.

"Yes, Keith Eastman called me twenty minutes ago."

"Then you'll know that one of my operatives was injured in the fiasco," Kolchinsky said angrily.

"Keith told me. How is she?"

"She needed seven stitches to a gash on her neck. She's being kept in hospital overnight for observation. She was lucky by all accounts. The doctor treating her said that had the projectile struck her on the head and not on her neck, it could have been fatal."

"I'm just glad she's all right."

"Michael Graham was absolutely livid when he phoned his report through to me earlier this evening. And he has every right to be. This is now the third time that the IRA have been quicker to the draw than us. In the first two instances there was an element of doubt over the IRA's source of information. It's possible that Graham could have been overheard talking to Roche in the bar. And they could have fled the boarding house after seeing the pictures of Mullen and Kerrigan on the front page of the morning newspaper. But after tonight, it all falls into place. You have a mole in your organization, Commander. And it's either Keith Eastman or John Marsh."

"Or one of your operatives," Palmer shot back.

"Michael and Sabrina were only given the address of the chalet once they touched down in Zurich," Kolchinsky was quick to reply. "And as Michael pointed out, all they needed to know in London was that McGuire was in Switzerland. The chalet's exact location wouldn't have meant anything to them. Only Eastman and Marsh knew the address from the very beginning. And before they left for Heathrow Airport either Eastman or Marsh had already made the call claiming that there was a bomb on board the Airbus, giving the IRA cell time to catch another flight to Switzerland ahead of them. Which puts Michael and Sabrina in the clear."

"Keith and John are two of my most trusted men. That's why I assigned them to the case. I still believe

the IRA obtained the address of the chalet from a
source outside this organization."

"Be that as it may, Commander, Jack Scoby arrives
in London tomorrow afternoon. We've already lost
McGuire, heaven help us if anything should happen
to Scoby."

"I'm still very skeptical about this theory of yours,
Mr. Kolchinsky. I mean, what would the IRA have to
gain by killing him? My God, it would be tantamount
to suicide. The American public would turn against
them in their droves and that would seriously affect
the financial support they receive from the States."

"We can't afford to be complacent, Commander. If
Scoby is killed over there and it comes out later that
both UNACO and the anti-terrorist squad had been
forewarned of a possible attempt on his life and
hadn't taken the necessary steps to protect him, then
heads will roll. Starting with ours."

"I may be skeptical but I'm still taking it seriously,
Mr. Kolchinsky. Very seriously." Palmer exhaled
deeply and raked his fingers through his hair. "I'll
have their offices and homes searched before they return from Switzerland tomorrow. Not that I expect to
find anything. But rest assured I'll call you if we do
come up with something."

"I'd appreciate that."

"Good night, Mr. Kolchinsky."

"Good night."

Palmer replaced the receiver then sat back in his
chair and chewed his lip pensively as he pondered
the best way to initiate the investigation. He decided
against using any of his own men. That could be mis-
construed as biased, especially if nothing was found
to incriminate either man, which he was certain
would be the case. He would bring in outside help;
another department. The Special Branch. He had
been in charge there before taking over at the anti-
terrorist squad. The head of Special Branch was an

old friend. And the men there still held him in high esteem. He knew he could count on them being impartial and, above all, discreet. He would have to clear it first with the Commissioner. But he saw that as little more than a formality. Obtaining search warrants would be a far more difficult task. Especially at that time of night. But he was determined to play it by the book. In the unlikely event of something being found that could link one of them to the IRA, it was imperative that the paperwork should be in order.

He had a feeling that he had a very long night ahead of him.

The Scobys lived in a two-story mansion on Long Island. It was surrounded by a ten-foot wall and guarded twenty-four hours a day by armed security men. One of the guards approached Whitlock's white BMW as he brought it to a halt in front of a pair of towering wrought-iron gates. A closed-circuit television camera, mounted on top of the wall, slowly panned the car while a security guard inside the house fed the BMW's registration number into a computer to check its ownership.

"Good evening," the guard said with a quick smile as he peered into the car. He looked from Whitlock to Paluzzi, who was in the passenger seat, then back to Whitlock. "Can I help you folks?"

"C. W. Whitlock. We have an appointment with Mr. Scoby at eight o'clock."

The guard checked both men's identity cards then handed them back. He unclipped a two-way radio from his belt and spoke into it. Moments later the gates were opened from inside the house. "Follow the road. It'll take you right into the courtyard."

Whitlock thanked him and drove into the grounds as the gates closed behind them. He kept to the driveway, which continued for another two hundred yards, until he reached the gravel courtyard.

A somber-looking butler was waiting for them in front of the house. "If you give me the keys, sir, I'll have the car parked in one of the garages for you."

Whitlock handed the keys to the butler who led them up the steps and into the house. The hall was lined with portraits of previous American Presidents. But as Whitlock cast his eyes over the gallery of faces he suddenly realized that all the pictures were of Republican Presidents. There wasn't a Democrat amongst them. He smiled to himself. It was typical of an outspoken right-wing Republican politician to hold all Democrats in contempt. Especially the Presidents . . .

The butler led them into a small lounge. "If you'd care to wait here, someone will be along shortly."

Whitlock picked up a copy of *Time* magazine from the coffee table and sat down in the nearest armchair. Paluzzi crossed to the window and looked out over the spacious lawn which led down to a diamond-shaped swimming pool. Although illuminated by a powerful overhead floodlight, the pool was empty. The tennis court beside it was in darkness.

"He must have a bit of money behind him to afford something like this," Paluzzi said at length.

Whitlock looked up and nodded. "Don't forget that he was one of the most successful lawyers in New York before he decided to run for the senate."

"His father was a judge, wasn't he?"

"Yes, Judge Arthur H. Scoby. Another outspoken Republican. He died last year."

The doors swung open and Ray Tillman entered the room. He shook hands with Whitlock who then introduced him to Paluzzi.

"The senator's not back yet, I'm afraid," Tillman told them. "He rang about an hour ago to say he'd be late. He asked me to apologize to you for not being here to meet you in person. He's stuck in a meeting with some of the city's leading financiers at a hotel over on Fifth Avenue. It's always the same when a new senator gets elected. The financiers want to test the water, see what kind of deals they can get out of him. But knowing Jack, they'll be coming out empty-handed tonight. They've leeched off the Democrats for too long. I'm sorry, you're not Democrats are you?"

"We're not Americans," Whitlock replied diplomatically.

"Neither are most Democrats, judging by their tepid foreign policies." Tillman laughed then clapped his hands together. "Please, why don't you come through to the lounge?"

They followed Tillman to a room at the end of the hallway. The doors were open. A tall, elegant woman was standing at the bay window. She looked around when Tillman ushered them into the room. Melissa Scoby, now in her late thirties, had lost none of the beauty and poise which had once made her one of the most coveted models in both Europe and America. She had married Scoby when she was twenty; a year later their son, Lloyd, had been born. He was now in his first year of reading law at Harvard University.

"Mr. Paluzzi will be traveling with us to London tomorrow," Tillman said once the introductions were over.

"Then I'm sure we'll be in very capable hands," she said with a faint smile, looping her hand through Paluzzi's arm and leading him to the sofa. "How long have you been in America, Mr. Paluzzi?"

"A couple of months," Paluzzi replied.

She sat down. "And which part of Italy are you from?"

"Pescara. It's a holiday resort on the east coast."

"I've heard of it," she replied. "I lived in Milan for

six months when I was modeling over there. Are you married?''

"Yes," he replied. "We have a six-month-old son, Dario."

She nodded then looked up at Tillman. "Ray, a drink for our guests."

"Of course. Gentlemen?"

"Just a soft drink for me," Whitlock replied. "I'm driving."

"Mr. Paluzzi?" Tillman asked.

"A beer would be fine," Paluzzi answered.

Tillman went to the sideboard and opened one of the doors. Inside was a mini-bar. He took a Budweiser and a Pepsi from the fridge then closed the door again. He had just handed the drinks to Whitlock and Paluzzi when the door opened and Jack Scoby entered.

"I'll have a Jack Daniels, Ray," Scoby announced, removing his jacket and draping it over the back of the nearest chair. "Make it a double. God, what a day." He kissed his wife lightly on the cheek then turned to Whitlock and extended a hand in greeting. "Good to see you again."

Whitlock shook Scoby's hand then introduced him to Paluzzi.

"He's going to be your bodyguard in London, darling," Melissa Scoby said, glancing at Paluzzi out of the corner of her eye.

There was a knock at the door and the butler entered the room. "There's a phone call for you, Mrs. Scoby."

"Who is it, Morgan?" she asked, mildly irritated.

"It's Master Lloyd. Would you like me to put the call through to you here, madam?"

"No, I'll take it in the hall." Melissa Scoby stood up, smoothed down her skirt, then followed the butler from the room.

Tillman handed Scoby his drink. "We need to talk."

"Sure," Scoby replied absently.

"Now, Jack. It's important." Tillman looked down at Whitlock. "Would you excuse us? It shouldn't take long."

"Please, go ahead," Whitlock said.

Scoby and Tillman left the room.

"I feel uncomfortable with her," Paluzzi said, looking across at the closed doors.

"She's known to be a bit of a flirt," Whitlock said. "Don't worry though, she wouldn't do anything to jeopardize her chance of becoming the First Lady one day. She's far too shrewd for that." He took a sip of the Pepsi then placed the glass on the table beside him. "What I'm going to tell you is strictly off the record."

"Of course," Paluzzi replied, sitting forward.

"You may have noticed earlier that Tillman didn't offer her a drink. She doesn't touch alcohol. Not anymore."

"Are you saying she was once an alcoholic?" Paluzzi said in amazement.

"Not in so many words. She did drink heavily for several years, but always in the privacy of her own home. That's why it never reached the Press. Her friends always rallied around her, protected her, and they eventually persuaded her to go to one of those clinics to dry out. She's now completely reformed."

"Why did she drink?"

"Boredom and loneliness. Well, that's how her friends saw it. Publicly, Jack and Melissa are the perfect couple. But it's only a pretense. The marriage is far from stable. Scoby's a workaholic. He's always put in a fourteen-, fifteen-hour day, ever since he graduated from Harvard. Which doesn't exactly leave much time for his wife. But she'll never leave him. She's far too smart for that. She'll stick by him because she's just as obsessed as he is about reaching the White House one day."

"And their son?"

"Like father, like son. And he doesn't get on too well with his mother by all accounts."

"Why wasn't any of this included in our assignment dossiers?" Paluzzi asked.

"Because it's irrelevant to the case. UNACO has a mole on Capitol Hill who knows everything there is to know about the different politicians up there. But it took some serious digging on his part to uncover any of this. Scoby has some very powerful connections on Capitol Hill who'll close ranks around him the moment there's a whiff of scandal about him, or any of his family. They're obviously protecting him for when he's ready to run for President."

Paluzzi sat back in his chair and took a sip of beer. "What if she tries to flirt with Mike? After all, he's the one with the looks."

A slow smile spread across Whitlock's face. "Now that would be worth paying to see."

Tillman removed the folder from his attaché case and placed it on the desk in front of Scoby. Scoby looked up at him but said nothing. He still couldn't believe what Tillman had just told him. They had gone to such extraordinary lengths to ensure that every meeting between Tillman and Miguel Cabrera was held in the utmost secrecy. Nothing had been left to chance. Why had they bothered? Hell, they might as well have met in Navarro's office for all the good it had done them. But his anger was still directed more at Navarro than it was at the Colombian. It was an anger born out of fear. He had devised the entire operation himself. He had negotiated his own percentage which would have been forwarded to the juntas in South and Central America. He had been in charge from the outset. Now it was Navarro who was calling the shots, and that frightened him. The manipulator had become the manipulated . . .

"Do you want to listen to any of the tapes?" Tillman asked.

"What the hell for?" Scoby shot back furiously.

"I just thought . . ." Tillman trailed off with a despondent shrug.

Scoby opened the folder and flicked through the photographs. He shook his head in disbelief then glared at Tillman. "I can't believe you let this happen under your very nose. Christ, Ray, how many meetings did you have with that bastard? Ten? Twelve? And each time he not only managed to get you on film, he also got everything you said on tape. Didn't you ever suspect anything?"

"Don't you think I'd have mentioned it if I had?" Tillman retorted angrily.

Scoby threw the photographs onto the desk then got up and moved to the window. "Well, thanks to your incompetence Navarro's now running the show. And there isn't a damn thing we can do about it without incriminating ourselves."

"We can still make it work, Jack. As Navarro said, the Mafia are going to be taking all the risks once the shipments are cleared through customs."

"Why don't I feel reassured?" Scoby closed the folder and looked across at Tillman. "So what happens now?"

"I'm meeting Navarro next Tuesday to give him our answer."

"You might as well have given it to him this afternoon. It's not as if we've got any say in the matter. We've been screwed and that's all there is to it." Scoby gestured to the box of tapes. "Burn them."

"And the folder?"

"No, I want to look at that more carefully. If we are

going to be forced to play by Navarro's rules, then the least we can do is give him a run for his money."

"Meaning?"

"Meaning he's dealing with Jack Scoby. I'm going to squeeze everything I possibly can out of this deal. It's not as if I've got anything to lose, is it?" Scoby smiled coldly then moved to the door. "Put the folder in my briefcase. I'll have a look at it once we get to London. I'll see you in the lounge. We mustn't forget our guests now, must we?"

"I can't believe it."

Maurice Palmer sat behind the desk in his study, his face drawn and pale. In front of him lay the evidence that he had been dreading from the moment he called in the Special Branch to check on Eastman and Marsh. One of them had been working in collusion with the IRA.

"I'm sorry, Maurice, but it's there in black and white," replied Commander Richard Carter, head of Scotland Yard's Special Branch. Carter lit a cigarette and tossed the match into the ashtray on the desk. "You thought a lot of him, didn't you?"

"A future departmental head at the very least. Who knows after that? He could have made it all the way to the top." Palmer indicated the cigarette in Carter's mouth. "Give me one of those, will you?"

"I thought you'd given up," Carter said, tossing the pack onto the desk.

"So did I," Palmer retorted, helping himself to a cigarette.

Carter lit it for him. "Well, at least he's been unmasked before he can do any more damage."

"He's done enough damage already," Palmer snapped, his anger showing through for the first time since Carter had broken the news to him. "I trusted him like a son, and this is how he repays that trust.

Who knows how much damage he's caused over th
years or how many innocent lives have been lost be
cause of his betrayal?"

"Only he can answer that, Maurice," Carter re
plied.

"Oh, he will," Palmer shot back, stabbing the ciga
rette at Carter. "You can be damn sure of that."

"Have you thought about how you're going t
break it to the Commissioner?"

"Very gently," Palmer replied tersely. "I'll inforr
him once they've returned from Switzerland. I wan
as much information as possible before I do speak t
him."

"I don't envy you," Carter said grimly. "It's .
pretty horrific breach of security."

"To say the least." Palmer tapped the ash from th
cigarette into the ashtray and glanced at his watch
Five-seventeen a.m. "You'd better get back hom
before Phyllis wakes up."

Carter stifled a yawn and nodded in agreement
He stubbed out the cigarette then got to his feet
"Keep me informed, will you?"

"You're just after the job, aren't you?" Palmer saic
with a forced smile.

"What else?" Carter replied, returning the smile
He reached across the desk and patted Palmer on th
arm. "You'll be OK. These things happen. The Com
missioner will make a lot of noise when you tell hin
but by the time you see him again he'll have forgotter
all about it."

Palmer walked Carter to the front door. "Thank
for coming round, Richard, I appreciate it."

"You'd have done the same for me. Give my lov
to Sheila, will you?"

"Of course. Good night, Richard."

"Night, Maurice," Carter said as he strode briskl
over to the unmarked police car which was waiting
for him.

Palmer closed the door and returned to the study. He gathered up the evidence, replaced it in the folder, then pulled the telephone toward him. He found Kolchinsky's home number then lifted the receiver and dialed out.

NINE

Sabrina had been discharged from hospital early that morning so that they could reach Zurich in time to catch the eleven o'clock flight back to London. She looked pale and tired, having refused the offer of sedatives the previous night, and within minutes of taking her seat on the plane she was asleep. Graham gave the stewardess strict instructions that she wasn't to be disturbed until they reached London.

Eastman and Marsh were also exhausted. They had been up most of the night compiling their reports for Palmer and, with Scoby due to arrive that evening, both were looking forward to catching a few hours' sleep in the comfort of their own beds once they arrived back in London . . .

Two members of the anti-terrorist squad were on hand to meet them at Heathrow and it quickly became apparent that sleep would have to wait. Palmer wanted to see them both urgently in his office at New Scotland Yard. Graham and Sabrina were taken in one of the cars to the Grosvenor House Hotel where Scoby would be based for the duration of his stay.

Palmer was on the telephone when Eastman and Marsh entered his office. He pointed to the two chairs in front of his desk. "I'll call back," he told the caller abruptly before replacing the receiver and reaching for the packet of cigarettes on his desk.

"I thought you'd given up, sir?" Eastman said in surprise as Palmer pushed a cigarette between his lips and lit it.

"I had, until last night," Palmer retorted sharply. He took a long drag on the cigarette and blew the smoke up toward the ceiling. "It was obvious after the débâcle in Switzerland last night that the IRA have a pipeline into the heart of this unit. How else could they have anticipated your every move?"

"It certainly looks that way, sir," Eastman agreed.

"The Special Branch were brought in last night to find this mole. You were both the first to be investigated. Your offices and your homes were raided simultaneously just after midnight." Palmer removed a computer disk from his drawer, placing it on the table in front of them. "This is yours I believe, John?"

Marsh picked it up and turned it around in his fingers. The number four was written on it in red pen. "Yes sir, it is. This is a backup copy of one of the disks in my office. I keep all backup disks in my safe at home. How did you come by it?"

"Your wife gave the Special Branch officers the combination of your personal safe. And before you say anything, she had no choice. They had search warrants."

"What about it?" Marsh asked, holding up the disk.

"According to the index on your office computer, this disk contains the names, addresses and telephone numbers of your contacts and informers. Is that correct?"

"Yes sir."

"Then tell me about 'Rebel Woman'."

" 'Rebel Woman'?" Marsh replied with a frown. "I don't know anyone who uses that codename."

"So how do you explain it being on this disk, but not on the disk that was taken from your office?"

"That's impossible, sir," Marsh replied in bewilderment. "I told you, I use my office disk to update this one. It's an exact copy."

Palmer removed two sheets of computer paper from the folder in front of him and put them in front of Marsh. "Printouts of the two disks. As you see, there's an extra entry on your backup disk. 'Rebel Woman.'"

Marsh ran his fingers through his blond hair. "It makes no sense, sir. It's impossible—"

"So you keep saying!" Palmer cut in. "But there's the evidence in front of you. And you'll also see that there are two telephone numbers listed under 'Rebel Woman.' They were checked out by Special Branch officers. The first is the number of a known IRA safe house in London. The second is a Belfast number. A flat registered in the names of Sean Farrell and Fiona Gallagher. So I'd say it was safe to assume that Fiona Gallagher is 'Rebel Woman'?"

"Sir, this is ludicrous," Marsh said, getting to his feet.

"Sit down!" Palmer thundered.

Marsh shot Eastman a despairing look then retook his seat.

"Then there's the ten thousand pounds which was found in your toolshed."

"What?" Marsh retorted in amazement. "God, what's going on? I don't know anything about any ten thousand pounds."

"Two bundles, five thousand in each bundle. The top and bottom notes of each bundle were dusted for prints. We were hoping to lift a print which would link the money to the IRA. We struck the jackpot. A print was positively matched to the copy of Kevin Brady's left thumbprint on our central computer. I don't have to tell you that Brady is the Chief-of-Staff of the Provos' Army Council. He's also the most wanted man in Britain. How do you explain his fingerprint being on the note?"

"I can't explain it," Marsh blurted out. "It's obviously been planted there so that I would take the fall."

"I could believe it about the money, but not the disk. How many people know the combination of your safe?"

"Only my wife and I," Marsh replied in desperation. He dug his fingers under his collar and pulled it away from his neck. "Somebody must have found out about it, sir. It's the only logical explanation."

"I suggest you keep your protestations for the jury. Perhaps they might look more favorably on them. But I certainly can't. God only knows how much damage you've done to this organization since you started working for the IRA. I only hope it's been worth it all, John."

"Sir, please listen—"

"Keith, there are two Special Branch men waiting outside," Palmer cut in. "Ask them to come in, will you?"

Eastman hesitated.

"Must I fetch them myself?" Palmer asked angrily.

Eastman reluctantly got to his feet and called the men into the room.

"John, you're suspended as of this moment. You know your rights, you can have a lawyer present when you're questioned by the Special Branch. And don't forget to leave your warrant card before you go. You won't be needing it again."

Marsh took the card from his pocket and handed it to Eastman. The two Special Branch men flanked Marsh and led him from the room.

Eastman sat down slowly after the door had closed behind Marsh and looked across at Palmer, the disbelief etched on his face. "The evidence may look conclusive, sir, but I still believe John's innocent. I probably know John better than anyone else at Scotland Yard. The anti-terrorist squad was his whole life. Everything else took second place."

"Now you know why," Palmer replied, stubbing out his cigarette and reaching for the packet again. He cursed angrily and tossed it aside. "Look at me. Chain-smoking like I'd never stopped. Don't you think I'm just as shattered about this as you are, Keith? John was one of the most promising officers I had in the unit. I wanted him to go far. But what really sticks in my throat is the thought that the lives of the men could have been put at risk because of his treachery. Who knows how much confidential information he's passed on to the IRA since he began working for them."

"Putting him on some show trial can only damage the image of the anti-terrorist squad and give the IRA an enormous publicity boost into the bargain."

Palmer lit another cigarette. "I'm well aware of the damage it'll do to the unit as a whole. Opposition MPs will be howling for a public inquiry. They always do at times like this. But what can we do? We can hardly push him out the back door and hope none of this ever reaches the Press."

"According to British law, a man is innocent until found guilty." Eastman tossed Marsh's warrant card on the desk then crossed to the door. He paused, his fingers resting lightly on the handle, and looked around at Palmer. "But that's not how a show trial works, is it, sir? There a man's guilty until found innocent. And that never happens, does it?"

"John will be given a fair trial," Palmer retorted, angry at the insinuation that he could influence the outcome of the trial in any way.

"It depends on your definition of fair, sir. Wouldn't you agree?" Eastman said, leaving the room before Palmer could muster a reply.

Graham was sitting up on the bed, a pillow propped up behind his back, watching the American wrestling on the cable channel. There was a knock at the door and he cursed irritably under his breath as he rose from the bed to answer it.

"C. W.!" he gasped in surprise. "What are you doing here? I thought you were flying over with Scoby later this afternoon."

"Can I come in before you fire any more questions at me?" Whitlock asked.

"Sure, buddy, come on in," Graham replied, opening the door for him. "You want a drink? There's a bar in here. Or I can make you a coffee if you want it."

"I know your coffee," Whitlock replied as Graham closed the door behind him. "You could patent it as an alternative to creosote."

"What good's coffee if you can't taste it?" Graham said, using the remote control to turn down the sound on the television set.

"I'll have a tea, thanks."

Graham pointed to a chair. "Sit down. So why aren't you flying over with Scoby?"

Whitlock eased himself into the chair. "I've got a meeting with the head of the anti-terrorist squad this afternoon. Fabio's coming over with the senator."

"When are they due in?" Graham asked, switching on the kettle.

"Tonight. About seven."

"Are we meeting the plane?"

Whitlock shook his head. "The anti-terrorist squad will be handling the security arrangements at the airport. I told Scoby we'd meet him here at the hotel. And anyway, a deputation from the Court of St.

James's will be on hand at the airport when he lands. Including the American ambassador. We'd only be in the way."

"I presume you heard about Marsh?"

Whitlock nodded. "Sergei told me before I flew out this morning. Seems he got a call in the middle of the night from a very distraught Maurice Palmer. Who told you? Eastman?"

"Yeah. He's well pissed off. He still thinks Marsh's innocent. The evidence seems pretty conclusive to me though." Graham held up the cup. "How strong do you want this tea?"

"Leave it to draw for a while," Whitlock replied. "Where's Sabrina?"

"She's asleep. She didn't get much sleep last night. But she did ask to be woken if anything cropped up."

"Let her sleep," Whitlock said.

"How's Sergei bearing up back home?" Graham asked, helping himself to a bottle of diet Pepsi from the mini-bar.

"Fed up. He wanted to come out and coordinate Scoby's security arrangements personally. You know how he loves to get involved in the fieldwork. But he's stuck at the UN. Meeting after meeting. He's hardly ever in the office these days. I know it's getting to him."

"What about you?"

"What about me?" Whitlock replied.

"You also pissed off?" Graham gave Whitlock his tea.

Whitlock took a sip and placed the cup on the table beside the chair before answering. "Sure I'm pissed off. I'm stuck behind a desk answering phone calls all day. Then at night it's off to some embassy to listen to the boring ramblings of a bunch of foreign ambassadors with names you can't even pronounce. And on the rare occasions when I do get out in the field, it's as a liaison officer. It's driving me up the wall."

"Have you told Carmen how you feel?"

Whitlock threw up his hands in despair. "Tell her what? That I want to give up my management position and return to the field? She'd throw a fit. Then she would instigate divorce proceedings against me."

"So you're just going to stick it out to please her?"

Anger flashed through Whitlock's eyes. "I saved my marriage by taking this position. Carmen and I are closer now than we've been for years. And I intend to keep it that way."

"You're living in a fantasy world, C. W. Do you honestly think you can be happy at home when you're so unhappy at work? You can only bottle up your frustration for so long before you reach breaking point. By then you'll have come to resent Carmen so much for having put you in that situation in the first place. And she'll resent you for not having confided in her. But by then it'll be too late. Your marriage *will* be over."

Whitlock got to his feet, his eyes blazing. "I don't need a lecture on marriage, especially not from you."

"Then get your act together and tell Carmen how you feel," Graham retorted. "You owe it to her just as much as you do to yourself."

Whitlock's hands balled into fists at his sides. Graham had never seen Whitlock so angry. He knew it was an anger that stemmed from frustration. But he still believed he was right to tell Whitlock how he felt.

"You let me worry about the state of my marriage," Whitlock said finally as he strode angrily to the door. "There's a meeting in my room at six-thirty tonight. Tell Sabrina. And Eastman."

"Sure," Graham replied gruffly.

Fiona Gallagher was wearing a pair of baggy patched jeans, a loose-fitting sweatshirt and her

favorite black trilby to hide her cropped blonde hair
when she entered St. Pancras Station. She wore no
make-up and carried a battered rucksack over her left
shoulder. It was imperative that she be as inconspicu-
ous as possible and, dressed as she was, she knew she
would be taken for just another student waiting for a
train. She went to Casey Jones, ordered a coffee, then
retreated to a corner table to wait for Mullen. She
looked at her watch. Three twenty-two. The rendezvous was for three-thirty. And, knowing him, he
would be late. Five, perhaps ten minutes. Never
more. Just enough to irritate someone as punctual as
she was. She opened the copy of the *Guardian* she'd
bought earlier. She despised it for its quasi-socialist
views but it was a favorite with the students and that
meant it would add credibility to her cover. She laid
it out on the table and began reading the lead story.

They had vacated the chalet early that morning
using the skis which had been left for them in the
helicopter. She had been skiing since her teens
whereas Mullen had only started in his twenties. It
showed. They had taken a taxi from Les Paccots to an
underground car park in Lausanne where a car had
been left for them. The keys were taped to the under-
side of the front bumper. Mullen had driven them to
Cointrin Airport in Geneva where they had caught a
mid-morning flight back to London. They traveled
separately on the plane, having previously agreed to
meet up again at St. Pancras that afternoon . . .

"Excuse me, is this seat taken?"

She looked up, startled by the voice. Then a grin
spread across her face. "I never thought I'd live to see
the day that Hugh Mullen actually arrived early for a
meeting."

Mullen chuckled and placed his coffee and cheeseburger on the table. He was wearing a pair of faded
blue jeans, torn at the knees, an Irish rugby jersey and
a red bandana tied around his forehead.

"I like the duds," she said, appraising Mullen's clothes.

"Thanks," Mullen replied, sitting down. "You did say formal wear, didn't you?"

She smiled, picked up his cheeseburger, and took a generous bite before handing it back to him.

"Are you sure you can spare this?" Mullen said, holding up his half-eaten burger. "Sean always said you had a big mouth. This proves it." He added milk and sugar to his coffee then took a sip before sitting back, his elbows resting on the back of the bench. "I'm sure looking forward to going back home. I'll need a week just to catch up on my beauty sleep."

"We're not going home," she said, her face suddenly becoming serious.

"Oh God, no. What's turned up now?"

Fiona took a manila envelope from the rucksack and placed it on the table. "I went to the usual drop this morning. There was an envelope for me. Inside was the key to the locker Sean always uses at Victoria Station. This was in the locker."

"I suppose it's too much to hope that it contains a couple of tickets for the next ferry out of Liverpool."

"No such luck." She removed a driver's license from the envelope and gave it to Mullen. "Your name's Daniel McKenna. I'm Marie Russell. We're both from Belfast. We've come down to London in your Toyota van for the weekend."

Mullen studied the license then slipped it into his pocket. She took a sheet of paper from the envelope and handed it to him. He put on his glasses. It was a typewritten directive signed by two members of the Army Council. He recognized one of the signatures: Kevin Brady. His eyes narrowed in disbelief as he read through it.

"This doesn't make any sense," he said softly after handing the paper back to her.

"On the contrary. I think it makes perfect sense. Are you going to eat that cheeseburger?"

Mullen shook his head. "How can you think of food at a time like this?"

"Because I'm hungry." She looked around. "Come on, we can talk in the van. I left it in a car park not far from here."

Mullen picked up his plastic coffee cup and led the way to the door as Fiona hurried after him, scoffing down the remainder of the cheeseburger. They walked to the car park in silence. She unlocked the passenger door and climbed in.

"That was an order to assassinate Senator Jack Scoby," Mullen said after he had got in behind the wheel and placed the cup on the dashboard. "We both know that the IRA never target foreign diplomats. And you say it makes sense to you. Well, would you like to share your reasoning with me? Because I'm damned if I can see any sense in it."

"You just said, the IRA *never* target foreign diplomats," Fiona repeated. "And that's the beauty of it. Who will the authorities blame when Scoby is assassinated?"

"Come on, Fiona, it won't take the authorities long to put two and two together, especially as Scoby's been shouting his mouth off about the IRA during his recent election campaign," Mullen retorted.

"The authorities may well suspect the IRA but there won't be any evidence linking us with the murder. And if they do accuse us in the Press you can be sure the Army Council will put out an immediate disclaimer, distancing the Revolutionary Army from any involvement. And they are also sure to contact senior Noraid members in the US to assure them that the IRA had no part in Scoby's murder. That way our support won't be harmed over there."

"But why target him? Shouting his mouth off about Noraid is one thing but he knows he can't shut down our operation over there. It would be unconstitutional. We have the right, as a political organization, to collect funds from our supporters in America."

"The Army Council obviously think differently," Fiona replied with a shrug. "And they make the policies. We're only here to carry out those policies to the best of our ability."

"I still don't like it," Mullen said.

"This has obviously been worked out well in advance. And as it said in the directive, it was originally Sean's operation. I think it's a great honor that they've asked us to carry it out in Sean's absence. And I know we can do it. But I'd understand if you wanted to back out."

"You'd do it by yourself?"

"If I had to," she replied somberly. "But I'd still prefer to work with a partner. Especially one I can trust."

"You know I'll be there," Mullen replied. "What have I got to lose apart from my life?"

"Ever the optimist," she said with a smile. "But we're not going to die. We'll hit Scoby and be back in Ireland before the weekend's out. And the Army Council are going to be waiting to welcome us back with open arms. Who knows, there may even be a promotion in it for us."

"You know what happened the last time I led a cell," Mullen replied glumly. "No, they won't risk it. And anyway, I don't want that kind of responsibility again. But if you get a promotion, I hope there will be a place for me in your cell."

"My first recruit," she replied.

He looked into the back of the van. A tarpaulin was spread over the floor. He knew from the appendix attached to the directive that underneath the tarpaulin were two Czech Skorpion machine-pistols and two Colt .45 revolvers. He was about to lift the

edge of the tarpaulin when Fiona grabbed his arm
and indicated the wing mirror on her side of the van
with a nod of her head. He checked in his wing mirror and a wave of fear surged through his body. Two
policemen were approaching the van on foot. She
dug the keys out of her pocket and handed them to
Mullen. He wiped a bead of sweat from his forehead
and wound down the window as one of the policemen approached the driver's door.

"Afternoon, officer," Mullen said with a friendly
smile.

"Good afternoon, sir," the policeman replied. "Is
this your vehicle?"

"I'm afraid it is," Mullen replied sheepishly. "It
may not be much to look at, but it gets us around."

"May I see your driver's license please, sir?"

Mullen took the license from his pocket and
handed it to the policeman. The policeman studied it
then looked up at Mullen. "Could you give me the
registration number of your vehicle please, sir?"

Mullen, who had already memorized it at the station, repeated it for the policeman.

The policeman checked the plates then held up the
driver's license. "Would you excuse me a minute,
sir?"

"There's nothing wrong is there, officer?" Mullen
asked anxiously.

"It's just a routine check, sir." The policeman unclipped his radio and turned away from the van as he
spoke into it.

The second policeman rapped on the passenger
window. Fiona wound it down. "Would you mind
opening the back, sir?"

Mullen took the keys out of the ignition and
climbed from the van. He walked around to the back
and unlocked the doors.

"Is there anything under the tarpaulin, sir?"

"Nothing, officer," Fiona called out from the passenger seat.

Mullen swallowed anxiously. What the hell was she doing? She knew what was underneath the tarpaulin. He noticed the jack on the floor by the door. He would have to use it. But why was Fiona acting so cool? It unnerved him. His fingers touched the jack as the policeman lifted the tarpaulin. Mullen had to check his surprise. There was nothing there. Satisfied, the policeman dropped the tarpaulin and told Mullen he could close the doors again.

Moments later the first policeman handed the driver's license back to Mullen. "Sorry to have troubled you, sir."

Mullen waited until the two policemen had disappeared from view before turning to Fiona. "I think you owe me an explanation. I was about to cosh that pig back there. Why didn't you tell me that you'd already taken the weapons out of the van?"

"I was interested to see how you'd react under pressure."

"Well I hope you're satisfied," he snapped angrily.

"You did well," she replied. "Come on, let's get out of here."

"Where to?" Mullen asked after they had got back into the van. "The safe house?"

"No, the Thames. Scoby's due to take a cruise on the river tomorrow afternoon. I want to take a closer look at the route the boat will be taking."

"Come," Palmer barked in response to the knock on the door.

Eastman opened the door. "Afternoon, sir. You wanted to see me?"

"Yes, come in, Keith," Palmer replied. "So you got my message all right? I hate those infernal answering machines."

"Frances always makes a point of switching it on when she gets home from the library. Most of the calls are for her anyway. But then that's what you get for being the secretary of the local amateur dramatics society."

"How is your wife?"

"She's fine, thank you, sir. Not that I've seen much of her these last few weeks. They're putting on one of those Russian tragedies later this month. That seems to be keeping her busy."

"I spoke to Whitlock earlier this afternoon. A good man to have on our side. He's holding a briefing at the hotel before Scoby gets there. Have you been told about it?"

"Graham left a message for me on the answering machine."

"I was hoping to be there as well but I've been summoned upstairs for a meeting with the Commissioner. God knows what time that will finish. I've already made my apologies to Whitlock but I wanted to see you before you went over there anyway." Palmer helped himself to a cigarette from the pack on his desk and lit it. "Earlier this afternoon two officers were on a routine patrol in the St. Pancras area when they spotted what they regarded as a suspicious vehicle near Euston Station. It was an old red Toyota van. There were two occupants: a man and a woman. The man's license was in the name of Daniel McKenna. The license and the plates checked out to an address in Belfast and the officers had to let them go. But both officers were suspicious and when they got back to the station they told their superior about the incident. He had them go through all known Irish villains on the computer and both positively identified Mullen as Daniel McKenna."

"So it's safe to assume that the woman must have been Fiona Gallagher?"

"It would have to be, wouldn't it?" Palmer re-

plied. "We've since checked on the real Daniel
McKenna. His van's been parked in his garage in Belfast for the last two days. So Mullen and Gallagher
must be using false plates. They're certainly canny,
I'll give them that."

"They could both have been in custody by now,"
Eastman said, shaking his head angrily to himself.

"There was nothing the officers could do. They
had to let them go."

"I'm not blaming them, sir," Eastman was quick to
point out. "On the contrary. If it hadn't been for their
vigilance, we wouldn't have known they were back
in the country. What about Kerrigan though? No sign
of him?"

"None at all. There were only the two of them."

"He's probably lying low somewhere, given how
distinctive he is in public."

"But what worries me is why they're here in London. Surely they'd want to get back to Ireland as soon
as possible? They'd be much safer over there."

"Unless they're planning another operation here
in London?"

"That seemed the most likely explanation to me as
well."

"Scoby?" Eastman said warily.

"It can't be ruled out, Keith," Palmer replied.
"Well, you'd better leave now if you want to get to
the hotel for six. You know what London traffic's like
at this time of the afternoon." Palmer watched Eastman cross to the door. "Oh, and Keith? Keep me informed."

"I will, sir," Eastman replied as he left the room.

"Can we talk?"

Whitlock nodded and gestured for Graham to
enter the room.

"I thought it best if I came by before the others got

here," Graham said. "I owe you an apology for my outburst earlier this afternoon. I was out of order."

"You spoke your mind, Mike, and that's something I've always liked about you." Whitlock closed the door. "It's often the best way. And what you said made a lot of sense once I'd sat down and thought about it."

"I was still out of order."

"Apology accepted, if that will make you feel any better," Whitlock said. "I'll talk to Sergei and the Secretary-General when I get back to New York. See what they have to say. That's the easy part. Then I'll have to sit down with Carmen and tell her how I feel about the situation. I can't say I'm really looking forward to that."

"It's best to clear the air."

"Best for who though?" Whitlock replied then indicated the kettle on the dresser. "Tea?"

Graham smiled. "I think I'll stick to creosote, thanks."

"Coming up," Whitlock replied, switching on the kettle.

There was a knock at the door and Whitlock answered it to admit Sabrina. Minutes later Eastman arrived and he briefed them about the incident near Euston Station that afternoon.

"So you agree with us now, do you?" Graham said, looking across at Eastman. "You think there will be an attempt on Scoby's life after all?"

"Nothing would surprise me after the events of the last twenty-four hours," Eastman replied.

"But where will they try and hit him?" Whitlock asked. "We've seen the senator's itinerary. It's not exactly a low-profile visit, is it?"

"He'll be at his most vulnerable when he's with the mayor on board the pleasure boat tomorrow afternoon," Graham replied. "I don't care how tight the security measures will be around the Thames, a good assassin could still take him out.''

"Agreed," Whitlock said.

"Any chance of cordoning off the boat's intended route tomorrow afternoon?''

"I suggested that to Senator Scoby last night," Whitlock replied. "But he wouldn't have any of it. He's determined to go ahead with the itinerary as planned.''

"So is the mayor," Eastman added. "He gave Commander Palmer the usual predictable speech about not giving in to threats of terrorism. We're just going to have to cope as best we can.''

"And have our letters of resignation ready if the IRA do breach our security measures," Sabrina said.

The telephone rang. Whitlock spoke briefly to the caller. "That was Fabio. They've just got into Heathrow. He thinks they should reach the hotel within the hour.''

Eastman finished his tea. "Well, if you'll excuse me, I've got to get back to the Yard. I'm due to give a briefing to my men at eight.''

"Will you be coming back here later?" Whitlock asked.

"That all depends on how long the briefing goes on for. I'll call you later and let you know what's happening. If not, I'll meet Scoby in the morning. That shouldn't be a problem, should it?''

"You can meet Scoby anytime. I was thinking more of the briefing we'll be holding after we've had a chance to talk to him. But if you can't make it, no matter. I'll call you and brief you on the phone.''

"I'll do my best to get back. But I can't make any promises.''

"I understand," Whitlock replied as he walked Eastman to the door.

"I'm starving," Sabrina announced after Eastman

had gone. "I haven't eaten a thing since breakfast. I think I'll grab a bite before Scoby gets here."

"And I'll call Sergei to let him know what's happening," Whitlock said. "Then I can start on the backlog of paperwork I've brought with me."

"Have you eaten yet?" Sabrina asked Graham.

"I guess I could force myself to eat something," Graham replied, following her to the door.

"Don't do me any favors," she replied, looking around at him.

"Get out, both of you," Whitlock chided good-humoredly. "I'll let you know when the senator gets here. *Bon appétit*."

"It's a pleasure finally to meet you," Scoby announced, taking Sabrina's hand in a gentle but firm handshake. "Mr. Whitlock told me last night that you were to be a part of my security team, but it wasn't until I read your dossier on the plane that I realized you were George Carver's daughter. He's still talked about on Capitol Hill to this day. It's a pity he was on the wrong side."

"That all depends on whose side you're on," Sabrina replied.

Scoby smiled politely. "So what is your father doing now? The last I heard he'd been appointed chairman of Sellers Marketing in Miami."

"He retired two years ago. My parents still live in Miami. In Coral Gables."

"Ah yes, a beautiful part of the city. It must be a good fifteen years now since your father was appointed American ambassador to Britain. I was still a student at Harvard in those days."

"Actually, it was eighteen years ago," Sabrina corrected him.

"Really, is it that long ago? And he was here for

eight years, I believe. That's a good innings by any standards."

"He was a good ambassador," Sabrina replied quickly.

"I'm sure he was," Scoby replied without much conviction. He shook Graham's hand. "Good to have you aboard."

"Thank you," Graham replied, tight-lipped.

"Isn't it strange that you should both have such prominent politicians in your family?" Scoby said. "Your father-in-law was Senator Howard Walsh. 'Hawk' Walsh. A fine man."

"As Sabrina said, that all depends on whose side you're on," Graham replied.

"I take it you don't share the senator's political views?"

"I don't share anything with Senator Walsh anymore," Graham said bitterly. "He's a narrow-minded, right-wing bigot who should have been dumped by the Republicans years ago."

Scoby's smile faltered. "Somehow, I never took you for a liberal."

Whitlock put a hand lightly on Graham's arm before he could reply. Tillman noticed the gesture and was quick to catch Scoby's eye. "The Ambassador and his wife are due here for drinks in half an hour. You said you wanted to change before they arrived."

"Ray will stay behind and sort out the security arrangements with you," Scoby said to Whitlock. "And if you should need me for anything, you know where to find me."

"I'm sure we'll be able to sort out everything with Mr. Tillman. But thank you anyway," Whitlock said.

"Where's Fabio?" Sabrina asked after Whitlock had seen Scoby out.

"He's making a phone call in his room," Whitlock

replied. "There was a message for him at reception when he checked in. He shouldn't be long now."

Paluzzi arrived a few minutes later. "I haven't been holding up the show, have I?"

"Actually, yes," Whitlock replied good-humoredly, "but perhaps now we can get down to business." He removed five folders from his attaché case and handed them around, keeping one for himself. "We're all familiar with the senator's schedule for the weekend by now. These folders contain a more detailed timetable of his intended movements. I want the three of you to study it carefully and, together with Inspector Eastman, work out a duty roster for the weekend. Commander Palmer has already detailed a dozen men to work with us. Inspector Eastman's briefing them now, using this same timetable. They will be answerable to him but, when he's not there, whichever of you is on duty will automatically assume command."

"What kind of shifts are we going to work?" Graham asked.

"That's for you to decide," Whitlock replied. "There will be a twenty-four-hour guard on the suite so, officially, you'll be off-duty once the senator's retired for the night. But one of you will be expected to be on call each night in case something should crop up. This doesn't involve Eastman as he won't be sleeping on the premises. Three nights, so you'll each have one night on call. OK?"

"It is for Eastman," Paluzzi replied, then looked across at Graham and Sabrina. "If it's all right with you, I'd prefer to take either tomorrow or Sunday. I'm still recovering from my little excursion to Milford last night."

"No problem," Sabrina replied. "I'll stay on call tonight. I think I've had more than enough sleep as it is today."

Graham nodded. "OK, then I'll take tomorrow night. Fabio, that leaves you with Sunday night."

"Perfect," Paluzzi said.

"There is one snag though," Whitlock announced. "The senator goes for a run every morning. Usually around six. So whoever's on call will have to be up bright and early to go with him."

"I don't have a tracksuit with me," Paluzzi complained.

"So buy one," Sabrina said with a shrug. "Gucci make good tracksuits. Stick it on your UNACO credit card. After all, that's what expense accounts are for." She winked mischievously at Whitlock. "Not so, C. W.?"

"You buy a Gucci tracksuit and it'll come out of your wages," Whitlock told Paluzzi bluntly. "You'll buy the cheapest one you can find."

"You know, C. W., you're sounding more like Sergei every day," Sabrina said.

"That's because I've seen our budget for the year." Whitlock turned his attention back to the folder in his lap. "There will only be two occasions when I want you all on duty. Tomorrow afternoon when the senator's on the pleasure boat, and Sunday when he'll be visiting the cemetery in Ireland. Apart from that, you make your own roster. Oh, there is one other matter. As you know, the senator's due to dine at the American ambassador's residence tomorrow night. The embassy wasn't too happy about the idea of either UNACO or the anti-terrorist squad being on US property. They wanted the Marines to take charge of the security operation. We finally reached a compromise. They can use their Marines provided UNACO is still in charge of the overall security operation. I'll be there, but in my official capacity as deputy director of UNACO. And that means I won't be able to give my full attention to the security arrangements. I want two of you to be there with me. Sabrina, you're at ease amongst diplomats. I think you . . ." he trailed off when he saw the smile tug at the corners of her mouth. "Don't tell me, you don't have an evening gown with you."

She shook her head innocently.

"Then hire one."

"Hire one?" she replied in disbelief. "That's like borrowing somebody else's clothes."

"You're not buying one," Whitlock told her firmly. "And that's final."

"OK, I'll hire one," she hissed through clenched teeth.

"Mike, I want you there as well."

Graham nodded.

Whitlock looked across at Tillman. "Is there anything you want to add?"

Tillman shook his head. "No, you seem to have covered everything. Although I would like a copy of the duty roster once your team has sorted it out."

"Of course," Whitlock replied.

"We can't make out the shifts until we've seen Eastman," Graham said to Whitlock.

"Forget about Eastman," Whitlock replied. "He'll just have to fit in with your arrangements. I want the duty roster made out tonight."

Tillman closed the folder, stood up, and made his way to the door. "That certainly went a lot quicker than I'd anticipated. I'll be in Senator Scoby's suite if you should need me again tonight."

Whitlock closed the door behind him and turned back to the others. "Well, I've still got a lot of paperwork to wade through before I turn in for the night. Let me have a copy of the roster once you've worked it out." They headed for the door. "Oh, Mike, can I have a word before you go?"

"We'll be in my room," Sabrina told Graham as she left with Paluzzi.

"Don't antagonize Scoby like that again," Whitlock said once they were alone.

"I wasn't out to antagonize him, C.W. He asked me about 'Hawk' Walsh—"

"Mike, you know very well that Scoby's just as right-wing as Walsh," Whitlock cut in. "And you went out of your way to try and mix it with him tonight."

"So what was I supposed to do?" Graham retorted. "Agree with him that 'Hawk' Walsh's a fine man? Forget it."

"If you're going to spar with politicians, the first lesson to learn is the art of diplomacy."

"And what is the art of diplomacy?" Graham asked with a hint of sarcasm in his voice.

"I used to have a poster on my wall when I was a student. It said simply: Diplomacy is telling someone to go to hell in such a way that they look forward to the trip."

Graham grinned. "I like it."

"Then bear it in mind next time." Whitlock opened the door. "Go on before Sabrina and Fabio bag all the best shifts."

Mullen moved quickly to the window as a pair of headlights swept across the front of the safe house in Finsbury Park. A white Mazda estate had turned into the drive and was pulling up in front of the closed garage door. Mullen grabbed the Colt from the table behind him and switched off the light. He took up a position in the hall with the revolver trained on the front door. His finger tightened around the trigger as the footsteps drew closer. They stopped in front of the door. The bell rang three times, each with a two-second interval. It was the code he had agreed to earlier with Fiona. But if it was her, where was the red

Toyota van? He moved cautiously to the door, still wary of some kind of trap.

A fist banged sharply on the door. "Hugh, open up!"

Mullen unlatched the door then stepped back, waiting. "It's open."

Fiona opened the door and found herself staring down the barrel of the revolver. Mullen looked behind her and, satisfied there wasn't anyone with her, lowered the gun. She closed the door and switched on the light.

"Where's the van?" he demanded as she brushed past him and disappeared into the lounge.

"I dumped it," she said, looking around at Mullen who was standing hesitantly in the doorway. "So that's what all this was about. You thought I was the cops?"

"What was I supposed to think?" he retorted, stung by the sarcasm in her voice. "Why did you dump the van?"

She held up three large padded envelopes. "These were at the dead-letter drop in Kensington Gardens. They're from Brady. The Fortune Teller contacted him this morning to say the cops knew about the van. The Fortune Teller was due to call him again late this afternoon. Nothing. It's possible that his cover could have been blown. There was always that chance after the information he passed on to us about McGuire being in Switzerland."

"So it looks like we might have lost our backup. That means we'll be going in naked tomorrow afternoon."

"We wouldn't have needed him tomorrow anyway," she replied, removing a sheet of paper from the envelope. "Brady's already worked everything out. We'll have three chances to hit Scoby over the weekend: when he goes for his run tomorrow morning, when he's on the pleasure boat tomorrow afternoon, and when he goes to Ireland on Sunday to visit his grandparents' graves." She handed him a sheet of paper. "This sets out details of the plan to hit him on the river tomorrow."

"And if that fails?" Mullen asked, casting a cursory look over the typewritten page.

"The other plans are in here," she replied, tapping the two envelopes in her hand. "We're only to open these if we need them. Those are my orders." She looked at her watch. "It's almost ten. I'm going to have a bath, then we'll run through the plans for tomorrow before we turn in for the night. We've got an early start in the morning."

"How early?"

"He goes for his morning run around six. We still have to get hold of a getaway car beforehand so we'll have to be out of here no later than three-thirty. The full details are there," she said, indicating the paper in Mullen's hand. "Read it through while I'm having my bath. Then we can go through it together. We can't afford to make any mistakes on this one . . ."

Whitlock was working on one of the files he had brought with him from New York when he was interrupted by a knock at the door. He groaned then got to his feet and answered it.

Paluzzi held out a sheet of paper. "You asked for a copy of our shifts for the weekend."

"Thanks, Fabio," Whitlock said, taking the timetable from Paluzzi.

"Are you busy right now?"

Whitlock's answer was to gesture to the files spread out over the bed.

"I was wondering if you could spare me five minutes?"

"Of course. Come in," Whitlock replied. "What's up?"

"It's about that message that I got when I checked in earlier this evening."

"It's nothing serious, is it?" Whitlock asked anxiously. "Nothing's happened to Claudine or little Dario, has it?"

"No, nothing like that," Paluzzi replied, quick to allay Whitlock's sudden concern. "The message was from the head of the Joint Chiefs-of-Staff in Italy. They want me to go back home and take over as the new Commander-in-Chief of the *NOCS*."

"But you left because you couldn't get on with your superiors," Whitlock said.

"Only my immediate superior, Brigadier Michele Pesco. But he was relieved of command last night. They want me to take his place."

"And?"

"And nothing," Paluzzi replied despondently. "Well, not yet anyway. I told them I needed time to think it over. I'm torn on this one, C.W. Half of me wants to catch the next flight back to Rome and assume command first thing in the morning. But the other half wants to stay on here with UNACO. I know it's something only I can decide, but I just needed to get it off my chest. That's why I came to you. You're the senior man around here. I just wanted to put my cards on the table so that if I did decide to take the post it wouldn't come as a bolt out of the blue to either you or Sergei. I respect you both too much for that."

"It sounds like you've made up your mind already," Whitlock said with a smile.

"Far from it. It's something I'll need to discuss with Claudine when I get back to the States."

"I know what she'll say."

"I know she's never settled properly in New York, which is obviously something I'll need to bear in mind when I'm weighing up the situation. There are other considerations but I'm still determined to make the decision myself.''

Whitlock suddenly thought of Carmen. What would she say when he announced that he wanted to go back into the field? Just how independent would his decision be when it came down to it? Knowing Carmen, she'd play a big role in the outcome. And although Paluzzi wasn't admitting it, he knew Claudine would also play an important part in his final decision. Which meant that Paluzzi was already as good as the new Commander-in-Chief of the Italian elite anti-terrorist squad.

''I just thought I'd let you know,'' Paluzzi said, breaking the sudden silence.

''I'm glad you did. And if you need to talk, you know where I am.''

Paluzzi nodded then left the room. Whitlock sat down on the edge of the bed and picked up the telephone. Should he tell Kolchinsky now, or wait until he returned to New York? Kolchinsky would have enough to worry about as it was with the Secretary-General on his back every few minutes. No, he had to tell him. And if Paluzzi did leave, he knew exactly who he'd want to replace him . . .

TEN

Sabrina reached out a hand for the telephone on the bedside table, fumbling in the darkness until she felt her fingers curl around the receiver. She picked it up.

"Good morning, Miss Carver, this is your five o'-clock wake-up call," a friendly female voice announced on the other end of the line.

"Uh-huh," Sabrina muttered sleepily, dropping the receiver back into its cradle.

All she wanted to do was turn over again and go back to sleep. She forced herself to sit up, then, switching on the bedside lamp, she pulled back the covers and swung her legs out of the bed. She had been on call that night and was wearing a gray tracksuit. Her plimsolls lay within easy reach of the bed. But there had been no calls. At least that had been some consolation . . .

She ran her fingers through her disheveled hair and rubbed her hands slowly over her face. She *hated* getting up early in the morning. And that meant any time before eight-thirty. She was essentially a night person. She finally stood up and switched on the kettle. If she had to start the day at such an obscene hour, then a cup of strong, black coffee would help to make it that little bit more bearable.

The telephone rang. She groaned then reached over and answered it.

"Morning. I hope I didn't wake you."

"Mike?" she said in surprise. "What are you doing up at this godforsaken hour? And why do you sound so bloody cheerful?"

Graham chuckled. "Sounds like someone got out of the wrong side of the bed this morning."

"You know I'm never at my best this early in the morning," she retorted gruffly. "Why are you calling?"

"You want some company on your run this morning?"

"I thought you usually went for your run around eight?" she replied.

"Yeah, usually. But I thought, what the hell, I might as well run with you guys this morning."

"I've got an idea. Why don't you run with Scoby and I'll go back to bed?"

"Nice try, Sabrina. Now get your butt out of bed. I'll be around in ten minutes."

"Make it twenty and you've got a deal," she replied.

"OK. Twenty minutes." The line went dead.

She replaced the receiver and stifled a yawn. She hated jogging almost as much as being forced to get out of bed at five in the morning. Almost. She knew Graham and Whitlock were both avid joggers but she couldn't see the point of running from one spot to another. What purpose did it serve? She preferred to work out in aerobic classes four times a week. And, when she wasn't on assignment, she taught karate to housewives two nights a week at a community center in Manhattan. She had gained her black belt in karate when she was still in her teens.

Pushing any thoughts of aerobics and karate from her mind, she reluctantly got to her feet and went through to the bathroom.

Cross and Johnstone, the two anti-terrorist squad detectives who had also been assigned to accompany Scoby on his early morning run, were already waiting in the corridor when Graham and Sabrina arrived punctually to meet Scoby at five forty-five outside his suite. Graham, as usual, was wearing his New York Giants tracksuit and a white headband knotted loosely at the back of his head.

"Is he ready?" Graham asked, gesturing to the door.

"Dunno," Cross replied with a shrug. "We just got here."

Graham rapped on the door and moments later Scoby answered it, still wearing his dressing gown. He appraised Graham's shellsuit slowly. "A liberal and a Giants fan?"

"Mike used to play for the Giants," Sabrina said, coming to Graham's defense.

Graham shot her a dirty look.

"Really?" Scoby said in surprise. "Why wasn't there any mention of it in your dossier?"

"It wasn't relevant to the case," Graham replied brusquely.

"Graham? I can't say I remember the name. What position did you play?"

"Quarterback. But I never played at senior level. I was sent to 'Nam a month after I signed for them. I picked up a shoulder injury over there and that was the end of my playing career."

"Sounds like you had a narrow escape. Let's face it, there is only one team to play for in New York. And that's the Jets."

"The Jets did try to sign me when I got back from

'Nam," Graham replied poker-faced. "I was told that even with my screwed-up arm, I was a damn sight better than any of their regular quarterbacks. But, much as I loved the game, I just couldn't bring myself to sink that low. Not the Jets."

"That's very good," Scoby said with a forced smile then, excusing himself, went to change. He returned a few minutes later wearing a black and red shellsuit and a black peaked cap.

"Do you always wear that when you go running?" Graham asked.

"This, or a black and yellow shellsuit. Why, what's wrong with it?"

Graham and Sabrina exchanged glances.

"You thinking what I'm thinking?" Graham asked.

She nodded.

"Can you drop the telepathy act and tell me what's going on?" Scoby demanded.

They told him.

"Stop that!" Fiona snapped at Mullen.

"What?" Mullen retorted.

"Drumming your fingers on the wheel."

"Was I?" Mullen replied with a shrug. He folded his arms across his chest then looked across the road at the entrance of the Grosvenor House Hotel. "I thought you said he always went for his run at six. He's already ten minutes late."

They were sitting in a light blue Volkswagen Polo which Mullen had stolen from an estate in Notting Hill earlier that morning. By the time the owner reported it missing, they would already have dumped it on the other side of town. They had thought about torching it but decided it would only draw unnecessary attention to themselves. Not that there would be any prints. Both had on gloves. Fiona was also wearing a shoulder-length red wig. A pair of dark sunglasses lay on the dashboard in front of her. Mullen's long, straggly hair was hidden under her black trilby. He also had a pair of sunglasses which were tucked into the top pocket of his corduroy jacket. Fiona looked at her watch. They had been there for the last forty minutes. So where was Scoby? It wasn't like him to be late.

"Hey, look," Mullen suddenly blurted out, pointing to Cross and Sabrina as they emerged from the hotel. "That could be Scoby's security team."

"Could be," Fiona replied absently, without taking her eyes off them.

Cross and Sabrina looked around them slowly then indicated to the third figure in the doorway behind them.

"It's Scoby," Mullen hissed, immediately recognizing the distinctive black and red tracksuit which had been mentioned in the directive.

Fiona retrieved the Skorpion machine-pistol from under her seat. Checking it was loaded, she cradled it in her lap, her eyes fixed on the three figures standing in front of the hotel. They crossed the road, heading in the direction of Grosvenor Gate. Fiona tightened her grip on the machine-pistol. She had the perfect shot. Suddenly she cursed under her breath and ducked down out of sight, pushing Mullen down as she did so. As soon as she judged that they had entered Hyde Park, she sat up again.

"Why didn't you take him out?" Mullen demanded.

"Because it wasn't Scoby," she snapped. "It was a decoy."

"A decoy? That means Scoby's probably ducked out through another entrance while we've been sitting here watching this lot."

"Exactly."

"Where to?" Mullen asked, reaching for the key in the ignition.

"Nowhere. I've got a feeling they're all going to meet up somewhere in Hyde Park. We can't miss them if we stay here."

Mullen looked at her but said nothing.

Barely a minute had elapsed when Fiona spotted two figures emerging from Upper Grosvenor Street at the side of the hotel. Both were wearing tracksuits.

"We're in luck," she murmured, smiling to herself.

One of them was Scoby.

Sabrina, Cross and Johnstone, who was wearing Scoby's shellsuit and black peaked cap, stopped running when they reached the Ring Tea House inside Hyde Park.

Sabrina unclipped the two-way radio attached to her belt. "Come in, Mike."

"Yeah, Graham here," came the breathless reply.

"Where are you?" she asked.

"We're at Brook Gate," he told her. "Did you attract any attention?"

"No, everything's quiet. Well, as quiet as can be expected around here. But no sign of any trouble."

"OK, we're moving on," Graham said. "We'll meet you, as arranged, at the Fountains in ten minutes."

"Right. Over and out."

Cross rubbed his gloved hands together. "It's a bit parky out here this morning."

"Parky?" Johnstone snorted. "It's bloody freezing. Why would anyone in their right minds want to be out jogging on a morning like this?" He looked at Sabrina. "I know where I'd like to be."

The insinuation wasn't lost on her. She gave him a mock innocent smile. "Me too."

"Yeah?" Johnstone said, grinning knowingly at Cross.

"Sure. The Fountains. Let's go."

Cross laughed at Johnstone's pained expression as Sabrina led the way to their rendezvous.

"They've stopped," Mullen said, reducing speed. "What do you want me to do?"

"Stay in the slow lane," she told him, activating the electric window. "And put on those sunglasses."

Mullen snatched the sunglasses off the dashboard and slid them over his eyes. They were less than forty yards away from their target when a white Rover appeared behind them. It passed them and swung into the lane in front of them. Inside were two men, one of whom waved them on as the Rover crawled along, keeping pace with the joggers.

Mullen swore angrily. "It's got to be part of his security team. Now what?"

"Stay behind them," Fiona replied, tightening her grip on the machine-pistol. "We're almost in range."

"We'll never outrun that Rover even if you do manage to hit Scoby," Mullen wailed. "It's too risky, Fiona. We've got to abort."

"Pull out after the next car," Fiona said, glancing behind her. It shot past them. "Now!"

Mullen swung out from behind the Rover and Fiona waited until they were almost parallel with Scoby and Graham before raising the machine-pistol to fire.

Graham saw the Skorpion at the last possible moment and grounded Scoby with a bruising football tackle a split second before a row of bullets ripped into the tree behind them. The Rover immediately ac-

celerated after the Polo as it sped away from the two
crumpled figures on the pavement.

Fiona leaned out of the window and fired a burst
at the Rover before ducking back inside the car. The
bullets dimpled the bullet-proof windscreen but the
Rover stayed with them. She wiped the sweat from
her forehead and looked around desperately as the
Rover continued to gain on them. It would only be a
matter of time before the Rover managed to force
them off the road. Mullen eased his foot on the brake
pedal as they reached the Cumberland Gate. Marble
Arch loomed up ahead of them. He swung out from
behind a black taxi and, as he turned into the bend,
Fiona fired a burst at the taxi's tires. She scored a direct hit on the left tire and the taxi skidded out of control, forcing the Rover's driver to slam on his brakes.
The wheels locked on the icy road and the Rover
plowed into the side of the taxi which mounted the
pavement and smashed head-on into a wrought-iron
fence. By the time the driver had managed to regain
control of the wheel the Polo had already maneu-
vered around Marble Arch and on to the other side of
Park Lane. Seconds later it disappeared up North
Row.

Graham reholstered his Beretta at the back of his
tracksuit then helped Scoby to his feet. "Are you all
right, senator?"

"I think so," Scoby replied, still visibly shaken by
what had happened.

Graham radioed Sabrina and told her what had
happened. She arrived minutes later with Cross and
Johnstone, all of them still breathless from the run.

"Where's Corbyn and Turnball?" Cross asked.

"They went after the car," Graham told him. "I
heard gunfire but they haven't reported in yet."

"May I borrow that?" Cross said, gesturing to the

two-way radio in Graham's hand. He managed to get through to Turnball.

"The bastards got away," Turnball hissed furiously as he told Cross what had happened.

"Have you called for backup?" Cross asked.

"It's on its way. I've also radioed in for an ambulance for the cabbie. Is the senator all right?"

Cross glanced at Scoby. "He's a bit shaken up but otherwise unharmed."

"We almost had them, Pete. Another ten seconds and we would have rammed them off the road."

"Yeah, I know," Cross said despondently and handed the radio back to Graham.

"The first thing we've got to do is get you back to the hotel," Graham said to Scoby.

"There should be a car along from headquarters any time now," Johnstone added.

"Forget it," Sabrina said. "We're exposed out here in the open. What if the assassins decide to come back?"

"What do you suggest?" Johnstone asked her.

"Simple," she replied, then moved to the edge of the road and flagged down the first black taxi that came along.

Whitlock was waiting for them in the foyer. "Senator, are you all right?" he asked anxiously as they entered the hotel.

"Yeah, thanks to Mike. If he hadn't sacked me when he did, I'd be on the way to the mortuary right now."

So now it's Mike again, Graham thought sarcastically to himself. Until the next time they crossed words and it would be back to Graham again. Not that it bothered him what Scoby called him. He didn't like the two-faced son-of-a-bitch one little bit and he'd be glad to see the back of him after the weekend.

As long as he survived that long. But irrespective of
his feelings toward Scoby, he'd make damn sure no
harm came to him while he was under UNACO's
protection. He knew Sabrina and Paluzzi shared
those sentiments. Sabrina seemed to dislike the man
even more than he did, regarding him as conceited,
arrogant, devious and self-opinionated. All necessary
attributes to become a future President of the United
States.

"Sabrina, why don't you and Mike come up to the
suite and have a coffee with us?" Scoby said. "I know
Melissa would like to meet you both."

"Go on," Whitlock said. "I've called Eastman, he's
already on his way. We'll sort out everything with
the local boys. I'll see you back here in a couple of
hours."

Sabrina shot Whitlock a *thanks-for-nothing* look
then followed Scoby and Graham to the lift.

Melissa Scoby was still in the bedroom when they
arrived at the suite. Scoby went through to explain
what had happened and a few moments later she followed her husband into the lounge. Sabrina noticed
that her eyes immediately went to Graham, who was
standing by the window, appraising him carefully
and smiling faintly to herself. Suddenly aware of Sabrina's watchful gaze, Melissa Scoby eyed her coldly,
then looked away sharply and extended a hand of
greeting toward Graham. "Jack told me what happened this morning. Thank you."

Graham shrugged it off awkwardly, easing his
hand from her lingering grip. Scoby then introduced
her to Sabrina. She shook Sabrina's hand with a grip
that was hard and uncompromising. Sabrina could
sense the animosity toward her and knew it stemmed
from Melissa Scoby's interest in Graham. But Graham and Scoby seemed unaware of the atmosphere:
only Sabrina had seen through the facade straight
away. And Melissa Scoby knew that . . .

Scoby ordered four coffees from room service. Graham and Sabrina declined the offer of breakfast. They would eat later with Whitlock.

"Please, sit down," Scoby said, gesturing to the chairs behind them.

Graham sat on the nearest sofa. Sabrina was quick to sit beside him and immediately noticed the sharp look from Melissa Scoby. She smiled pleasantly as she met Melissa Scoby's eyes.

Scoby sat down in the armchair opposite them. "I have to admit I initially thought UNACO had got it wrong when your Mr. Whitlock told me that the IRA might try and assassinate me when I came to Britain. But it would seem you've been right all along. I still don't see what they hope to achieve by killing me though. It would only serve in turning even more Americans against the IRA. The funds would dry up overnight. It doesn't make any sense to me."

"It doesn't make any sense to us either," Sabrina told him. "But until we get some answers, we've got to treat the situation very seriously. That much is apparent after what happened this morning."

"I refuse to cancel any of my engagements," Scoby was quick to tell them.

"It would be a major propaganda victory for them," Melissa Scoby said, perching on the edge of the armchair beside him.

"Not just for them," Scoby replied, taking her hand. "Imagine what damage the Democrats could do with that kind of propaganda in a future Presidential election. But it's more than just that. I've always believed that the only way to defeat terrorism is to confront it head on. Because the more we avoid confrontation, the stronger they become."

"We're not suggesting you cancel your engagements, senator," Sabrina assured him. "But there will be a tighter security presence around you for the rest of your stay here in Britain."

There was a knock at the door. Johnstone answered it and took the tray from the room service waiter and brought it through to the lounge. Having poured the coffees, Melissa Scoby handed them around. There was another knock at the door. This time it was Tillman who, clearly agitated, brushed past Johnstone and entered the lounge. "Jack, are you all right?" he asked, approaching Scoby.

"Sure," Scoby replied with a quick smile. "Sit down, Ray. You want a coffee?"

"Jack, why didn't you call me when you got in?" Tillman crossed to the window then turned back to Scoby, his fingers tapping nervously against the side of his legs. "Whitlock told me what happened. You should have told me, Jack."

"What's there to tell you? They took a shot at me and missed," Scoby said with surprising calmness. "And that's all there is to it. I didn't see any need to wake you up just to tell you that. You'd have found out soon enough."

Tillman turned on Graham. "Why wasn't the car picked up before it reached the senator? It sounds like a serious breach of security on your part."

"Ray, sit down!" Scoby snapped, pointing to the armchair by the window.

Tillman glared at Graham then sat down, his hands now clenched tightly in his lap. "I still say your men should have spotted them earlier."

"There will be an inquiry," Graham assured him. "And if you're right, those responsible will be reprimanded. Does that satisfy you?"

Tillman said nothing.

Graham finished his coffee then stood up. "Well, if you'll excuse me, I'd like to take a shower and change out of these clothes."

"Me too," Sabrina said, leaving her coffee and getting to her feet.

Scoby walked them to the door. "Mike, I know

there's nothing I can ever do or say to repay you for saving my life this morning. But thank you."

Graham shook Scoby's extended hand and followed Sabrina from the room.

"I'd watch Melissa Scoby if I were you," Sabrina said once they had reached the lift and were out of earshot of the two detectives on duty outside the suite.

"What are you talking about?" Graham asked, pressing the button.

"It's obvious she fancies you."

"What gives you that idea?" he replied in amazement.

"Call it intuition."

"Intuition?" he said sarcastically. "I should have guessed."

She bit back her anger. "I'm just telling you what I saw, that's all."

"Well you saw wrong," he told her firmly.

The doors opened onto their floor and they walked down the corridor toward their rooms.

She took her key card from her tracksuit pocket as she reached her door. "I know I'm right about this, Mike."

"No, you're not right about it. You've obviously latched on to what C.W. told us last night about Melissa Scoby being a bit of a flirt back home and now you're reading all sorts of nonsense into it. I suggest you put your personal feelings to one side and get on with the job."

"Don't flatter yourself, Mike Graham," she snapped angrily as she pushed the key card into the lock and shoved open the door.

He waited until the door had closed behind her then shook his head sadly to himself and made his way to his room.

* * *

"Can we talk, Jack?" Tillman asked once Scoby had seen off Graham and Sabrina.

"Sure," Scoby replied. "What about?"

Tillman glanced at Melissa Scoby. She got the message and disappeared into the bedroom, closing the door behind her.

"So talk," Scoby said, extending a hand toward Tillman.

"You were dealt a friendly card this morning, Jack. Next time you might not be so lucky. I want to make sure that you get back home in one piece. And that means your security team will have to be a lot more vigilant than it was today."

"Why don't you just come out and say what you really mean, Ray?" Scoby said icily. "That if I die, you'll suddenly be caught between the Colombians and the Mafia. Am I right?"

"That's not true, Jack," Tillman replied sharply. "I've always had your best interests at heart. You know that."

"I can't say I've ever taken you for an altruist, Ray," Scoby said scornfully. "You're in this for yourself just as much as I'm in it for myself. So let's not kid each other, shall we? And if it's any consolation to you, I'd also like to get back to New York in one piece."

Tillman ran his fingers through his hair. "Just listen to us. We're squabbling like a couple of schoolkids over a date."

"And if I remember correctly, I was always the one who won those arguments," Scoby said with a satisfied smile.

"Yeah you did, didn't you?" Tillman said between clenched teeth. "But then you've always had the looks and I've always had the brains."

"Well, if you're so brainy, why didn't you sort out the security arrangements properly last night?"

Scoby demanded. "You had every opportunity to do so."

"I'm not a security consultant," Tillman shot back. "I assumed Whitlock knew what he was doing."

"Then I suggest you check again. It's for your protection just as much as it is for mine. Remember that. Because without me, there is no deal between either the Colombians or the Mafia. And that would leave you very isolated indeed, wouldn't it?"

Tillman wiped the sweat from his forehead. "I'll talk to Whitlock when he gets back to the hotel."

"You do that, Ray. Now, if you'll excuse me, I'd like to take a bath before I go downstairs for breakfast."

"What time are you having breakfast?"

Scoby patted Tillman on the arm. "Don't worry, Ray, I'll make sure I call you this time and let you know."

Tillman bit back his anger and strode from the room.

Fiona and Mullen abandoned the stolen car near Claridges then took the tube back to the safe house in Finsbury Park. Once there she opened the wall safe, hidden behind a Van Gogh print in the lounge, and removed the envelope marked "B," the plans for the hit on Scoby on the pleasure-boat trip that afternoon. She sat down and tore open the envelope. Inside was a sheet of paper and a single key on a plastic key ring. She put the key ring on the table beside her and unfolded the sheet of paper. She read through the details of the operation then used the remote control to switch on the television set in time to watch the early morning news.

Mullen appeared with two mugs of tea. He put them on the table beside her and gestured to the screen. "Anything about us?"

She shook her head then held out the sheet of paper to him. "Read this."

Mullen sat down on the sofa and read through the text carefully. "Brady's gone to a lot of trouble to set this one up for us."

"My thoughts exactly," she replied. "So we've got to make sure we don't screw up again."

Mullen took a sip of tea and smiled to himself. "We won't. We've got him this time, Fiona. We've really got him."

"I'll believe it when he's dead," Fiona replied, then indicated the mug in his hand. "Drink up, we've still got a lot to do this morning."

Whitlock phoned Graham and Sabrina once he returned to the hotel and told them to come to his room. Graham arrived first. Eastman and Paluzzi were already there.

"There's food there if you're hungry," Whitlock said, gesturing to the trolley by the bed.

Graham helped himself to three rashers of bacon which he layered between two slices of toast. He then poured himself a coffee and sat down on the bed.

When Sabrina arrived Whitlock again indicated toward the trolley.

"I'll just have a coffee, thanks," she replied.

"Mike, pour Sabrina a coffee," Whitlock said.

"I'll get it myself," she retorted brusquely, crossing to the trolley.

"OK, what's going on?" Whitlock demanded.

"Nothing," Sabrina replied innocently.

Whitlock's eyes flashed angrily as he looked from Sabrina to Graham. "Mike?"

"I've got no beef with Sabrina," Graham replied truthfully.

"You'd better sort out your differences smartish. Both of you. Because if you can't work together, I'll bring in a team that can. Do I make myself understood?"

Sabrina gave Whitlock her best winning smile as she sat down beside Paluzzi. "There's no problem, C.W."

"This is me you're talking to, Sabrina. I know when the two of you are squabbling. I saw enough of it when I worked with you. Just see that it's sorted out by this afternoon." Whitlock held up his hand before she could say anything. "That's all I have to say. Now, can we get down to the briefing? Keith's just received word from Scotland Yard that the getaway car's been found."

Eastman nodded. "It was abandoned in Brook Street, about fifty yards from Claridges. The area's been sealed off in case there were any booby trap devices left in the car. There's a team of ATOs, a bomb-disposal unit, at the scene now."

"How far's Brook Street from where we lost the car?" Sabrina asked.

"A mile, if that," Eastman replied. "The car was obviously abandoned in a hurry. The doors were unlocked and the keys were still in the ignition."

"They must have known it would only be a matter of time before they were spotted from the air," Paluzzi deduced.

"Did anyone see them fleeing the car?" Sabrina asked.

"The car was left outside a shop. The owner said they went up Binney Street in the direction of Oxford Street. Binney Street is also a couple of blocks away from Bond Street tube station. We've got uniformed officers there now with pictures of Mullen, hoping someone may have seen them entering the station. The tube seems to be the most logical escape route."

"And they could have gone anywhere once they reached the tube station," Paluzzi said.

"We can only keep asking, hoping to jog someone's memory," Eastman replied with a shrug. "We're concentrating mostly on the London Underground staff."

"Yeah, that red hair of hers was pretty distinctive," Graham said thoughtfully. "Guys would notice something like that."

"You saw her?" Eastman said in surprise.

"I caught a glimpse of her hair, that's all."

"And her face?" Eastman asked.

Graham shook his head. "It all happened too quickly."

Whitlock poured himself another cup of tea. "I had a visit from Ray Tillman before I called you here. He wasn't too happy with the security arrangements this morning."

"Yeah, he had a go at us as well," Graham said, looking across at Sabrina.

"Personally, I don't know what else we could have done to protect the senator apart from sealing off Park Lane and the surrounding streets. I advised him even before we left New York not to go running in the mornings. But he wouldn't have any of it. He was adamant he would go for his morning run."

"Do you want me to double the security tomorrow morning?" Eastman asked.

"He's not going running in the morning," Whitlock retorted sharply.

"Did he tell you that?" Paluzzi said.

"No, I told him after I'd thrown Tillman out."

Graham smiled. "What did he say?"

"He wasn't too happy about it at first but when I pointed out that although I couldn't stop him from running in the morning, I could stop you from going with him, that seemed to do the trick. So at least that's one area we don't have to worry about anymore." Whitlock took a folder from his attaché case and opened it. "I spoke to Commander Palmer earlier to finalize the security arrangements for this afternoon.

It's been decided that the Metropolitan Police will be responsible for security around the Thames. Commander Palmer will be taking charge of the operation himself. I'll be in charge of security on the river itself." He turned to Paluzzi. "Fabio, you're the only one here who can fly a chopper. I want you as an eye in the sky this afternoon. Mike will be with you. You'll be in an unmarked police helicopter. There will be other police helicopters up there as well but they'll be covering a much wider area. I want you to stay as close to the boat as possible."

"I assume that means I'm on the boat with Scoby," Sabrina said.

"We'll both be on the boat," Whitlock told her. "Well, that's all for now. Sabrina, we're due at Charing Cross Pier for nine to check over the boat with the River Police and a team from the bomb-disposal unit."

"If you'll excuse me, I've got to get back to the Yard," Eastman said, getting to his feet. "I assume you'll be at the pier if I do need to get in touch with you?"

"I should be there for the rest of the morning. But if not, I'll leave a number where I can be contacted," Whitlock replied.

"Fine. See you later." Eastman left the room.

"And where will we be?" Paluzzi asked, gesturing to Graham.

"You two have got a briefing with the Air Police at ten. They're sending a car over for you." Whitlock picked up his attaché case and moved to the door. "You may as well finish that breakfast since it's been paid for. Just make sure you close the door behind you when you leave. Come on, Sabrina, we've got work to do."

She shot the others a despairing look then jumped nimbly to her feet and hurried after Whitlock.

* * *

Fiona and Mullen took the tube to Great Portland Street Station. From there they walked the short distance to a nearby car park where they found the white Peugeot estate with the registration number which corresponded to the numbers printed on the plastic key ring in her bag. They both slipped on gloves but when Mullen held out his hand for the key ring Fiona shook her head and climbed behind the wheel. Mullen just shrugged and got in beside her.

She had already memorized their route on an A to Z of London before they left the house and she drove to a deserted warehouse off Grosvenor Road, close to the Pimlico Gardens. The lock-up garage was annexed to the building. The doors were padlocked. Fiona handed Mullen the key. He got out of the car, looked around slowly, then crouched down and unlocked the doors. He waited until Fiona had driven the Peugeot into the garage then replaced the padlock and opened the door leading into the warehouse and went inside, closing it again behind him. The warehouse had been abandoned for more than two years. Most of the windows had been smashed and graffiti covered the walls. The floor was littered with empty wooden crates, many still bearing the company logo. He crossed to the door which connected the warehouse to the lock-up garage to join Fiona. The garage was a lot bigger than it looked from the outside. No wonder the company had gone bankrupt if the managing director needed a place this big just for his car, Mullen thought to himself.

Preparations for the operation had been meticulous. A plaid rug had been spread out over the floor of the Peugeot's boot. Underneath it were two Ingram MAC II machine-pistols; a radio transmitter, not much bigger than a cigarette packet; two wetsuits; two sets of closed-circuit oxygen breathing apparatus;

two plastic-handled knives and a pair of autofocus
binoculars. Mullen unloaded the gear then Fiona
lifted the floor covering. Lying beside the spare wheel
was a hermetically sealed case containing an eight-
kilogram Russian RPG-7 anti-tank launcher and two
OG-7 high-explosive grenades. Like the machine-
pistols, they were secured in waterproof wrapping.
Mullen lifted out the case and Fiona replaced the covering and closed the boot.

"Put this on," Fiona said, tossing one of the wetsuits to Mullen.

"Here? Together? We're not . . ." Mullen said uncomfortably. "I mean, you and Sean—"

"For God's sake, Hugh, this is a job, not a seduc-
tion." Briskly she pulled off her T-shirt to reveal a
white vest underneath, but Mullen was still staring
awkwardly at her. "Go into the warehouse if it'll
make you feel better."

Mullen blushed and disappeared into the warehouse, closing the door behind him. She pulled on the
wetsuit and zipped it up to her chin. She was still adjusting the hood when there was a discreet knock on
the door.

"Come in, Hugh," she called out.

As Fiona had done, Mullen stuffed his clothes into
a hold-all on the backseat of the car. Fiona picked up
the binoculars and crossed to a row of rusted metal
stairs which led up onto a catwalk. Once on the catwalk she crouched beside one of the broken windows
and slowly scanned the river with the binoculars.
Mullen watched her from the foot of the stairs.

"Well?" he asked as she lowered the binoculars.

"Brady was right. You can see Lambeth Bridge
from here with these binoculars."

"And the barge?"

"It's there. Exactly where Brady said it would be."
Fiona scanned the NCP car park on the opposite

side of the river. The blue transit van was in position. The small explosive charge would already have been attached to the undercarriage of the vehicle, close to the petrol tank. She instinctively glanced at the transmitter on her belt. The explosion would be the perfect diversionary tactic. And in the confusion they could slip unnoticed onto the barge and set up the rocket launcher. She descended the stairs and crossed to a pile of empty crates which had been tossed haphazardly in the corner of the room. Mullen helped her move them. They had been concealing a small, wooden trapdoor. She eased it open. A rusted ladder led down to the water. She switched on her torch and shone the beam into the semi-darkness. Two cigar-shaped swimmer delivery vehicles, both four feet in length, were secured to the ladder. She glanced at her watch. The pleasure boat was due to leave Charing Cross Pier shortly.

"Get the scuba gear," she said to Mullen. "We've got to be ready to move the moment the boat reaches Lambeth Bridge."

He nodded and hurried back to the car. She returned to the window and trained the binoculars back onto the water. All they could do now was wait . . .

John Moody was a true Cockney, having been born within the sound of the bells of St. Mary-le-Bow church in the Cheapside area of London. Now in his late fifties, he had been piloting pleasure boats on the Thames for the last forty years. He was an instantly recognizable figure with his white peaked cap tugged down firmly over his bald head and a brier pipe clenched firmly between his nicotine-stained teeth. Both items were on show as he stood in the wheelhouse of his boat, the *Merry Dancer*, which was berthed at Charing Cross Pier.

He had taken an instant liking to both Whitlock and Sabrina when he had met them earlier that morning. They had been honest with him from the very beginning and that was a characteristic he had always admired in people. At eleven-thirty the mayor and his entourage arrived at the pier with Jack and Melissa Scoby. The paparazzi had a field day. They had even hired a pleasure boat of their own, hoping to keep close to the *Merry Dancer* in case a second attempt on Scoby's life was more successful than the first. The cameras were primed and ready . . .

Moody smiled at Sabrina when she appeared at the wheelhouse door. "Ready when you are, luv."

"We're ready," she replied then gestured to the saloon directly beneath them. "Not that I think any of them would know whether the boat was in motion or not. They're all tucking in to the buffet."

Moody guffawed, then leaned out of the wheelhouse window and shouted at a teenage youth to cast off the ropes.

"I'd better get back to keep an eye on the senator," Sabrina announced, then descended the stairs and entered the saloon where the food had been laid out on three trestle tables in the center of the room.

Scoby approached her. "I'd like a word if you've got a minute. In private." He gestured to the stairs. "Could we go on deck?"

"You know you're not to take any unnecessary risks," she reminded him. "You were told that even before you got here. If the IRA do have an assassin somewhere out there—"

"OK, we'll stay down here," Scoby replied with a dismissive shrug, taking her arm and leading her across the room until they were out of earshot of the others. "Are you happy at UNACO?"

"Sure. Why?"

"I'd like to offer you a job. Head of my security team."

"I didn't realize you could choose your own security team," she replied with a faint hint of sarcasm in her voice.

Scoby smiled. "I've got contacts in the right places. In fact I could get you transferred to the Secret Service on the same day as you tendered your resignation to UNACO. What do you say?"

She could see through his scheme straight away. He wasn't interested in her talent but rather in the fact that she was a woman. What better way to win over more of the female vote than by having a woman as head of his security team? But she doubted women would go for it anyway. It was too transparent for someone like him. She smiled to herself—would he have been so quick to offer Whitlock a position on his security team? It might win him a few more liberal votes but she doubted the Ku Klux Klan would be too pleased about it. Then again, to be fair to Scoby, there had never been any proof of his involvement with the Klan and his lawyers had already issued a writ against the newspaper which had published the article suggesting there was.

"You find my offer amusing?" Scoby said.

"No, I'm flattered that you asked but I think I'll stick with UNACO."

"And what happens if UNACO's disbanded? It's certainly a possibility after the events of the last few days. What will you do then?"

"The only way UNACO would be disbanded is if we slipped up and let the IRA get to you. That's why we're living in your shadow until you're returned to the protection of the Secret Service back home. So it wouldn't really be in your interests if that were to happen, would it?"

Scoby eyed her intently then the familiar smile creased his face. "Well then, let's hope UNACO isn't disbanded. At least not until I get home."

Melissa Scoby approached them. She shot Sabrina

a disdainful look then addressed her husband. "Darling, the mayor's already making noises about your absence from the table. Can we humor him, please?"

Scoby kissed his wife on the cheek then looked at Sabrina. "What would I do without her? The voice of my conscience. And always there when I need her."

"Jack," she hissed.

Scoby followed his wife back to the table. Sabrina went up on deck and leaned her arms on the railing. They were passing the Jubilee Gardens. She looked at the second boat tagging along in the wake of the *Merry Dancer*. The Press. Vultures, waiting for the kill. The River Police had forbidden them to travel beside the *Merry Dancer* because two of the police's own launches would be flanking it for the duration of its journey on the river. She looked up at the white helicopter twenty yards ahead of the boat. Paluzzi and Graham. She couldn't see either of them in the cockpit. As she turned back to the stairs she noticed Moody in the wheelhouse. Moody smiled and gave her a wave. She returned the wave and went below again.

Eastman saw Palmer's car from the window of the mobile police van and went out to meet it.

"Morning, sir," Eastman said.

Palmer looked at his watch. "Actually, it's afternoon, Keith."

Eastman acknowledged his mistake with a forced smile. It was barely ten minutes into the afternoon. But he knew better than to say anything. The old bastard was obviously in one of his moods.

"I was hoping to get over here before the boat left but unfortunately I was held up at the Yard. The Commissioner wanted to see me. And when he gets talking, there's no stopping him." Palmer fumbled in his overcoat pocket for his cigarettes. "Cigarette?"

"Thank you, sir," Eastman replied then took out his lighter and lit both cigarettes.

"Did the boat get off on time?" Palmer asked.

"Yes, sir."

"What about the security arrangements? Is everything going according to plan?"

"It's all under control, sir," Eastman replied. "I'm in constant touch with Whitlock. I've also deployed our men at regular intervals along the route so if something should happen I can bring them into play at a moment's notice."

"And who's running the helicopters?"

"I am, sir. I've got three police choppers up there and UNACO have an unmarked chopper sticking close to the boat. And on top of that, there are two police launches flanking the boat and another five patroling the route. The IRA won't be able to make a move without it being spotted either from the air or from the water."

"I'm glad to hear it." Palmer took a long drag on his cigarette then looked up as a police helicopter swooped low overhead, heading toward Lambeth Bridge. "Dave Thompson rang me this morning."

"Dave Thompson of the *Guardian?*"

"Yes. He received a call earlier today from Kevin Brady."

"So the IRA have accepted responsibility for the attempt on Scoby's life this morning?"

"On the contrary, Brady was quite insistent that the IRA had nothing whatsoever to do with it. He claims the IRA don't have a contract out on Scoby."

"And I suppose he's just as insistent that Gallagher, Mullen and Kerrigan aren't members of the IRA."

"Kerrigan's dead," Palmer said.

"Did Brady say that?"

"No, I received word of it this morning from the Swiss authorities. The helicopter that they used in

Switzerland was found abandoned near a chalet about ten miles outside Lucerne. Kerrigan's body was found in the chalet. He'd been shot."

"First Lynch and now Kerrigan," Eastman said, chewing his lip thoughtfully. "What do you make of it, sir?"

"I don't know. Not yet."

"You don't think there could be some kind of internal power struggle going on within the IRA, do you, sir? It's no secret that Brady and Lynch never got on. That was one of the main reasons why Lynch chose to settle in Switzerland when he got married. And Kerrigan was always close to Lynch. What if Lynch was planning to return to Ireland to launch a campaign to oust Brady as Chief-of-Staff of the Army Council?"

"It's a possibility," Palmer conceded. "But it still doesn't explain where Scoby fits into all of this."

"Dom Lynch was close to Sean Farrell and Fiona Gallagher. What if Lynch and Farrell planned to kill Scoby and then blame Brady for it? After all, a directive like that would have to come from the head of the Army Council. Farrell's arrested before Scoby gets here so it's handed down to Gallagher to carry on in his place. I know it's all hypothetical, sir, but it would give a motive for the murders of Lynch and Kerrigan."

"But Farrell and Gallagher would be implicated as well."

"Not if they were supposedly carrying out an order from the Army Council," Eastman replied.

A rare smile touched the corners of Palmer's mouth. "You know, Keith, you might just have something there. We'll discuss it further this afternoon." The smile vanished as quickly as it had appeared. "I've got to get back to the Yard. I've got a meeting with my opposite number in Special Branch at one o'-

clock. I want to be kept up to date on the situation here."

"Even if nothing's happening, sir?"

"Especially if nothing's happening. At least if I know it's all quiet it might help me to cut down on these damn things." Palmer dropped the cigarette onto the ground, crushed it underfoot, then got back into the car.

Eastman returned to the mobile van. There were five uniformed officers seated in the back of the van, each wearing a pair of headphones, who were in constant touch with the various arms of the Metropolitan Police involved in the security arrangements on and around the river. One of the men caught Eastman's attention and informed him that Whitlock was waiting to talk to him. Eastman sat down in his chair by the door, slipped on a pair of headphones, and was patched through to Whitlock.

"Where have you been?" Whitlock asked.

"The Commander's just been here," Eastman replied. "I had to brief him."

"Well, it's all quiet out here. The highlight so far was when the mayor's wife spilt a glass of red wine down the front of her dress."

"Sounds nasty," Eastman said with a smile. "Oh, by the way, I've got a bit of news for you. Kerrigan's dead. The Swiss authorities found his body in a chalet earlier today. He'd been shot."

"First Lynch, now Kerrigan. Do you think the murders are somehow linked?"

"There doesn't seem to be any evidence to suggest it at present but I've got my own little theory which I've already put to Commander Palmer. I'll discuss it with you later over a beer."

"You're on. Well, I'd better check in with the launches. I'll talk to you again soon."

"Right. Over and out."

* * *

Mullen wiped the sweat from his face with the back of his hand. The wetsuit had become uncomfortably warm. Or was it just his nerves? Fiona looked ice cool as she crouched on the catwalk, scanning the river with the binoculars. He had already tried to talk to her but she had held up a hand to silence him without taking her eyes off the river. He now paced the floor, anxiously waiting for her to give them the go-ahead to move out.

She suddenly cursed loudly.

"What is it?" he asked, pausing mid-stride to look up at her.

"There's a police chopper coming this way," she hissed, pressing herself against the wall as it buzzed low over the warehouse. She waited until the engine had died away then peered cautiously out of the window.

"Can you see it?" Mullen called out.

"It's heading toward the Albert Bridge. It's the first time it's been this far down river which means the *Merry Dancer* can't be too far behind."

She trained the binoculars back on to the Lambeth Bridge. The unmarked white helicopter was already hovering close to the bridge. She smiled to herself as the bow of the *Merry Dancer* came into view. There were two men in the wheelhouse. One was Whitlock. The other was Moody. She watched as he removed his sweat-stained peaked cap, ran his arm across his forehead, then tugged it back over his bald head. She lowered the binoculars and looked round at Mullen, the smile still fixed on her face. She didn't need to say anything. He crossed to the trapdoor and began to strap on his breathing apparatus. The waiting was over . . .

◆ CHAPTER

ELEVEN

Stephen Tanner was one of the most experienced officers in the Air Police. He was a former RAF helicopter pilot who had joined the Metropolitan Police at the end of the Falklands War. In contrast, Bruce Falconer was a rookie who had graduated from the police college only a month before. He was a quiet, soft-spoken youth whose self-assuredness had impressed his superiors and they had decided to put him with Tanner to help toughen up his character. Now, two weeks later, Falconer was already more assertive and Tanner was beginning to warm to his new partner . . .

"Hey, isn't that Stamford Bridge down there?" Tanner said with a wicked grin, pointing to the football stadium in the distance as the helicopter approached Albert Bridge.

"Very funny," Falconer retorted.

"Oh, I'm sorry, I forgot," Tanner said, the grin widening. "You've got tickets for the match this afternoon, haven't you?"

"Yeah, and much good they'll do me now."

"Don't worry, kid, it won't be the last time your day off will be canceled at such short notice," Tanner said, easing the stick to the left, arcing the helicopter in a graceful one-hundred-and-eighty-degree turn.

"You're all heart . . ." Falconer trailed off and grabbed the binoculars.

"What is it?" Tanner asked, his face suddenly serious.

"I thought I saw something down there," Falconer replied without lowering the binoculars.

"Where?"

"In that deserted warehouse over there," Falconer replied, pointing it out.

"I'll take her in for a closer look," Tanner said, banking the helicopter away sharply to the left. "What did you see?"

"I don't know. I thought I saw a movement through one of those broken windows." Falconer cursed angrily and lowered the binoculars as the helicopter descended toward the warehouse. "I'm sorry, I should have been concentrating more carefully on the surroundings."

"Forget it. You say you thought you saw something, that's good enough for me. We'll get the place checked out."

"I'm going to look pretty stupid if it turns out to have been nothing."

"You're going to look a lot more stupid if we don't report it and it turns out to have been that IRA cell." Tanner indicated the radio. "Call it in, kid."

Falconer nodded and reached for the radio.

Fiona lay on the lead swimmer delivery vehicle as it powered its way silently through the cold, murky water toward the barge. Mullen, who was carrying the hermetically sealed container, kept close behind her. They were guided by the powerful lights built into the nose of the SDVs and by the directional beacon detector which was set on the same wavelength as the homing device attached to the hull of the barge.

When they reached the barge, moored in the center of the river, she tethered her SDV to the anchor chain and switched off the light. Then, keeping close to the hull, she removed an optical fiber periscope from her belt and pushed its tip out of the water. It took her a few seconds to get her bearings. She focused on Vauxhall Bridge, which was two hundred yards away from the barge. The *Merry Dancer* was due to turn at the bridge before heading back toward Tower Bridge. The boat was now only a few hundred yards from the bridge. It would begin to turn within the next minute. She slipped the periscope back into its protective sheath then took the transmitter from the pouch on her belt and extended its short aerial. She released the protective cap covering the detonator and pressed the button.

Whitlock was the first person on board the *Merry Dancer* to react to the explosion. Grabbing Scoby by the arm he shoved him roughly to the floor.

"Lie down," Sabrina shouted to the bewildered guests. "And keep your heads down." Then, unholstering her Beretta, she ran, doubled-over, to the window. She could see the source of the explosion. Smoke billowed into the sky as the remains of the blue transit van burned fiercely less than fifty yards away from the bridge.

Whitlock hurried across to where she was crouched and followed her gaze. His radio suddenly crackled into life. "Whitlock here. Over."

"C.W., get everybody off the boat now!" Eastman yelled. "Use the police launch on your starboard side. Do it now!"

Sabrina hurried across to the stairs and began ushering the terrified guests up onto the deck.

"Sabrina's already moving them out as quickly as possible. What's going on out there?"

"All I know at the moment is that two figures have been spotted aboard a barge a couple of hundred yards away from the bridge. And it looks as if one of them's assembling what could be a rocket launcher. I've already instructed the chopper pilot and two police launches to close in on the barge. Hopefully it'll distract them long enough for you to evacuate the *Merry Dancer*."

"Understood. Call Fabio, tell him to get over there as well. He's no use to us hovering over the boat."

"Will do. Over and out."

Whitlock clipped the radio back onto his belt then hurried up the stairs and onto the deck where Sabrina was busy helping the last of the women onto the launch. The men had yet to be transferred. Whitlock looked anxiously behind him. He still couldn't see beyond the police launch which was protecting the boat's exposed flank. And he knew time was running out fast . . .

"For God's sake, hurry up!" Fiona snarled at Mullen.

"Almost finished," Mullen retorted as he attached the tail section to the high-explosive round.

Fiona had unwrapped the two Ingram MAC II machine-pistols as soon as they had boarded the barge and she held one in each hand, waiting for the police helicopter to come within range. Mullen slotted the round into the barrel of the RPG-7 launcher and hoisted it onto his shoulder.

"Can you get in a clear shot?" she asked, glancing at Mullen.

Mullen squinted through the sights. "No, but if I

take out the police launch in front of the boat, the
force of the blast should be enough to take out the
Merry Dancer as well. These are high-explosive
rounds, remember?"

"Then do it," she snapped.

The helicopter buzzed low over the barge. Forced
to duck, Mullen tried to concentrate again on the target. Fiona fired a burst upward as it wheeled away.
When the helicopter dived low again Fiona opened
fire with both machine-pistols but could make no impression on the bullet-proof fuselage. Again Mullen
had to take evasive action. Cursing loudly, he lined
up the retreating helicopter in the sights of the
launcher, then squeezed the trigger. The stabilizing
fins snapped open the moment the missile left the
barrel, giving it a slow roll as it homed in on its target.
The warhead automatically armed itself after five
meters and the helicopter was still trying desperately
to turn out of the path of the grenade when it struck
the side of the fuselage. The helicopter partially disintegrated in a hail of searing debris that rained down
onto the water. The twisted remains of the fuselage
spiraled grotesquely downward into the river, sink-
ing within seconds in a bubbling hiss of molten
metal.

Mullen punched the air triumphantly then
reached for the second grenade, screwed the tail onto
the missile, then slotted it into the breech. Fiona
looked around as two police launches were closing in
on them fast.

Suddenly the unmarked helicopter wheeled away
from the *Merry Dancer* and arced in front of the barge,
forcing Mullen to jerk his finger off the trigger. For a
second his anger got the better of him and he lined up
the helicopter in his sights. But he quickly checked
himself. He only had one round left. He had to use it
on the boat. As the helicopter came back into range,
Fiona sprayed it with both machine-pistols. The clips

ran out and she hurriedly replaced them with fresh ones but before she could shoot, a burst of machine-gun fire raked the barge. She flung herself to the floor as the bullets peppered the side of the boat. Fiona watched in horror as a bullet caught Mullen in the arm and the launcher slid from his hands, disappearing into the water. Mullen looked around at her, his expression a mixture of pain and disbelief. She immediately strapped on her self-breathing apparatus again and slipped the mask back over her face.

Mullen stumbled over to where his kit lay, crying out in agony as he tried to use his injured arm to pick it up. He turned to Fiona for help and his eyes widened in disbelief at the sight of the Ingram levelled at his chest. "What are you doing?" he stammered.

"You're no use to me anymore," she replied contemptuously.

"Fiona . . . please," he said desperately. "It's only a flesh wound. I can manage. I won't hold you up. We can still get Scoby."

"I don't need you for the next stage of the operation."

"You don't know that until you've opened the envelope."

"I don't need to open it. I've known the details of all three operations from the start. The envelopes were only for your benefit. I'd have killed you irrespective of what happened here today."

Mullen met her eyes. There was no recognition. No remorse. Only disdain. What a fool he'd been . . .

She fired. The bullet ripped across his chest, knocking him back against the side of the barge. He dropped to his knees, the disbelief still mirrored in his eyes, then toppled face forward onto the tarpaulin in front of him. She fired another burst at the approaching helicopter then discarded the machine-pistol and disappeared into the water. Police divers, who were already closing in on the barge, immediately made for the spot where she'd disappeared.

"She just gunned him down in cold blood," Graham said, still fanning the water with the Uzi he had withdrawn from Scotland Yard that morning.

Paluzzi didn't reply.

Graham looked at Paluzzi and realized something was wrong. He was sweating and his face was twisted in pain. "Fabio, what is it?"

"He's not the only one she shot," Paluzzi hissed through clenched teeth.

"Where are you hit?" Graham asked anxiously.

"My side. It feels like the bullet's smashed through my rib cage. Christ, it hurts." Paluzzi looked at Graham. "I'm going to try and put down on that abandoned wharf further down river. I don't know if I'll make it though. I'll take the chopper down close to the water so you can bail out. OK?"

"Like hell I will," Graham retorted sharply. "We're both going to make it to the docks."

Paluzzi shook his head and lowered the helicopter toward the water. "OK, jump."

"Quit wasting time and get the hell over to those docks," Graham snapped.

Suddenly Paluzzi reached over and unbuckled Graham's safety belt. Graham was still fumbling with the belt when Paluzzi tilted the helicopter sharply to the side. Losing his grip, Graham tumbled headlong through the open doorway and into the water.

Paluzzi levelled out the helicopter and headed toward the abandoned docks. He knew there were other areas closer where he could try and put down, but if the helicopter were to crash it might endanger innocent people. No, he had to keep to the river and make for the docks. He gritted his teeth as the pain seared through his body with every move he made. The sweat stung his eyes but he made no attempt to wipe it away. He needed both hands for the controls.

He felt himself slipping over the abyss of consciousness. The control panel blurred in front of him and he squeezed his eyes closed then opened them again. They were in focus again. Keep your mind active. He thought about Claudine. And Dario. Stay awake for them. If he pulled through this he'd take more notice of what Claudine had to say in future. That was a promise. He knew she wanted to go back to Italy. They could go. He'd take the post with the *NOCS*. But he had to stay awake. The dials blurred again. He blinked rapidly. This time they remained blurred. His hand slipped off the stick and the helicopter swiveled sharply to one side before he managed to regain control of it. The pads skimmed across the water. He couldn't move his hands. They felt like lead. He wouldn't make the docks. He was going to crash . . .

Graham was picked up by a police launch. He refused any medical attention but did accept a blanket which he threw around his shoulders. The water had been freezing. He was glad of the warmth. He remained on deck as the launch sped after the retreating helicopter. They lost sight of the helicopter as it disappeared around a bend in the river. Seconds later there was an ear-splitting explosion and they watched in horror as plumes of thick, black smoke spiraled hundreds of feet up into the sky. But it was only when the launch negotiated the bend that the full extent of the carnage became apparent. The helicopter had plowed into a mobile crane on the wharf where Paluzzi had hoped to put down. The helicopter had exploded on impact, and the twisted remains of the tail section now lay on the other side of the wharf. The fuselage was already a blackened shell as the flames continued to lick around it.

Graham sank slowly onto the bench behind him

and buried his face in his hands. The captain put a consoling hand on Graham's shoulder. Nobody could have survived that.

"Sir!" the look-out shouted to the captain from his vantage point above the bridge. "There's someone in the water."

Graham discarded the blanket and hurried over to the railing.

"My God, he's right," the captain said in disbelief, staring at the motionless figure floating in the water thirty yards away from the boat's starboard bow.

Graham dived into the water before the captain had a chance to stop him. He swam with powerful strokes to where Paluzzi was floating, his head lolling on the front of his life jacket. He gently lifted Paluzzi's head. Blood was streaming down his face from a gash under his hairline.

The police launch came alongside the two men and willing hands reached down to pull Paluzzi out of the water. He was already stretched out on the deck when Graham scrambled back onto the launch. A blanket was immediately thrown around Graham's shoulders again.

"Is he alive?" Graham asked anxiously, standing over the inert figure.

"Yes, but he's lost consciousness and his pulse is very weak," the medic replied.

"He must have bailed out at the last possible moment," the captain said, staring at Paluzzi.

"Yeah," Graham agreed. "He could have put down earlier but he specifically made for that abandoned pier knowing that if he did pass out before he reached it there would be no risk of any innocent casualties."

"And that's obviously why he dumped you in the river first," the captain said.

Graham nodded. "Where are we headed?"

"Cadogan Pier. I've already radioed ahead for an

ambulance. He'll be taken straight to Guy's Hospital."

The medic stood up. "His weak pulse is only to be expected due to the amount of blood he's lost. The head wound's my main concern. It's a deep laceration. He'll certainly need a brain scan once he reaches the hospital."

"What about the bullet wound?" Graham asked.

"The bullet passed straight through him. It's my guess he's probably broken a couple of ribs as well, judging by the angle of the bullet. I can't be sure, you understand, not without the proper equipment." The medic indicated Graham's wet clothes. "I suggest you change out of those. You'll have pneumonia before you know it. There are clothes below. I'll get one of the crew to show you."

Graham looked at Paluzzi once more then followed the man down the hatchway.

Fiona had already adjusted the directional beacon detector before she went over the side of the barge. So, while the police divers scanned the area around the barge with powerful underwater lights, she had already made good her escape on the swimmer delivery vehicle. Her destination was a row of houseboats further down river. She had never intended to return to the warehouse. She knew the authorities could have stumbled on to the car while they were away. It would have been too risky.

She used the detector to home in on the beacon secured to the side of the houseboat belonging to a couple who, according to the directive, had been on holiday for the past ten days. They weren't expected back for another week. She tethered the SDV to the anchor chain then unloaded the oxygen cylinders and flippers into the water before clambering onto the deck. It didn't matter if she was seen. In the unlikely event of someone raising the alarm, she would be long gone before the authorities arrived.

She discarded the mask over the side then hurried down the stairs and used a duplicate key to get into the main cabin. Stripping off her wetsuit she went, as instructed, to the built-in cupboard. A hold-all had been placed there, containing a pair of jeans, a sweater and a pair of moccasins. She dressed quickly, stuffed the wetsuit into the hold-all and carried the bag down the gangplank to the shore. She walked to the nearest tube station where she boarded a train for Finsbury Park.

Graham got to his feet when he saw Whitlock hurrying down the hospital corridor toward him.

"I got here as fast as I could," Whitlock said breathlessly. "How is he?"

"He's going to be OK," Graham replied, patting Whitlock's arm reassuringly.

"What did the doctor say?"

"The bullet entered his side and exited through his back. Amazingly, there's no real damage other than a couple of cracked ribs. And he needed twenty-two stitches for the gash on his head."

"But no brain damage?"

"No."

"Thank God for that," Whitlock said with a relieved sigh. "So have you been in to see him yet?"

"No, not yet. He's still under sedation. The nurse said she'd call me when he came around."

Whitlock sat down on the bench and dabbed his forehead with his handkerchief. "I've been on the phone to Sergei for the last forty minutes. That's why I'm so late. He's been taking some heavy flak since the news broke over there, and not only from the Secretary-General. He's also had a call from the White House. The man himself."

"You'd think Scoby was already worm bait judging by the reaction," Graham snorted.

"Most of this is down to Tillman. He's been on the phone ever since they got back to the hotel. And he's not being very complimentary about UNACO."

"What do you expect?" Graham retorted, his lips curled in disgust. "He's been on our case from the start. But what can you expect from a lackey? He's kissing butt wherever he can to keep on Scoby's good side. He knows Scoby's on the up. And he'll do anything to stick with him."

"The remains of the chopper have been found in the Thames," Whitlock said. "But still no sign of Tanner and Falconer."

"The missile scored a direct hit on the cockpit," Graham said grimly. "There's no chance they survived that."

"I still don't understand why she killed Mullen," Whitlock said, scratching his head.

"All I know is that she must have pumped a good twelve rounds into him before she went over the side," Graham replied. "But what got me was how cool she was. She just turned the Skorpion on him and gunned him down. Hell, he didn't stand a chance."

The door opposite swung open and a nurse emerged into the corridor. She smiled at Graham. "Mr. Paluzzi's just regained consciousness. You can go in now if you like. But not for long. He's still very weak."

"Can we both go in?" Whitlock asked.

"Yes. Is either of you called C. W.?" she asked.

"Yes, I am," Whitlock replied in surprise. "Why?"

"He's been asking for you ever since he came round. I'll be back in a few minutes to give him another sedative."

Whitlock waited until the nurse had left then pushed open the door and peered into the ward.

"It's not contagious," Paluzzi said in a croaky voice. His face was pale and his eyes were still glazed from the effects of the anesthetic. He managed a weak smile when Graham entered the room behind Whitlock. "Hey, Mike, how you doing?"

"Better than you by the looks of it," Graham replied, pulling up a chair and sitting down. "How you feeling, buddy?"

"How do I look?"

"Like a stiff," Graham replied with a grin.

"Then you know how I feel." Paluzzi looked at Whitlock. "Did Gallagher get away?"

Whitlock nodded. "Yes."

"And what about Scoby?" Paluzzi asked.

"He's fine," Whitlock replied. "He asked me to send you his best wishes for a speedy recovery."

"What can I say?" Paluzzi retorted facetiously.

"Say it in Italian," Graham said disdainfully. "That way you won't offend any of the nurses."

"That's enough, you two," Whitlock said with a reprimanding scowl.

"Where's Sabrina?" Paluzzi asked.

"She's at the hotel. Somebody has to keep an eye on the senator," Whitlock told him. "But she did say she'd be along to see you sometime before we go over to the ambassador's house tonight."

"Does Claudine know I'm here?"

Whitlock shook his head. "I thought it best to talk to you first about that. Do you want me to call her?"

"I would rather do it myself," Paluzzi replied. "If I know Claudine, she won't take it well. But if I can reassure her personally that I'll be OK, it'll help to soften the blow."

"If she wants to fly out, tell her to book the flight and UNACO will reimburse her for the ticket."

"I'll tell her, thanks," Paluzzi replied.

The door opened and the nurse entered the room.

"I'm sorry, gentlemen, but you'll have to leave now. You can come back again during visiting hours."

"Of course," Whitlock replied.

"C. W., wait," Paluzzi said. He looked across at the nurse. "Could you give us another couple of minutes, please? It's very important."

"The doctor was very insistent that you get as much rest as possible," the nurse replied.

"Please, it's very important," Paluzzi pleaded weakly.

"OK. Two minutes. But then I'm coming back to give you another sedative."

Paluzzi waited until the nurse had gone before looking up at Graham. "Mike, I need to talk to C. W."

"Sure thing," Graham replied, getting to his feet.

"Wait a minute, Mike," Whitlock said, putting a restraining hand lightly on Graham's arm. He turned back to Paluzzi. "You're going back to Italy, aren't you? It's OK to talk in front of Mike, he'll find out about it soon enough."

"Yes," Paluzzi said softly. "How did you know?"

"I've known since you first mentioned it to me," Whitlock replied with a smile. "You'd have been crazy to have turned it down. And obviously what happened earlier this afternoon has made the decision that much easier for you."

"Hey, could somebody tell me what this is all about?" Graham cut in before Paluzzi could reply.

"You remember my boss at the *NOCS*, Brigadier Michele Pesco?" Paluzzi asked Graham.

"I heard about him but I never actually met him," Graham replied. "He was one of the reasons why you left the *NOCS* to come over to us."

"That's right," Paluzzi agreed. "Well, he was relieved of his command two days ago. The Joint Chiefs-of-Staff offered the job to me. It's something I'd always wanted ever since I joined the *NOCS*. And much as I want to stay with UNACO, I know the chance may never come again."

"C. W.'s right, you'd have been crazy to turn it down," Graham said. "Have you told Claudine yet?"

"She doesn't even know I've been offered the position. I'll tell her when I see her. I know she'll be thrilled. She's never really settled in New York."

"He made the right decision," Graham said once they were in the corridor.

"I know."

"Who'll be sent out to replace him?"

"Nobody's being sent out," Whitlock replied.

"Give us a break, C. W.," Graham shot back. "We were stretched as it was even before Fabio was injured. How do you expect Sabrina and me to carry the workload by ourselves?"

"I never said Fabio *wasn't* being replaced," Whitlock corrected him. "What I did say was that nobody's being sent over to replace him."

Graham stopped in his tracks and eyed Whitlock suspiciously. "You?"

"It was the obvious solution. I cleared it with Sergei before I came over here."

"Does Sabrina know?"

"Not yet. But then it's not for me to tell her. That's your job as head of Strike Force Three."

"What are you talking about, C. W.? You're still the senior man around here."

"I'm still the Deputy Director of UNACO, but you call the shots in your team. And I'm now part of your team."

"You mean I now have rank over you in the field?" Graham said with obvious delight.

"As long as I'm a part of your team, yes." Whitlock paused at the entrance and wagged a finger of warning at him. "But don't push it or I'll have your arse the moment we get back to New York."

Yeah, you probably would, Graham thought to

himself as he hurried after Whitlock, who was already making his way back to the car.

When Fiona left the safe house for the last time she was wearing a plain black skirt, a baggy red sweater and the familiar black trilby which was tugged down firmly over her spiky blonde hair. She took the tube to Heathrow Airport and was told that the Belfast flight was scheduled to leave on time. After checking in she bought a copy of the *Independent* then went through to the cafeteria and treated herself to a coffee and a sandwich. She found a seat by the window then opened her overnight bag and withdrew the envelope containing the third plan for the assassination of Scoby: the letter "C" was inscribed on its cover. She didn't bother opening it. Instead she put it down on the table then turned her attention to the front page of the *Independent*.

She was on her second coffee when her flight was announced over the loudspeaker. She picked up her overnight bag and made her way to the departure lounge, leaving the unopened envelope on the table.

The envelope was discovered by a cleaner after the flight had taken off. She handed it in to her supervisor who opened it, hoping to discover an address so he could forward it on to the owner. He looked inside. It was obviously some prank: it was empty. He tossed the envelope into the bin at the side of his desk and went back to his paperwork.

◆ CHAPTER

TWELVE

The rain pummeled the Mercedes as it hurtled along a deserted road in County Armagh. Inside were three men. The driver, Hagen, and McAuley, who sat beside him, had both served time for their part in an IRA bombing campaign on the British mainland in the early eighties. McAuley was armed. The third man, who was seated in the back of the car, was in his late thirties with thinning brown hair and a pale, cadaverous face. Kevin Brady was the Chief-of-Staff of the IRA's military wing, the Army Council. He was a cold, dispassionate man who had an unnerving habit of speaking in an unvarying monotone. Quick to reward initiative and even quicker to punish failure, he had been known to order the execution of entire families simply by a nod of his head or a snap of his fingers if he thought it would prove a point. The majority of those on the Army Council were prepared to overlook his faults because of his tactical successes in the field, but there were a small number who were fiercely opposed to his brutal methods, especially those relating to internal discipline, and who felt that the only way to displace him would be to have him killed . . .

The Mercedes turned off the main road and sped through an open gate onto a dirt road. An armed Provo, his face hidden under a black balaclava, ghosted out from behind a bush and closed the gate behind the car. They continued along the dirt road for another three hundred yards until they reached a farmhouse. Hagen brought the car to a halt. Two masked Provos stood outside, both armed with Armalite rifles. Jumping out of the car, McAuley opened the back door for Brady while one of the armed Provos knocked on the farmhouse door. Brady was ushered inside and led to a room at the end of the corridor. His escort rapped twice on the door then gestured for Brady to enter.

The three men sitting behind a table at the far end of the room were all senior members of the Army Council: Pat Taylor, an Enniskillen businessman and a former Army Council Chief-of-Staff; Michael Kelly, once a leading Sinn Fein councillor; and Kieran O'Connell, the former editor of the official IRA newspaper, *An Phoblacht*.

Taylor pointed to the wooden chair in the middle of the room. "Sit down."

Brady crossed to the chair and sat down.

"You know why you've been called here, don't you?" Taylor said as he tamped a wad of tobacco into the bowl of his pipe.

"Yes."

"Did you issue a directive to Fiona Gallagher to assassinate Senator Jack Scoby?" O'Connell asked.

Brady's lifeless eyes locked onto O'Connell's face. "No."

"Then who issued the directive?" O'Connell demanded.

"You tell me," Brady replied in his deadpan voice.

"Now you listen to me—"

"Kieran," Taylor cut in quickly. "We aren't going to get anywhere by squabbling amongst ourselves like this." He looked across at Brady. "An order like that would have had to come from the Chief-of-Staff or one of his senior officers."

"I didn't give the order and neither did any of my senior officers," Brady told him.

Kelly got to his feet and crossed to the window. "There's been a rumor going around these last few weeks that Dominic Lynch intended to come back from Switzerland to try and oust you, not only as Chief-of-Staff, but also from the Army Council as well."

"I've also heard that rumor," Brady replied.

Kelly looked around at Brady. "Lynch and Farrell were close friends, weren't they?"

"And you think they planned this to discredit me?" Brady sat forward and stared at the wooden floor. His face remained expressionless. "It's possible. But then who killed Lynch?"

"Gallagher, probably," Kelly said after a thoughtful pause. "That way it would leave the door open for Farrell to challenge you instead. She kills Kerrigan and Mullen because they know too much and all the time the finger's pointing at you because he'd already given the order to silence McGuire."

"That's pure fantasy and you know it," O'Connell said, coming to Farrell's defense. "Sean and Dom were inseparable. It's inconceivable that Sean would allow Fiona to murder his best friend. I just don't buy it."

Taylor's worst fears were being realized. It was fast becoming a conflict of personalities. O'Connell, the moderate who would certainly have backed Lynch had he returned to challenge Brady; and Kelly, the hard-liner who was Brady's most vociferous supporter in the Army Council. He had to steer the issue back on course. "Who gave the order is irrelevant right now. What we have to do is stop Gallagher before she does manage to take Scoby out."

"Can you find her?" Kelly asked Brady.

"I don't think he should be in on this," O'Connell said before Brady could answer. "What if he really is the mastermind behind this whole conspiracy? He'd be able to make sure she was always one step ahead of us."

"You're out of line, Kieran," Kelly snapped. "What proof do you have to substantiate these allegations?"

"That's enough," Taylor cut in, glaring at both men. "We've got enough problems as it is without you two bickering like this." He turned back to Brady. "I want her stopped. And if you can't do it, we'll find someone who can. Do I make myself understood?"

"Perfectly." Brady stood up. "And I can employ any methods I see fit to find her?"

"Yes," Taylor replied bluntly. "But just make sure you bring her in alive."

"That may not be possible—"

"Alive," Taylor interceded sharply. "She's our one chance of getting to the bottom of this."

Brady left the room without another word. Moments later they heard the Mercedes drive off.

"You don't honestly think he'll bring her in alive, do you?" O'Connell said contemptuously, breaking the lingering silence. "He'll put a bullet in her the first opportunity he gets. It's the only way he'll be sure of silencing her."

"You're sailing close to the wind, Kieran," Kelly said, levelling a finger at him. "You've been on Kevin's back ever since this story broke this afternoon."

"That's because I believe he's behind it. We both know that Fiona's not a maverick and that she wouldn't touch something like this unless the authorization had come from the very top. And that means Brady." O'Connell turned to Taylor. "I think it was a mistake to send Brady after her, Pat."

"We'll see, Kieran," Taylor replied thoughtfully. "We'll see."

Brady had spent much of his adult life either in jail or on the run. He had spent seven years at Belfast's Long Kesh prison, more popularly known as "The Maze," for his part in the murder of an off-duty policeman in the late seventies. It was while he was there that he had first met Sammy Kane. They had become good friends and Brady now regarded Kane as the one man in the Revolutionary Army he could trust implicitly. He had rewarded that trust by appointing Kane as his Adjutant-General, his second-in-charge in the Army Council.

Kane was three years Brady's junior with a burly physique and cropped blond hair. He was Brady's conscience and had, on more than one occasion, talked Brady out of a course of action which he felt could have been detrimental not only to his future as Chief-of-Staff, but also to the Cause in general. Kane claimed to be the only person who really understood him. Well, most of the time . . .

Kane had already been at the safe house on the outskirts of Keady for over an hour when the Mercedes pulled up outside. As Hagen drove off, McAuley and Brady entered the house. McAuley disappeared into the kitchen while Brady went through to the lounge and closed the door behind him.

"How did it go?" Kane asked.

"I've been told to find Gallagher."

"And?"

"I've got to bring her in alive." Brady took off his

overcoat and draped it over the back of the sofa. "I'll take a drop of whiskey if there's any. I'm frozen."

Kane took a bottle of whiskey and two glasses from the sideboard. He poured out two generous measures and handed one of the glasses to Brady. "There was a phone call for you while you were out. Martin Navarro, calling from New York."

"Navarro? What did he want?"

"He didn't say, only that you were to call him back as soon as you got in."

Brady dialed out on a secure line then sat down on the arm of the sofa. When the call was answered he asked for Navarro, taking a sip of whiskey as he waited for Navarro to come to the phone.

"Brady?" Navarro snapped down the line.

"Speaking," came the toneless reply. "What do you want?"

"I want to know what the hell's going on over there. Why is there an IRA contract out on Jack Scoby?"

"Why are you suddenly so interested in Scoby's welfare?"

"That doesn't concern you," Navarro shot back indignantly. "Just get the contract lifted."

"I can't."

"What do you mean you can't?" Navarro snarled.

"I can't because I never authorized it."

"Then who did?"

"We don't know that," Brady replied.

"So what you're saying is that you've got a renegade cell running around trying to kill Scoby?"

"It would seem so."

"And what do you intend to do about it?" Navarro yelled.

"We're looking into it. Now, if that's all—"

"No it's not all," Navarro cut in angrily. "You don't seem to be taking this very seriously, Brady. Well, let me put it to you another way. We know of at least ten of your operatives who are currently in hiding over here in the United States. Some of your top field operatives, I believe. As of this morning, contracts have been put out on all of them. We also have them under twenty-four-hour surveillance. So if anything should happen to Scoby, all ten would be hit simultaneously. But that would only be the beginning. All future arms shipments from the United States, bound for Ireland, would be frozen. Then your Noraid offices around the country would be mysteriously fire-bombed. Then your Noraid employees would be targeted, their families threatened, their property vandalized. I could go on indefinitely. But I think you get the picture, don't you?"

"I get the picture. Scoby must be worth a lot of money to you if you're prepared to go to these lengths to protect him."

"More than you could ever imagine. Call me if there're any further developments."

The line went dead. Brady replaced the receiver then drank the remainder of the whiskey.

"Why are the Mafia suddenly so interested in Scoby?" Kane asked.

"Why indeed?" Brady replied thoughtfully. "He's obviously worth a considerable amount of money to them."

"And if Gallagher takes him out, they lose it all?"

"So do we."

Kane frowned but didn't push for an explanation. He knew Brady would tell him what he needed to know. In his own time. "So how do we go about trying to find her?"

"We don't," Brady replied.

Kane frowned. "What do you mean?"

"When you're drowning, you'll grab hold of any lifeline if there's a chance it'll save you." Brady picked up the receiver then looked around at Kane.

"Close the door behind you on your way out,
Sammy."

Kane knew better than to argue. He left the room,
closing the door behind him.

Palmer opened a fresh pack of cigarettes, lit one
then sat back in his chair and stared at the two tele-
phones on his desk. One red. One white. The white
phone was his outside line which had remained virtually silent for most of the day. He had drafted in
three senior officers to deal with the deluge of Press
inquiries he knew would follow the attempt on
Scoby's life earlier that afternoon. Scotland Yard's
switchboard had indeed been besieged by reporters
desperate to get a story for the next edition. But he
had given the officers strict instructions to stonewall
all inquiries. He would give a press conference later
in the afternoon.

The red phone was his scrambler line. He had
rarely been off it in the last two hours. He had already
spoken to Kolchinsky on two separate occasions. The
first call had been outwardly cordial, but tense. Neither of them was prepared to shoulder the blame for
what had happened. The second call, an hour later,
had been franker and more constructive. By then
they'd both been briefed in greater detail by their re-
spective operatives and were able to reflect more
clearly on the situation. They had decided that they
would stand together. After all, it had been a joint operation from the start. A responsibility shared . . .

The Police Commissioner had rung demanding
that the results of a full inquiry were to be on his desk
no later than Monday morning. Palmer had been
quick to assure him that a detailed investigation into
the incident was already under way.

Palmer rubbed his eyes wearily and reached for
the cigarette smouldering in the ashtray. The white

phone rang. He groaned then reached over and picked up the receiver.

It was one of the officers he'd assigned to fend off the Press. "I'm sorry to trouble you, sir, but I've got someone on the other line who claims to be Kevin Brady. He insists on speaking to you."

"What?" Palmer said in amazement. "Did he say what he wanted?"

"No, sir. Only that he wouldn't speak to anyone other than you."

"Have you put a trace on the call?"

"Yes, sir."

"Good. Put him through." Palmer waited until he heard the connection then immediately transferred the call to his scrambled line. He picked up the red receiver. "Commander Palmer speaking."

"This is Brady," came the impassive reply. "I assume we're speaking on a secure line?"

"Of course," Palmer replied, a suspicion still lingering in his mind that the caller may yet turn out to be some ingenious Press reporter out to get an exclusive for his paper. He knew only too well the lengths they would go to in order to scoop their rivals.

"I'm sure you've already put a trace on this call so I'll get straight to the point. We want to find Fiona Gallagher as much as you do."

"So your Press officer said in his statement to the media," Palmer replied contemptuously. "But frankly I don't buy it for one minute."

"If you want to talk about it further I'll be in Warrenpoint tonight. It's a town close to the border with Southern Ireland. The Stills Hotel. Eight o'clock. Ask at the desk for Pat Gorman. Come alone. And unarmed. And don't waste your time by sending in any of your strong-arm boys because I won't be there until I know the area's been declared safe. The ball's in your court, Palmer."

Palmer slowly replaced the receiver. Moments

later the telephone rang again. The call had been traced to Keady in County Armagh, but there hadn't been time to pinpoint its exact location.

Palmer stubbed out the cigarette then lit another one. There was no doubt in his mind now that he had been speaking to Kevin Brady. Michael Nelson had been one of the anti-terrorist squad's top undercover operatives in Belfast in the late eighties. He had disappeared suddenly and a week later his body had been found in an alley in west Belfast. He had been tortured then shot in the back of the head. His murder had never been solved. Nelson was his undercover name. It had never been revealed to the Press that his real name was Patrick Gorman . . .

He dialed the Grosvenor House Hotel and asked the switchboard operator to put him through to Whitlock's room. It was urgent.

Half an hour later, Whitlock was sitting in Palmer's office.

"It could be a trap," Whitlock said when Palmer had finished telling him about Brady's call.

"Don't you think I know that?" Palmer replied. "But what if he's on the level? What if he's genuinely as much in the dark about this as we are? More importantly, what if he knows something that could lead us to her?"

"And *what if* you're wrong?"

"I know I'm an IRA target. It goes with the job. But I've got a feeling about this. It goes against everything I've learnt in this business, but I think he's on the level."

"Was there anything in his voice to suggest that?"

Palmer managed a rare smile. "You obviously don't know Kevin Brady. He never shows any emotion, either on his face or in his voice. It's uncanny. You'll see."

"I'll see?" Whitlock retorted suspiciously.

"I'd like you to fly to Warrenpoint with me later this afternoon. I know you're supposed to be attending the banquet at Winfield House tonight but I'm sure your operatives can cover for you. If, as I believe, Fiona Gallagher is the last remaining member of this cell still alive, then it's hardly likely that she will try anything at the ambassador's house tonight. No, it's my bet that she'll try and take the senator out at the church tomorrow." Palmer tapped the ash from his cigarette into the ashtray. "Of course the decision's entirely up to you whether you accompany me or not."

"It's a long shot but I guess right now we should be grabbing at anything that comes our way. OK, I'll make the necessary excuses to the senator and the American ambassador. Are we taking a backup team in with us?"

"I don't think that would be a good idea, do you?"

"We could take Keith Eastman."

"He's flying out to Dugaill tonight. I want the area around the church secured by the time the senator's helicopter arrives tomorrow morning. We can't afford any more slip-ups."

"What time will we leave for Warrenpoint?"

"I can have a light plane ready for take-off in an hour. Do you need to go back to the hotel for anything?"

"No, I can arrange things with Mike over the phone."

"Help yourself," Palmer said, pushing the white telephone toward Whitlock. "I'll have a word with Keith. Then I'll have to clear it with the Commissioner. I'm not quite sure how he's going to react to the idea of us holding a clandestine meeting with Britain's most wanted criminal, but right now I don't see that we've got much choice."

* * *

Sabrina knocked on the door of Paluzzi's private ward. He immediately folded over the copy of the *London Evening Standard* he had been reading and beckoned her into the room.

"How are you feeling?" she asked as she pulled up a chair and sat down.

"My ribs still hurt like hell but at least the headache's gone. That was driving me mad." Paluzzi eyed the magazines in her hand. "Are they for me?"

She handed them to him. "I picked them up on the way over here. I know how boring it can get stuck in a hospital bed."

"These are great. Thanks." He put them on the bedside table. "You were laid up in hospital a few years ago, weren't you?"

"Don't remind me," she replied, pulling a face. "I spent four months at the American Hospital of Paris."

"What happened exactly?"

"I was involved in an accident at Le Mans." She nodded when she saw the surprise on his face. "I was very rebellious in those days. I'd do anything to spite my parents. So when they told me not to enter the race I naturally went and did the exact opposite. I lost control of the car and ended up in hospital. I got off lightly. A punctured lung and multiple fractures. The car was a complete write-off. But it was just the sort of jolt I needed to bring me to my senses. I decided it was time to grow up and do something constructive with my life. So I joined the Feds . . ." She trailed off with a sheepish grin. "I haven't been here two minutes and I'm already boring you to death with my life history."

"Hardly boring," Paluzzi replied.

"Well, enough of me. I hear congratulations are in

order. Mike told me you're going back to Italy to head the *NOCS*. We'll be sorry to lose you."

"I'm sorry to be going. But it's for the best in the long term."

"Have you told Claudine yet?"

"I phoned her earlier this afternoon. She's thrilled to be going back home again."

"What did she say when you told her you were in hospital?"

"You know what . . ."

"Women are like?" Sabrina finished with a smile. "There's a maternal instinct in all of us. Mike's on at me about it all the time."

"I guess it's just a woman's way of showing that she cares," Paluzzi said, watching her closely for any reaction.

"I guess," she replied with a quick shrug. "Is Claudine coming over?"

"Yes. And she's bringing Dario with her. The flight's due in at Heathrow around eleven tonight. So I'll probably get to see them in the morning."

"I bet you're really looking forward to seeing them again."

"Of course. Especially little Dario. He's changed my life. Kids, they're really fantastic."

"I know," she replied with a smile.

"Have you ever thought about having kids of your own one day?"

"My parents keep hinting that I should find a husband and settle down. I know my mother would kill for a grandchild. But it would mean leaving UNACO, especially if I did decide to have kids. And I'm not ready for that. I sometimes wonder if I'm ever going to be ready for it. They say you'll know when the right person comes along. Well, he hasn't shown yet."

"Hasn't he?" Paluzzi said, casting a questioning look in her direction.

"Mike?" She shook her head. "He's great as a friend. But that's as far as it goes."

"As far as who's concerned?"

"As far as we're both concerned. And even if I did want to take it further, which I don't, I know he wouldn't be interested. There will only ever be one woman for Mike. And that's Carrie. He was absolutely crazy about her." She glanced at her watch. "Well, if you've quite finished playing matchmaker, I'd better be getting back to the hotel. I've still got to get ready for this do tonight."

"I wish I was going with you guys."

"I don't know why. These embassy functions are always a major yawn. I'll be glad when it's over."

"I'd still rather be there than stuck in this damn bed," he said.

"Hey, you've got Claudine and Dario here from tomorrow. I'm sure you can survive one night by yourself. Read those mags I brought for you."

"I hope I'll see you and Mike before you head back to the US on Monday."

"You can count on it," she told him. "We'll drop by after we get back from Ireland tomorrow night. Promise. OK, I've got to go."

"Thanks for coming round," Paluzzi said.

"Sure," she replied as she crossed to the door.

"I still say you two would make a good couple," he called out after her.

"And I still say you're wrong. See you tomorrow."

He smiled to himself. He had been intrigued to know whether Sabrina's feelings for Graham went deeper than just friendship. Now he had his answer. Well, he thought he did . . .

◆ CHAPTER

THIRTEEN

The Piper Seneca touched down on a deserted field on the outskirts of Warrenpoint and taxied to within a few feet of the white Rover parked at the end of the field.

When Palmer and Whitlock disembarked from the plane they were met by an RUC officer who introduced himself as Detective-Inspector Duncan Reeves. Although Palmer didn't know him personally, he had been recommended by Eastman who had worked with him on several operations in the past.

"I heard about John Marsh," Reeves said as they walked toward the unmarked police car. "He always seemed a very dependable sort. I was absolutely staggered when Keith told me he'd been arrested on suspicion of being an IRA mole."

"A lot of us were staggered by the news," Palmer replied as they reached the car.

"I thought it better if we dispensed with a driver," Reeves said, opening the back door for them. "This way we can talk freely."

"Good thinking," Palmer said. "So tell us about the Stills Hotel."

"It's a dive, sir," Reeves replied, starting the engine. "It's owned by a Provo by the name of Joseph Meehan. He's got a form as long as your arm. A particularly nasty piece of work."

"Aren't they all?" Palmer retorted, tight-lipped.

"He's worse than most. He's a heavy drinker who'll go out of his way to pick a fight. And he knows how to handle himself even when he's tanked up to the lip."

"Sounds like he could liven up the evening," Whitlock said.

Reeves turned the car out onto the main road into Warrenpoint. "I doubt you'll come across him tonight. He's usually out playing poker on a Saturday night."

"Any sign of Brady?" Palmer asked.

"Nothing so far, sir. But that's to be expected. He won't make a move until he's satisfied the area's safe. Kane was seen entering the hotel earlier this evening and, as far as we know, he's still there. He's obviously going to be Brady's point man at the rendezvous."

It was another ten minutes before they reached the RUC roadblock which had been set up just inside the town. Reeves pulled up behind a police Land Rover and switched off the engine. The hotel was situated a couple of hundred yards further down the road.

Palmer asked Reeves for the car phone and dialed the number of the Stills Hotel. When it was answered he asked to speak to Pat Gorman. He was told there was nobody there by that name. Then he asked to speak to Kane. Silence. Several seconds elapsed before he was patched through to another connection.

The receiver was picked up at the other end. "Who is this?" a voice demanded.

"I want to speak to Brady."

"You've got the wrong number."

"I don't think so. You tell him that if he hasn't called me back in five minutes, the meeting's off." Palmer gave the number of the car phone then hung up.

The phone rang almost immediately. Palmer answered it.

"This is Gorman."

Palmer was satisfied he was speaking to Brady. "Commander Palmer here. There's been a change of plan. There will be two of us coming over to the hotel. I've got the head of the senator's security team with me. I want him in on this as well."

"No deal, Palmer. You come in alone."

"Then no deal," Palmer retorted and broke the connection. He had anticipated Brady's reaction. Now he wanted to see just how desperate Brady was to meet with him. And if his plan backfired, he would have a lot of explaining to do to his superiors. They had only sanctioned the meeting after careful negotiations with both the RUC and the army to minimize the chances of anything happening to him while he was there. He looked from Whitlock to Reeves then back to the phone, willing it to ring again. Had he underestimated Brady? No, Brady had obviously wanted to meet with him otherwise he wouldn't have taken such an enormous risk by calling Scotland Yard in the first place. So why wasn't he calling back to renegotiate? He couldn't afford any more setbacks after the disastrous events of the day. If he blew this, he'd better start contemplating life outside the force . . .

The phone rang.

He resisted the temptation to reach over and snatch up the receiver. No, he had to be seen to be the one calling the shots. He'd be damned if he'd dance to Brady's tune. He let the phone ring for a few seconds then lifted the receiver.

"Palmer?"

"Yes," Palmer replied.

"Scoby's minder can come with you. Use the un-marked Rover. No driver. Both of you sit up front. Park outside the hotel. A space has been cordoned off for you. Go into the hotel and ask at the reception for Sammy Kane. We'll take it from there."

"I'm glad to see you've got it all worked out so well, Brady. If I didn't know better, I'd be inclined to think you were running scared."

There was a hesitant pause. "You just make sure those pigs stay behind their little roadblock. The area around the hotel is completely secured and my men have strict orders to open fire if any pig is stupid enough to venture within range. Make sure you pass that message on to Reeves." The line went dead.

Palmer recounted Brady's demands.

"We're obviously under close surveillance," Whit-lock said.

"We have been ever since we got here," Reeves told him. "The men have already spotted several Provos in prominent positions overlooking the hotel. They're the ones we're supposed to see. It's the ones we can't see that worry me. They'll be the ones with the artillery."

Palmer checked his watch. Seven forty-two. "I'd say it was time to go in."

"He did say eight," Reeves reminded him.

"If we're playing by his rules," Palmer replied. "And I have no intention of doing that."

Whitlock nodded in agreement. "Commander Palmer's right. We've got to take the initiative. The more we unsettle Brady, the better it'll be for us when it comes to making any kind of deal with him."

"Why do you think I waited until now to tell Brady that I'd be taking Mr. Whitlock in with me?" Palmer said. "This way we undermine his control of the situation. It gives us the edge. And that's vital in these circumstances."

Palmer and Whitlock moved to the front of the car and Reeves handed Palmer the keys through the driver's window.

"You know the drill," Palmer said to Reeves. "Stick to it and if something should go wrong, move in and get Brady."

"Yes sir," Reeves replied.

Palmer started up the car and pulled out from behind the Land Rover. They drove in silence to the hotel. It was a drab gray building with the name illuminated in garish neon lights above the revolving doors. Not surprisingly, the road seemed totally deserted. They were in Provo territory. And the Provos had already cleared the area until the meeting was over. Palmer parked in front of the hotel and they made their way up the steps, through the revolving doors, and into the foyer. Reeves had been right. It was a dive. A teenage receptionist sat behind the desk watching a Colombo repeat on a black and white television set. She glanced up at them without interest as they approached the desk then reached back and knocked on the door behind her, immediately returning her attention to the screen. The door opened and two masked Provos appeared. They came around from behind the desk and frisked them. Satisfied that both men were unarmed one of the Provos picked up the telephone on the desk and called Kane.

"What have we got here?"

Whitlock and Palmer looked around simultaneously. Joseph Meehan, who had appeared from the deserted bar lounge behind them, was in his mid-fifties with an unshaven face and thinning, greasy black hair. The front of his shirt was stained and it hung untidily out of his trousers. He was obviously drunk. The masked Provos stood uncertainly by the desk, neither sure what to do.

"Are you telling me I had to close my hotel for these two?" he demanded of the two Provos.

"I think you should go back into the bar," one of the Provos said to Meehan.

"This is my hotel and I'll do what I bloody well like in it," Meehan snarled back angrily. He levelled a finger at Palmer. "You, I don't mind being here. But nobody said anything about any nigger coming here."

Palmer stepped forward but Whitlock quickly put a restraining hand on his arm.

"Or perhaps you're just here looking for work," Meehan jibed at Whitlock. "Is that it? Are you here for a job?"

Whitlock stared back impassively at Meehan but said nothing.

"Nice suit," Meehan said, reaching out to feel the cloth.

"Don't touch me," Whitlock hissed menacingly.

"Are you talking to me?" Meehan snapped. "Because if you are, you'd better call me 'sir'."

"I've had enough of this." Palmer bristled indignantly.

"It's OK," Whitlock said soothingly. "Let it go."

It was then that Meehan grabbed Whitlock's lapel. Whitlock broke the grip and brought his elbow up viciously into the side of Meehan's face. Meehan crashed backward against the wall and slid slowly to the floor, cradling his jaw in both hands. The two Provos made a move toward Whitlock.

"Leave him!" Kane snapped from the top of the stairs. "Get Meehan out of here. And sober him up. Mr. Brady will want to have a word with him about this later."

The two Provos carried Meehan back into the bar as Kane gestured for Palmer and Whitlock to follow him. They climbed to the top of the stairs and Kane led them to an open door further down the passage. Palmer and Whitlock exchanged suspicious glances. If they were walking into a trap, it was too late to turn back now. They had to go on. Kane stepped aside to let them enter then closed the door behind them.

The room consisted of a single bed, a battered wardrobe and two high-back armchairs. One was facing the window.

"You're early," a voice said from behind a chair. Brady stood up slowly and turned to face them.

Whitlock eyed Brady contemptuously. Was this the man who had sanctioned the coldblooded murder of three of his UNACO colleagues? He felt a sudden anger surging through him but he was quick to check himself. This was neither the time nor the place to confront Brady. The time for retribution would come later . . .

"Let's get something straight right from the start, Brady," Palmer said. "Detective Inspector Reeves will be calling the hotel every five minutes to speak to me. If, for some reason, I'm not able to answer the phone, or if I should give him a code word which would imply that we were in some kind of trouble, his men will immediately storm the building. You would be their main target. Dead or alive."

"When I want you dead, I'll arrange to have it done on the mainland," Brady replied. "Not on my own doorstep with the RUC only a few hundred yards away. So put your mind at rest, this isn't a trap."

"As long as we understand each other," Palmer said.

Brady rang the reception desk and gave instructions that any calls for Palmer were to be put through to the room. He then crossed to the second armchair, which was facing into the room, and sat down. "Now, to business. The IRA has no quarrel with

Senator Jack Scoby and neither do we have a contract out on him," he announced, addressing himself to Whitlock. "The events of the last fourteen hours have been very damaging to our organization and it's for that reason that I asked to meet with Commander Palmer."

"Do you deny Fiona Gallagher is a member of the IRA?" Whitlock asked, sitting beside Palmer on the bed.

"We've never denied that. What we do deny is any involvement in her actions against Senator Scoby. The operation wasn't sanctioned by the Revolutionary Army."

"Get to the point, Brady," Palmer snapped. "We've already heard all this rhetoric from your Press officer this afternoon. Why did you call this meeting?"

"It galls me to have to admit this, but right now we need each other. If the senator is assassinated in Dugaill tomorrow, our heads will be the first to roll."

The telephone rang. Brady made no move to answer it. Palmer reached over and picked up the receiver. It was Reeves. They spoke briefly then Palmer replaced the receiver.

"What are you suggesting?" Whitlock asked.

"That we mount a joint security operation in Dugaill tomorrow," Brady replied impassively.

"Out of the question!" Palmer shot back indignantly. "My God, imagine what the Press would make of it. Our security forces working in league with the IRA? They would crucify us. And rightly so. It would be a betrayal of all those innocent people the IRA have butchered since the conflict in Ireland began."

"Don't get me wrong, Commander, I'm not suggesting that masked freedom fighters should stand side by side with the security forces. That would be a betrayal of our principles as well. No, the church and village would be patrolled by the security forces and we would operate in the woodland situated directly behind the church. The area could be cordoned off for security reasons so the Press would never need to know we were there. Don't forget, we have people who know those woods like the back of their hands. They know all the places where Fiona could hide while she awaited Scoby's arrival at the church. Granted, the security forces will find most of them. But not all of them. And you can be sure that if Fiona does use the woods, she'll have done her homework. They won't find her."

"You seem very sure that she will use the woods," Whitlock said suspiciously.

"I would if I were in her shoes. It's the one area where she could hide without being detected." Brady turned his attention back to Palmer. "The IRA are just as concerned as you are about the senator's safety. His death would seriously damage our reputation abroad. That's why we're prepared to work with you under these unique circumstances."

"And what a propaganda coup that would be for the IRA if you were instrumental in thwarting Gallagher before she could get to Scoby," Palmer said disdainfully. "It's very transparent, Brady. And I'll have nothing to do with it. I have every confidence in the security forces. We don't need your help."

"You're overlooking one important point here, Commander Palmer. None of your people knows what Fiona looks like, do they? I do. So would the people I'd use to search the woods. We'd be able to spot her straight away."

"If you were serious about helping us, you'd let us have a photograph of her to circulate amongst the men," Whitlock told him.

"I can't let you have something I haven't got," Brady replied.

"You expect us to believe that the IRA don't have

any photographs of her?'' Palmer retorted indignantly. "I don't believe that for a minute."

"You believe what you want, Commander. I can assure you that we don't have any photographs of her. The only known picture of her was taken at Dominic Lynch's wedding. And even then she insisted on keeping it. She's always been obsessively camera-shy."

"Did she kill the Lynches?" Whitlock asked.

"I believe so. But right now I don't know why. Or why she killed Kerrigan and Mullen for that matter. We want those questions answered just as much as you do. Probably more so. That's why we're prepared to compromise on this one occasion and help you find her."

"Why, so that you can silence her before she can say anything to us?" Palmer retorted.

"You still believe we're behind this, don't you?"

"I don't believe she's working alone. She's had far too much assistance along the way. And not just from John Marsh."

"I've heard about this John Marsh from a source of ours at Scotland Yard. He's supposed to be working for us, isn't he? It's an interesting theory, but not one I have the time or inclination to pursue right now."

"I'm sure you don't," Palmer said. "It must have come as quite a shock to you when you heard your man had been busted."

"It was more of a shock when I heard he was supposed to have been working for us. But then, it doesn't bother me one way or the other what happens to him. He's only a cop."

The telephone rang again. Palmer answered it, spoke to Reeves, then replaced the handset.

"I was hoping we could have come to some arrangement about the security for Senator Scoby's visit to Dugaill tomorrow. Obviously I was wrong."

"Obviously," Palmer retorted. "And let me tell

you this, Brady, if we find any of your Provos near Dugaill tomorrow they'll find themselves behind bars so quickly they won't have time to draw breath. See that you pass the message on to the Army Council."

"I'm sorry you see it that way," Brady said as he got to his feet and crossed to the door. He called Kane into the room. "Sammy will show you back to your car. You'll be given safe passage out of here. I only hope your faith in the security forces is justified, Commander. Because if Scoby is assassinated in Dugaill tomorrow, you'll only have yourself to blame. We held out the olive branch. You refused it. Remember that."

Palmer left the room without a word. Whitlock stared at Brady as if he were branding the face into his memory. When it came to finding out who was behind the hit on his colleagues, he knew which face would first come to mind. He followed Kane and Palmer back to the foyer.

"Mr. Brady has agreed to give you safe passage back to the roadblock. We would hope you will reciprocate the gesture and pull your men out of the area before we leave. The cease-fire will last for exactly ten minutes after you've reached safety but if your men haven't withdrawn by then, then we'll open fire. As you can imagine, our soldiers are heavily armed. Your people wouldn't stand a chance. And by the time you'd called in for reinforcements, we'd be gone. We don't want any bloodshed. I would hope you feel the same."

"He'll be free to leave," Palmer replied. "You have my word on that."

Kane waited until the Rover had pulled away from the front of the hotel before he called Brady to let him know they had gone.

When Brady came downstairs into the foyer Kane told him about the incident with Whitlock and Meehan. As usual, Brady listened impassively before asking to see Meehan. Kane led him into the bar where one of the Provos, his balaclava now discarded on the counter, was plying Meehan with black coffee.

Meehan looked up slowly at Brady and managed a weak smile. "Good evening, Mr. Brady. Have you finished your meeting? Can I open the hotel again?"

"Are you sober yet?" Brady asked.

"I'm feeling a lot better now," Meehan replied obsequiously.

"I hear you insulted one of my guests tonight. That's something I will not tolerate."

"I . . . I got what I deserved, Mr. Brady," Meehan said, touching his bruised chin gingerly. "I've nothing against black people. It was just the drink talking."

"You drink too much, Meehan."

"I . . . I enjoy a drink, Mr. Brady."

"Not anymore. You're on the wagon as of now. But obviously you'll need some kind of incentive to stop drinking. Something to take your mind off it." Brady nodded to Kane. "Break the fingers on his right hand."

"Mr. Brady, please . . ." Meehan screamed in terror as Kane moved toward him. "I'll never drink again. Honestly. I've learned my lesson."

"Consider this your first and last warning, Meehan," Brady told him. "If I ever hear that you've been drinking again, you'll end up in some alley with the back of your head blown away. Sammy, I'll see you back at the house. I've got some business to attend to first."

Brady left the bar. Seconds later an agonized scream came from behind the closed doors. The receptionist looked around from the television set, her eyes wide and uncertain.

"I'd start looking for a new job if I were you," Brady said to her. "I've got a feeling that Mr. Meehan won't be running this hotel for very much longer."

The receptionist swallowed nervously but said nothing. Brady pushed his hands into the pockets of his leather jacket then disappeared through the revolving doors and out into the night.

"The men are in position, sir," Reeves said as Palmer pulled up behind the Land Rover. "Do you want me to give the order for them to move in?"

"No," Palmer replied, switching off the engine. "Brady's to be allowed to leave of his own accord."

"But sir, we've got them—"

"I gave my word," Palmer cut in angrily. "And I intend to keep it."

"Yes, sir, of course," Reeves said, immediately regretting his sudden outburst. "I'm sorry, sir, I didn't mean to question your authority. It's just that . . . he's been responsible for the deaths of five of my colleagues over the last eight months. And now that we've got a chance to nail him, we have to stand by and watch him drive away."

"I understand your frustration," Palmer replied, getting out of the car. "Believe me, I'd like nothing better than to give the order to grab him the moment he leaves the hotel. But we can't. It's not just that I gave my word. The whole area's crawling with Provos. And God knows what kind of artillery they've got with them. If you move in, they've threatened to open fire. We've lost more than enough young men in this conflict as it is without adding any more to the list. I want you to give the order for all patrols to pull out of the area." He looked at his watch. "They've got eight minutes left in which to do it. And I mean every patrol. I don't want any of our boys in the area for the next few hours. Is that understood?"

"Perfectly understood, sir." Reeves saluted then hurried off to carry out Palmer's orders.

"He's a good copper, that one," Palmer said as he watched Reeves give the order to his men to pull out.

"Sure," Whitlock replied thoughtfully. "I know just how he feels though. As you know, we lost three men when the cell first tried to take out McGuire in London. I'm just glad I wasn't armed when I went into that hotel room tonight. I'd gladly have put a bullet in him."

Palmer took the pack of cigarettes from his pocket and lit one. It was the first cigarette he'd had since getting off the plane and he inhaled deeply, savoring it.

Whitlock rested his arm on the roof of the car and stared thoughtfully at the hotel in the distance. "Something just doesn't ring true about Brady's motives tonight."

"He was obviously out for personal glory. Some way to worm his way back into favor with the Army Council. And it would have been a major propaganda coup if he'd managed to bring the IRA in on the security operation tomorrow." Palmer noticed the consternation on Whitlock's face as he continued to stare at the hotel. "You're not convinced, are you?"

"Not about bringing the IRA in on the security operation. I can't believe he would have taken these kinds of risks to lay something like that on you. He would have known you'd never have gone along with it. So why did he bring you here?"

"You mean apart from trying to ingratiate himself with me?" Palmer said with a half-smile. "When we spoke earlier on the phone it was Palmer. Then, to my face, it suddenly became Commander this, Commander that. The way he was addressing me—"

"Of course," Whitlock cut in and banged his fist

angrily on the roof. "Now it all makes sense. The son-of-a-bitch."

"Well, spit it out, man," Palmer demanded.

"Think back to the points he raised tonight. The IRA have never had a contract out on Senator Scoby. They're just as concerned for his safety as we are. They want to stop Gallagher to save themselves any further embarrassment. But we don't know what she looks like. They do. And they're prepared to go out on a limb to help us track her down before she can get to the senator. But he knows you'd never go for it. And you don't. In fact, you turned him down flat."

"So?" Palmer said, frowning.

"What if everything we said in there tonight was recorded onto tape so that if the senator is assassinated in Dugaill tomorrow, Brady can produce a copy of the meeting and give it to the Press? But it won't be the original tape. It'll be an edited version of the original. A version designed to highlight the fact that although the IRA were our last chance of finding Gallagher you refused even to consider working with them. In other words, he'd be trying to shift the blame for the senator's death on to the anti-terrorist squad."

"The public would see through it straight away," Palmer said.

"But with the maximum amount of embarrassment to Scotland Yard. They would demand to know why the head of the anti-terrorist squad was meeting secretly with the Chief-of-Staff of the IRA's Army Council. A man who's been responsible for an intensive bombing campaign on the British mainland over the last year which has cost the lives of innocent women and children. Were you trying to make a deal with him? If not, what were you doing talking to him in the first place? And by making the edited version public in the US he'll also be allaying the fears of many of their Noraid supporters who'll naturally be worried that the IRA have gone back on their word never to target foreigners.

"He's anticipated the worst possible scenario and this is his contingency plan not only to discredit Scotland Yard but also to minimize the damage abroad. Killing two birds with one stone, so to speak. That's why he was being so ingratiating to you tonight. It's going to sound really good on tape, isn't it?"

"I see now why Sergei Kolchinsky talks so highly of you," Palmer said after a long, thoughtful silence.

"It's only a theory," Whitlock was quick to point out. "And that's all it can be until we know for sure."

"Well if you're right about this and that tape does reach the Press, we're going to be crucified. We'll be lucky to keep our pensions. We have to stop him before he leaves the hotel."

"No," Whitlock said, putting a restraining hand on Palmer's arm. "Let him go."

"What are you talking about? We have to stop him before he can get the tape edited."

"Trust me," was all Whitlock would say.

The Land Rover started up in front of them and drew away from the curb, disappearing up an adjoining street.

Reeves crossed to where Palmer and Whitlock were standing. "I've pulled all the men out, sir."

Palmer glanced anxiously at Whitlock but Whitlock just shook his head. "Has the plane been refuelled, Reeves?" he asked calmly.

"Yes, sir, I would think so."

"Good," Whitlock replied, clapping his hands together. "Then we can get back to London."

"What about Brady?" Palmer demanded. "Are you just going to let him walk?"

"Yes," Whitlock replied bluntly.

"Look, if you're right—"

"Trust me," Whitlock said with a reassuring smile. "Now, shall we get back to the plane?"

* * *

The complement of Marines on duty that evening at Winfield House, the official residence of the American ambassador in Regent's Park, were under the direct command of a second lieutenant called Kowalski. Kowalski, who had only recently graduated from the Officers' Training College at Quantico, Virginia, had made no attempt to hide his contempt for Graham and Sabrina when they arrived at the embassy with the Scoby party. Sabrina had taken an immediate dislike to him, finding him both arrogant and condescending. Graham had been more tolerant. As an ex-soldier he knew that the young officer felt his authority was being undermined by a couple of outsiders. He would have reacted similarly had it happened to him at Delta. Kowalski had shown them around the grounds and made the point several times that security at the embassy was always on full alert. And it would be no different that night. Graham and Sabrina certainly couldn't find fault with what they had seen. Which meant there wouldn't be much for them to do other than keep an eye on the Scobys inside the embassy building.

Sabrina had made it plain to Graham from the outset that she thought it best if he shadowed the senator whilst she stayed with Melissa Scoby. It was obvious that she still harbored the bizarre belief that Melissa Scoby fancied him and that, by keeping them apart, she was acting in his best interests. He knew it was ridiculous and although as head of Strike Force Three he could technically overrule her, he wasn't about to start making waves. It wasn't worth the aggravation. He went along with it, if only to keep the peace.

Scoby had mingled freely with the guests, establishing as many new contacts as possible. Ambassadors, chargés d'affaires, businessmen. Anyone he felt could be useful to him at some point in his future.

Graham was quick to pick up on Scoby's thought pattern. The more important the contact, the more quality time he would spend talking to them. Those who had nothing to offer him were rewarded with a cursory smile and a handshake before he set off to weed out another potential target. Scoby's cunning intrigued Graham. He was a scheming bastard. But also a clever one.

At dinner Graham, now the senior UNACO representative there, found himself sandwiched between the wives of two senior European ambassadors and he spent much of the meal tactfully fending off a barrage of questions about both UNACO and the events on the Thames earlier in the day. The secret had been to keep visualizing the poster Whitlock had had on his bedsit wall when he was at Oxford. *Diplomacy is telling someone to go to hell in such a way that they look forward to the trip . . .*

The end of the meal couldn't come quickly enough for him. He caught up with Sabrina as she was leaving the room with one of the European ambassadors and, grabbing her arm, he gave the ambassador a conciliatory smile before propelling her out into the corridor.

"You looked like you were having fun in there," she said with a mischievous grin.

"Yeah, sure," he retorted. "And talking of fun, it's your turn to check in with Kowalski."

"I went the last time," she complained.

"Nice try. Now go on."

She pulled a face. "Keep an eye on Melissa Scoby for me. The last I saw of her she was with the American ambassador. I shouldn't be long."

Graham went through to the lounge but there was no sign of either Jack or Melissa Scoby. He was about to double back and check the dining room again when Melissa Scoby appeared from a doorway further down the hall. The door closed behind her.

Graham crossed to where she was standing. "Where's the senator?"

"He's in there with Ray and the ambassador," she replied, gesturing to the door behind her. "It's the first chance he's had all night to have a word with the ambassador in private. Where's Sabrina?"

"She's just gone to have a word with the duty officer. She'll be back shortly."

"Good," Melissa Scoby said, then slipped her hand under his arm. "Now you can tell me why you've been avoiding me all evening."

"I haven't been . . ." He trailed off when he noticed her teasing smile.

"I could do with a breath of fresh air," she announced. "Come, walk with me, Mike."

"Will you be warm enough?" Graham asked as they walked toward the patio.

"I'll be fine. It's mild out tonight." She smiled at a couple sipping liqueurs on the patio then led him down the steps and out into the spacious garden. "I had a long talk with Sabrina earlier this evening. I know that she and I didn't exactly hit it off from the start. But I realize now that I've misjudged her. You've got a very smart partner there, Mike. And a very loyal one too."

"Yeah, I know," came the hesitant reply.

"She knew straight away that I was flirting with you yesterday. I know Jack didn't notice. He never does." Melissa Scoby smiled at Graham's surprised look. "Sabrina said you hadn't noticed either."

"No, I hadn't," Graham replied uncertainly.

"I've always been a bit of a flirt. It's all a game to me. But completely harmless as far as I'm concerned. I've never cheated on Jack and I never would. It's Jack's ambition to reach the White House some day. And when he does eventually decide to run for President, the last thing I want to do is give the Democrats any ammunition to use against him. And infidelity is a serious crime in the eyes of the American electorate. There're enough discredited politicians around to testify to that. I realized afterwards that it could have been a bit awkward for you and when I saw that you were going to stick with Jack tonight I thought you'd decided purposely to stay out of my way to avoid any further embarrassment. But it turns out it was Sabrina's idea all the time."

"She can be very maternal at times," Graham replied.

Sabrina and Scoby emerged from the house and crossed to where they were standing.

"Have you finished talking to the ambassador?" Melissa Scoby asked her husband.

"Yes. There wasn't much to discuss. Just a few minor points." Scoby looked at his watch. "I want to get back to the hotel. Ray and I have still got a lot of documents to sift through tonight. You stay on here if you want. Mike or Sabrina can take you back to the hotel later."

"No, it's been quite a day already," she replied. "I'm ready for an early night."

"Then we'd better make our apologies to the ambassador and his wife," Scoby said.

"I'll have the cars brought round to the front of the house for you," Graham said to Scoby. "Sabrina will call the anti-terrorist squad and let them know we're on our way back to the hotel. The last thing you need is a foyer full of reporters to deal with when we arrive there."

"Well, we'll leave you to it," Scoby said, escorting his wife back to the house.

Graham and Sabrina followed discreetly behind them.

Cross and Johnstone, two of the anti-terrorist squad detectives on duty at the hotel that night, hur-

ried over to the first of the two black Mercedes as it
drew up in front of the hotel. Inside were Jack and
Melissa Scoby. Ray Tillman was in the second car.
The passenger door of the lead car swung open and
Graham jumped out. He looked around him quickly.
To his right was the usual circus of Press photogra-
phers jostling amongst themselves for the best vantage points to catch Scoby on film as he exited the car.
To his left were a small group of about a dozen anti-
American protesters. Most of them carried placards
denouncing American foreign policy in Central
America. They were penned in behind a police cordon which was being marshaled by five uniformed
officers. Sabrina got out of the second car and crossed
to where Graham was standing. Graham nodded to
Cross who then opened the back door. The flashlights
popped incessantly as Scoby got out of the car. He
waved in the general direction of the photographers
then offered his hand to his wife as she climbed out
after him.

A movement caught Graham's eye as he turned to
usher the Scobys into the hotel. A young woman,
dressed in a pair of jeans and an army flak jacket,
broke through the police cordon and ran toward the
car. Sabrina was still closing in on her when she
hurled an egg in the direction of the first car. A cheer
went up from the protesters as it splattered against
the windscreen. Sabrina took the woman's legs from
underneath her then reached down and twisted her
arm savagely behind her back. The woman screamed
abuse as she struggled to break free from Sabrina's
viselike grip. Two uniformed policemen quickly intervened and hauled the woman to her feet. She was
immediately handcuffed and dragged off toward a
waiting panda car.

"Are you all right, sir?" Graham asked Scoby after
they had reached the safety of the foyer.

"Yes," Scoby replied brusquely. He glared at the

protesters who had now turned their anger on the departing panda car. "It's the same old story, isn't it? Students and welfare junkies who think they can change the world with their outmoded brand of socialism. Look at them. A bunch of pseudo-commies and pinkos. What the hell do they know anyway?"

Graham eyed Scoby warily. It was like listening to "Hawk" Walsh all over again. But the difference was Jack Scoby was destined to reach the White House one day . . .

Tillman grabbed Graham's arm, interrupting his thoughts. "Why was that protester allowed to get so close to the senator? What if that had been a grenade instead of an egg?"

"Then we'd all be dead, wouldn't we?" Graham replied, easing his arm from Tillman's grasp.

"Now you listen—"

"Ray, that's enough," Scoby hissed under his breath. "We can discuss this further in the morning. But right now we've still got a lot of work to get through before either one of us can get any sleep. So the sooner it's done, the sooner we can go to bed."

Tillman said nothing as he followed Jack and Melissa Scoby to the lift. Graham glanced over his shoulder. The flashlights were still popping furiously outside the hotel. Again the security had been wanting. Another embarrassment for UNACO. But he was only too well aware that it could have been much worse . . .

"I'm sure glad that's over," Graham said after they had seen the Scobys safely back to their suite. "I don't know how much more I could have taken at the ambassador's house."

"Oh come on, it wasn't that bad," Sabrina replied as they walked toward the lift.

"You would say that, you grew up in that environment." Graham loosened his bow tie and opened the top button of his shirt. "Your father must have thrown hundreds of dinner parties like that."

"Sure," Sabrina agreed, pressing the button for the lift. "But that doesn't mean I went to any of them. I was only a kid at the time. In fact, I wasn't invited to my first embassy party until after I'd left the Sorbonne."

"The point is, that it's your crowd, not mine."

"No, it's not *my* crowd," she shot back indignantly, falling suddenly silent as the lift doors opened onto an elderly couple. She smiled politely at them as she stepped into the lift and didn't speak again until they alighted on their floor. "You've always had the preconception of me being this poor little rich girl who spends all her leisure time mixing with New York's rich and famous. I don't deny I enjoy the occasional glitzy party, but, believe it or not, I'm much more at home in a pair of jeans and a sweater at a smoke-filled jazz club than I am in an expensive designer dress at some swanky nightclub. I only wish I could make you understand that."

"Be that as it may, you're still more at ease with a bunch of politicians than I am."

"I'm more at ease with most people than you are," she replied with a half-smile. She paused outside her room. "Fancy a nightcap?"

"Yeah, OK," came the indifferent reply.

"Are you sure you can spare the enthusiasm?" she said, opening the door to her room. "You know where the drinks are. I'll have a diet Coke."

"Where are you going?"

"To change out of this," she replied, indicating her evening dress. "I've felt uncomfortable in it all night."

"You're still smarting because C.W. wouldn't let you buy a new dress for tonight, aren't you?"

"I don't like hiring clothes, that's all. It's gross. I

don't know who's worn this before me." She shuddered at the thought then disappeared into the bathroom.

Graham took a diet Coke and a Perrier water from the mini-bar then noticed the red light flashing on the telephone. "There's a message for you at reception," he called through the bathroom door.

"Ring down and get it for me, will you?" she replied.

When she re-emerged from the bathroom she was wearing a white towelling robe. "Who was it from?"

"C.W.," Graham replied, pouring the diet Coke into a glass and handing it to her. "He doesn't know when he'll get back to the hotel tonight. We're not to wait up for him."

"I didn't know we were expected to," she replied, sitting on the bed.

"Well now it's official." Graham sat down. He turned the bottle around slowly in his hands then looked across at her. "I guess I owe you an apology."

"For what?" she replied, suddenly intrigued. It wasn't often Mike Graham admitted he was wrong.

"I spoke to Melissa Scoby tonight." He shifted uncomfortably in his chair. "You were right, she did have the scope on me. And I didn't believe you. But then I guess you know more about these things than I do."

"Gee thanks, Mike," came the bemused reply.

"You know I don't mean it like that." He frowned at her. "Was it really that obvious?"

"It was to me. I could hear it in her voice and in the way she kept glancing in your direction. Why do you think she took such an instant dislike to me when we were first introduced? Because she knew I'd seen through her. And that worried her."

"You could hear it in her voice? And in the way she kept looking at me? You're way ahead of me here, Sabrina." Graham stared disconsolately at the bottle in his hand. "And I didn't notice a damn thing."

"And neither did Scoby."

"Isn't it great? A woman flirts with you and you don't even know she's doing it." Graham managed a wry smile. "I guess I've been out of circulation too long."

"She isn't your type anyway."

"Damn right." He noticed a faint smile touch the corners of her mouth. "What is it?"

"I was just thinking."

Graham waited for her to continue and when she didn't asked, "Is that it? You were just thinking?"

"It was something Fabio said when I went to see him at the hospital this afternoon. He reckons you and I would make a good couple."

"I think he's been overdoing the tranquilizers. We work well together as a team. But that's purely on a professional level."

"And it's only been in the last few months that we've actually clicked as a team. I can remember the days when we used to be at each other's throats over every little thing."

"Banging heads at every turn. We were too independent for our own good in those days."

"You were," she corrected him.

"You weren't exactly blameless yourself." He took a sip of the Perrier water. "What gets me is this idea that a man and a woman can't work together without there being some sexual stigma attached to it."

"I know," she replied with a shrug.

"It's not even as if we've got anything in common."

"Apart from a love of jazz," she was quick to point out.

"Well, yeah," he conceded.

"I had a great time at Sweet Basil's the other night."

"Me too. The band was great. Perhaps we can do it again sometime?"

"I'd like that," she said softly.

"But just as long as you don't go shouting your mouth off again to everyone at work like you did the last time."

She rolled her eyes. "Sarah and Fabio hardly constitute everyone."

"It's sure to get around."

"Why does that worry you so much, Mike?"

"It doesn't worry me. I just don't like to fuel any rumors. Especially amongst the other Strike Force teams. They'd have a field day if they thought for a moment that there was something going on between us." He quaffed the last of the Perrier water then stood up and put the empty bottle on the table beside him. "Well, I'd better be off."

"Before you fuel any more rumors?" she said with a smile, then got to her feet and kissed him lightly on the cheek. "Night, Mike."

He reached out and brushed a strand of loose hair back over her shoulder. She tried to read something, anything, in his eyes as he held her gaze. But she couldn't. She had never known anyone capable of masking their emotions better than Mike Graham. Then the moment was gone.

"See you in the morning," he said softly.

She stared at the door for some time after he'd gone. "Don't even think it, girl," she suddenly snapped to herself then went through to the bathroom to run herself a bath.

It had just gone midnight when the motorbike pulled up outside the house on the outskirts of Warrenpoint. The rider, dressed in a pair of jeans and a black leather jacket, switched off the engine and hurried to the front door. The door opened before he could press the bell. Sammy Kane held out his hand. The man removed a package from inside his jacket and gave it to Kane. The door closed again and the man returned to his bike. He kick-started it and drove off into the night.

Neither he nor Kane had noticed the Mercedes which had been parked beside a tangle of undergrowth thirty yards away from the house for the past two hours. All four men inside the car were dressed in black. Three of them climbed out of the car, disappeared into the undergrowth and came out at the back of the house. Their faces were now hidden under black balaclavas. They paused to survey the house. A single light came from behind the drawn curtains in the lounge. They knew Kane was alone.

One of the men was carrying a hold-all. He opened it and three sawed-off shotguns were produced. He then ghosted around to the back of the house to disable the security system. When he returned a few minutes later the job was done. A glass-cutter was used to remove one of the panes and a hand snaked through the hole and unlatched the window. They clambered silently into the house, closed the window again behind them, then made for the lounge.

The door was kicked open with such force that the bottom hinges were torn from the frame. Kane made a desperate grab for the automatic in the desk drawer in front of him.

"Don't even think it, Sammy!" one of the men commanded in a strong Belfast accent, the shotgun aimed at Kane's head.

Kane's eyes flickered to the other two shotguns aimed at him then he slowly brought both hands up into view.

"Move away from the desk!" the Belfast voice snapped.

"Who the hell are you?" Kane demanded. "And why—"

"I said move away from the desk!"

Kane did as he was told.

The Belfast man approached Kane and slammed the butt of the shotgun viciously into his midriff. "The Army Council send their regards."

Kane crumpled to the floor, his hands clutched over his stomach in agony. When he finally managed to get up on his knees one of the men moved behind him and pressed the shotgun against the back of his head.

"My God, what's all . . . this about?" Kane stammered, still struggling to catch his breath.

"It's about a meeting you and Brady had with Commander Maurice Palmer of Scotland Yard's antiterrorist squad earlier this evening," the Belfast voice told him.

"The Army Council knew about that," Kane blurted out. "Kevin cleared it with them before he made the arrangements with Palmer."

"Brady never informed the Army Council about any meeting tonight."

"That's absurd," Kane retorted. "He told me that he'd cleared it all with them and that they had sanctioned the meeting. He would never have done it behind their backs."

"The Army Council only found out about the meeting from one of their touts inside the RUC. They also heard a rumor from the same source that Brady taped the whole meeting. Is that true?"

Kane swallowed nervously as he felt the barrel of the shotgun press harder against the back of his head. He said nothing.

"Your loyalty to Brady's very misguided, Sammy," the Belfast voice said disdainfully. "The Army Council are well pissed off with him right now. And if he is relieved of his command because of what happened tonight, you can be sure they'll be very critical of those around him as well. And as you virtually live in his shadow, you'd be the first to go down with him. Think about it, Sammy."

Kane used his sleeve to wipe the sweat from his forehead. "Yes, he taped the meeting. But how would the RUC know about that?"

"Because Brady's lost his touch. He used to be innovative. Now he's just predictable. And it seems that the RUC are very interested in hearing those tapes."

"Tapes?" Kane said hesitantly.

"Don't piss us about, Sammy. It's obvious that Brady intended to send an edited version of the tape to the Press just so that he could save his own miserable skin. As I said, he's become very predictable. Why else would he have taped the meeting? And if those tapes do fall into the hands of the RUC the Army Council are going to have a hell of a job explaining the deception to our supporters abroad. You received a delivery not five minutes ago from a courier on a motorbike. And it wasn't a bloody pizza. So where are the tapes?"

"How do I even know the Army Council sent you? I don't recognize your voices. You won't even show your faces. You could be from the RUC for all I know."

"We've got our orders," the man behind Kane said to the Belfast man.

The Belfast man shook his head slowly. "I don't like it. He's one of us."

"You tell that to Pat Taylor!" the man snarled.

"Sammy, for God's sake, man. We were given strict instructions to execute anyone who tried to stop us from getting those tapes. I don't want to have to give that order."

"You kill me and you'll never get the tapes," Kane replied coldly, sensing he now had the edge.

"We know that package contained the tapes," the man behind Kane announced. "It had to be. So they're obviously somewhere in the house. Probably here in this room. So if I have to kill you, I will. It'll just take longer for us to find them. It's your move, Sammy!"

The radio in the hold-all suddenly crackled into life. The third man, who had been watching the street from the window, was quick to answer it.

"I can hear police sirens in the distance," the man in the car shouted over the radio. "And they're headed this way. We've got to move out."

"OK, Sammy. Decision time," the Belfast voice told him. "Either you give us those tapes now or else we find them ourselves and leave the remains of your head on the wall for the constabulary to scrape off."

"Bottom drawer of the desk," Kane said sullenly.

The Belfast man jerked open the drawer and withdrew a sealed brown envelope. "What's inside it?"

"The original and a copy of the edited version."

"How many copies are being made?"

"We've got the tapes, now let's go," the man behind Kane hissed.

"How many copies did Brady want made?" the Belfast man repeated, his eyes riveted on Kane's face.

"A dozen." Kane's eyes narrowed anxiously when he heard the approaching police sirens. "Come on, we've got to get out of here. There's a secret tunnel in the cellar. We can use that."

The Belfast man nodded to the man behind Kane, who cracked the butt of his shotgun against the side of Kane's head. Kane was already unconscious before he slumped forward onto the carpet.

The look-out tossed the radio to the Belfast man and crossed to the telephone to dial out as the first of the police cars screeched to a halt outside the house. It was answered immediately at the other end.

He pulled off his balaclava and wiped his hand across his sweating face. "Detective-Inspector Reeves here, sir. Mr. Whitlock's plan worked a treat." He glanced across at the other two policemen who had already discarded their balaclavas, and grinned triumphantly. "We've got the tapes."

Whitlock's plan had worked solely on the premise that Brady *had* taped the meeting at the hotel. It would have been a very different story had he been wrong . . .

But he had never entertained that idea. It was the obvious ploy. Why else would Brady have dragged Palmer to Ireland knowing that he would never agree to his terms? Whitlock had decided on using the two Belfast policemen with Reeves as an added precaution. If the Army Council hadn't known about the meeting they would have sent in a cell from out of town, knowing that they couldn't trust the locals in case they tried to tip off Kane in advance. But he didn't know whether the meeting had the Army Council's approval. It obviously did. And he knew Brady would have dealt with that himself. So by casting doubt on Brady's word, that would throw Kane off-guard.

Brady had been allowed to leave Warrenpoint, as Palmer had promised. But Kane had been tailed to the safe house on the outskirts of the city by the four policemen. They had orders to wait until the tapes were delivered to Kane. Whitlock had been positive that Brady would put the tapes in the care of the one man he knew he could trust. It had just been a question of when the tapes would arrive . . .

All three men had been wired when they went into the house so that both the "look-out" and the local RUC, who were parked a few hundred yards away from the house, would know exactly when to make their moves.

With Kane unconscious, the RUC could claim either not to have found the three masked men when

they entered the house or else to have lost them in a
subsequent chase. Whitlock had left that decision to
the police. Kane would be none the wiser. And with
Kane in custody, Brady would have lost his one real
ally. It would isolate him even further. And when the
Army Council found out that Kane had lost the original tape, the noose would tighten a little more around
Brady's neck . . .

◆ CHAPTER

FOURTEEN

The young constable flagged down the Mazda as it neared the RUC roadblock on the outskirts of Dugaill. "Morning," he said politely, crouching down beside the open driver's window. "I'm afraid this road won't be opened again until early this afternoon. Where are you headed?"

"The church," came the friendly reply. "My name's Sabrina Carver. I'm with the senator's security team."

"Do you have any identification on you?"

She unclipped a laminated identity card from the pocket of her white blouse and handed it to him. He checked the seal. It was authentic. He returned it to her then consulted the clipboard in his hand. "I thought you were flying in with the senator?"

"That was the idea. But with so much at stake, I was sent on ahead to liaise with Inspector Eastman. My partners will be flying in with the senator later this morning. It was thought I'd be more use on the ground than up there with them. Any idea where I might find Inspector Eastman?"

The constable shrugged. "I don't, I'm sorry. It's best if you ask someone when you get to the church. The turn-off to the church is about a hundred yards further down the road. You can't miss it."

"Thank you."

The constable signaled to his colleague and the boom gate was raised. She put the car into gear and drove through.

The constable grinned at his colleague. "She can protect me any time she wants."

"She's some looker, isn't she?"

The constable nodded in agreement then turned his attention to the next car as it approached the boom gate.

She was stopped again on the slip road, but after showing her card was allowed to continue. She parked close to the cemetery. It was crawling with armed RUC officers. She got out of the car but instead of going into the cemetery she made her way across to the church. When she opened the front door she was immediately challenged by a uniformed police sergeant.

"I'm Sabrina Carver," she told him, indicating the ID card clipped to her blouse. "I'm part of the senator's security team. I've been sent ahead to take charge of the security here in the church."

"Inspector Eastman didn't say anything about it," the sergeant replied.

"That's because he doesn't know I'm here. The decision to send me here ahead of the others was only taken earlier this morning. How many men do you have here in the church?"

"Two."

"Only two of you?" she shot back.

"If you've got a problem with that then I suggest

you take it up with the Inspector," came the gruff reply. "He gives the orders around here, not me."

"I'm sorry," she said with a placating smile. "I'm just surprised that there isn't a stronger security presence in here."

"It's not necessary. The church was searched thoroughly last night and then again this morning. Then it was sealed off. The doors are all guarded from the outside. Nobody's going to get in here without being seen."

"Where's the second man?"

"Paul Reilly's up in the belfry. It's got a great view overlooking the cemetery. So if a sniper was going to use the belfry they would first have to get past the police cordon outside the church and then past the two of us in here. No chance. We've got the situation well under control here, Miss . . ."

"Carver," she replied. "I'm glad to hear it."

"Is the senator due to arrive on time?" the policeman asked.

"As far as I know. The helicopter should already be on its way from Belfast by now. ETA is about ten minutes."

"You might as well have come with them, miss. I'm just surprised you didn't check with Inspector Eastman before you came here. It would have saved you a wasted journey."

"Hardly wasted," she replied then chopped him hard on the side of the neck. She grabbed him as he fell and lowered him silently to the floor. Then, after locking the front door, she took a small metal case from her pocket and opened it. Inside was a hypodermic needle and a vial of sodium pentothal. She drew half of the sodium pentothal into the syringe and injected it into the unconscious man. He'd be out for the next few hours.

She pocketed the case again and made for the belfry.

* * *

Paul Reilly took the pack of cigarettes from his tunic pocket and lit the last one. He crumpled the empty packet in his hand and was about to toss it over the side of the catwalk when he remembered where he was. He wasn't particularly religious but some things were still sacrosanct. He stuffed it into his pocket then took a long drag on the cigarette.

The small belfry was dominated by a heavy bell which hung from the center of the hammer-beam roof. Each of the four walls in the tower contained a narrow, elongated window. None was glazed. He stood by the window which overlooked the cemetery, a Heckler & Koch machine-pistol slung over his shoulder. He'd been there since early morning. Well, not much longer to wait now . . .

He looked around when he heard the spiral staircase creaking behind him. He called out his colleague's name. No reply. He unslung the Heckler & Koch machine-pistol and moved cautiously along the catwalk to the top of the staircase. It was impossible to see past the first few stairs from where he was standing. He gripped the railing and peered down, hoping to get a better look. It was no better. All he could see was the sheer, hundred-foot drop to the tiled floor below. He shuddered then stepped away from the railing. The creaking had stopped. It was probably the wind. Or his imagination. Pull yourself together, he chided himself, and moved back to the window.

"Morning."

He swung around, the machine-pistol at the ready.

"Sorry, I didn't mean to startle you. I thought you would have heard me coming up the stairs. I made enough noise to wake the dead."

"Who are you?" Reilly demanded.

"Sabrina Carver. I'm part of the senator's security

team. I do have ID on me. It's here under my jacket."

Reilly kept the Heckler & Koch trained on her. "Show me."

She removed the disc and held it out toward him. He moved forward for a closer look. The Heckler & Koch was finally lowered.

"I'm glad we cleared that up," she said with a smile.

"I'm just doing my job, Miss Carver. What are you doing up here?"

"I'm checking on the security arrangements before the senator arrives. Your colleague downstairs assures me you've both got the situation under control in here."

"Sure we do," Reilly replied confidently. "Especially from up here. You can see for miles in all directions. Come, I'll show you."

As he turned away from her she chopped him hard on the back of the neck. He crumpled to the catwalk. She removed the hypodermic needle from the metal case and injected the remaining sodium pentothal into his arm.

Then, taking a switchblade from her pocket, she crouched down and eased the blade between two floorboards. One of them was loose and she was able to prize it open. Underneath was an L96 sniper rifle wrapped inside a protective layer of plastic sheeting. She removed the plastic sheet then snapped the ten-round magazine into place and moved to the window. Reilly had been right. She could see for miles in all directions. But she was only interested in the cemetery. She looked at her watch. The helicopter was due to land in the next few minutes.

She peeled off the honey-blonde wig she had been wearing, then put on Reilly's tunic and peaked cap. If anyone did see her from the ground they would assume it was him.

Fiona Gallagher smiled to herself. All she had to do now was wait . . .

"I've left an envelope in the safe in our room back at the hotel. If anything should happen to me in Dugaill today, it's imperative that you give it to Whitlock as soon as possible. Promise me you'll do that, Melissa. You must promise me."

Melissa Scoby had promised her husband that she would comply with his wishes. And that had been an end to it. He had refused to discuss it any further. He had then spent the rest of the flight from London to Belfast staring absently out of the window, lost in a world of his own. He had hardly spoken to her. He had hardly spoken to anyone. She had even tried to touch his hand to reassure him that she was there if he needed her but he had quickly pulled his hand away. It had been cold. And trembling. It wasn't the Jack Scoby she knew. It was almost as if he had resigned himself to the fact that he wouldn't leave Dugaill alive . . .

"That's the church down there."

"Sorry?" she said, startled by the voice behind her.

"The church is down there," Whitlock repeated, pointing it out through the side window.

She nodded then cast a sidelong glance at her husband. He was staring ahead of him, his hands clenched tightly in his lap. If he had noticed her, he didn't show it.

The helicopter slowly descended toward the clearing at the edge of the cemetery. Graham and Sabrina were the first out of their seats as the wheels touched down on the ground. A group of armed policemen had already formed a cordon around the helicopter by the time Graham had opened the cabin door. He pushed the steps out from the cabin and they were anchored firmly on the ground by one of the policemen. Sabrina was the first to disembark and ran, doubled-over, to where Eastman was standing clear of the rotors.

"Has everything gone according to plan?" Eastman asked her.

"So far," she replied then jabbed her thumb in the direction of the helicopter. "A word of warning. Scoby seems a bit preoccupied today."

"Any particular reason?"

"Not that I know of," she replied, then looked around as Graham hurried over to them. "I was just telling Keith that Scoby's got out of the wrong side of bed this morning."

"Judging by those bags under his eyes, I doubt he even got into bed last night." Graham turned to Eastman. "How's the security operation going?"

"A gnat couldn't get within a hundred yards of this place without the proper security clearance."

"I hope you're right," Graham replied softly.

"The senator's agreed to the revised schedule," Sabrina told Eastman. "He'll lay a wreath at his grandparents' grave then head straight over to the Town Hall for lunch with the mayor."

"So the priest won't be saying a few words at the grave?" Eastman asked.

"No," she replied.

"Does *he* know that?"

"We thought we'd let you tell him." Graham gestured behind him. "Come on, Scoby's about to disembark."

They crossed to the helicopter and stood on either side of the steps as first Melissa Scoby, then her husband, alighted from the cabin. Whitlock brought up the rear. The Scobys were introduced to the elderly parish priest who was hovering at the foot of the steps.

"It's a pleasure to meet you," the priest said, shaking Scoby's hand. "I'm only sorry your visit to our country has had to be conducted under such a tight security blanket. Tell me, senator, is this your first visit to Ireland?"

"Yes, it is," Melissa Scoby said when it became evident that her husband wasn't going to answer. "And from what we've seen of it so far, it's certainly a beautiful country."

"That it is," the priest agreed.

Whitlock put a hand lightly on the priest's arm. "Father, could we proceed to the cemetery?"

"Of course. If you'll follow me."

Eastman fell in line beside Whitlock as he followed the Scobys into the cemetery. "Where's Tillman? Didn't he fly over with you?"

"No, he decided to stay behind in London." Whitlock looked across at the photographers who were massed behind a police cordon at the edge of the cemetery. "It is supposed to be a personal visit, after all."

The priest stopped beside the double grave of Kieran and Estelle Scoby. Jack Scoby removed his sunglasses and stood over the grave, his head bowed as he read the epitaph which had been carved into the headstone more than a hundred years earlier.

Graham and Sabrina exchanged anxious glances. Scoby was the perfect target. Stationary and exposed. She caught Whitlock's eye. He wiped a bead of sweat from his forehead then looked across at the thick woodland a couple of hundred yards beyond the cemetery. He knew there were over forty policemen combing the area. But what if Fiona Gallagher had still managed to evade them, assuming she was ever in there? Eastman followed Whitlock's gaze for several seconds then looked toward the church. His eye finally settled on the belfry and the window which looked out over the cemetery. It all seemed so peaceful . . .

* * *

The heat was stifling in the belfry. Fiona wiped her forearm across her face then reached underneath the tunic and pulled her damp blouse away from her back. But within seconds it was clinging uncomfortably to her skin again. She had monitored Scoby's progress from the time he had left the helicopter but it was only when he stopped in front of the grave that she reached for the rifle which was propped against the wall beside her. She wound the strap tightly around her arm then kneeled down on one knee and pressed the butt firmly against her shoulder. She lined up the top of Scoby's bowed head in the cross hairs and, after making a minor adjustment to the Schmidt & Bender telescopic sight, she slowly curled her finger around the trigger. She knew she had only one shot. She had to make it count . . .

Scoby stood silently in front of the headstone for over a minute before he finally looked up at the RUC officer standing on his right. The policeman handed him the flowers he'd brought with him from London. He placed them across the grave then stood up and caught Melissa's eye. He smiled gently at her then reached out and took her hand.

The soft-nosed bullet hit him above the right eye and exploded through the back of his head. His flailing arm caught Whitlock painfully on the side of the face as he was knocked off his feet as if hit by a hammering punch to the jaw. He landed heavily on the ground, his arms outstretched, the blood streaming down the side of his face. Melissa Scoby screamed in horror then fell to her knees beside her husband and cradled his bloodied head in her lap. Whitlock yelled at the nearest RUC officer to get the paramedics whose vehicle had been parked discreetly out of view of the cemetery.

Eastman, Graham and Sabrina exchanged glances then started running toward the church. The shot had to have come from there. A dozen armed policemen had already surrounded the building by the time they got there.

"The sniper's in the belfry," a senior officer told them breathlessly. "But the doors are locked and the keys are with the sergeant inside the church."

"I got a spare front door key from the priest last night," Eastman said, taking it from his pocket. "You take the back, Sabrina. Take some men with you and break the door down if necessary."

Sabrina quickly picked out half a dozen men and disappeared around the side of the church. Eastman unlocked the front door and eased it open. Graham pushed past him and went inside, Beretta drawn. Calling to the remaining policemen to cover the door and windows, Eastman hurried after Graham who had already reached the foot of the stairs.

"Hey, wait up," Eastman hissed, grabbing Graham's arm. "I know these stairs better than you. Let me lead the way."

Graham pulled his arm from Eastman's grip and reluctantly let him go first. Eastman unholstered his Browning then began to climb the stairs. Graham winced every time Eastman stepped on a creaky floorboard. So much for him knowing the stairs! Gallagher would certainly know they were coming.

Eastman suddenly held up his hand and whispered to Graham that they would be visible from the belfry as of the next turn in the staircase. Graham watched as Eastman pivoted around sharply, training the Browning on the top of the stairs. He held up his hand again to halt Graham. Eastman negotiated the last few stairs by himself.

"Mike, up here," he called out anxiously over his shoulder. "Hurry."

Graham hurried up onto the catwalk and immediately swung his Beretta on Fiona. In that instant Eastman pressed the Browning into Graham's back and quickly disarmed him. He pushed the Beretta into his belt.

"What the hell's going on?" Graham demanded, looking from Eastman to Fiona.

"You don't recognize me, do you?" Fiona said, watching Graham's face closely.

"Should I?" Graham replied hesitantly.

"You saw me talking to Keith outside the pub in Soho the day you arrived in London. What we didn't know was whether you'd seen my face. If you had you'd have been the one person still capable of blowing this whole operation. We couldn't afford to take that chance." She levelled the sniper rifle at Graham's chest.

"It's a simple scenario, Mike. You reached the belfry first and Fiona shot you before I managed to overpower her." Eastman stepped away from Graham. "Kill him."

Fiona's finger curled around the trigger.

"Drop the gun!" Sabrina yelled from beneath the belfry, a Heckler & Koch machine-pistol trained on Fiona.

"Take her out," Fiona snarled at Eastman without taking her eyes off Graham.

"I can't see her from here," Eastman snapped back, peering over the railing. "Dammit, I can't see her."

"Fiona, drop the rifle," Sabrina ordered. "Now!"

Fiona suddenly swung the rifle downward. Sabrina fired. The bullet took Fiona high in the shoulder, knocking the rifle from her hands. Clutching her shoulder in agony, Fiona stumbled back against the railing which gave way under her weight and she screamed in terror as she lost her footing and fell from the catwalk. She caught the side of her head on the bell as she fell and her body hit the floor with a sickening crunch of breaking bones.

Graham brought his elbow up sharply into Eastman's midriff and the Browning clattered onto the catwalk. As he stumbled backward Eastman pulled the Beretta from his belt but Graham managed to grab his wrist as he pulled the trigger. The bullet fired harmlessly into the roof. Graham delivered two hammering blows to Eastman's stomach, knocking the wind out of him. The Beretta slipped from Eastman's fingers when he dropped to his knees, coughing and spluttering as he struggled to catch his breath. Graham quickly retrieved both weapons and when the first two uniformed policemen appeared on the catwalk they found him standing over Eastman, who was on his knees, his hands clutched tightly over his stomach.

"What the hell are you waiting for?" Graham demanded as the two policemen hovered hesitantly at the top of the stairs. "Get him out of here."

Moments later Whitlock arrived breathlessly with a senior RUC officer. "OK, Mike, let the police take it from here. Sabrina's told us what happened."

Graham reluctantly handed Eastman's Browning to the RUC officer then followed Whitlock back down the stairs. He crossed to where Sabrina and a paramedic were crouched over Fiona Gallagher. "Is she dead?" he asked.

Sabrina nodded then unclipped the laminated identity disc from the front of Fiona's blouse and held it up. "This is obviously how she got in."

"I can't say I'm surprised," Graham replied bitterly. "Not now. Eastman must have got it for her. Christ, the bastard was in charge of the whole operation. No wonder she was always slipping through our hands with such ease."

"We'll leave you to tidy up in here," Whitlock said to the paramedic. "Mike, Sabrina, let's go."

"Scoby's dead, isn't he?" Graham asked once they were outside.

Whitlock nodded grimly. "The bullet blew away the back of his head. It looks like she used a dumdum bullet. He didn't stand a chance."

"How's Melissa Scoby?" Graham asked.

"She's been sedated and taken to a local hospital." Whitlock watched as Eastman was led from the church to a waiting police car. "I'll get on to Commander Palmer as soon as possible. Hopefully he'll let us have first crack at Eastman when he's returned to the mainland."

"We really screwed this one up, C. W.," Graham said.

"It looks like Fabio got out just in time," Sabrina added. "At least he's got a future to look forward to back in Italy."

"I hear the pay's good for military advisers in the Gulf," Graham said. "I always thought my Delta years would come in handy again some day."

"We're not beaten yet," Whitlock reminded him. "I don't know about the two of you, but I'm damned if I'm going to give our critics at the UN the satisfaction of seeing UNACO on its knees. And that means we've still got a lot of work to do if we're going to pull this round in our favor. Are you with me?"

Graham patted Whitlock on the shoulder. "We're with you, buddy. Come on, let's go."

It was five-thirty in the morning when the telephone woke Kolchinsky. It was Whitlock. Five minutes later Kolchinsky replaced the receiver then reached for the pack of cigarettes on the bedside table. He lit one, took his first drag of the day, and began coughing violently. Donning his dressing gown and slippers he went into the lounge. He had to tell the Secretary-General about Scoby before one of his aides either heard it on the radio or saw it on the six o'clock news. He sat down in his favorite armchair and dialed the number of the Secretary-General's scrambled line at his home in Rhode Island. It was answered by an aide who patched the call through to the Secretary-General's bedroom, but Kolchinsky's worst fears were realized: the Secretary-General had been up since five and had already heard of the shooting on the radio. Repeating all he knew, Kolchinsky promised to keep him posted on any new developments, then replaced the receiver and used the remote control to switch on the television set in the corner of the room.

He lit another cigarette as the news began but it smouldered untouched in the ashtray for the duration of the lead story: the assassination of Senator Jack Scoby at a church in Ireland. Impatiently he switched off the set, stubbed out the remains of the cigarette, then sat back in the chair and ran his hand over his thinning hair. Nothing had gone right since he had taken over from Philpott. It had been an endless catalog of catastrophic errors. And now UNACO had just handed their critics the ammunition they needed to destroy them. He knew the Secretary-General would stand by UNACO. But how long could he hold out against the inevitable tide of condemnation that was sure to break once the news of Scoby's death spread through the United Nations? It was imperative that Kolchinsky try and minimize the damage to the organization. The Secretary-General needed a scapegoat to appease their opponents.

He knew now who that would have to be. He would tender his resignation to the Secretary-General when he met with him later that morning.

* * *

Tillman had originally been scheduled to travel with the Scobys to Ireland but had pulled out earlier that morning, citing a backlog of paperwork as his reason for staying at the hotel. The real reason for his change of heart, however, had nothing to do with work. He knew that even with the added security which had been drafted in to protect Scoby in Dugaill, the threat to Scoby's life was still very real. And if anything were to happen to Scoby, he would have to move fast to save his own skin . . .

Scoby was the linchpin in the deal with the Colombians and the Mafia. Without him, the deal became worthless. That meant both parties would have to move quickly to distance themselves by removing all incriminating evidence which could possibly link them to Scoby. And Tillman would be top of their list. He had spent the last couple of days pondering the different options open to him if Scoby were assassinated. And when it came down to it, there were only really two options open to him. Agree to turn State's Evidence in return for a place on the Witness Protection Program. But there was no guarantee that he wouldn't spend time in prison before he was allocated a new identity under the program. And if that happened, he knew he'd never get out alive. Or he could use the five hundred thousand dollars he'd received as "sweeteners" from the Colombians and the Mafia to start a new life in some distant corner of the world. It would be his only chance if worse came to worst . . .

And it had. After Palmer had called he'd immediately put his emergency plan into action. He'd hurriedly packed his suitcase then checked out of the hotel and taken a taxi to Heathrow where he'd used his diplomatic status to secure a seat on the next flight back to New York. He knew the anti-terrorist officers on duty at the hotel would tell their superiors that he'd gone. But he wasn't worried about them. He was worried about Jorge Cabrera and Martin Navarro. It would only be a matter of time before they found out that he had returned to the States, but hopefully by then he'd have already collected the money and fled the country. Hopefully . . .

As was his custom every morning, Martin Navarro woke at six then spent half an hour working out in his mini-gymnasium before swimming a dozen lengths of his indoor pool.

A bodyguard handed him his towelling robe as he climbed out of the pool. He slipped it on as he walked through to the patio which overlooked the spacious gardens of his double-story mansion in Rhode Island. A glass of freshly squeezed orange juice and a copy of the *New York Times* lay on the table in the center of the patio. He sat down and opened the paper.

"Excuse me, sir," the butler said, appearing in the doorway behind him. "Mr. Varese's in the lounge. He asked if he could have a word with you. He seems rather agitated."

"Tony's here at this time of the morning?" Navarro said with a frown. He folded the paper over again and tossed it back onto the table. "Show him in."

The butler bowed and left. He returned moments later with Varese and ushered him into the patio. "Can I get you anything, Mr. Varese? Coffee? Orange juice?"

Varese shook his head.

Navarro dismissed the butler then looked up at Varese. "Well?"

"You haven't heard, have you?" Varese said, pacing the floor anxiously.

"I don't know unless you tell me what it is you're talking about," Navarro shot back.

"Scoby's dead. It's the lead story on every news

bulletin. I know you only watch the news on your way to work. That's why I came straight round when I heard about it."

"Tell me what you know," Navarro said, clasping his hands behind his head as he listened to Varese. "Well, at least the damage is minimal. Nobody else in the family knew about the deal we made with Scoby. And I intend to keep it that way."

"What about Tillman?"

"I'd say that all depends on him. If he goes for a deal with the DA, he's probably already under police protection. That's going to make a hit that much more difficult. But if he tries to make a run for it, then we can find him. What's the name of the hotel he's staying at in London?"

"The Grosvenor House."

Navarro pulled the telephone toward him, lifted the receiver, and asked the operator for the number of the hotel. He dialed the number in London, spoke briefly to the switchboard operator, then replaced the receiver. "He checked out of the hotel an hour ago."

"He's obviously panicked."

Navarro allowed himself the luxury of a smile. "Good. And it's my guess that he's already on his way back here to pick up the money. It won't take me long to find out which flight he's on and when he's due to touch down in New York. I want you to tail him from the airport."

"When do you want me to make the hit?"

"When he's led you to the money, of course. And no mistakes, Tony, or we'll both be answerable to the family."

"No mistakes," Varese replied as he left the room.

Navarro sat impassively for some time as the anger slowly began to build up inside him. He'd told Brady to deal with the situation. And he'd blown it. And now with Scoby dead, his chance of pulling off a major coup against the Colombians had gone. It was back to square one again. He'd warned Brady what would happen if he failed him. Well, it was payback time. He'd see to that.

"Come," Maurice Palmer called in response to the sharp rap on the door.

The door opened and Whitlock entered the room. "Is it a bad time?"

"It's been a bad time ever since you called me from Ireland," Palmer replied despondently. "Come in, C.W. Sit down."

Whitlock closed the door behind him and sat down. "We got in to Heathrow an hour ago. I told Mike and Sabrina to wait for me downstairs."

"The Commissioner's agreed to let you question Keith first. Initially he wanted Special Branch in on it as well but I managed to talk him out of it. You've got an hour before Special Branch take over. I've given specific orders that none of my men are to go near Keith until we know whether any of them were in collusion with him as well. We can't rule that out at present. And find out about John Marsh. If he is innocent, I want him back on the case as quickly as possible."

"Sure, if Eastman agrees to talk to us."

"He'll talk," Palmer replied confidently. "I spoke to him briefly after he was brought over here from the airport. He said then he was prepared to answer any questions. He actually seemed quite chirpy under the circumstances."

"I'm not surprised he's chirpy. Scoby's dead. The IRA have achieved what they set out to do. And you can bet they'll see to it that he'll be looked after on the inside. They've beaten us, haven't they?"

Palmer took a cigarette from the packet in front of him and lit it. "I want a transcript of the interrogation

on my desk as soon as possible after you're through
so that I can brief the Commissioner."

"I'll see that you get one," Whitlock replied as he
got to his feet and left the office.

Eastman was ushered into the interview room by
two Special Branch officers. How many times had he
grilled villains in this very room? The irony wasn't
lost on him. He was led to the table in the middle of
the room and told to sit down. On the table was a por-
table tape recorder and two microphones. He sat
down and clasped his manacled hands in his lap. The
two policemen remained in the room until Whitlock
arrived.

"Tell them to take these cuffs off me," Eastman
said without looking around.

Whitlock stared at the back of Eastman's head then
nodded his consent. One of the policemen removed
the handcuffs and gave them to Whitlock. Eastman
was still massaging his chafed wrists when Graham
and Sabrina entered the room and the two policemen
withdrew, closing the door behind them.

Whitlock sat opposite Eastman and Graham and
Sabrina took their places on either side of him. Eastman looked up slowly at them. His right eye was almost closed and a dark, discolored bruise had spread
across the surrounding skin.

"I'm impressed," Graham said, eyeing the bruise
with evident satisfaction. "I never realized you en-
couraged that kind of initiative amongst your men."

"Unfortunately the same can't be said for
UNACO, can it?" Eastman replied coldly, holding
Graham's stare. "You've all been blundering about in
the dark like a bunch of headless chickens. It certainly
made our task that much easier."

Whitlock grabbed Graham's arm as he was about
to jump to his feet. "Let it go, Mike." He turned back

to Eastman. "You know the procedure. The questioning begins when I switch on the tape recorder."

"Be my guest," Eastman replied.

Whitlock positioned a microphone in front of Eastman then switched on the machine. "How long have you been working for the IRA?"

Eastman sat back in the chair. "There you go again, blundering about in the dark."

"Then perhaps you'd care to enlighten us?" Whitlock said.

"I have *never* worked for the IRA."

"Then let me rephrase the question," Whitlock said. "How long has the IRA been paying you to pass information on to them?"

"I have never worked for, passed any information on to, or ever received any money from, the IRA. This whole operation was set up to discredit the IRA, not assist them."

"So who exactly was behind this operation?" Whitlock asked.

"There were three of us. Patrick Gorman, Fiona Gallagher and myself."

"Gorman, the undercover cop who was murdered in Belfast last year?" Sabrina asked.

"The same. The plan has always been to discredit the IRA. At the time we didn't have a particular target in mind. Pat was murdered before we could finalize the details. That meant Fiona and I had to rethink our strategy. We decided to put the operation on ice until we found the right target. And when Scoby announced that he was coming over to the UK we knew we'd found it."

"Gallagher's still the mystery figure in this case," Whitlock said. "Commander Palmer claims she'd never been a member of the anti-terrorist squad and yet she obviously worked closely with the two of you, both senior officers in the unit. Where exactly did she fit into all this?"

"Palmer's right. She'd been a Provo since Mullen recruited her at Bristol University. But after a few years she became disillusioned with the movement. That's when Pat turned her. When I first met her I suggested she take up with Farrell because he was then the blue-eyed boy of the movement. She reeled him in perfectly. He was absolutely besotted with her. And all the time she was with him she was passing info back to us. Then Pat was killed. She took it badly. Not that she ever showed it in front of Farrell or any of his cronies. She was every inch the professional. The best."

"Did Marsh know about her?" Whitlock asked.

"Only Pat and I knew about her. It was vital for her own protection."

"So where does Marsh come into it?" Graham asked.

"John?" Eastman managed a faint smile. "John was what you Americans would call a patsy."

"So you set him up?" Whitlock said.

"It wasn't very difficult. Fiona managed to get Brady's thumbprint on a tenner when she last saw him. And I got the combination to John's safe when I went over to his house a couple of weeks ago on the pretext of borrowing one of his disks. Not the one that was used to trap him, mind. That would have been too obvious. I planted the evidence a couple of days before he was arrested."

"You knew he'd be arrested?" Sabrina said.

"I knew we were going to be investigated. That was obvious. So I had to make sure John took the fall."

"Let's turn now to McGuire," Whitlock said. "How did he find out about the plot to assassinate Senator Scoby?"

"He overheard Fiona talking to me on the phone. But he obviously thought she was talking to someone in the IRA because she also mentioned that Farrell

was returning to the UK after meeting with a cell in
Germany. He then tipped you off that Farrell was
due back in the UK and you, in turn, told Palmer. But
that suited us perfectly: if Farrell hadn't been put behind bars when he was, we'd have had to kill him. It
was absolutely essential for our plan to have any
chance of succeeding, that Fiona be put in temporary
charge of the cell so that Mullen and Kerrigan would
think that she was taking her orders directly from the
Army Council.''

"Did the IRA sanction McGuire's murder?" Whitlock asked.

"Yes. When Fiona realized that McGuire had overheard her and was planning to meet with Swain she
told the Army Council that McGuire was a tout. They
gave her instructions to kill him. And by doing that
she could then introduce the second part of the plan
to assassinate Scoby, without raising any suspicion
amongst either the members of her cell, who would
automatically have assumed that it was another IRA
directive, or amongst the Army Council, who would
still think she was tidying up the McGuire affair.''

"And you had Grogan silenced because he could
have led us to McGuire?" Sabrina deduced.

"At the time we didn't know how much Grogan
knew for the simple reason we didn't know where he
was. That's why I had Mike get the information from
Roche. The car was bugged so when he told me the
address, Fiona was able to get there before us. I
removed the bug before I brought the car back here.''

"And presumably it was you who also made the
hoax bomb call to the airport?" Whitlock said.

Eastman nodded. "I had to give her time to get to
McGuire first and take him out. It was touch and go
for a while because of the weather. But Mullen did an
unbelievable job to get them to the chalet just ahead
of us. It was certainly a close call.''

"Why did she kill Lynch?" Whitlock asked.

"Two reasons. Lynch and Kerrigan had hatched a plan to tell the Army Council that she wasn't capable of running the cell in Farrell's absence. If she'd been relieved of her command, that would have ruined everything. Secondly, Lynch was one of the senior Provos in Europe. Kill him and you damage the network. Which it's done by all accounts."

"Why did she kill Kerrigan and Mullen?" Whitlock asked.

"Kerrigan was becoming increasingly rebellious. It came to a head at the chalet where they were hiding out after the hit on McGuire. He pulled a gun on her and she shot him. She killed Mullen for the simple reason that she didn't need him after the botched attempt on the *Merry Dancer*. She needed to operate alone at the church. And with both of them dead, there would be no witnesses to contradict her in court."

Whitlock nodded to himself. "I get it now. You intended to arrest her after she'd killed Mike, then when she appeared in court she'd have claimed that she shot Scoby on the orders of the IRA. That would have caused an international outcry and the IRA would have been discredited publicly. That alone would have seriously damaged their image abroad."

"It's already damaged their image abroad," Eastman corrected him. "They're sure to regroup and rebuild again from within but you can still bet that heads are going to roll. And the first head to roll will be Brady's. And that will be a major coup in itself."

"How can you be so sure?" Sabrina asked.

"Because Brady was Fiona's superior. And the IRA are going to need a scapegoat if they're going to win back their supporters. He knew that when he came up with that idea to edit the tape for public release. It was the one ace he still had up his sleeve. But Whitlock outwitted him. Probably the only person who ever has.

"You must understand that when we originally devised this plan, we had Brady very much in mind. He's been responsible for the deaths, either directly or indirectly, of more British soldiers in Ireland than any other Chief-of-Staff in the history of the organization. And this was one way of getting him. Discredit him in the eyes of his superiors. Let them deal with him."

"She'd have got life if she'd ever stood trial," Sabrina said. "Didn't that bother her?"

"She'd have got several life sentences," Eastman corrected her. "But that doesn't mean she'd have spent long in jail. There was a contingency plan to spring her after a few weeks. She'd have left the country and started a new life somewhere out of the reach of the IRA."

"And I suppose it doesn't bother you that three of our colleagues and an innocent American senator were murdered as a result of your vigilante operation?" Graham snapped.

"Scoby's death was an essential part of the operation. I make no excuses for that. But your colleagues . . ." Eastman trailed off and shook his head. "That wasn't part of the operation. Fiona specifically gave orders to hit only McGuire but Kerrigan overstepped the mark. There was nothing she could do about it. I know she was just as gutted about their deaths as I was. As we were when Mullen shot that chopper down over the Thames."

"You sound just like the IRA now," Graham shot back. "When they kill someone by mistake they always make some lame apology to the family. It doesn't wash, Eastman. It just doesn't wash."

"I don't expect you to believe me," Eastman replied softly. "But it's true."

"Who put up the money for the operation?" Sabrina asked.

"The IRA. Unwittingly, of course. As a senior officer, Farrell had access to the funds. It wasn't difficult for Fiona to skim money off over the last year and attribute it to Farrell. Always small amounts. But it all added up in the end. She bought the weapons and equipment herself and used a couple of ex-pats to help her put it in place. She paid them well and swore them to silence. Who were they to argue, especially as they thought they were in on an IRA operation?"

Whitlock stared at the microphone in front of him, his brow creased in thought. He finally looked up at Eastman. "So had we been questioning Fiona Gallagher now instead of you, none of this would have come out, would it? She'd have stuck to the story about it being an IRA operation. So why have you changed the script?"

"Fiona was a Provo. There's no question of that. Her background would have added credibility in a courtroom. And she'd have made a very convincing witness. After all, she pulled the trigger in Dugaill. She killed Scoby. What have I done? I planned the hit with her and Pat. It doesn't have the same punch, does it?"

"That still doesn't answer the question," Sabrina said.

"I think it does," Graham replied. "By coming clean he's putting the authorities in a major dilemma. Do they keep to the story that's been splashed across the front page of every newspaper this morning that the IRA were responsible for Scoby's death, or do they put him on trial and admit that the whole thing was really planned by a couple of maverick Scotland Yard detectives out to discredit the IRA? Imagine the public outcry. They'll be screaming about unlawful vigilantes within the British police. It would do irreparable harm to Scotland Yard's image. But more importantly, it would completely exonerate the IRA of any blame. And their support would be sure to increase. How am I doing, Eastman?"

"I couldn't have put it better myself," Eastman replied.

"That's pretty ingenious," Whitlock said after a moment's thought.

"There's one thing that I still don't understand," Sabrina said, breaking the sudden silence. "Why didn't Gallagher kill me after they'd taken out Grogan?"

Eastman leaned his elbows on the table and rested his chin on his clenched fists. "I told you, our plan was to discredit the IRA; it was never our intention to kill those working against them. Fiona seemed to admire you for what you'd managed to achieve with UNACO. I guess you could say that she saw in you a mirror image of what she would have liked to be, had things turned out differently for her. But that doesn't mean she wouldn't have killed you had you threatened either her or the success of the operation. It's all irrelevant now though, isn't it?"

Whitlock switched off the tape recorder. He recalled the two Special Branch detectives and Eastman was handcuffed again and escorted from the room. He then ejected the two cassettes from the machine. "I'm going to get this transcribed for Sergei as soon as possible. I'll fax the text through to him as soon as it's finished. In the meantime I'll take this one over to Commander Palmer."

"Do you think Eastman will ever stand trial?" Sabrina asked Whitlock as he crossed to the door.

"What do you think?" Whitlock replied contemptuously before leaving the room.

Sabrina turned back to Graham. "Gallagher took us down to the wire, didn't she? She anticipated our every move and countered them with moves of her own. And she so nearly outfoxed us at the finish. Eastman was right. She could have been me."

"She was good. Granted. But she was never in

your league. If she was, she'd still be alive, wouldn't she?''

"Flatterer," Sabrina said with a grin.

"I'm just stating the obvious, that's all," Graham replied matter-of-factly.

"Thanks, Mike," she said with a resigned sigh as she left the room.

Graham frowned. She knew he wasn't into flattery or any of that kind of ingratiating nonsense. Surely honesty was a compliment in itself? He shrugged to himself then went after her.

Melissa Scoby woke to find herself in a hospital bed. It was obviously a private ward. She had been undressed and was now wearing a white nightgown. She tried to sit up but the effects of the sedative administered to her in Dugaill made her feel giddy and light-headed. She lay back on the pillow and stared at the ceiling.

Then it all came flooding back to her. The shot. The blood. Jack being knocked off his feet. Falling. Falling . . .

The tears came quickly but she made no attempt to wipe them away. They streamed down the side of her face and onto the pillow. She had known Jack was dead even before Whitlock had gently helped her to her feet. She had struggled fiercely with him, wanting to stay with her husband. Then the paramedics had arrived. They had gone over to where her husband lay sprawled on the ground, the grass around his head already soaked in blood. So much blood. It had stained her jacket. Her blouse. Her skirt. She remembered wiping her hand across her face. Her palm was streaked with blood. She had screamed and her legs had gone from underneath her. Someone had caught her. Whitlock? She didn't know. Then one of the paramedics had appeared beside her. She didn't want a sedative. No sedative. She had tried to tell him. But her throat was dry. She couldn't speak. Then she had felt the needle prick her skin. She had initially fought against the drowsiness. But within seconds it had taken effect and she had felt herself going.

She struggled again to sit up. She took a tissue from the box on the bedside table and wiped her eyes. Still the tears came. Tears of disbelief. Tears of sorrow. Tears of loss. Tears of guilt . . .

She knew their marriage had been far from perfect but, despite that, she had never been unfaithful to her husband. Her flirtations had been harmless enough, just an attempt to attract his attention. But he'd never noticed, he had been too busy with his career. It had always come first. And it had ultimately cost him his life. Suddenly all those dreams were gone. The Presidency. The White House. Everything he'd ever wanted. Everything she'd ever wanted . . .

"Mrs. Scoby?" A nurse stood in the doorway. She smiled gently. "How are you feeling?"

"Numb," came the reply.

"Yes, I can understand that," the nurse replied, entering the room.

"Can you?" Melissa Scoby bit her lip as she fought back the tears. "Where am I?"

"You're in the Armagh County Hospital. It's the nearest hospital to Dugaill. The American embassy is sending someone over to take you back to London. They should be here within the next hour."

Melissa Scoby dabbed her eyes with the tissue. "Please, just leave me alone."

"Would you like anything to drink. Tea? Coffee?"

"No."

The nurse left the room, closing the door quietly behind her.

Melissa Scoby propped the two pillows against the headboard then leaned her head against them and closed her eyes. She suddenly saw her husband's face in her mind. It was so clear. So real. Then she remembered what he had said to her at the airport before they set out for Belfast. *I've left an envelope in the safe in our room back at the hotel. If anything should happen to me in Dugaill today, it's imperative that you give it to Whitlock as soon as possible. Promise me you'll do that, Melissa. You must promise me.*

She had promised him. She sat up abruptly in bed and lifted the telephone off the bedside table and placed it in her lap. She picked up the receiver, dialed the switchboard, and asked the operator to ring the Grosvenor House Hotel in London.

◆ **CHAPTER**

FIFTEEN

Tillman was sweating as he made his way through customs at John F. Kennedy Airport. He wasn't stopped, which surprised him. If anyone looked nervous, he did. His luck seemed to be holding. He looked anxiously around him as he strode briskly through the concourse. Once outside he made for the nearest yellow cab and told the driver to take him to Grand Central Station. The driver finished the Hershey bar he was eating then switched on the meter and started the engine.

Tony Varese had tailed Tillman discreetly through the airport from the moment he was cleared through customs. He climbed into the back of another yellow cab and told the driver to follow Tillman. The driver, an expatriate Italian who regularly worked for the Germino family, put the cab into gear then pulled out into the road and followed the quarry at a safe distance.

* * *

Tillman told the driver to wait for him once they reached Grand Central Station. He wouldn't be long. When he returned he had a pale blue hold-all with him. He thought momentarily about going back to his apartment to collect a few personal things but quickly dismissed the idea. It would be too dangerous. He couldn't afford to take any unnecessary risks. He still hadn't decided on his ultimate destination. El Salvador? Guatemala? Honduras? It didn't matter. He could decide that later. All that mattered now was getting out of the country. He knew he couldn't use any of the major airlines. How would he explain away the five hundred thousand dollars in the hold-all? No, it was time to call in a favor. He told the driver where he wanted to go.

Judd Miller's boast was that if it had wings and an engine, he could fly it. He had yet to be proved wrong. He had flown helicopter gunships in Vietnam in the sixties, Hercules transport planes in war-torn Africa in the seventies and a variety of light aircraft in Central America in the eighties. During that time he had also served a total of fourteen years in prisons around the world on a variety of charges ranging from gun-running to attempted murder.

He had returned to the States in the late eighties and opened a small flying school outside New York, but a costly divorce a year later and mounting debts had taken the company to the brink of bankruptcy. He had been forced to sell one of his planes earlier in the year to pay off some of his creditors and then the previous month had laid off his secretary and two of his three mechanics because he couldn't afford to pay their wages anymore. He knew it would only be a matter of time before the company was wound up. Not that it bothered him. He'd had enough of teaching anyway. It was time to move on again. He knew he could get a job in any number of countries. He'd already put out feelers and now all he had to do was wait until the right offer came along . . .

He was sitting in his office, his feet on the desk, when the yellow cab pulled up outside the door. The driver removed a suitcase from the trunk and dumped it on the ground. Miller cursed angrily. He wasn't running a charter service. He was about to swing his legs off the desk and go outside when Tillman got out of the cab. Miller recognized him straight away. He raked his fingers through his greasy hair. What the hell was going on?

He had first met Tillman in the early eighties. He had been serving a three-year sentence in a Nicaraguan jail for running arms to the Contras; Tillman had been a highly respected foreign correspondent with the *New York Times*. Even though they had little in common, apart from a mutual hatred of international communism, their paths had crossed several times over the next few years. Then Tillman had returned to the States and Miller hadn't heard of him again until a recent NBC special about Jack Scoby's historic victory in New York State. Tillman was there. The brains behind the campaign. The puppeteer. But now it seemed that the strings had suddenly been cut from underneath him . . .

Tillman paid the driver then waited until the taxi had left before entering the small office. "You remember me, don't you?"

Miller nodded slowly. "Sure. The smart-assed journalist turned political manipulator. You did a good job on Scoby. You even got me to vote for him. And I've never voted before in my life. Pity it turned out to have been a wasted vote though."

"Then you know what happened?"

"It's all they've been reporting on the radio this morning." Miller clasped his hands behind his head. "I'd have thought you'd have been big news right now. There must be journalists out there who'd sell their children to get an exclusive with you. So what the hell are you doing here?"

"I'm calling in the favor you owe me," Tillman replied sharply.

"And which favor would that be?"

"Don't screw me about, Miller. You know damn well what I'm talking about. I got you out of Honduras after your plane had been shot down by the guerrillas. If they'd have got hold of you, you wouldn't be here today."

"Oh, *that* favor? I guess I do owe you something for bailing out my ass. What do you want?"

"I want you to fly me to Central America. It doesn't matter where at the moment. Just get me out of the States."

A look of disbelief crossed Miller's face. "Fly you out to Central America? Just like that?"

Tillman cleared a space on the desk for the hold-all then opened it and removed two packs of ten thousand dollars and tossed them into Miller's lap. "That's for the hire of the plane, all fuel expenses and for your time. I think you'd agree that twenty grand is a more than reasonable amount."

Miller picked up one of the packs and fanned the money with his thumb. "I'm intrigued. Scoby's assassinated and suddenly you have to flee the country in a hurry. What the hell's going on, Tillman?"

Tillman tossed another ten thousand dollars on the table. "Thirty grand. No questions asked."

"How much blood money have you got in there?"

"I said no questions asked," Tillman snapped.

"You must have quite a bit there if you can afford to throw around thirty Gs. Let's say fifty Gs and you pay for the fuel as well. Deal?"

"Deal," Tillman replied tersely.

"How can you make a deal with money that doesn't belong to you?" Varese said, appearing in the doorway. He had a silenced Heckler & Koch automatic in his hand.

"Who the hell are you?" Miller snapped, swinging his legs off the desk.

Varese eyed Miller disdainfully then raised the automatic and shot him. Tillman stumbled backward against the wall, the hold-all clasped to his chest as if it would somehow shield him from the next bullet.

"Fifty grand to take you to Central America?" Varese said, glancing down at Miller's body. "I'd say he was dealing you from the bottom of the deck on that one."

"We can make a deal, Varese," Tillman said in desperation, stuffing the thirty thousand dollars back into the hold-all. "You can say you never found me. That way you'd get to keep all the money for yourself. Half a million. It's a lot of money. I won't talk. You know that. I'm in this just as deep as you are. I don't want to spend the rest of my life in a prison cell. Take the money. Take it all. Just let me go."

"I know you wouldn't sing to the authorities but what if the Colombians got hold of you? They'd certainly torture you and you'd end up telling them all about Mr. Navarro. And then they'd be sure to retaliate against the family. The Colombians are particularly bad losers. And then we'd have to retaliate so as not to lose face. It could all turn very nasty. And all because I let you go."

"They could torture me, I wouldn't talk," Tillman replied, using his cuff to wipe the sweat from his forehead.

"The Colombians are masters of torture. I know I'd talk rather than have to endure that kind of agony. And so would you. You'd tell them everything they wanted to know. And more. Just to make them stop." Varese levelled the automatic at Tillman's head. "This way there can't be any misunderstandings.

And you'll be spared an agonizing death at the hands of the Colombians.''

Tillman lashed out with the hold-all, catching Varese full in the face. The bullet smashed harmlessly into the wall behind the desk. Tillman darted past Varese and out through the open doorway. Cursing angrily, Varese moved to the door. Tillman was making for the hangar a couple of hundred yards away from the office. Varese raised the automatic, steadied his aim, then fired. The bullet took Tillman in the leg. He stumbled and fell heavily to the ground. He looked around in horror as Varese walked toward him. He tried to get up but a sharp pain speared through his leg. He gritted his teeth in agony and finally managed to get up onto his one good leg. But after a couple of unsteady steps he overbalanced and fell to the ground again. He clawed at the ground, dragging himself toward the hangar. When Varese caught up with him he raised the automatic and shot him through the back of the head. He used his foot to roll Tillman over onto his back. Satisfied Tillman was dead, he picked up the hold-all and walked back to the taxi which had been parked out of sight at the back of the hangar. He told the driver to take him to West Side Electronics. He wanted to break the news personally to Navarro. Their troubles were over . . .

Kolchinsky punched a code into the bellpush then opened the door and entered the room. Sarah wasn't behind her desk. And the sliding door leading into the Director's office was open. Although she had access to the spare miniature transmitter which was kept in the wallsafe behind her desk, she knew she was only to use it in an emergency if either he or Whitlock wasn't in the office. Those were the rules. So why was she in there? Was it an emergency? Another crisis? He hurried into the room and froze when he saw Malcolm Philpott seated behind the desk.

"Afternoon, Sergei," Philpott said, looking up at him. He turned back to Sarah who was standing in front of the desk. "Thanks for doing those photocopies for me."

She smiled at him and left the room.

Philpott used the spare miniature transmitter to close the door again behind her. "Sit down and I'll tell you what's going on."

"I would but you're sitting in my chair."

"This is the Director's chair." Philpott took the envelope containing Kolchinsky's letter of resignation from his pocket and placed it on the desk. "I believe you gave this to the Secretary-General this morning?"

Kolchinsky sat down slowly on one of the black leather sofas, his eyes never leaving Philpott's face. "This smacks of an old-style Soviet coup. The ink isn't even dry on my letter of resignation and already the bureaucrats have moved me out."

"You haven't been moved out, Sergei." Philpott picked up his pipe and turned it around thoughtfully in his hands. He hadn't used it since he suffered the heart attack earlier in the year. Now it was just a memento. He put it down again. "The Secretary-General called me this morning after you'd handed in your letter of resignation and asked if I'd consider returning to UNACO. It was a bolt out of the blue. Not that I needed any persuading. As you already know, the boredom's been driving me mad. But I haven't come back to wind UNACO down. On the contrary, I intend to fight tooth and nail to ensure it survives. I've spent most of the morning studying the reports of the Scoby case. There's no use fooling ourselves. UNACO is in a lot of trouble. But there are loopholes. And I intend to exploit them to the full to get UNACO back on an even keel. But I'm going to need support on this. And I hope you'll be there to give me that support, old friend. Of course you're going to take some flak from the politicians. It's only to be expected. But that doesn't mean you were to blame for what's happened. It would still have happened even if I'd been here. None of us is infallible. But my main concern at the moment is that UNACO will fragment at the top. A point borne out by your resignation this morning. That's why I'm asking you to reconsider your decision. I can understand why you did it. But I don't think it's the answer. At least not at the moment. If we appear solid then it's going to be that much harder for our critics to find the chinks in our armor.

"I've already spoken to C.W. and he's indicated that he wants to stay with UNACO on the condition that he can return to the field. I've certainly got no problem with that. He's one of the best field operatives we've ever had. He's obviously never settled properly on the management side." Philpott held up the envelope. "We've always been honest with each other, Sergei. If you still want to stick by your decision, I won't try and change your mind. I respect you too much for that. It's entirely up to you."

Kolchinsky stared at the carpet for some time then sat back on the sofa and clasped his hands in his lap. "In retrospect, what you say makes sense. The organization does need to stand together at a time like this. Perhaps I was a bit hasty in tendering my resignation this morning. But I still intend to reconsider my position again once all the hubbub has died down."

"Then I'd better hang on to this," Philpott said, slipping the envelope into the drawer in front of him.

"Why didn't the Secretary-General tell me you were coming back? I've been with him for the last three hours."

"I asked him not to say anything. I thought it would be better if I told you myself."

"It's good to have you back again, Malcolm," Kolchinsky said at length. "I only wish it were under different circumstances."

"The cards have been dealt. It's now up to us to play our hand as best we can."

"Some hand," Kolchinsky retorted.

"We've still got an ace to play," Philpott replied, tapping the folder in front of him. "Jack Scoby left instructions with his wife to forward an envelope to C. W. if anything happened to him while they were in Ireland. C. W. faxed the contents through to the office while you were still in conference with the Secretary-General. It makes chilling reading. The question now is how best to play it for maximum effect."

"What was in the envelope?" Kolchinsky asked, his interest stimulated.

Philpott briefly outlined the five pages of handwritten text in which Scoby had explained, in meticulous detail, the agreement he'd made with the Colombians, later to be hijacked by the Mafia, to import cocaine into the United States using New York State as the port of entry.

"Tillman's obviously the key to this now that Scoby's dead," Kolchinsky said. "Has he been arrested yet?"

"Tillman fled the hotel in London as soon as he found out that Scoby was dead. By the time this came through he'd already arrived back in New York. The DEA have staked out his apartment and there's an APB out on him as well but so far there's been no sign of him. He seems to have vanished."

"I'm not surprised. He must know it'll only be a matter of time before both the Colombians and the Mafia catch up with him. But why would he come back here? If I was in his shoes I'd have fled as far away from the States as I possibly could."

"We'll only know that after he's been arrested," Philpott replied.

"Did Scoby give any reason for leaving such a damaging confession behind?"

"To protect his wife. It's possible that the Colombians or the Mafia might put a contract out on her if they believed Scoby had let her in on the deal as well. But Scoby was very insistent in his notes that she knew nothing about it. If these allegations were made public then everything would be out in the open. It's the best protection she could have."

"It's going to damage the image of the Republican Party enormously if these allegations reach the Press," Kolchinsky said. "They could lose the next election with a skeleton like this in their closet."

"Which is why the President's sending one of his senior aides down from Washington tomorrow morning. And I intend to use this situation to its fullest advantage."

"You mean you'd actually blackmail the President?" Kolchinsky said in amazement.

"Perish the thought," Philpott replied in mock horror. "Let's just say I intend to negotiate a deal in our favor."

"What's the deal?"

"You'll find out soon enough," Philpott replied, pushing the folder to one side. "Now tell me about your meeting with the Secretary-General."

After Whitlock had settled the accounts at the hotel, the three of them had taken a taxi to Heathrow Airport where they checked in for their flight back to New York then went through to the cafeteria for a coffee.

"I'll be glad to get back home," Sabrina said after they'd sat down.

"Me too," Graham said, adding milk to his coffee.

"The Giants are playing at Meadowlands tomorrow night. Should be a great game."

"I know I'm going to regret asking this, but who are they playing?" Sabrina said.

"The Washington Redskins. It should be a really tight game. I reckon it could even be decided on a single touchdown."

"I'm regretting it already," Sabrina said with a despairing look in Whitlock's direction.

"Why don't you come along?" Graham said. "You might learn something. I've got a few contacts in the game. I should be able to get another ticket even at this late stage."

"You know I don't know the first thing about football, Mike," she replied. "You'd just be wasting your money."

"OK, I'll make a deal with you. For the price of a cheap exercise book I'll teach you the basics of the game on the flight back home. And if you still don't understand the plays by the time we reach JFK, then I'll concede defeat. But I guarantee that you'll want to come to Meadowlands tomorrow night. Is it a deal?"

"Me and my big mouth." She shrugged. "It's not as if I've got much else to do for the next couple of hours."

"We'll make a Giants fan out of you yet."

"I can hardly wait," she replied, pulling a face.

"What do you think, C. W.?" Graham's smile faded when he saw the consternation etched on Whitlock's face. "C. W.?"

Whitlock snapped out of his reverie and grinned ruefully at Graham. "Sorry, Mike, I was far away. What was that you said?"

"It doesn't matter. Are you OK?"

"Sure," Whitlock replied. But he knew he hadn't fooled either of them. He exhaled deeply and sat back in his chair. "When I spoke to the Colonel earlier on the phone I told him that I wanted to be transferred back into the field. I'm just not cut out for management. He was great about it. He said we could finalize the details once I got back to New York. But I haven't told Carmen yet. She's going to throw a fit when she finds out."

"Don't judge her too quickly, C. W."

"Come on, Sabrina, you know how she feels about all this. She wanted me out of the field because she feared for my safety. It got to a point where she threatened to leave because she couldn't bear the anxiety every time I went off on another assignment. Why else do you think I took a management job? It was the one chance to save the marriage. And it's worked. So far." Whitlock indicated Graham beside him. "Mike and I discussed this over the weekend. And he was right. It was a short-term solution. I can't be unhappy at work and happy at home. Sooner or later something would have to give. And I could feel the tension rising these last few days. The three of you were in the thick of the action while I was stuck by the phone writing God knows how many reports to fax through to the UN. I'm not cut out to be a desk jockey. I can't live the lie anymore. But how am I going to convince Carmen?"

"Tell her what you've just told us," Graham said. "From what you've told me about her I'm pretty sure she'll understand the dilemma you've been in since you left the field. The main thing is you've tried management but you just couldn't hack it. And you did it for her. What else can she ask of you? That you grin and bear it for the sake of your marriage? That's no formula to save a marriage. You've got to be honest with her, C. W. It's the only way.

"I know what you're going through," Graham continued. "Carrie and I went through exactly the same thing. She also wanted me out of the field when I was with Delta. And every time she raised the subject, I would refuse to talk about it. There wasn't anything to talk about as far as I was concerned. It was my life. My decision. And I was damned if I was going to push a pen for the rest of my days. Well, it finally got to the point where we had to confront our feelings. And we did. No holds barred. And I'll tell you something, we learned more about each other that day than we had in the previous four years of marriage. It sure cleared the air. And it also saved our marriage, I've no doubt of that."

"Thanks," Whitlock said at length. "I feel better for having talked this through."

"I'll bill you," Graham said with a smile.

Sabrina suddenly noticed Marsh standing in the entrance of the cafeteria. "Don't look now, but we've got company."

Marsh greeted them then pulled up a chair and sat down. "You should have given me a bell at the Yard, I'd have brought you over here myself."

"I think we've caused enough trouble as it is," Whitlock replied. "We thought it best if we just slipped out quietly and went back to the States."

"I'm glad I caught you anyway. I just wanted to thank you for what you did for me."

"We didn't do anything," Whitlock said. "Eastman was the one who cleared your name."

"What's the latest on the son-of-a-bitch?" Graham asked.

"He's still being held at Brixton Remand but it's my guess he'll walk, especially in light of Scoby's drug activities."

"Any more news on Brady?" Whitlock asked.

Marsh shook his head. "Nothing's been seen of him since he left the hotel."

"So it's conceivable that the IRA could already have killed him and dumped his body in a ditch somewhere?" Graham said.

"It's possible, yes. But I think Keith's seriously underestimated Brady's support inside the Army

Council. Sure, this whole operation's damaged the IRA's standing abroad and it's going to take a lot of hard talking by the Army Council to reassure their supporters, especially those over in America, but it's far from being the mortal blow the Press are maintaining in the papers this morning. The IRA will bounce back from it. They always do. And I believe there's even a chance that Brady might come out of this unscathed.

"But if he is killed then I'd be more inclined to think that the order would have come from dissatisfied members within the Army Council rather than from the body as a whole. I guess we'll just have to wait and see, won't we?"

The flight was announced over the public address system. They shook hands with Marsh then picked up their overnight bags and made for the boarding gate. Marsh waited until they had disappeared from view then headed back across the foyer to the main doors. His work wasn't over yet . . .

Seamus Finnegan had been the landlord of the Castle Tavern in Carrickfergus for over twenty-five years. He was a staunch Republican who listed prominent Sinn Fein councillors and senior members of the IRA amongst his close friends. Although the premises were used regularly for Republican meetings and for harboring wanted men from the authorities, he had never been convicted of anything more serious than a speeding offense. Such was the frustration amongst the local RUC that they now regularly raided the pub, claiming to have received an anonymous tip-off that there was a fugitive on the premises. And they invariably chose Saturday nights when the pub was full. The previous night had been no exception. And, as on all the other occasions, they had gone away empty-handed.

Sunday mornings were always quiet. The regulars would converge on the pub after lunch for their customary pint and a game of dominoes. Finnegan glanced at the clock on the wall behind him. It would be another half hour before the first of the regulars began to arrive. There were only four customers in the pub, all seated at the bar watching a recorded game of football on the television. Their glasses were full. His wife had called down five minutes earlier to tell him that his lunch was ready. He decided to go upstairs and fetch it before it went cold. As he turned away from the television screen the door opened and a figure entered the room, his head bowed against the driving rain which had been lashing Carrickfergus since the early hours of the morning. He closed the door behind him and looked up slowly at Finnegan.

"Dear mother of God," Finnegan muttered in disbelief.

Kevin Brady turned down the lapels of his leather jacket and crossed to the far end of the counter, out of earshot of the other customers. "Good to see you, Seamus," he announced in his deadpan voice.

Finnegan pumped Brady's hand vigorously. "And you, lad. How are you?"

"Bearing up," Brady replied, running his fingers through his matted hair.

"The phone hasn't stopped ringing since that American senator was assassinated in Dugaill yesterday afternoon. The Army Council were asking after you. I suppose they assumed that as you grew up in this neighborhood, you'd probably come back here sooner or later. You want to talk to them, lad. Put their minds at ease."

"I will," Brady replied.

"Why not come upstairs? There's a hot meal on the table. You look like you could use it."

"No, but thanks anyway. I'll settle for a pint of

Guinness and a cheese roll. I need to get my thoughts together before I call the Army Council."

Finnegan poured a pint of draft Guinness and placed it on the counter. "There's been talk around these parts that you were involved in that shooting yesterday. It's not true, is it, lad?"

"No."

"That's what I said." Finnegan took a cheese roll from a basket at the back of the bar and handed it to Brady. "I still can't believe that Fiona pulled the trigger. I can't remember the number of times she came in here with Sean for a few drinks and a game of pool. I honestly thought she was one of us."

"We all did."

"Are you sure you won't eat something hot, lad? I can bring you down a plate."

Brady shook his head then crossed to a corner table and sat down. He had always prided himself before on his ability to operate single-handedly but he had never felt so isolated and alone as he had in the last twenty-four hours. Not only was Kane in custody but his plan to publicly discredit the authorities had backfired badly on him. They now had the tapes. But that was nothing compared to the death of Jack Scoby. As a cell leader, Fiona was theoretically under his command. And every Sunday newspaper had fingered him as the mastermind behind the assassination. He knew the authorities wouldn't stop searching until they had found him. It would be the only way they could hope to stem the international outcry. But what worried him more was the reaction of the Army Council. Would they stand by him or would they use him as a scapegoat to appease their supporters abroad? He knew he had strong support in the Army Council but would it be enough to save him? He couldn't keep running. He had to face the truth sooner or later . . .

He looked up when the door opened and instantly

recognized the tall, gangly figure of Kieran O'Con
nell, his fiercest critic on the Army Council. O'Con
nell brushed his windswept hair away from his face
as he crossed the room to where Brady was sitting.
His eyes were cold and malicious.

"Have you come to take me back to face the wrath
of the Army Council?" Brady asked, holding O'Con
nell's penetrating stare.

"The Army Council have voted overwhelmingly
to stand by you until an internal investigation has
been carried out. And now I'm facing expulsion from
the Council because of my friendship with Fiona.
There's nothing left for me anymore."

Brady had always loathed O'Connell for his
wishy-washy liberal views. How many times had
O'Connell's veto wiped out one of his meticulously
planned operations to hit at the very heart of the Brit
ish forces? The Army Council were obviously going
to take a tougher stance in the future. And Brady
knew he was the man to spearhead that campaign.
Revenge was sweet.

O'Connell suddenly stepped back and pulled a
Browning Mk2 from his overcoat pocket. Brady
kicked back the chair, looking wildly around him for
a means of escape. O'Connell fired. The bullet took
Brady in the stomach, punching him back against the
wall. Brady clutched his stomach and stared in horror
as the blood seeped through his fingers. He looked
up slowly at O'Connell but as he tried to open his
mouth to speak, three more bullets were pumped
into him. The blood trickled from the corners of
Brady's mouth and the disbelief was still mirrored in
his eyes when he fell forward onto the table, toppling
it sideways, as his body crashed to the floor.

Finnegan, who had been alerted by the sound of
the first shot, had grabbed his revolver from the bed
room and bounded downstairs, but by the time he
burst through the door behind the counter Brady was

already dead. He was momentarily taken aback by the sight of O'Connell. Another regular. Another friend.

"Put down the gun, Kieran," he ordered, levelling the revolver at O'Connell.

O'Connell looked around slowly at Finnegan. There was no recognition in his eyes. Then, almost as if in slow motion, O'Connell pushed the barrel against the roof of his mouth and pulled the trigger.

◆ CHAPTER

SIXTEEN

It was nine o'clock on Monday morning when Whit
lock pulled up behind the white Ford which was
parked a block away from West Side Electronics. As
he climbed out of the car the Ford's passenger door
swung open and a man got out. Thirty-eight-year-old
Frank Grecco had been one of the Drug Enforcement
Agency's top UCs, undercover cops, in New York for
over twelve years before his cover was blown by an
overzealous journalist out for a scoop. He had to be
withdrawn from the field for his own protection and
after a successful stint as the Assistant Division Chief
in Los Angeles he returned to New York as its youngest ever Division Chief.

Whitlock locked the driver's door and smiled as
Grecco approached him. He had worked with Grecco
on a number of joint DEA-UNACO operations over
the years and it was hard to believe that it was the
same man he had come to regard as one of the best
UCs he'd ever encountered outside UNACO. Gone
was the shoulder-length hair, the stubble and the
dirty jeans. Now Grecco sported a short back and

sides, a neatly trimmed black moustache and an expensive Armani double-breasted suit.

"Hey, goombah, long time no see," Grecco said with a wide grin as he pumped Whitlock's hand. "How you doing?"

It was the same old Frank Grecco. No frills, no graces. And that was why his return to New York two months earlier had been greeted so enthusiastically by his former colleagues.

"I'm fine, Frankie. How's the new job going?"

"It's days like these that make it all worth while," Grecco replied. "I still can't believe that we've finally got the chance to take Navarro down. All these years and we haven't been able to get close to him. Every time we've brought him in for questioning we've never been able to make anything stick. I tell you, I haven't been this excited since Scott Norwood missed that field goal for the Bills with eight seconds left of Superbowl Twenty-Five. That was a hell of a night for the Giants."

"So Mike constantly reminds me."

"How is that lunatic?"

"As ever," Whitlock replied.

"And how's my favorite UC?" Grecco said with a knowing grin.

"Sabrina's fine. They both send their regards."

"Thanks. Where are they?" Grecco asked.

"They had some business to attend to out of town."

"Tell Mike I'll call him sometime. I haven't been to a game with him for a while." Grecco rapped on the Ford's rear window and gave the occupants a thumbs-up sign. Two men emerged from the back of the car. The rear doors of a second white Ford in front of it also swung open and two more plainclothes men got out. Grecco turned back to Whitlock. "I didn't want to take any chances. Not when we're dealing with a slippery customer like Navarro. If he does try anything, we've got the backup to deal with it."

"Well, are you ready?"

"I've been ready for this for years," Grecco replied with a grin.

The brunette looked up from her computer and gave Whitlock and Grecco a warm smile when they entered the room. "Good morning. May I help you?"

"We're here to see Martin Navarro," Grecco told her.

"Do you have an appointment, sir?" she asked, feeding a code into the computer to call up a list of Navarro's appointments for the day.

"You won't find our names on there, sweetheart," Grecco told her, holding up his warrant card. "DEA. We try not to make appointments. That way we can catch the scumbags by surprise."

"Mr. Navarro's not due in until later this morning."

"Your loyalty's touching, sweetheart, but we saw him arrive half an hour ago with his hatchet man, Varese," Grecco told her. "Don't worry, we'll see ourselves in."

Whitlock opened the door and entered Navarro's spacious office. Navarro looked up sharply from behind his desk and was about to challenge Whitlock when Grecco entered the room behind him.

The receptionist hovered anxiously in the doorway. "I'm sorry, Mr. Navarro, I did try to stop them."

"It's OK, Marsha. I'll deal with this."

She nodded nervously and closed the door behind her.

"This is Special Agent Whitlock, he's come down all the way from our Washington office just to see you," Grecco said to Navarro, indicating Whitlock behind him.

Whitlock held up the false DEA warrant card he'd been issued earlier that morning. Varese, who had been sitting on the sofa, got to his feet and took the card from Whitlock. He studied it carefully then nodded to Navarro before handing it back to Whitlock.

"I'm getting very tired of this continual DEA harassment, Grecco. Your people tail me wherever I go. My house is under constant surveillance. Not to mention the fact that I've been hauled in for questioning five times in this last year alone and on each occasion I've been released without charge. Doesn't that say something to you?"

"Yeah, that maybe we've been concentrating on the wrong man." Grecco turned to Varese. "I know you're carrying, Tony. I want you to take your piece out very slowly and toss it onto the floor in front of me. And I wouldn't do anything stupid. Special Agent Whitlock's never been known to miss from that range."

Varese's eyes flickered to the automatic in Whitlock's hand but he made no move to comply with Grecco's instructions.

"Do you want me to come over there and take it from you, Tony?" Grecco said icily.

"Why don't you try it, Grecco?" Varese hissed, balling his fists at his sides.

"Just do as he says!" Navarro snapped at Varese.

Varese glared at Navarro then took the Heckler & Koch P9S from his shoulder holster and tossed it onto the floor in front of Grecco.

Grecco looped his pen through the trigger guard and slipped it into a plastic evidence bag he'd produced from his pocket. "I assume this is the same Heckler & Koch you used to kill Judd Miller and Ray Tillman?"

"What are you talking about?" Varese asked contemptuously.

"Are you denying that you were at the Paramus Flying School yesterday afternoon?"

"I've never even heard of the Paramus Flying School," Varese retorted disdainfully. "I was here all afternoon. Mr. Navarro can verify that."

"Can you?" Grecco asked Navarro.

There was something in Grecco's voice that unsettled Navarro. Confidence? He wasn't sure but he decided to play it safe. "You seem very sure of yourself, Grecco. What have you got on Tony?"

"Judd Miller, the owner of the Paramus Flying School, recently installed video surveillance equipment on the premises in an attempt to catch the vandals who'd twice broken into the hangar in the last month and tampered with his planes," Grecco told him. "Tillman's murder was captured on film. If you want, I can even tell you to the second when Varese actually pulled the trigger."

Whitlock opened his attaché case and tossed a brown envelope onto Navarro's desk. "Those are just a few of the stills which have been lifted from the film. Each one identifies Varese as the killer."

Navarro removed the photographs from the envelope. He only needed to look at the first one. It showed Varese standing over Tillman, the Heckler & Koch raised to fire. That alone would put him away for twenty years. "I'm calling my lawyer."

"Tell him to meet you both down at DEA headquarters," Grecco replied.

Suddenly Varese rushed at Whitlock, knocking him aside as he ran to the door. Swiftly unclipping his two-way radio from his belt, Grecco warned his men in the corridor that Varese was headed their way. Varese's attempt to escape was hopeless: they grabbed him the moment he appeared and wrestled him to the floor. Snapping a pair of handcuffs around his wrists, they led him back into Navarro's office.

Navarro had spoken to the family's senior lawyer,

dward Brasco; now he looked across at Varese who
as slumped dejectedly on the sofa, a trickle of blood
unning down the side of his chin. "Brasco's on his
ay over to DEA headquarters. Don't say anything
ntil he's briefed you."

"You've made your call, Navarro. Now on your
et." Grecco nodded to one of his men. "Cuff him,
ead him his rights, then get him out of here."

"And what are the charges against me?" Navarro
emanded as he was handcuffed.

"Accessory to murder and conspiracy to import
nd sell illegal drugs in this country," Grecco told
im.

"What the hell have drugs got to do with any of
is?" Navarro demanded.

"Senator Scoby left a detailed outline of the deal
e'd made with the Colombians, as well as the one he
ntended to make with you on his return to New York
oday. That, in itself, might not have stood up in
ourt. But by having Tillman killed, you've admitted
our guilt. Unless, of course, you intend to deny that
ou had anything to do with his murder and let
arese take the rap by himself. Do you?"

Navarro knew what Grecco was trying to do. He
urned to Varese. "Tony, now listen to me. Grecco's
oing to try and offer you immunity from prosecu-
on in return for testifying against me. Sure, it's
oing to sound good. You won't serve time. You and
our family will be given a new identity. A new life.
on't believe him. They won't keep their word. They
ever do. They'll use you then throw you to the
olves once they've got what they want. Don't be
mpted. Talk to Brasco. You know he'll see you
ght. Promise me you won't say anything until
ou've spoken to Brasco, Tony. Promise me."

There was uncertainty in Varese's eyes. He looked
own at the carpet.

"Tony, look at me! Tony!"

"Take him away," Grecco said disdainfully.

Two of Grecco's men led Navarro from the roor Whitlock closed the door behind them.

"You're facing a murder rap, Tony," Grecco sai sitting next to Varese. "That's life. You'd be lucky be out in twenty years. More like twenty-fiv Navarro knows that. Why do you think he didn speak up for you when he was here? Twice I put hi on the spot and twice he weaseled his way out of giv ing me a straight answer. Why? Because he knows I can wriggle his way out of this by claiming he kne nothing of Tillman's murder. And it's his wor against yours. Brasco's brief will be to get him of You're of secondary importance to the family. Th family need him. They don't need you. Trigger me can easily be replaced. But Navarro's the brains b hind the New York operation. He's being groomed take over from Carmine Germino one day. Do yc honestly think Germino would risk losing his be lieutenant for the next twenty years just because you?"

"I can't cop on Martin," Varese said without tal ing his eyes off the carpet.

"Can't, or won't?" Whitlock asked.

Varese remained silent.

"I hear you've just become a father, Tony," Grecc said. "How old's your daughter now? A month? Tw months? When you go down you'll miss the chan of watching her growing up. Those are the best yea of your life. I know. I've got a son of my own. Cou you live with yourself knowing you'd missed h first step? Or her first word? Or with the fact th you'd only get to see her when your wife brought h on visits to the prison at weekends? And who's to sa she'd still come to visit you when she gets older an finds out that you're serving life for murder? You' got to make a choice here, Tony. Which family's mo mportant to you? Your wife and daughter or the Mafia?''

Varese continued to stare at the carpet as the reality of his situation slowly began to sink in. He finally looked up at Grecco. "You'd protect me if I testified against the family?"

"You'd immediately be put on the Witness Protection Program. New identities. New lives. You'd be safe."

"Would I serve time first?" Varese asked, the uncertainty still evident in his voice.

"That would depend on what you could give the DA. The more you gave him, the more flexible he'd be."

"I can give you Carmine Germino. I've got enough on him to put him away for life. And his lieutenants. I've sat in on their strategy meetings for the last five years. I can give you numbers of bank accounts all around the world that the Germino family are using to launder their drug money. And I can give you names of senior politicians Germino has in his back pocket. But I won't cop on Martin. Not directly. You'll build up enough evidence against him from what I've got on Germino and his lieutenants. But before I do say anything to your DA I want a guarantee that I won't spend time in jail. Because I know I'd never come out of there alive. Even if I was put in solitary they'd find a way to get to me. That's the deal."

"Why this obsessive loyalty to Navarro?" Whitlock asked.

"Because they're related," Grecco told him.

Varese nodded. "Martin's my half-brother. We had the same mother. I was the tough one. Martin had the brains. He'd always try and talk our way out of trouble but if that failed, I'd use my fists. I guess you could say I always looked after Martin when we were growing up. But that all changed when we joined the family. Then it was his turn to look after

me. Martin insisted that he wanted me as his right
hand man. Germino wanted to keep him happy so h⌐
agreed. Family loyalty means a lot to Italians, Mr
Grecco. You should know that."

"I do."

Varese looked from Grecco to Whitlock. "Yo⌐
know my terms. Put them to the DA. You shouldn'
have too much trouble finding me when you've go
the answer."

Grecco turned to Whitlock after Varese had bee⌐
taken away. "Now I've got to convince my superior
and the DA to go along with this. Let's face it, keep
ing Varese out of jail's a small price to pay for landin⌐
the top echelon of the Germino family. But I guess i⌐
the end it's all down to politics, isn't it?"

"Isn't it always?" Whitlock replied as he followe⌐
Grecco from the room.

Graham and Sabrina flew to Milford by helicopter
They were met there by Jim Kingsland, a recent grad
uate of the FBI academy who'd been sent down fron
the Bureau's New York headquarters earlier tha⌐
morning to liaise with the local police department
All he'd been told was that Graham and Sabrina wer⌐
"affiliated" to the Bureau and that he was to giv⌐
them his full cooperation. He didn't like the vague
ness of his orders but he knew better than to questio⌐
them.

Kingsland drove them to the docks. Graham an⌐
Sabrina were determined to nail Killen and his me⌐
for the murder of Billy Peterson and the attempte⌐
murder of their colleague. And if that led to informa
tion about the link between the *Ventura*'s cargo an⌐
the IRA, then so much the better. Two patrol car⌐
were already waiting for them outside the mai⌐
gates. One of the patrol cars followed them into th⌐

compound and parked next to them in front of the harbor master's office.

"Kingsland, you and the two uniforms get Woods and Natchett," Graham said, getting out of the car. "Sabrina and I will deal with Jess Killen ourselves."

When they reached Killen's office Graham knocked and entered. Killen was on the telephone, his feet propped up on the desk. He nodded to Graham, his eyes instinctively flickering past him to Sabrina. He wet his lips as his eyes scanned the length of her body.

Graham reached over and yanked the telephone from Killen's hand. "Yeah, he'll call you back in twenty years' time." He slammed the receiver back into its cradle. "Are you Jess Killen?"

"Yeah, I'm Killen. What the hell's going on? You can't just come—"

"Special Agents Graham and Carver," Graham said. He held up his ID card then took a warrant from his pocket and placed it on the desk. "Jess Killen, you're under arrest for the murder of William Peterson. Anything you—"

"Spare me the lecture," Killen snarled. "I want my lawyer."

Graham put his hand on the receiver and finished reading Killen his rights. "On your feet, Killen. Hands against the wall, feet apart."

"You thinking I'm packing?" Killen said in disbelief. "I'm the foreman of a dockyard, not some gunslinger."

"Just do it!" Graham hissed menacingly.

Killen swore angrily then stood up and assumed the position. Graham frisked him quickly. He was clean.

"Satisfied, G-man?" Killen snapped. "Who is this William Peterson anyway?"

"Billy Peterson," Sabrina said. "He used to work

here, remember? Then, one night, he just disappeared. Nobody's seen or heard of him since."

"So, what's that got to do with me?"

"You killed him. First you beat him senseless then you put a bullet in the back of his head," Graham told him.

"You got a witness to prove it?"

"As a matter of fact we do," Sabrina replied, taking a photograph from her pocket and holding it out toward Killen. "Fabio Paluzzi. One of us. Only you'd know him as Pasconi, the Italian journalist."

"He didn't drown when you and your two huskies pushed the car into the water," Graham told him. "Our colleagues are at this very moment reading Woods and Natchett their rights. I'd suggest this was as good a time as any to call your lawyer, Killen."

Killen picked up the receiver then suddenly lashed out at Graham, catching him across the side of the face. Graham stumbled backward against Sabrina, knocking the gun from her hand. It skidded under the desk. Killen shoved past them and disappeared out through the doorway. Sabrina squinted under the desk for the gun. It was out of reach and there wasn't time to retrieve it. She went after Killen.

Graham got to his feet and gingerly touched the side of his face. A cut had opened up at the corner of his right eye. He cursed angrily then went outside. There was no sign of either Killen or Sabrina. He looked around, deciding which way he would have gone if he'd been in Killen's place. The warehouse? The back of the warehouse. Yeah, he'd probably duck behind the warehouse. There was a lot of foliage there. A good place to move without being seen. He drew his holstered Beretta and was about to make his way around to the back when he noticed a movement out of the corner of his eye. He swung around, Beretta raised.

Killen slowly emerged from the warehouse, his

arm wrapped around Sabrina's neck. He was holding a screwdriver to her throat. "Okay, G-man, drop the piece."

Graham kept the Beretta trained on Killen. He couldn't risk the shot, not with the tip of the screwdriver pressed so close to Sabrina's throat. "Let her go, Killen!"

"I said drop the piece," Killen snapped back.

"Don't do it, Mike," Sabrina said to Graham.

"Shut up!" Killen snapped at her, pressing the tip of the screwdriver harder against her throat. It broke her skin and a trickle of blood ran onto her sweatshirt. Killen swallowed nervously. "I want a car brought round here now. Then the lady and I are going for a ride. Then once I'm outta here, she goes free."

"The lady's not going anywhere with you," Sabrina said calmly. "So you'd better kill me now."

It was then that Kingsland and one of the uniformed policemen appeared behind Killen, their weapons drawn.

"Put the weapon down!" Kingsland ordered.

"Easy, Killen," Graham shouted, holding up his hand as Killen looked anxiously over his shoulder.

Kingsland moved slowly toward Killen. "I want you to put the screwdriver down. Very slowly."

"Back off, kid," Graham hissed furiously. "Just back off."

Kingsland's eyes flickered toward Graham. "I'm trained—"

"Back off!" Graham yelled and swung the Beretta on Kingsland. "You take another step and I'll put you down."

Kingsland froze.

Graham turned back to Killen. "She wouldn't go with you even if I did get you the car. So then what would you do? Kill her? You do that and I'll empty this Beretta into you. And I promise you it'll only be the last bullet that will kill you."

"I'll kill her, G-man, I swear I'll kill her."

"Do it," Graham retorted. "Or don't you have the guts?"

"Wait," Kingsland shouted, staring at Graham in disbelief. "Killen, we'll get whatever you want. Just don't harm the woman."

"The kid doesn't have the authority to get you anything." Graham slowly raised the Beretta until it was in line with Killen's head. "I'm going to count to five. If you haven't released her by then, I'll kill you. It's your choice, Killen."

"You kill me and she dies," Killen replied, blinking his eyes furiously as the sweat streamed down his face.

"One."

Killen swallowed nervously as he stared at the Beretta in Graham's hand.

"Two."

"You wouldn't do it," Killen said, adjusting his grip on the handle. "She's your partner. You wouldn't risk her life like that."

"Three."

Graham fired. The bullet took Killen in the forehead. The screwdriver sliced across the side of Sabrina's neck as he fell. She knocked his hand away and stumbled backward, the blood pouring from the gash on her neck. She dropped to her haunches then pulled a handkerchief from her pocket and pressed it against her neck. Kingsland immediately holstered his automatic and hurried toward her but she recoiled when he tried to help her to her feet.

"Leave her," Graham snapped then turned to the policeman who was crouched over Killen, trying to find any signs of life.

The policeman finally shook his head then got to

his feet and began to disperse the group of onlookers who had been alerted by the sound of gunfire.

"Kingsland, radio in for an ambulance."

Kingsland glared at Graham but knew better than to argue. He ran off toward the unmarked police car.

Graham crouched beside Sabrina then tilted her head back gently and eased the handkerchief away from her neck. "It looks worse than it is. But we'll get you over to a hospital all the same."

"That was some shot," she said, wincing as she pressed the handkerchief against her neck again.

"Yeah, some shot," Graham retorted, helping her to her feet. "I nearly got you killed."

"You'd have got me killed if you'd let the count go on to five. It was obvious Killen was desperate. I could feel it." She put a hand on his arm. "I'm still alive, aren't I? That makes it some shot."

Kingsland returned breathlessly. "The ambulance is on its way."

"Good," Graham replied.

"This is far from over, Mr. Graham. Not only did you show a blatant disregard for your partner's life, you also threatened my life when I was trying to negotiate with Killen. Then, on top of all that, you didn't even give Killen the chance to surrender. You shot him without warning. You can be sure all this will be going in my report."

"I'm sure it will," Graham said contemptuously.

"And I have a witness who'll corroborate my statement." Kingsland turned to the policeman. "You were here. You saw everything."

"I saw Mr. Graham save his partner's life."

"You heard him tell Killen he'd count to five. He didn't even give him a chance to surrender."

"Count?" The policeman shrugged. "I didn't hear any count."

"What are you talking about?" Kingsland demanded.

"You may be the one who's just graduated from some fancy college but I'm the one with twenty years' service behind me," the policeman said coldly. "This is the real world, not one of your textbook simulations. Wise up, kid, or you won't last very long in this business."

Kingsland glared at the policeman then strode off.

"Thanks for the support, pal," Graham said to the policeman.

"You had to make a split-second decision. And that's what this game's all about, isn't it?" The policeman looked around as more workers emerged from the warehouse to get a closer look at Killen's body. "Excuse me. I'd better get something to put over the body."

Graham crossed to where Sabrina was sitting on a wooden crate, the blood-soaked handkerchief still pressed against her neck. He sat down beside her. "How you doing?"

"I could be a lot worse," she replied, watching as the policeman draped a tarpaulin over Killen's body.

Graham looked at his watch. "I don't think we're going to make the Colonel's briefing at this rate. I'll call him from the hospital and tell him we're going to be delayed."

"That's guaranteed to put him in a good mood. You know how he hates to be kept waiting."

"I still can't believe he's back at the helm again. He may be a cantankerous old fossil at times but he's still the only person capable of saving the organization right now."

"As long as it's not already too late."

Graham and Sabrina arrived forty minutes after the briefing was due to have started.

"I'm sorry we're late, sir," Graham said. "I hope

you got my message: Sabrina had to get some medical attention before we flew back from Milford."

"Yes, I've heard all about the incident at the docks," Philpott replied, then looked at Sabrina. "How is your neck?"

Sabrina's hand instinctively went to the scarf she was wearing. "It's nothing serious, sir. Just a few stitches."

"How did you hear about it, sir?" Graham asked.

"I received a call from a senior official in the local FBI. He tells me you threatened to kill his man and that you shot a suspect without warning."

"They sent down a fresh-faced kid straight out of the academy, sir," Sabrina cut in before Graham had a chance to defend himself. "He was playing it by the book. If Mike hadn't intervened when he did Killen would almost certainly have stabbed me. Mike saved my life, sir. I don't think he has to explain himself for that."

Philpott nodded slowly in agreement. "No, he doesn't. I've since spoken to a Sergeant Kelley of the Milford Police Department." He looked at Graham. "He spoke very highly of you, Mike. From what I can ascertain, you took a decision under pressure when Sabrina's life was threatened. Sabrina's alive so, as far as I'm concerned, that's an end to it. Now sit down, both of you."

Graham and Sabrina exchanged suspicious glances as they sat down on the nearest sofa. Philpott was being unusually understanding. It was a far cry from the often dictatorial Philpott of old. Had the heart attack mellowed him?

"Is something the matter?" Philpott asked.

"No, sir," Graham replied with a quick smile.

Philpott opened the folder in front of him. "I've received some good news and bad news in the last hour. I thought it best to wait until you were all here before I told you. The bad news is that the powers-that-be in London have decided that Eastman won't stand trial."

"So the bastard walks," Graham hissed angrily.

"What choice did they have? Imagine what the Press would have made of it had it ever come out that Scoby's assassination had actually been masterminded by a senior officer in the anti-terrorist squad. It would have destroyed public confidence in the British police."

"What will happen to him?" Sabrina asked.

"He's already been stripped of his rank and dismissed from the force. Who knows what will happen to him in the future? If the IRA ever got a whiff of what really happened they'll have him killed without a moment's hesitation. And that's something he'll have to live with for the rest of his life. I certainly wouldn't want to be in his shoes."

"And the good news?" Sabrina said.

"I met with one of the President's senior aides earlier today. I explained our position to him and asked that he pass it on to the President. Well, I received a call from the President a short time ago. He assured me that UNACO will continue to operate, as before, under the auspices of the United Nations. So there's no need for any of you to start preparing your CVs."

"How did you manage to get him on our side, sir?" Whitlock asked in amazement.

"We came to an understanding. The President wanted the Scoby affair buried. I wanted an assurance that UNACO wouldn't be sacrificed for what happened in Ireland. It means, however, that as far as we're concerned, neither Scoby nor Tillman ever made a deal with the Colombians to import cocaine into this country. Nor did the meeting between Tillman and Navarro ever take place. Not even Melissa Scoby will know the truth. That's how the President wants it and as no drugs ever changed hands on

American soil, I'd say we got the better end of the deal."

"What about Navarro and Varese? Are they just going to be allowed to walk?"

Philpott let Whitlock answer Graham's question.

"Tony Varese's made a deal with our old buddy, Frankie Grecco," Whitlock told them. "The DEA have persuaded the DA to drop all charges against Varese in return for testifying against the Germino family. Carmine Germino and four of his senior lieutenants have already been taken into custody. The only stipulation Varese made was that he wouldn't testify against Navarro. It's a personal thing. But with the evidence against the others the DEA are confident that they can make a solid case against Navarro anyway. They'll go down for a long time."

"What about Tillman's murder?" Graham asked.

"It'll become another unsolved statistic on the books of the NYPD," Philpott replied. "The videotape will be destroyed once Varese's testified and been given a new identity under the Witness Protection Program."

"There's another interesting twist to the case," Kolchinsky said. "We received a fax this morning from our contact in Medellín. Miguel Cabrera, Navarro's inside man in the Medellín cartel, was killed in a car bomb explosion late last night. His murder was almost certainly ordered by Navarro to silence him after the deal went sour. It seems highly unlikely that his father could have found out that he was working for Navarro and had him killed."

"If he had, he wouldn't have been killed by a car bomb," Graham said. "You can be sure Miguel Cabrera would have died a slow and agonizing death. The Colombians don't take too kindly to informers."

Philpott ran his finger down the list in front of him. "There is one last point which actually brings us back full circle to the arms which were found on

Nantucket Island last week. Varese's already told Grecco that the Germino family was one of the main suppliers of arms to the IRA. The cache of Armalite rifles on board the *Ventura* was destined for Sean Farrell. So Scotland Yard will now have ample evidence to nail Farrell on gun-running charges. Not that he'll be much of a threat anymore. His liaison with Fiona Gallagher has not only destroyed his credibility but also his future within the IRA. Rumor has it he'll go the same way as Brady."

"That can't be a bad thing, can it?" Whitlock said.

Philpott leafed through the papers in front of him until he found the one he wanted. "Now, about Fabio's replacement."

"I thought C. W. was being brought back into the field?" Graham said, looking at Whitlock.

"He is," Philpott agreed. "But I'll need a team leader when we come to rebuild Strike Force Seven. And C. W. is the perfect choice."

"I thought I'd be back with Mike and Sabrina," Whitlock said in surprise.

"In case you've forgotten, Mike was promoted to team leader when you came over on to the management side," Philpott reminded him. "There can't be two team leaders in one unit."

"In that case I resign my leadership," Graham said. "I know I speak for Sabrina when I say we want C. W. back in Strike Force Three. Let's face it, UNACO are going to need to be at their sharpest over the next few months if we're to regain our credibility amongst the other intelligence services around the world."

"Mike's right, sir," Sabrina added. "It would be crazy to break up the team at a time like this. We need to consolidate our position amongst the intelligence community and we can't do that by rebuilding another team. Recruit from the outside and, where necessary, promote from within. I can think of half a dozen operatives you could bring in to replace Dave Swain. And it would be good for morale.''

"Have you both quite finished lecturing me on the concepts of good management practice?'' Philpott said, looking at each of them in turn.

They both nodded somberly.

"You obviously feel strongly about this. And, surprisingly enough, there is an element of common sense in what you both said. C. W., you're reinstated as leader of Strike Force Three.''

"Thank you, sir,'' Whitlock said, beaming.

"This doesn't mean that you've pulled one over on the old fossil,'' Philpott said, looking directly at Graham. "Just remember that.''

"Sir, you're not suggesting that I call you . . .'' Graham trailed off with a helpless shrug but when he turned to Sabrina for support she was looking down at her feet, struggling not to laugh.

"I'm sure it's meant as a term of endearment,'' Philpott said with a knowing smile. He closed the folder. "That's all, thank you. You have the rest of the week off but just make sure you have your beepers with you at all times in case something should crop up. Mike, that includes taking it with you to the game tonight.''

"That goes without saying, sir,'' Graham replied. "But how did you know I was going to the game?''

"The Giants against the Redskins at Meadowlands? I know you wouldn't miss that for the world.''

"No, sir,'' Graham said with a smile.

"But I still want those outstanding reports on my desk first thing in the morning. I can't delay the Secretary-General any longer.''

"You'll have them, sir,'' Graham assured him.

Philpott activated the sliding door then turned his attention to one of the folders on his desk.

Whitlock touched Graham's arm as he turned to leave. "Frankie said to tell you he'd ring you sometime and arrange for the two of you to go to a game together."

"Frankie's always going to ring me and arrange for us to go to a game together," Graham replied. "He never does though."

"Why don't you ring him today and see if he's going to the game tonight?" Sabrina said to Graham. "Perhaps we can meet up with him there."

"Why don't you ring him?" Graham replied. "You're a lot closer to him than I am."

"What's that supposed to mean?" she shot back.

"It's no secret that you've been out with Frankie a few times since his divorce came through."

"Sure I have. But it's always been a purely platonic friendship."

"That's not what Frankie says," Graham replied.

"Then Frankie's a goddamn liar," she snapped angrily. "And you can tell him that when you see him at the game tonight. It would be a shame to waste the spare ticket after all the trouble you've gone to to get it."

She stormed out of the room before Graham could say anything.

"I'm glad to see you haven't lost your touch while I've been away, Mike," Philpott said, looking up from the folder on his desk. "Still as subtle as ever."

"You were way out of line there, Mike," Whitlock said. "You know Frankie and his big mouth. I think you owe Sabrina an apology."

"OK," Graham said defensively and hurried from the room. He caught up with Sabrina as she was about to press the button for the lift. "Hey, wait up a minute, will you? Look, I was out of order back there. I'm sorry."

Her finger hovered over the button then she sighed deeply and let her arm fall to her side. "Frankie was a great UC. One of the best. But he was a completely different person outside work. He had this macho side to his personality that always seemed to surface whenever he was around women. That wasn't for me. So I stopped seeing him. It's as simple as that. And now you say he claims that we had something going? It's really sad that a guy like Frankie has to make up these kind of stories to bolster his own ego."

"Yeah. But then that's Frankie for you. I should have known better than to say what I did. I'm sorry." Graham gave her a questioning look. "You still want to come to the game tonight?"

"Are you going to invite Frankie?"

"Not a chance," Graham said.

"Then you're on." She chuckled to herself. "It would have been a pity if I hadn't got to see the game after spending three hours over the Atlantic learning about nickel defenses, slot formations, shotguns, sacks and turnovers."

"You'll have a good time, you'll see."

Whitlock left the UNACO offices and walked over to where they were standing. "Truce?"

"For the moment," Sabrina replied.

"Talking of truces, have you spoken to Carmen yet?" Graham asked.

"I broke the news to her gently last night. Very gently in fact."

"And?" Sabrina pressed.

"Well, she didn't exactly do a jig of delight. But then she didn't pack her bags and leave either. I think she's accepted it, albeit reluctantly. I'm taking her out to dinner tonight at her favorite restaurant, Le Chantilly. I'm sure she'll have something to say about it then."

"I'm sure she will."

"Thanks for making me feel better, Sabrina." Whitlock pressed the button for the lift. "Anyone for a beer over at McFeely's?"

"You buying?" Graham asked as the lift doors opened onto the floor.

"Why not?" Whitlock replied and followed them into the lift.

◆ EPILOGUE

Eastman knew exactly where Marsh meant when he had said to meet him at the "usual place" at two that afternoon. A clearing in a remote area of woodland near Chadwell Heath which they had used in the past to meet with informers. He also knew exactly why Marsh wanted to see him . . .

Marsh's Toyota MR2 sports car was already there when Eastman arrived. Eastman parked his Rover beside it and got out. A cold wind had whipped up since he'd left home and as he zipped up his blouson he glanced up at the sky. Rain was imminent.

"John?" he called out, digging his hands into his pockets.

Marsh emerged from a cluster of beech trees. He was dressed in a pair of jeans and a baggy antique-style leather jacket. He smiled coldly at Eastman. "It's good to see you, Keith. Thanks for coming."

"As I said to you on the phone, I was going to call you anyway."

"Let's walk," Marsh said, indicating the trees behind him.

"Sure," Eastman replied, falling into step behind him. "Have you been reinstated yet?"

"Yesterday. But I doubt Palmer will ever fully

trust me again. I think you owe me an explanation, Keith."

"What has Palmer told you about me?" Eastman asked.

"Nothing. He's playing it close to the chest. The unit was told that you'd been relieved of your command and that you were no longer a member of the force. It's all been cloak and dagger stuff as far as we're concerned."

"You must know what happened otherwise you wouldn't be here, would you?" Eastman replied, pausing at the edge of the trees and looking out over the river in front of him.

Marsh moved down to the water's edge then turned back to look at Eastman. "What's that supposed to mean? All I know is that you were arrested in Dugaill, questioned by UNACO, then kicked off the force. There's a major cover-up going on and because you put me in the frame I'm now a part of it. The least you can do is tell me what really happened."

"Why, so that you can report back to your superiors?" Eastman replied disdainfully.

"Obviously my superiors already know what's going on, otherwise they wouldn't have initiated the cover-up in the first place, would they?" Marsh replied, picking up a stone and skimming it across the water.

"I wasn't talking about those superiors. I was talking about your paymasters in the IRA."

"What?" Marsh replied in disbelief as his hand slipped inside his jacket.

"Don't even think it, John," Eastman replied, pulling a Browning from his pocket.

Marsh swallowed nervously and slowly withdrew his hand. "How did you know?"

"Fiona found out," Eastman replied, then nodded when he saw the surprise on Marsh's face. "Oh, I know your recruitment was supposed to have been a closely guarded secret known only to the senior members of the Army Council, but Kieran O'Connell made the mistake of telling Farrell about it. And Fiona had Farrell twisted around her little finger. He told her everything. Pillow talk I believe it's called."

"How long have you known I was working for the Provos?"

"Since Fiona discovered that it was you who blew Pat Gorman's cover. You never saw what Brady did to Pat before he finally killed him, did you? It was barbaric. Why did you turn?"

"I was in debt. Real debt. And I couldn't cover those debts on my police pay. So I turned informer."

"And how much of your debt did you pay off by blowing Pat's cover?"

Marsh remained silent.

"I hope it was worth it, Johnny. I really hope it was worth it."

"If you've known about this all along, why didn't you just let me rot in jail when you had the chance?"

"That was the idea," Eastman replied. "Fiona had enough on you to put you away for life. And she intended to finger you in court. But without her the case would probably have collapsed. And I wasn't going to risk it. So I told Whitlock you were the fall guy. That way they would have to release you."

"So that you could kill me?" Marsh shot back.

"I promised myself that I'd avenge Pat's death. Brady's already dead. You're the last piece in the jigsaw, Johnny."

"You knew I intended to kill you today, didn't you?"

"I knew the authorities would never let me walk. I know too much. So what better way of silencing me than by using the Provos to do their dirty work for them? All it needed was an anonymous call to the

Army Council to set me up. I presume that is how they found out about me?"

Marsh nodded.

"How much were they told?"

"Enough to put a contract out on you," Marsh replied.

"But obviously not enough to link me with either Pat or Fiona," Eastman deduced. "Which means the public will always hold the IRA responsible for Scoby's murder. Perfect."

"Killing me won't solve anything. They'll just send someone else after you. They won't stop until they've found you. I'm your one chance of getting out of this alive. If I report back to them that I've killed you, the contract will be lifted. You need me, Keith, can't you see that?"

"I had a plan to get Fiona out of the country. Well, now I'm going to use it myself. I've got all the contacts in place. All the details have already been finalized. I guarantee you that the IRA will never find me. So, you see, I don't need you at all."

Marsh clawed desperately for his holstered Browning. Eastman pumped three bullets into him. Marsh's body spun grotesquely as he fell backwards into the river. Eastman stared impassively at the lifeless body as it wallowed, facedown, in the water then pushed the Browning into his pocket and hurried back to his car.

He saw the red motorbike parked behind Marsh's Toyota as he emerged into the clearing. The two figures standing beside the car were dressed in black leathers with helmets obscuring their faces. Both were armed with Armalite rifles. He knew then he was going to die. He was still reaching for the Browning in his pocket when they shot him.

Alistair MacLean, who died in 1987, was the best-selling author of thirty books, including world famous novels such as *The Guns of Navarone* and *Where Eagles Dare*.

Alastair MacNeill was born in Scotland in 1960. His family moved to South Africa when he was six years old, where he showed a growing interest in writing, winning several school competitions. He returned to Britain in 1985 to pursue a full-time writing career.